Portrait *of an* Unknown Woman

Also by Daniel Silva

DANIEL Silva

Portrait *of an* Unknown Woman

HARPER

An Imprint of HarperCollins*Publishers*

PORTRAIT OF AN UNKNOWN WOMAN. Copyright © 2022 by Daniel Silva. All rights reserved. Printed in the United States of America. No part of this book may be used or reproduced in any manner whatsoever without written permission except in the case of brief quotations embodied in critical articles and reviews. For information, address HarperCollins Publishers, 195 Broadway, New York, NY 10007.

HarperCollins books may be purchased for educational, business, or sales promotional use. For information, please email the Special Markets Department at SPsales@harpercollins.com.

FIRST EDITION

Library of Congress Cataloging-in-Publication Data has been applied for.

ISBN 978-0-06-283485-0 (Hardcover)
ISBN 978-0-06-283533-8 (International Edition)

22 23 24 25 26   LSC   10 9 8 7 6 5 4 3 2 1

For Burt Bacharach

*And, as always, for my wife, Jamie,
and my children, Lily and Nicholas*

All that glisters is not gold.

—William Shakespeare, *The Merchant of Venice*

PART ONE

———

Craquelure

1

Mason's Yard

On any other day, Julian would have tossed it straight into the rubbish bin. Or better yet, he would have fed it into Sarah's professional-grade shredder. During the long, bleak winter of the pandemic, when they had sold but a single painting, she had used the contraption to mercilessly cull the gallery's swollen archives. Julian, who was traumatized by the project, feared that when Sarah had no more needless sales records and shipping documents to destroy, it would be his turn in the machine. He would leave this world as a tiny parallelogram of yellowed paper, carted off to the recycler with the rest of the week's debris. In his next life he would return as an environmentally friendly coffee cup. He supposed, not without some justification, there were worse fates.

The letter had arrived at the gallery on a rainy Friday in late March, addressed to *M. JULIAN ISHERWOOD*. Sarah had nevertheless opened it; a former clandestine officer of the Central Intelligence Agency, she had no qualms about reading other people's mail. Intrigued, she had placed it on Julian's desk along with several inconsequential items from the morning's post, the only sort of correspondence she typically allowed him to see. He read it for the first time while still clad in

his dripping mackintosh, his plentiful gray locks in windblown dis-
array. The time was half past eleven, which in itself was noteworthy.
These days Julian rarely set foot in the gallery before noon. It gave
him just enough time to make a nuisance of himself before embarking on the three-hour period of his day he reserved for his luncheon.

His first impression of the letter was that its author, a certain Madame Valerie Bérrangar, had the most exquisite handwriting he had
seen in ages. It seemed she had noticed the recent story in *Le Monde*
concerning the multimillion-pound sale by Isherwood Fine Arts of
Portrait of an Unknown Woman, oil on canvas, 115 by 92 centimeters,
by the Flemish Baroque painter Anthony van Dyck. Apparently, Madame Bérrangar had concerns about the transaction—concerns she
wished to discuss with Julian in person, as they were legal and ethical
in nature. She would be waiting at Café Ravel in Bordeaux at four
o'clock on Monday afternoon. It was her wish that Julian come alone.

"What do you think?" asked Sarah.

"She's obviously mad as a hatter." Julian displayed the handwritten
letter, as though it proved his point. "How did it get here? Carrier
pigeon?"

"DHL."

"Was there a return address on the waybill?"

"She used the address of a DHL Express in Saint-Macaire. It's
about fifty kilometers—"

"I know where Saint-Macaire is," said Julian, and immediately regretted his abrupt tone. "Why do I have this terrible feeling I'm being
blackmailed?"

"She doesn't sound like a blackmailer to me."

"That's where you're wrong, petal. All the blackmailers and extor-
tionists I've ever met had impeccable manners."

"Then perhaps we should ring the Met."

"Involve the police? Have you taken leave of your senses?"

"At least show it to Ronnie."

Ronald Sumner-Lloyd was Julian's pricey Berkeley Square attorney. "I have a better idea," he said.

It was then, at 11:36 a.m., with Sarah looking on in disapproval, that Julian dangled the letter over his ancient metal dustbin, a relic of the gallery's glory days, when it was located on stylish New Bond Street—or New Bondstrasse, as it had been known in some quarters of the trade. Try as he might, he couldn't seem to let the damn thing slip from his fingers. Or perhaps, he thought later, it was Madame Bérrangar's letter that had clung to him.

He set it aside, reviewed the remainder of the morning post, returned a few phone calls, and interrogated Sarah on the details of a pending sale. Then, having nothing else to do, he headed off to the Dorchester for lunch. He was accompanied by an employee of a venerable London auction house, female, of course, recently divorced, no children, far too young but not inappropriately so. Julian astonished her with his knowledge of Italian and Dutch Renaissance painters and regaled her with tales of acquisitional derring-do. It was a character he had been playing to modest acclaim for longer than he cared to remember. He was the incomparable Julian Isherwood, Julie to his friends, Juicy Julie to his partners in the occasional crime of drink. He was loyal as the day was long, trusting to a fault, and English to the core. English as high tea and bad teeth, as he was fond of saying. And yet, were it not for the war, he would have been someone else entirely.

Returning to the gallery, he found that Sarah had adhered a fuchsia-colored sticky note to Madame Bérrangar's letter, advising him to reconsider. He read it a second time, slowly. Its tone was as formal as the linenlike stationery upon which it was written. Even Julian had to admit she sounded entirely reasonable and not at all like an extortionist. Surely, he thought, there would be no harm in merely listening to what she had to say. If nothing else, the journey would provide him with a much-needed respite from his crushing workload at the gallery. Besides, the weather forecast for London called for several days of nearly uninterrupted cold and rain. But in the southwest of France, it was springtime already.

———

Among the first actions that Sarah had taken after coming to work at the gallery was to inform Ella, Julian's stunning but useless receptionist, that her services were no longer required. Sarah had never bothered to hire a replacement. She was more than capable, she said, of answering the phone, returning the emails, keeping the appointment book, and buzzing visitors upstairs when they presented themselves at the perpetually locked door in Mason's Yard.

She drew a line, however, at making Julian's travel arrangements, though she consented to peer over his shoulder while he performed the chore himself, if only to make certain he didn't mistakenly book passage on the Orient Express to Istanbul rather than the Eurostar to Paris. From there, it was a scant two hours and fourteen minutes by TGV to Bordeaux. He successfully purchased a first-class ticket and then reserved a junior suite at the InterContinental—for two nights, just to be on the safe side.

The task complete, he repaired to the bar at Wiltons for a drink with Oliver Dimbleby and Roddy Hutchinson, widely regarded as London's most disreputable art dealers. One thing led to another, as was usually the case when Oliver and Roddy were involved, and it was after 2:00 a.m. by the time Julian finally toppled into his bed. He spent Saturday tending to his hangover and devoted much of Sunday to packing a bag. Once he would have thought nothing about hopping on the Concorde with only an attaché case and a pretty girl. But suddenly the preparations for a jaunt across the English Channel required all of his powers of concentration. He supposed it was but another unwanted consequence of growing old, like his alarming absentmindedness, or the strange sounds he emitted, or his seeming inability to cross a room without crashing into something. He kept a list of self-deprecating excuses at the ready to explain his humiliating clumsiness. He had never been the athletic type. It was the bloody lamp's fault. It was the end table that had assaulted *him*.

He slept poorly, as was frequently the case the night before an important journey, and awoke with a nagging sensation that he was about to make yet another in a long series of dreadful mistakes. His spirits lifted, however, as the Eurostar emerged from the Channel Tunnel and surged across the gray-green fields of the Pas-de-Calais toward Paris. He rode the *métro* from the Gare du Nord to the Gare Montparnasse and enjoyed a decent lunch in the buffet car of the TGV as the light beyond his window gradually took on the quality of a Cézanne landscape.

He recalled with startling clarity the instant he had seen it for the first time, this dazzling light of the south. Then, as now, he was riding a train bound from Paris. His father, the German Jewish art dealer Samuel Isakowitz, sat on the opposite side of the compartment. He was reading a day-old newspaper, as though nothing were out of the ordinary. Julian's mother, her hands knotted atop her knees, was staring into space, her face without expression.

Hidden in the luggage above their heads, rolled in protective sheets of paraffin paper, were several paintings. Julian's father had left a few lesser works behind at his gallery on the rue la Boétie, in the elegant Eighth Arrondissement. The bulk of his remaining inventory was already hidden in the château he had rented east of Bordeaux. Julian remained there until the terrible summer of 1942, when a pair of Basque shepherds smuggled him over the Pyrenees to neutral Spain. His parents were arrested in 1943 and deported to the Nazi extermination center at Sobibor, where they were gassed upon arrival.

Bordeaux's Saint-Jean station lay hard against the river Garonne, at the end of the Cours de la Marne. The departure board in the refurbished ticket hall was a modern device—gone was the polite applause of the updates—but the Beaux-Arts exterior, with its two prominent clocks, was as Julian remembered it. So, too, were the honey-colored Louis XV buildings lining the boulevards along which he sped in the back of a taxi. Some of the facades were so bright they seemed to glow with an interior light source. Others were dimmed by grime. It was the porous quality of the local stone, his father had explained. It absorbed soot from the air like a sponge and, like oil paintings, required occasional cleaning.

By some miracle, the hotel hadn't misplaced his reservation. After pressing an overly generous tip into the palm of the immigrant bellman, he hung up his clothes and withdrew to the bathroom to do something about his ragged appearance. It was gone three o'clock when he capitulated. He locked his valuables in the room safe and debated for a moment whether to bring Madame Bérrangar's letter to the café. An inner voice—his father's, he supposed—advised him to leave it behind, concealed within his luggage.

The same voice instructed him to bring along his attaché case, as it would confer upon him a wholly unwarranted patina of authority. He carried it along the Cours de l'Intendance, past a parade of exclusive shops. There were no motorcars, only pedestrians and bicyclists and sleek electric trams that slithered along their steel tracks in near silence. Julian proceeded at an unhurried pace, the attaché case in his right hand, his left lodged in his pocket, along with the card key for his hotel room.

He followed a tram around a corner and onto the rue Vital Carles. Directly before him rose the twin Gothic spires of Bordeaux Cathedral. It was surrounded by the scrubbed paving stones of a broad square. Café Ravel occupied the northwest corner. It was not the sort of place frequented by most Bordelais, but it was centrally located and easily found. Julian supposed that was the reason Madame Bérrangar had chosen it.

The shadow cast by the Hôtel de Ville darkened most of the café's tables, but the one nearest the cathedral was sunlit and unoccupied. Julian sat down and, placing his attaché case at his feet, took stock of the other patrons. With the possible exception of the man sitting three tables to his right, none appeared to be French. The rest were tourists, primarily of the package variety. Julian was the café's sore thumb; in his flannel trousers and gray sport jacket, he looked like a character from an E. M. Forster novel. At least she would have no difficulty spotting him.

He ordered a café crème before coming to his senses and requesting a half bottle of white Bordeaux instead, brutally cold, two glasses. The waiter delivered it as the bells of the cathedral tolled four o'clock. Julian reflexively smoothed the front of his jacket as his eyes searched the square. But at four thirty, as the lengthening shadows crept across his table, Madame Valerie Bérrangar was still nowhere to be found.

––––––––

By the time Julian finished the last of the wine, it was approaching five o'clock. He paid the bill in cash and, taking up his attaché case, moved from table to table like a beggar, repeating Madame Bérrangar's name and receiving only blank stares in return.

The interior of the café was deserted save the man behind the old zinc-topped bar. He had no recollection of anyone named Valerie Bérrangar but suggested Julian leave his name and phone number. "Isherwood," he said when the barman squinted at the spidery lines scrawled on the back of a napkin. "Julian Isherwood. I'm staying at the InterContinental."

Outside, the bells of the cathedral were tolling once more. Julian followed an earthbound pigeon across the paving stones of the square, then turned into the rue Vital Carles. He realized after a moment that he was berating himself for having come all the way to Bordeaux for no reason—and for having permitted this woman, this Madame Bérrangar, to stir up unwanted memories of the past.

"How dare she?" he shouted, startling a poor passerby. It was another unsettling development brought about by his advancing years, his recent propensity to say aloud the private thoughts running through his head.

At last the bells fell silent, and the pleasing low murmur of the ancient city returned. An electric tram glided past, sotto voce. Julian, his anger beginning to subside, paused outside a small art gallery and regarded with professional dismay the Impressionist-inspired paintings in the window. He was aware, vaguely, of the sound of an approaching motorbike. It was no scooter, he thought. Not with an engine note like that. It was one of those low-slung beasts ridden by men who wore special wind-resistant costumes.

The gallery's owner appeared in the doorway and invited Julian inside for a closer look at his inventory. Declining, he continued along the street in the direction of his hotel, the attaché case, as usual, in his left hand. The volume of the motorcycle's engine had increased sharply and was a half step higher in register. Suddenly Julian noticed an elderly woman—Madame Bérrangar's doppelgänger, no doubt—pointing at him and shouting something in French he couldn't make out.

Fearing he had once again uttered something inappropriate, he turned in the opposite direction and saw the motorcycle bearing down on him, a gloved hand reaching toward his attaché case. He drew the bag to his chest and pirouetted out of the machine's path, directly into the cold metal of a tall, immovable object. As he lay on the pavement, his head swimming, he saw several faces hovering over him, each wearing an expression of pity. Someone suggested calling an ambulance; someone else, the gendarmes. Humiliated, Julian reached for one of his ready-made excuses. It wasn't his fault, he explained. The bloody lamppost attacked *him*.

2

Venezia

It was Francesco Tiepolo, while standing atop Tintoretto's grave in the church of the Madonna dell'Orto, who had assured Gabriel that one day he would return to Venice. The remark was not idle speculation, as Gabriel discovered a few nights later, during a candlelit dinner with his beautiful young wife on the island of Murano. He offered several considered objections to the scheme, without conviction or success, and in the aftermath of an electrifying conclave in Rome, the deal was concluded. The terms were equitable, everyone was happy. Chiara especially. As far as Gabriel was concerned, nothing else mattered.

Admittedly, it all made a great deal of sense. After all, Gabriel had served his apprenticeship in Venice and had pseudonymously restored many of its greatest masterpieces. Still, the arrangement was not without its potential pitfalls, including the agreed-upon organizational chart of the Tiepolo Restoration Company, the most prominent such enterprise in the city. Under the terms of their arrangement, Francesco would remain at the helm until his retirement, when Chiara, who was Venetian by birth, would assume control. In the meantime she would occupy the position of general manager, with Gabriel serving as the director of the paintings department. Which meant that, for all intents and purposes, he would be working for his wife.

He approved the purchase of a luxurious four-bedroom *piano nobile* overlooking the Grand Canal in San Polo but otherwise left the planning and execution of the pending move in Chiara's capable hands. She oversaw the apartment's renovation and decoration long-distance from Jerusalem while Gabriel served out the remainder of his term at King Saul Boulevard. The final months passed quickly—there always seemed to be one more meeting to attend, one more crisis to avert—and in late autumn he embarked on what a noted columnist at *Haaretz* described as "the long goodbye." The events ranged from cocktail receptions and tribute-laden dinners to a blow-out at the King David Hotel attended by espiocrats from around the globe, including the powerful chief of the Jordanian Mukhabarat and his counterparts from Egypt and the United Arab Emirates. Their presence was proof that Gabriel, who had cultivated security partnerships across the Arab world, had left an indelible mark on a region torn by decades of war. For all its problems, the Middle East had changed for the better on his watch.

Reclusive by nature and uncomfortable in crowded settings, he found all the attention unbearable. Indeed, he much preferred the quiet evenings he passed with the members of his senior staff, the men and women with whom he had carried out some of the most storied operations in the history of a storied service. He begged Uzi Navot for forgiveness. He dispensed career and marital advice to Mikhail Abramov and Natalie Mizrahi. He shed tears of laughter while telling uproarious tales about the three years he had spent living underground in Western Europe with the hypochondriacal Eli Lavon. Dina Sarid, archivist of Palestinian and Islamic terrorism, beseeched Gabriel to sit for a series of exit interviews so that she might record his exploits in an unclassified official history. Not surprisingly, he declined. He had no wish to dwell on the past, he told her. Only the future.

Two officers from his senior staff, Yossi Gavish of Research and Yaakov Rossman of Special Ops, were regarded as his most likely successors. But both were overjoyed to learn that Gabriel had chosen Rimona Stern, the chief of Collections, instead. On a blustery Friday afternoon in mid-December, she became the first female director-general in the history of the Office. And Gabriel, after affixing his signature to a stack of documents regarding his modest pension and the dire consequences he would suffer if he ever divulged any of the secrets lodged in his head, officially became the world's most famous retired spy. His ritual disrobing complete, he toured King Saul Boulevard from top to bottom, shaking hands, drying tear-streaked cheeks. He assured his heartbroken troops that they had not seen the last of him, that he intended to keep his hand in the game. No one believed him.

That evening he attended one final gathering, this time on the shore of the Sea of Galilee. Unlike its predecessors, the encounter was at times contentious, though in the end a kind of peace was made. Early the next morning he made a pilgrimage to his son's grave on the Mount of Olives—and to the psychiatric hospital near the old Arab village of Deir Yassin where the child's mother resided in a prison of memory and a body ravaged by fire. With Rimona's blessing, the Allon family flew to Venice aboard the Office's Gulfstream, and at three that afternoon, after a windblown ride across the *laguna* in a gleaming wooden water taxi, they arrived at their new home.

Gabriel headed directly to the large light-filled room he had claimed as his studio and found an antique Italian easel, two halogen work lamps, and an aluminum trolley filled with Winsor & Newton sable-hair brushes, pigment, medium, and solvent. Absent was his old paint-smudged CD player. In its place was a British-made audio system and a pair of floor-standing speakers. His extensive music collection was organized by genre, composer, and artist.

"What do you think?" asked Chiara from the doorway.

"Bach's violin concertos are in the Brahms section. Otherwise, it's absolutely—"

"Amazing, I think."

"How did you possibly manage all this from Jerusalem?"

She waved a hand dismissively.

"Is there any money left?"

"Not much."

"I'll line up a few private commissions after we get settled."

"I'm afraid that's out of the question."

"Why?"

"Because you shall do no work whatsoever until you've had a chance to properly rest and recuperate." She handed him a sheet of paper. "You can start with this."

"A shopping list?"

"There's no food in the house."

"I thought I was supposed to be resting."

"You are." She smiled. "Take your time, darling. Enjoy doing something *normal* for a change."

The closest supermarket was the Carrefour near the Frari church. Gabriel's stress level seemed to subside a notch with each item he placed in his lime-green basket. Returning home, he watched the latest news from the Middle East with only passing interest while Chiara, singing softly to herself, prepared dinner in the apartment's showplace of a kitchen. They finished the last of the Barbaresco upstairs on the roof terrace, huddled closely together against the cold December air. Beneath them, gondolas swayed at their moorings. Along the gentle curve of the Grand Canal, the Rialto Bridge was awash with floodlight.

"And if I were to paint something original?" asked Gabriel. "Would that constitute work?"

"What did you have in mind?"

"A canal scene. Or perhaps a still life."

"Still life? How boring."

"In that case, how about a series of nudes?"

Chiara raised an eyebrow. "I suppose you'll need a model."

"Yes," said Gabriel, tugging at the zipper of her coat. "I suppose I will."

———————

Chiara waited until January before taking up her new position at Tiepolo Restoration. The firm's warehouse was on the mainland, but its business offices were located on the fashionable Calle Larga XXII Marzo in San Marco, a ten-minute commute by vaporetto. Francesco introduced her to the city's artistic elite and dropped cryptic hints that a succession plan had been put in place. Someone leaked the news to *Il Gazzettino*, and in late February a brief article appeared in the newspaper's Cultura section. It referred to Chiara by her maiden name, Zolli, and pointed out that her father was the chief rabbi of Venice's dwindling Jewish community. With the exception of a few nasty reader comments, mainly from the populist far right, the reception was favorable.

The story contained no mention of a spouse or domestic partner, only two children, twins apparently, of indeterminate age and gender. At Chiara's insistence, Irene and Raphael were enrolled in the neighborhood *scuola elementare* rather than one of Venice's many private international schools. Perhaps fittingly, theirs was named for Bernardo Canal, the father of Canaletto. Gabriel deposited them at the entrance at eight o'clock each morning and collected them again at half past three. Along with a daily visit to the Rialto Market, where he fetched the ingredients for the family dinner, the two appointments represented the sum total of his domestic responsibilities.

Forbidden by Chiara to work, or to even set foot in the offices of Tiepolo Restoration, he devised ways of filling his vast reservoir of available time. He read dense books. He listened to his music collection on his new sound system. He painted his nudes—from memory, of course, for his model was no longer available to him. Occasionally she came to the apartment for "lunch," which was the way they referred to the ravenous sessions of midday lovemaking in their glorious bedroom overlooking the Grand Canal.

Mainly, he walked. Not the punishing clifftop hikes of his Cornish exile, but aimless Venetian wanderings conducted in the unhurried manner of a flaneur. If he were so inclined, he would drop in on a painting he had once restored, if only to see how his work had held up. Afterward, he might slip into a bar for a coffee and, if it was cold, a small glass of something stronger to warm his bones. More often than not, one of the other patrons would attempt to engage him in conversation about the weather or the news of the day. Where once he would have spurned their overtures, he now reciprocated, in perfect if slightly accented Italian, with a witticism or keen observation of his own.

One by one, his demons took flight, and the violence of his past, the nights of blood and fire, receded from his thoughts and dreams. He laughed more easily. He allowed his hair to grow. He acquired a new wardrobe of elegant handmade trousers and cashmere jackets befitting a man of his position. Before long he scarcely recognized the figure he glimpsed each morning in the mirror of his dressing room. The transformation, he thought, was nearly complete. He was no longer Israel's avenging angel. He was the director of the paintings department of the Tiepolo Restoration Company. Chiara and Francesco had given him a second chance at life. This time, he vowed, he would not make the same mistakes.

In early March, during a bout of drenching rains, he asked Chiara for permission to begin working. And when she once again denied his request, he ordered a twelve-meter Bavaria C42 yacht and spent the next two weeks preparing a detailed itinerary for a summer sailing trip around the Adriatic and Mediterranean. He presented it to Chiara over a particularly satisfying lunch in the bedroom of their apartment.

"I have to say," she murmured approvingly, "that was one of your better performances."

"It must be all the rest I've been getting."

"Have you?"

"I'm so rested I'm on the verge of becoming bored stiff."

"Then perhaps there's something we can do to make your afternoon a bit more interesting."

"I'm not sure that would be possible."

"How about a drink with an old friend?"

"Depends on the friend."

"Julian rang me at the office as I was leaving. He said he was in Venice and was wondering whether you had a minute or two to spare."

"What did you say to him?"

"That you would meet him for a drink after you were finished having your way with me."

"Surely you left the last bit out."

"I don't believe so, no."

"What time is he expecting me?"

"Three o'clock."

"What about the children?"

"Don't worry, I'll cover for you." She glanced at her wristwatch. "The question is, what shall we do until then?"

"Since you're not wearing any clothing..."

"Yes?"

"Why don't you come to my studio and pose for me?"

"I have a better idea."

"What's that?"

Chiara smiled. "Dessert."

3

Harry's Bar

Standing beneath a cascade of scalding water, drained of desire, Gabriel rinsed the last traces of Chiara from his skin. His clothing lay scattered at the foot of their unmade bed, wrinkled, a button ripped from his shirt. He selected clean apparel from his walk-in closet, dressed quickly, and headed downstairs. As luck would have it, a Number 2 was nudging against the pier of the San Tomà stop. He rode it to San Marco and at three o'clock sharp entered the intimate confines of Harry's Bar.

Julian Isherwood was pondering his mobile phone at a corner table, a half-drunk Bellini hovering beneath his lips. When Gabriel joined him, he looked up and frowned, as though annoyed by an unwanted intrusion. Finally his features settled into an expression of recognition, followed by profound approval.

"I guess Chiara wasn't joking about how you two spend your lunch hour."

"This is Italy, Julian. We take at least two hours for lunch."

"You look thirty years younger. What's your secret?"

"Two-hour lunches with Chiara."

Julian's eyes narrowed. "But it's more than that, isn't it? You look as though you've been . . ." His voice trailed off.

"What, Julian?"

"Restored," he answered after a moment. "You've removed the dirty varnish and repaired the damage. It's almost as if none of it ever happened."

"It didn't."

"That's funny, because you bear a vague resemblance to a morose-looking boy who wandered into my gallery about a hundred years ago. Or was it two hundred?"

"That never happened, either. At least not officially," added Gabriel. "I buried your voluminous file in the deepest reaches of Registry on my way out the door of King Saul Boulevard. Your ties to the Office are now formally severed."

"But not to you, I hope."

"I'm afraid you're stuck with me." A waiter delivered two more Bellinis to their table. Gabriel raised his glass in salutation. "So what brings you to Venice?"

"These olives." Julian plucked one from the bowl at the center of the table and with a flourish popped it into his mouth. "They're dangerously good."

He was dressed in one of his Savile Row suits and a blue dress shirt with French cuffs. His gray hair was in need of a trimming, but then it usually was. All things considered, he looked rather well, except for the plaster adhered to his right cheek, perhaps two or three centimeters beneath his eye.

Cautiously Gabriel asked how it got there.

"I had an argument with my razor this morning, and I'm afraid the razor got the better of me." Julian fished another olive from the bowl. "So what do you do with yourself when you're not lunching with your beautiful wife?"

"I spend as much time as possible with my children."

"Are they bored with you yet?"

"They don't appear to be."

"Don't worry, they will be soon."

"Spoken like a lifelong bachelor."

"It has its advantages, you know."

"Name one."

"Give me a minute, I'll think of something." Julian finished his first Bellini and started in on the second. "And what about your work?" he asked.

"I painted three nudes of my wife."

"Poor you. Any good?"

"Not bad, actually."

"Three original Allons would fetch a great deal of money on the open market."

"They're for my eyes only, Julian."

Just then the door opened, and in walked a handsome dark-haired Italian in slim-fitting trousers and a quilted Barbour jacket. He sat down at a nearby table and in the accent of a southerner ordered a Campari and soda.

Julian was contemplating the bowl of olives. "Cleaned anything lately?"

"My entire CD collection."

"I was referring to paintings."

"The Tiepolo Restoration Company was recently awarded a contract by the Culture Ministry to restore Giulia Lama's four evangelists in the church of San Marziale. Chiara says that if I continue to behave myself, she'll let me do the work."

"And how much will the Tiepolo Restoration Company receive in compensation?"

"Don't ask."

"Perhaps I could tempt you with something a bit more lucrative."

"Such as?"

"A lovely Grand Canal scene that you could knock into shape in a week or two while gazing upon the real thing from your studio window."

"Attribution?"

"Northern Italian School."

"How precise," remarked Gabriel.

The "school" attribution was the murkiest designation for the origin of an Old Master painting. In the case of Julian's canal scene, it meant that the work had been produced by *some*one working *some*where in the north of Italy, at some point in the distant past. The designation "by" occupied the opposite end of the spectrum. It declared that the dealer or auction house selling the painting was certain it had been produced by the artist whose name was attached to it. Between them lay a subjective and oftentimes speculative series of categories ranging from the respectable "workshop of" to the ambiguous "after," each designed to whet the appetite of potential buyers while at the same time shielding the seller from legal action.

"Before you turn up your nose at it," said Julian, "you should know that I'll pay you enough to cover the cost of that new sailboat of yours. Two sailboats, in fact."

"It's too much for a painting like that."

"You funneled a great deal of business my way while you were running the Office. It's the least I can do."

"It wouldn't be ethical."

"I'm an art dealer, petal. If I was interested in ethics, I'd be working for Amnesty International."

"Have you run it past your partner?"

"Sarah and I are hardly partners," said Julian. "My name might still be on the door, but these days I am largely underfoot." He smiled. "I suppose I have you to thank for that, too."

It was Gabriel who had arranged for Sarah Bancroft, a veteran covert operative and overeducated art historian, to take over day-to-day control of Isherwood Fine Arts. He had also played a facilitating role in her recent decision to wed. For reasons having to do with her husband's complicated past, the ceremony was a clandestine affair, held at an MI6 safe house in the countryside of Surrey. Julian had been one of the few invited guests in attendance. Gabriel, who was late in arriving from Tel Aviv, had given away the bride.

"So where's this masterpiece of yours?" he asked.

"Under armed guard in London."

"Is there a deadline?"

"Have you another pressing commission?"

"That depends."

"On what?"

"How you answer my next question."

"You want to know what really happened to my face?"

Gabriel nodded. "The truth this time, Julian."

"I was attacked by a lamppost."

"Another one?"

"I'm afraid so."

"Please tell me it was a foggy night in London."

"Actually, it was yesterday afternoon in Bordeaux. I went there at the invitation of a woman named Valerie Bérrangar. She said she wanted to tell me something about a painting I sold not long ago."

"Not the Van Dyck?"

"Yes, that's the one."

"Is there a problem?"

"I wouldn't know. You see, Madame Bérrangar died in an automobile accident on the way to our meeting."

"And the incident involving the lamppost?" asked Gabriel.

"Two men on a motorcycle tried to steal my briefcase as I was walking back to my hotel. At least I think that's what they were doing. For all I know," said Julian, "they were trying to kill me, too."

4

San Marco

In the Piazza San Marco, a string quartet wearily serenaded the day's last customers at Caffè Florian.

"Are they incapable of playing anything other than Vivaldi?" asked Julian.

"What have you got against Vivaldi?"

"I adore him. But how about Corelli for a change of pace? Or Handel, for heaven's sake?"

"Or Anthony van Dyck." Gabriel paused before a shop window in the arcade on the square's southern flank. "The original story in *ARTnews* didn't mention where you found the painting. It didn't identify the buyer, either. The price tag, however, received prominent play."

"Six and a half million pounds." Julian smiled. "Now ask me how much I paid for the bloody thing."

"I was getting to that."

"Three million euros."

"Which means your profit was in excess of one hundred percent."

"But that's how the secondary art market works, petal. Dealers like me search out misattributed, misplaced, or undervalued paintings and bring them to market, hopefully with enough flair and panache to attract one or more deep-pocketed buyers. And don't forget, I had my expenses, too."

"Long lunches at London's finest restaurants?"

"Actually, most of the lunches took place in Paris. You see, I bought the painting from a gallery in the Eighth. The rue la Boétie, of all places."

"Does this gallery have a name?"

"Galerie Georges Fleury."

"Have you done business with him in the past?"

"A great deal. Monsieur Fleury specializes in French paintings from the seventeenth and eighteenth centuries, but he deals in Dutch and Flemish works as well. He has excellent relationships with many of France's oldest and wealthiest families. The ones who live in drafty châteaux crammed with art. He contacts me when he finds something interesting."

"Where did he find *Portrait of an Unknown Woman*?"

"It came from an old private collection. That's all he would say."

"Attribution?"

"Manner of Anthony van Dyck."

"Which covers all *manner* of sins."

"Indeed," agreed Julian. "But Monsieur Fleury thought he saw evidence of the master's hand. He called me for a second opinion."

"And?"

"The instant I laid eyes on it, I got that funny feeling at the back of my neck."

They emerged from the arcade into the fading afternoon light. To their left rose the Campanile. Gabriel led Julian to the right instead, past the ornate facade of the Doge's Palace. On the Ponte della Paglia, they joined a knot of tourists gawking at the Bridge of Sighs.

"Looking for something?" asked Julian.

"You know what they say about old habits."

"I'm afraid that most of mine are bad. You, however, are the most disciplined creature I've ever met."

On the opposite side of the bridge lay the *sestiere* of Castello. They hurried past the souvenir kiosks lining the Riva degli Schiavoni, then followed the passageway to the Campo San Zaccaria, home of the Carabinieri's regional headquarters. Julian had once spent a sleepless night in an interrogation room on the second floor.

"How's your old friend General Ferrari?" he asked. "Still pulling the wings off flies? Or has he managed to find a new hobby?"

General Cesare Ferrari was the commander of the Carabinieri's Division for the Defense of Cultural Patrimony, better known as the Art Squad. It was headquartered in a palazzo in Rome's Piazza di Sant'Ignazio, though three of its officers were stationed full-time in Venice. While not searching for stolen paintings, they kept tabs on the former Israeli spymaster and assassin living quietly in San Polo. It was General Ferrari who had arranged for Gabriel to receive a *permesso di soggiorno*, a permanent Italian residence permit. Consequently, Gabriel tried to stay on his good side, no easy feat.

Adjacent to the Carabinieri headquarters was the church for which the square was named. Among the many monumental works of art adorning the nave was a crucifixion executed by Anthony van Dyck during the six-year period he spent studying and working in Italy. Gabriel stood before it, a hand to his chin, his head tilted slightly to one side.

"You were about to tell me about the painting's provenance."

"It was good enough for me."

"Meaning?"

"It depicted a portrait that had been executed in the late sixteen twenties and had made its way over the centuries from Flanders to France. There were no glaring holes and no red flags."

"Did it require restoration?"

"Monsieur Fleury had it cleaned before he showed it to me. He has his own man. Not your caliber, mind you. But not bad." Julian crossed to the opposite side of the nave and stood before Bellini's majestic *San Zaccaria Altarpiece*. "You did a lovely job with it. Old Giovanni would have approved."

"You think so?"

Julian cast a glance of mild reproach over one shoulder. "Modesty doesn't suit you, my boy. Your restoration of this painting was the talk of the art world."

"It took me longer to clean it than it did for Giovanni to paint it."

"There were extenuating circumstances, as I recall."

"There usually were." Gabriel joined Julian in front of the altar-piece. "I assume that you and Sarah got a second opinion about the attribution after the painting arrived in London."

"Not just a second opinion. A third, a fourth, and a fifth as well. And all of our gold-plated hired guns concluded that the painting was the work of Anthony van Dyck and not a later follower. Within a week we had a bidding war on our hands."

"Who was the lucky winner?"

"Masterpiece Art Ventures. It's an art-based hedge fund run by one of Sarah's old contacts from her days in New York. Someone called Phillip Somerset."

"The name rings a distant bell," said Gabriel.

"Masterpiece Art Ventures buys and sells an enormous number of paintings. Everything from Old Masters to contemporary. Phillip Somerset routinely shows his investors twenty-five-percent annual returns, from which he takes a substantial cut. And he can be quite litigious if he thinks someone has wronged him. Suing people is his favorite pastime."

"Which is why you went running to Bordeaux when you received a rather ambiguous letter from a perfect stranger."

"Actually, it was Sarah who convinced me to go. As for the letter, the men on the motorbike obviously thought it was in my briefcase. That's why they tried to steal it."

"They might have been ordinary thieves, you know. Street crime is one of the few growth industries in France these days."

"They weren't."

"How can you be sure?"

"Because when I got back to the hotel after being discharged from *l'hôpital*, it was quite obvious that my room had been searched." Julian patted the front of his jacket. "Fortunately, they didn't find what they were looking for."

"Searched by whom?"

"Two well-dressed men. They paid the bellman fifty euros to let them into my room."

"How much did the bellman get from you?"

"A hundred," answered Julian. "As you might expect, I passed a rather restless night. When I woke this morning, there was a copy of *Sud Ouest* outside my door. After reading the story about a fatal single-vehicle accident south of Bordeaux, I hastily packed my things and caught the first train to Paris. I was able to make the eleven o'clock flight to Venice."

"Because you were craving the olives at Harry's Bar?"

"Actually, I was wondering—"

"Whether you might prevail upon me to find out what Valerie Bérrangar wanted to tell you about *Portrait of an Unknown Woman* by Anthony van Dyck."

"You *do* have friends in high places in the French government," said Julian. "Which will enable you to conduct an inquiry with absolute discretion and thus reduce the chance of a scandal."

"And if I'm successful?"

"I suppose that depends on the nature of the information. If there is indeed a legal or ethical problem with the sale, I will quietly refund

Phillip Somerset's six and a half million quid before he drags me into court and destroys what's left of my once glittering reputation." Julian offered Gabriel Madame Bérrangar's letter. "Not to mention the reputation of your dear friend Sarah Bancroft."

Gabriel hesitated, then accepted the letter. "I'll need the attribution reports from your experts. And photographs of the painting, of course."

Julian produced his smartphone. "Where shall I send them?"

Gabriel recited an address at ProtonMail, the Swiss-based encrypted email service. A moment later, secure mobile phone in hand, he was scrutinizing a high-resolution detail image of the unknown woman's pale cheek.

At length he asked, "Did any of your experts take a close look at the craquelure?"

"Why do you ask?"

"You know that funny feeling you got when you saw this painting for the first time?"

"Of course."

"I just got it, too."

———

Julian had booked a room for the night at the Gritti Palace. Gabriel saw him to the door, then made his way to the Campo Santa Maria del Giglio. There was not a tourist in sight. It was as if a drain had opened, he thought, and washed them out to sea.

On the western side of the square, next to the Hotel Ala, was the entrance to a narrow, darkened *calle*. Gabriel followed it to the vaporetto station and joined three other passengers—a prosperous-looking Scandinavian couple in their late sixties and a world-weary Venetian woman of perhaps forty—waiting beneath the shelter. The Scandinavians were huddled over a map. The Venetian woman was watching a Number 1 crawling up the Grand Canal from the direction of San Marco.

When the vessel nudged against the jetty, the Venetian woman boarded first, followed by the Scandinavians. All three claimed seats in the cabin. Gabriel, as was his habit, stood in the open-air passage behind the pilothouse. There he was able to observe a single late-arriving passenger emerging from the *calle*.

Dark hair. Slim-fitting trousers. A quilted Barbour jacket.

The man from Harry's Bar.

5

Canal Grande

He entered the passenger cabin and lowered himself into a blue-green plastic seat in the first row. He was taller than Gabriel remembered, formidably built, in the prime of life. Early thirties, thirty-five at most. The malodorous trail he left in his wake indicated he was a smoker. The slight bulge in the left side of his jacket suggested he was armed.

Fortunately, Gabriel was in possession of a gun as well—a Beretta 92FS 9mm pistol with a walnut grip. He carried it with the full knowledge and consent of General Ferrari and the Carabinieri. Nevertheless, it was his intention to resolve the situation without having to draw the weapon, as an act of violence, even one in self-defense, would likely result in the immediate revocation of his *permesso*, which in turn would endanger his standing at home.

The most obvious course of action was to shed the man as quickly as possible. In a city like Venice, with its labyrinthine streets and gloomy *sotoportegi*, it would not prove difficult. It would, however, deprive Gabriel of the opportunity to determine why the man was following him. It was better to have a quiet word with him in private, he reasoned, than to lose him.

The Palazzo Venier dei Leoni, home of the Peggy Guggenheim Collection, slid right to left through Gabriel's field of vision. The two Scandinavians disembarked at the Accademia; the Venetian woman, at Ca' Rezzonico. San Tomà, Gabriel's stop, was next. He stood stock-still behind the pilothouse as the vaporetto alighted long enough to collect a single passenger.

As the vessel withdrew, he lifted his gaze briefly toward the soaring windows of his new apartment. They were aglow with amber-colored light. His children were doing their schoolwork. His wife was preparing dinner. Doubtless she was troubled over his prolonged absence. He would be home soon, he thought. He had one small matter to attend to first.

The vaporetto crossed the canal to the Sant'Angelo stop, then returned to the San Polo side and docked at San Silvestri. This time Gabriel disembarked and, leaving the platform, entered an unlit *sotoportego*. From behind him came the sound of footsteps—the footsteps of a formidably built man in the prime of life. Perhaps, thought Gabriel, a small measure of violence was called for, after all.

———

He fell into the easy, unhurried pace of his afternoon sojourns through the city. Even so, he twice had to loiter outside shop windows in order to keep his pursuer in the game. He was no professional surveillance artist; that much was obvious. Nor did he seem to be familiar with the streets of the *sestiere*, a shortcoming that would provide Gabriel with a distinct home-field advantage.

He continued in a northwesterly direction—across the Campo Sant'Aponal, along a succession of slender alleyways, over a humpbacked bridge—until he came to a *corte* bordered on three sides by apartment buildings. He knew with certainty that the dwellings had fallen into a state of disrepair and were unoccupied, which is why he had chosen the courtyard as his destination.

He moved to a darkened corner and listened to his pursuer's approaching footfalls. A long moment passed before the man blundered into view. He paused in a puddle of moonlight, then, realizing there was no way out, turned to leave.

"Looking for something?" asked Gabriel calmly in Italian.

The man wheeled around and reached reflexively toward the front of his jacket.

"I wouldn't do that if I were you."

The man froze.

"Why are you following me?"

"I'm not."

"You were in Harry's Bar. You were on the Number One. And now you're here." Gabriel stepped from the shadows. "Twice is a coincidence. Third time is the charm."

"I'm looking for a restaurant."

"Tell me the name, and I'll take you there."

"Osteria da Fiore."

"Not even close." Gabriel took another step across the courtyard. "Please reach for your gun again."

"Why?"

"So I won't feel guilty about breaking your nose, your jaw, and several of your ribs."

Wordlessly the young Italian turned to one side, raised his left hand defensively, and bunched his right fist against his hip.

"All right," said Gabriel with a sigh of resignation. "If you insist."

The Israeli martial arts discipline known as Krav Maga is characterized by constant aggression, simultaneous offensive and defensive measures, and utter ruthlessness. Speed is prized above all else. Typically contests are short in duration—no more than a few seconds—and decisive in outcome. Once launched, an attack does not cease until the adversary has been completely incapacitated. Permanent injury is commonplace. Death is not out of the question.

No part of the body is off-limits. Indeed, practitioners of Krav Maga are encouraged to focus their attacks on vulnerable, sensitive regions. Gabriel's opening gambit consisted of a vicious kick to his opponent's exposed left kneecap, followed by a crushing downward heel strike on the instep of the left foot. Next he ventured north to the groin and solar plexus before directing several rapid elbows and side-handed blows to the throat, the nose, and the head. At no point did the younger, larger Italian manage to land a punch or kick of his own. Still, Gabriel did not emerge unscathed. His right hand was throbbing painfully, probably from a minor fracture, the Krav Maga equivalent of an own goal.

With the fingers of his left hand, he checked his fallen opponent for evidence of a pulse and respiration. Finding both, he reached inside the front of the man's jacket and confirmed that he was indeed armed—with a Beretta 8000, the standard-issue sidearm for officers of the Carabinieri. Which explained the credentials that Gabriel found in the unconscious man's pocket. They identified him as Capitano Luca Rossetti of the Venice division of Il Nucleo Tutela Patrimonio Artistico.

The Art Squad . . .

Gabriel returned the gun to its holster and the credentials to their pocket, then rang the regional headquarters of the Carabinieri to report an injured man lying in a *corte* near the Campo Sant'Aponal. He did so anonymously, with his phone number concealed, and in perfect *veneziano*. He would deal with General Ferrari in the morning. In the meantime, he had to concoct a plausible cover story to explain his injured hand to Chiara. It came to him as he crossed the Ponte San Polo. It wasn't his fault, he would tell her. The bloody lamppost attacked him.

6

San Polo

Five minutes later, while climbing the staircase toward the door of the apartment, Gabriel encountered the tantalizing fragrance of veal simmering in wine and aromatics. He entered the passcode into the keypad and turned the latch, performing both tasks with his left hand. His right was concealed in the pocket of his jacket. It remained there as he entered the sitting room, where he found Irene stretched upon the carpet, a pencil in her fist, her tiny porcelain brow furrowed.

Gabriel addressed her in Italian. "There's a lovely desk in your room, you know."

"I prefer to work on the floor. It helps me concentrate."

"What sort of work are you doing?"

"Math, silly." She looked up at Gabriel with the eyes of his mother. "Where have you been?"

"I had an appointment."

"With whom?"

"An old friend."

"Does he work for the Office?"

"Wherever did you get an idea like that?"

"Because it seems like all your old *friends* do."

"Not all of them," said Gabriel, and looked at Raphael. The boy was sprawled on the couch, his long-lashed, jade-colored eyes focused with unnerving intensity on the screen of his handheld video console. "What's he playing?"

"Mario."

"Who?"

"It's a computer game."

"Why isn't he doing his schoolwork?"

"He's finished." With the tip of her pencil, Irene pointed toward her brother's notebook. "See for yourself."

Gabriel craned his head to one side and reviewed Raphael's work. Twenty rudimentary equations involving addition and subtraction, all answered correctly on the first attempt.

"Were you good at math when you were little?" asked Irene.

"It didn't interest me much."

"What about Mama?"

"She studied Roman history."

"In Padua?"

"Yes."

"Is that where Raphael and I will go to university?"

"You're rather young to be thinking about that, aren't you?"

Sighing, she licked the tip of her forefinger and turned to a fresh page in her workbook. In the warmth of the kitchen, Gabriel found Chiara removing the cork from a bottle of Brunello di Montalcino. Andrea Bocelli flowed from the Bluetooth speaker on the counter.

"I've always loved that song," said Gabriel.

"I wonder why." Chiara used her phone to lower the volume. "Going somewhere?"

"Sorry?"

"You're still wearing your overcoat."

"I'm a little chilled, that's all." He wandered over to the gleaming stainless-steel Vulcan oven and peered through the window. Inside was the orange casserole dish that Chiara used for preparing osso buco. "What have I done to deserve this?"

"I can think of one or two things. Or three," she added.

"How long until it's ready?"

"It needs another thirty minutes." She poured two glasses of the Brunello. "Leaving you just enough time to tell me about your conversation with Julian."

"We'll talk after dinner, if you don't mind."

"Is there a problem?"

He turned abruptly. "Why do you ask?"

"There usually is one where Julian is concerned." Chiara regarded him carefully for a moment. "And you seem upset about something."

He decided, with no small amount of guilt, that the wisest course of action was to blame his edgy mood on Raphael. "Your son failed to notice my return home because he was hypnotized by that computer game of his."

"I gave him permission."

"Why?"

"Because it took him all of five minutes to finish his math homework. His teachers think he's gifted. They want him to begin working with a specialist."

"He certainly didn't get it from me."

"Nor from me." Chiara offered him a glass of the wine. "There's a package in your studio. It looks as though it might be from your girlfriend Anna Rolfe." She smiled coolly. "Listen to a bit of music and relax. You'll feel better."

"I feel just fine."

Gabriel accepted the wine with his left hand and withdrew to the master bathroom suite, where he subjected the injured extremity to a thorough examination by the light of Chiara's vanity. The sharp pain produced by a gentle probe indicated at least a hairline fracture to the fifth metacarpal. Significant swelling was plainly evident, but as yet there was no visible bruising. At a bare minimum, immediate immobilization and icing were required. Given the circumstances, however, neither was possible, leaving Gabriel no treatment option other than alcohol and pain reliever.

He took down a bottle of ibuprofen from the medicine chest, shook several emerald capsules into his palm, and swallowed them with a mouthful of the Brunello. Repairing to his studio, he found the package. It had been sent to him by the publicity department of Deutsche Grammophon. Inside was a two-CD survey of Mozart's five remarkable violin concertos, notable for the fact that the soloist had recorded the pieces with the same instrument upon which they had been composed.

Gabriel placed the first disc onto the tray of his CD player, tapped the PLAY button, and went to his easel. There he gazed upon a beautiful young woman draped nude across a brocade-covered couch, her melancholy gaze fixed upon the viewer—in this case, the artist who had painted her. *Is there a problem?* No, he thought as his hand throbbed with pain. No problem at all.

––––––––

Gabriel managed to listen to the first two concertos before Chiara summoned him to the dining room. The meal arrayed upon the table looked as though it had been staged for a photo shoot by *Bon Appétit*—the risotto, the platter of roasted vegetables glistening with olive oil, and, of course, the thick veal shanks drenched in a rich sauce of tomato and herbs and wine. As always, they were fork tender, allowing Gabriel to eat with one hand, keeping the other cradled protectively in his lap. The Brunello-and-Advil therapy had worked its magic; he was only vaguely aware of the pain. He was certain, however, it would return with a vengeance the instant the drug wore off, probably sometime around three in the morning.

Chiara's eyes shone with candlelight as she guided the conversation. Diplomatically she raised the subject of Raphael's mathematical prowess, which in turn led to a discussion of how his gifts might be put to good use. Irene, the family environmentalist, suggested that her brother consider pursuing a career as a climate scientist.

"Why?" probed Gabriel.

"Did you read the new UN report about global warming?"

"Did *you*?"

"We talked about it at school. Signora Antonelli says Venice will soon be underwater because the Greenland ice sheet is melting. She says none of it would have happened if the Americans hadn't withdrawn from the Paris Agreement."

"That's debatable."

"She also says it's too late to prevent a significant increase in global temperatures."

"She's right about that."

"Why did the Americans withdraw?"

"The man who was president at the time thought global warming was a hoax."

"Who would believe such a thing?"

"It's a rather common affliction among Americans of the far right. But let's talk about something pleasant, shall we?"

It was Raphael who chose the subject. "What does *woke* mean?"

Gabriel directed his gaze toward his son and, to the best of his ability, answered. "It's a word that emerged from the Black community in the United States. If someone is woke, it means they care about issues involving racial intolerance and societal injustice."

"Are you woke?"

"Evidently."

"I think I'm woke, too."

"I'd keep it to myself, if I were you."

At the conclusion of the meal, the children volunteered to clear away the plates and serving dishes, a feat they accomplished with minimal conflict and no breakage. Chiara poured the last of the wine into their glasses and held hers to the light of the candles.

"Where shall we begin?" she asked. "Your meeting with Julian or the new tattoo on your right hand?"

"It's not a tattoo."

"That's a relief. What is it?"

Gabriel removed his hand from his lap and laid it carefully on the tablecloth.

Chiara winced. "It looks dreadful."

"Yes," said Gabriel gloomily. "But you should see the other guy."

7

San Polo

Have you tried to hold a paintbrush?"

"I'm not sure I ever will again."

"How bad is the pain?"

"At the moment," said Gabriel, "I can't feel a thing."

He was perched on a stool at the kitchen island, his hand submerged in a bowl of ice and water. It had done nothing to reduce the swelling. If anything, it appeared to be growing worse.

"You really should have it X-rayed," said Chiara.

"And when the orthopedist asks how I broke it?"

"How did you?"

"I assume it was the knifehand strike."

"Where did it land?"

"I'd rather not say."

"Are you sure you didn't kill him?"

"He'll be fine."

"Will he?"

"Eventually."

With a sigh of dismay, Chiara took up Madame Valerie Bérrangar's letter. "What do you suppose she wanted to tell Julian?"

"I can think of several possibilities," said Gabriel. "Starting with the most obvious."

"What's that?"

"The painting was hers."

"If that were the case, why didn't she contact the police?"

"Who's to say she didn't?"

"Surely Julian checked the Art Loss Register before taking it to market?"

"No dealer ever acquires or sells a work of art without first checking to see whether it's been pinched."

"Unless the dealer doesn't want to know whether it's stolen."

"Our Julian is far from perfect," said Gabriel. "But he has never knowingly sold a stolen painting."

"Not even on your behalf?"

"I don't believe so."

Chiara smiled. "Possibility number two?"

"The work was seized from the Bérrangar family during the war and has been missing ever since."

"Do you think Valerie Bérrangar was Jewish?"

"Did I say that?"

Chiara set aside the letter. "Possibility number three?"

"Unlock my phone."

Chiara entered his fourteen-digit hard password. "What am I looking at?"

"A detail image from *Portrait of an Unknown Woman*."

"Is there a problem?"

"What does the craquelure pattern look like to you?"

"Tree bark."

"And what does that tell you?"

"I will defer to your superior knowledge."

"Surface cracks resembling tree bark are typical of Flemish paintings," explained Gabriel. "Van Dyck was a Flemish painter, of course.

But he worked with materials similar to those being used by his contemporaries in Holland."

"So his surface cracks appear more Dutch than Flemish?"

"Correct. If you look at *Lady Elizabeth Thimbelby and Her Sister* on the website of the National Gallery, you'll see what I mean."

"I'll take your word for it," answered Chiara, her thumbnails clicking against the surface of Gabriel's phone.

"What are you looking for?"

"The article in *Sud Ouest*." She dragged the tip of her forefinger down the screen. "Here it is. The accident happened yesterday afternoon on the D10, just north of Saint-Macaire. The gendarmes seem to think she somehow lost control of her car."

"How old was she?"

"Seventy-four."

"Married?"

"Widowed. Apparently, there's a daughter named Juliette Lagarde." Chiara paused. "Perhaps she'll agree to see you."

"I thought I was supposed to be resting."

"You are. But under the circumstances it's probably better if you leave Venice for a few days. With any luck, you'll be airborne before General Ferrari realizes you're gone."

Gabriel removed his hand from the ice water. "What do you think?"

"A splint should suffice. You can pick one up at the pharmacy on your way to the airport. But I would advise you to avoid striking anyone while you're in Bordeaux."

"It wasn't my fault."

"Whose fault was it, darling?"

It was Madame Bérrangar's, he thought. She should have simply telephoned Julian's gallery in London. Instead, she had sent him a letter. And now she was dead.

8

San Polo

Exhausted, Gabriel crawled into bed and, with his hand cradled gently against his chest, fell into a dreamless sleep. The pain roused him at four o'clock. He lay awake for another hour, listening to the barges making their way up the Grand Canal toward the Rialto Market, before padding into the kitchen and pressing the power button on the Lavazza *automatico*.

While waiting for the coffee to brew, he stirred his phone into life and was relieved to discover he had received no overnight correspondence from General Ferrari. A check of *Sud Ouest* confirmed that Valerie Bérrangar, seventy-four years of age, was still dead. There was a small update to the story regarding the arrangements for her funeral. It was scheduled for 10:00 a.m. on Friday, at the Église Saint-Sauveur in Saint-Macaire. Regardless of Madame Bérrangar's religious affiliation at the beginning of her life, thought Gabriel, it appeared as though she had ended it as a Roman Catholic.

He swallowed another dose of ibuprofen with his coffee. Then he showered and dressed and placed a few items of clothing into an overnight bag while Chiara, tangled in Egyptian cotton, slept on in the next room. The children spilled from their beds at half past six and demanded to be fed. Irene fixed Gabriel with an accusatory stare over her customary breakfast of muesli and yogurt.

"Mama says you're going to France."

"Not for long."

"What does that mean?"

"It means that your grandmother will be picking you up at school for the next few days."

"How many days?"

"To be determined."

"We like it when *you* pick us up," declared Raphael.

"That's because I always take you to the *pasticceria* on the way home."

"That's not the only reason."

"I like picking you up, too," said Gabriel. "In fact, it's one of my favorite parts of the day."

"What's your favorite?"

"Next question."

"Why do you have to leave again?" asked Irene.

"A friend needs my help."

"*Another* friend?"

"Same friend, actually."

She inflated her cheeks and stirred the contents of her bowl without appetite. Gabriel knew full well the source of her anxiety. Three times during his tenure as director-general of the Office he had been targeted for assassination. The last attempt had taken place on Inauguration Day in Washington, when he had been shot in the chest by a congresswoman from the American Midwest who believed him to be a member of a blood-drinking, Satan-worshipping cult of pedophiles. The two preceding attempts, though more prosaic, had both taken place in France. For the most part, the children pretended that none of the incidents, though widely publicized, had transpired. Gabriel, who still suffered from the unpleasant aftereffects, was similarly inclined.

"Nothing is going to happen," he assured his daughter.

"You always say that. But something *always* happens."

Having no retort at the ready, Gabriel looked up and saw Chiara standing in the doorway of the kitchen, an expression of mild bemusement on her face.

"She does have a point, you know." Chiara poured herself a cup of coffee and looked at Gabriel's hand. "How does it feel?"

"Good as new."

She gave it a gentle squeeze. "No pain at all?"

He grimaced but said nothing.

"I thought so." She released his hand. "Are you packed?"

"Almost."

"Who's taking Thing One and Thing Two to school?"

"Papa," sang the children in unison.

He returned to the bedroom and unlocked the safe concealed in the walk-in closet. Inside were two false German passports, €20,000 in cash, and his Beretta. He removed one of the passports but left the gun behind, as his arrangement with the Italian authorities did not permit him to carry firearms on airplanes. Besides, if circumstances warranted, he could acquire an untraceable weapon in France with a single phone call, with or without the connivance of his old service.

He deposited the bag in the entrance hall and at 7:45 a.m. followed Chiara and the children down the stairs of the palazzo. Outside in the street, Chiara set off toward the San Tomà vaporetto station. Then she stopped abruptly and kissed Gabriel's lips.

"You *will* be careful in France, won't you?"

"Cross my heart."

"Wrong answer, darling." She placed her palm on the left side of Gabriel's chest and felt the sudden pulse of his phone. "Oh, dear. I wonder who that could be."

9

―――

Bar Dogale

After entrusting Irene and Raphael to Signora Antonelli, their
environmentally conscious and reliably democratic socialist
teacher, Gabriel made his way through empty streets to the Campo
dei Frari. The square remained in morning shadow, but a benevo-
lent sun had established dominion over the red-tile rooftops of the
mighty Gothic basilica. At the foot of the bell tower, the second-
tallest in Venice, stood eight chrome tables covered in blue, the property of Bar Dogale, one of the better tourist cafés in San Polo.

At one of the tables sat General Ferrari. He had forsaken his blue
uniform, with its many medals and insignia, and was wearing a business suit and overcoat instead. The hand he offered in greeting was
missing two fingers, the result of a letter bomb he received in 1988
while serving as chief of the Carabinieri's Naples division. Nevertheless, his grip was viselike.

"Something wrong?" he asked as Gabriel sat down.

"Too many years holding a paintbrush."

"Consider yourself lucky. I had to learn how to do almost everything with my left hand. And then, of course, there's this." The gen-

eral pointed toward his prosthetic right eye. "You, however, appear to have come through your most recent brush with death with scarcely a scratch."

"Hardly."

"How close did we come to losing you in Washington?"

"I flatlined twice. The second time, I was clinically dead for nearly ten minutes."

"Did you happen to see anything?"

"Like what?"

"A brilliant white light? The face of the Almighty?"

"Not that I can recall."

The general seemed disappointed by Gabriel's answer. "I was afraid you were going to say that."

"It doesn't mean that there isn't a life after this one, Cesare. It just means that I have no memory of anything that happened after I lost consciousness."

"Have you given the matter any thought yourself?"

"The existence of God? An afterlife?"

The general nodded.

"The Holocaust robbed my parents of their belief in God. The religion of my childhood home was Zionism."

"You're entirely secular?"

"My faith comes and goes."

"And your wife?"

"She's a rabbi's daughter."

"I have it on the highest authority that the cultural and artistic guardians of Venice are quite smitten with her. It appears the two of you have a bright future here." The general's prosthetic eye contemplated Gabriel sightlessly for a moment. "Which makes your recent behavior all the more difficult to explain."

He entered the passcode into his smartphone and laid it on the tabletop. Gabriel lowered his eyes briefly to the screen. The bruised and swollen face depicted there bore little resemblance to the one he had seen the previous evening.

"His jaw had to be wired shut," said General Ferrari. "For an Italian, a fate worse than death."

"He'd be sitting down to a nice long lunch later today if only he'd identified himself."

"He says you didn't give him much of a chance."

"Why was he following me in the first place?"

"He wasn't," answered Ferrari. "He was following your friend."

"Julian Isherwood? Whatever for?"

"As a result of that unfortunate business in Lake Como a few years ago, Signore Isherwood remains on the Art Squad's watchlist. We keep an eye on him whenever he comes to Italy. Young Rossetti, who was assigned to Venice only last week, drew the short straw."

"He should have walked out of Harry's Bar the minute he saw Julian with me."

"I ordered him to stay."

"Because you wanted to know what we were talking about?"

"I suppose I did."

"That still doesn't explain why he followed me onto the vaporetto."

"I wanted to make certain you arrived home safely. And how did you repay this act of kindness? By beating one of my best young recruits to a pulp in a darkened *corte*."

"It was a misunderstanding."

"Be that as it may, I am left with a most difficult choice."

"What's that?"

"Immediate deportation or a lengthy incarceration. I'm leaning toward the latter."

"And what must I do to avoid this fate?"

"You can start by showing at least a trace of remorse."

"Mea culpa, mea culpa, mea maxima culpa."

"Much better. Now tell me why Signore Isherwood came to Venice. Otherwise," said the general, glancing at his wristwatch, "you're liable to miss your flight."

———

Over a breakfast of *cappuccini* and *cornetti*, Gabriel recounted the story as Julian had told it. Ferrari's artificial eye remained fixed on him throughout, unblinking. His expression betrayed nothing—nothing, thought Gabriel, other than perhaps mild boredom. The general was the leader of the world's largest and most sophisticated art crime unit. He had heard it all before.

"It's not so easily done, you know. Engineering a fatal car accident."

"Unless it was carried out by professionals."

"Have you ever?"

"Killed anyone with a car? Not that I can recall," said Gabriel. "But there's a first time for everything."

The general emitted a parched laugh. "Still, the most logical explanation is that the Bérrangar woman was running late for her appointment with Signore Isherwood and died in a tragic accident."

"What about the two men who tried to steal Julian's briefcase?"

Ferrari shrugged his shoulders. "Thieves."

"And the ones who searched his hotel room?"

"The search," acknowledged the general, "is harder to explain. Therefore, I would advise your friend to tell the French art crime unit everything he knows. It's a division of the Police Nationale called the Central Office for the Fight against Cultural Goods Trafficking."

"Catchy," remarked Gabriel.

"I suppose it sounds better in French."

"Most things do."

"I'd be happy to contact my French counterpart. His name is Jacques Ménard. He dislikes me only a little."

"Signore Isherwood has no wish to involve the police in this matter."

"And why is that?"

"An allergy, I suppose."

"A common affliction among art dealers and collectors. Unless one of their precious paintings goes missing, of course. Then we're suddenly quite popular." The general offered an approximation of a smile. "I assume that you intend to start with the daughter."

"If she'll agree to see me."

"Who could possibly resist the opportunity to meet with the great Gabriel Allon?"

"A woman who is mourning the death of her mother."

"What about the dealer in Paris?"

"Julian swears he's reputable."

"If you like, I can run his name through our database and see if anything turns up."

"I have contacts of my own in the Paris art trade."

"The dirty side of the trade, as I recall." General Ferrari expelled a lungful of air. "Which returns us to the topic of young Capitano Rossetti."

"Perhaps I should speak to him."

"I can assure you, Rossetti has no wish to see you. If the truth be told, he's rather embarrassed by the way things turned out last night. After all, you *are* half his size."

"And twice his age."

"That, too."

Gabriel checked the time.

"Going somewhere?" inquired the general.

"The airport, I hope."

"A Carabinieri patrol boat will collect you at San Tomà at ten o'clock."

"Ten is cutting it rather close, don't you think?"

"A representative from Alitalia will escort you through security and directly onto the plane. And don't worry about Chiara and the children," the general added as he ordered two more *cappuccini*. "We'll keep an eye on them while you're away."

10

Villa Bérrangar

In the Middle Ages, when English kings laid claim to all of France, the picturesque village of Saint-Macaire was designated a *ville royale d'Angleterre*. It seemed that little had changed in the intervening centuries. A medieval tower stood guard over the entrance to the old city, its clockface showing half past five. Next to it was a café called La Belle Lurette. Gabriel handed the waiter twenty euros and asked whether he knew the address of Madame Valerie Bérrangar.

"She was killed in an auto accident on Monday afternoon."

Gabriel wordlessly handed over another banknote.

"Her villa is near Château Malromé. About two kilometers to the east." The waiter slipped the money into the pocket of his apron. "The entrance will be on your left. You can't miss it."

The château stood on a broad hillside north of Saint-Macaire, in the commune of Saint-André-du-Bois. Renowned for the quality of its gravelly clay soil, the forty-hectare property was acquired in the late nineteenth century by Countess Adèle de Toulouse-Lautrec. Her son, a painter and illustrator who often found inspiration in the brothels and cabarets of Paris, had passed his summers there.

East of the château the road was dangerously narrow and lined on both sides with vineyards. With one eye on the instrument panel of his rented sedan, Gabriel drove two kilometers exactly and, as promised, glimpsed a dwelling on the left side of the road. Parked in the forecourt was a Peugeot estate car, metallic blue, Paris registration. Gabriel drew up next to it and switched off the engine. The instant he opened his door, a dog barked ferociously. But of course, he thought, and climbed out.

Warily he approached the entrance of the villa. As he stretched out a hand toward the bell push, the door opened to reveal a woman, dark in dress and demeanor, with the pale skin of someone who assiduously avoided the sun. She looked to be in her early forties, but Gabriel couldn't be sure. An Old Master painting he could reliably date to within a few years. But modern women, with their age-concealing balms and injections, were a mystery to him.

"Madame Lagarde?"

"*Oui*," she answered. "May I help you, monsieur?"

Gabriel introduced himself. Not with a work name, or one he plucked from thin air, but his real name.

"Have we met somewhere before?" asked Juliette Lagarde.

"I rather doubt it."

"But your name is very familiar." Her eyes narrowed. "Your face, too."

"You might have read about me in the newspapers."

"Why?"

"I used to be the chief of the Israeli intelligence service. I worked closely with the French government in the fight against the Islamic State."

"Not *that* Gabriel Allon."

He offered her an apologetic smile. "I'm afraid so."

"What on earth are you doing here?"

"I'd like to ask you a few questions about your mother."

"My mother—"

"Was killed in an accident on Monday afternoon." Gabriel glanced over his shoulder toward the large Belgian shepherd berating him from the forecourt. "Would it be possible for us to talk inside?"

"You're not afraid of dogs, are you?"

"*Non*," said Gabriel. "Only dogs like that."

————————

As it turned out, Juliette Lagarde didn't much care for the dog, either. It belonged to Jean-Luc, the caretaker. He had worked for the Bérrangar family for more than thirty years, looking after the house when they were in Paris, tending to the small vineyard. Juliette's father, a prosperous commercial lawyer, had planted it with his own hands. He had died of a massive heart attack while Juliette was still a student at the Paris-Sorbonne University. Having earned a useless degree in literature, she now worked in the marketing department of one of France's largest fashion houses. Her mother, unnerved by the jihadist terrorist attacks in Paris, had lately been spending most of her time in Saint-André-du-Bois.

"She wasn't an Islamophobe or a follower of the far right, mind you. She just preferred the countryside to the city. I worried about her being alone, but she had friends here. A life of her own."

They were standing in the villa's spacious kitchen, waiting for the water to boil in the electric kettle. The house around them was silent.

"How often did you speak to her?" asked Gabriel.

"Once or twice a week." Juliette Lagarde sighed. "Our relationship had been strained of late."

"May I ask why?"

"We were quarreling over the question of remarriage."

"She was involved with someone?"

"My mother? God, no." Juliette Lagarde held up her left hand. It was absent a wedding ring. "She wanted me to find another husband before it was too late."

"What happened to the first one?"

"I was so busy at work that I failed to notice he was involved in a passionate *cinq à sept* with a young woman from his office."

"I'm sorry."

"Don't be. These things happen. Especially in France." She poured boiling water from the electric kettle into a flowered teapot. "What about you, Monsieur Allon? Are you married?"

"Happily."

"Children?"

"Twins."

"Are they spies, too?"

"They're in elementary school."

Juliette Lagarde took up the tray and led Gabriel along a central corridor, into a sitting room. It was formal, more Paris than Bordeaux. The walls were hung with oil paintings in ornate French antique frames. They were works of high quality but moderate value. Someone had chosen them with care.

Juliette Lagarde placed the tray on a low wooden table and opened the French doors to the chill afternoon air. "Do you know who lived there?" she asked, pointing toward the distant silhouette of Château Malromé.

"A painter whose work I've always admired."

"You're interested in art?"

"You might say that."

She sat down and poured two cups of tea. "Are you always so evasive?"

"Forgive me, Madame Lagarde. But I've only recently traded the secret world for the overt one. I'm not used to talking about myself."

"Try it once."

"I was an art student when I was recruited by Israeli intelligence. I wanted to be a painter, but I became a restorer instead. For many years, I worked in Europe under an assumed identity."

"Your French is excellent."

"My Italian is better." Gabriel accepted a cup of tea and carried it to the fireplace. Photographs in handsome silver frames lined the mantel. One depicted the Bérrangar family in happier times. "You bear a striking resemblance to your mother. But then I'm sure you realize that."

"We were very much alike. Too much, perhaps." A silence fell between them. At length Juliette Lagarde said, "Now that we're properly acquainted, Monsieur Allon, perhaps you can tell me why her death is of any possible interest to a man like you."

"She was on her way to Bordeaux to meet a friend of mine when she had the accident. An art dealer named Julian Isherwood." He handed Juliette Lagarde the letter. "It arrived at his gallery in London last Friday."

She looked down and read.

"Is that your mother's handwriting?"

"Yes, of course. I have boxes and boxes of her letters. She was very old-fashioned. She loathed email and was forever misplacing her mobile phone."

"Do you have any idea what she might have been referring to?"

"The legal and ethical problems concerning your friend's painting?" Juliette Lagarde rose abruptly to her feet. "Yes, Monsieur Allon. I think I might."

———

She led him through a pair of double doors and into an adjoining sitting room. It was smaller than its neighbor, more intimate. It was a room where books were read, thought Gabriel, and letters to London art dealers written. Six Old Master paintings, beautifully framed and illuminated, adorned its walls—including a portrait of a woman, oil on canvas, approximately 115 by 92 centimeters, quite obviously Dutch or Flemish in origin.

"Does it look familiar?" asked Juliette Lagarde.

"Very," said Gabriel, and placed a hand thoughtfully to his chin. "Do you happen to remember where your father purchased it?"

"A small gallery on the rue la Boétie in Paris."

"Galerie Georges Fleury?"

"Yes, that's the one."

"When?"

"It was thirty-four years ago."

"You have a good memory."

"My father gave it to my mother on her fortieth birthday. She always adored this painting."

With his hand still pressed to his chin, Gabriel tilted his head to one side.

"Does she have a name?"

"It's called *Portrait of an Unknown Woman.*" Juliette Lagarde paused, then added, "Just like your friend's painting."

"And the attribution?"

"I'd have to check the paperwork in my father's files, but I believe it was a follower of Anthony van Dyck. To be honest, I find the various categories of attribution rather arbitrary."

"So do many art dealers. They generally select the one that will earn them the most money." Gabriel drew his phone, snapped a photograph of the woman's face, and enlarged the image.

"Are you looking for something in particular?"

"The pattern of the surface cracks."

"Is there a problem?"

"No," said Gabriel. "No problem at all."

11

Villa Bérrangar

Together they lifted the painting from its hangers and carried it into the next room, where the natural light was more abundant. There Gabriel removed it from its frame and subjected it to a preliminary examination, starting with the image itself—a three-quarter-length portrait of a young woman, late twenties or early thirties, wearing a gown of gold silk trimmed in white lace. The garment was identical to the one worn by the woman in Julian's version of the painting, though the color was less vibrant and the subtle folds and wrinkles in the fabric were less persuasively rendered. The subject's hands were awkwardly arranged, her gaze vacant. The artist, whoever he was, had failed to achieve the lifelike penetration of character for which Anthony van Dyck, among the most sought-after portraitists of his day, was renowned.

Gabriel turned over the painting and examined the back of the canvas. It was consistent with other seventeenth-century Dutch and Flemish paintings he had restored. So, too, was the stretcher. It looked to be the original woodwork, with the addition of two twentieth-century horizontal reinforcements. In short, there was nothing out

of the ordinary or suspicious. By all outward appearances, the painting was a copy of the original Van Dyck portrait that Julian had sold
to Phillip Somerset, the New York art investor, for the sum of six and
a half million pounds.

There was, however, one glaring problem.

Both works had emerged from the same gallery in the Eighth Arrondissement of Paris, thirty-four years apart.

Gabriel propped the Bérrangar family's version of the painting
against the coffee table and sat down next to Juliette Lagarde. After a silence she asked, "Who do you suppose she was, our unknown
woman?"

"That depends on where she was painted. Van Dyck maintained
successful studios in both London and Antwerp and shuttled between them. The London studio was known as the beauty shop. It
was a rather well-oiled machine."

"How much of the portraits did he actually paint?"

"Usually, just the head and face. He made no attempt to flatter
his subjects by altering their appearance, which made him somewhat
controversial. We think he produced about two hundred portraits,
but some art historians believe the real number is closer to five hundred. He had so many followers and admirers that authentication
can be a tricky business."

"But not for you?"

"Sir Anthony and I are well acquainted."

Juliette Lagarde turned to the painting. "She looks Dutch or
Flemish rather than English."

"I agree."

"She was a rich man's wife or daughter?"

"Or mistress," suggested Gabriel. "In fact, she might well have
been one of Van Dyck's lovers. He had a lot of them."

"Painters," said Juliette Lagarde with mock disdain, and added tea to Gabriel's cup. "So let's say, for argument's sake, that Anthony van Dyck painted his original portrait of our unknown woman sometime in the sixteen forties."

"Let's," agreed Gabriel.

She nodded toward the frameless canvas. "So who painted that one? And when?"

"If he was a so-called follower of Van Dyck, he was someone who worked in Van Dyck's style but wasn't necessarily a member of his immediate circle."

"A nobody? Is that what you're saying?"

"If this piece is representative of his oeuvre, I doubt he was terribly successful."

"How would he have gone about it?"

"Copying a painting? He might have attempted to do it freehand. But if I were in his shoes, I would have traced Van Dyck's original and then transferred that image to a canvas of the same dimensions."

"How would you have accomplished that in the seventeenth century?"

"I would have started by poking tiny holes along the lines of my tracing. Then I would have laid the paper atop my ground and sprinkled it with charcoal dust, leaving a ghostly but geometrically accurate rendering of Van Dyck's original."

"An underdrawing?"

"Correct."

"And then?"

"I would have prepared my palette and started to paint."

"With the original close at hand?"

"It was probably on a nearby easel."

"So the artist forged it?"

"It would have only been a forgery if he had tried to sell his version as an original Van Dyck."

"Have you ever done it?" asked Juliette Lagarde.

"Copied a painting?"

"No, Monsieur Allon. Forged one."

"I'm an art conservator," said Gabriel with a smile. "There are some critics of our profession who claim that we restorers forge paintings all the time."

The room had turned suddenly cold. Juliette Lagarde closed the French doors and looked on while Gabriel secured the painting to its frame. Together they carried it into the adjoining room and returned it to its place on the wall.

"Which one is better?" asked Juliet Lagarde. "This one or your friend's?"

"I'll let you be the judge." Gabriel held his phone next to the painting. On the screen was a photograph of Julian's version of *Portrait of an Unknown Woman*. "What do you think?"

"I must admit, your friend's is much better. Still, it's rather unsettling to see them side by side like that."

"What's even more troubling," said Gabriel, "is that both paintings passed through the same gallery."

"Is it possible it's a coincidence?"

"I don't believe in them."

"Neither did my mother."

Which is why, thought Gabriel, she was now dead.

He slipped his phone into the breast pocket of his jacket. "Have the gendarmes returned her personal effects?"

"Last night."

"Did anything appear out of the ordinary?"

"Her mobile phone seems to be missing."

"She didn't have it with her when she was driving to Bordeaux?"

"The gendarmes say not."

"You've searched the house?"

"I've looked everywhere. The truth is, she rarely used it. She much preferred her old landline phones." Juliette Lagarde pointed toward the room's elegant antique writing table. "That's the one she used the most."

Gabriel went to the table and switched on the lamp. Stored in the phone's memory he found five incoming calls from Galerie Georges Fleury and three more from a Police Nationale number in central Paris. He also discovered, in Madame Bérrangar's desk calendar, a reminder for an appointment at four in the afternoon, on the last day of her life.

M. Isherwood. Café Ravel.

He turned to Juliette Lagarde. "Have you tried calling her mobile phone recently?"

"Not since this morning. I have a feeling the battery is dead."

"Do you mind if I give it a try?"

Juliette Lagarde recited the number. When Gabriel dialed it, the call went directly to voice mail. He severed the connection and held the unfaltering gaze of the unknown woman, certain for the first time that Valerie Bérrangar had been murdered.

"Did your mother have a computer?"

"Yes, of course. An Apple."

"It's not missing, is it?"

"*Non.* I checked her email this morning."

"Anything interesting?"

"On the same day my mother died in an automobile accident, she received a notification from her insurance agency that they intended to raise her rates. For the life of me, I can't imagine why. She was an excellent driver," said Juliette Lagarde. "Never so much as a parking ticket."

––––––––––

The skies poured with rain during the drive back to Saint-Macaire. Gabriel checked into his hotel, then walked to La Belle Lurette for dinner, a book beneath his arm for company. After placing an order of *poulet rôti* and *pommes frites*, he rang Chiara in Venice. Their phones were Israeli-made Solaris models, the world's most secure. Even so, they chose their words with care.

"I was beginning to get worried about you," she said.

"Sorry. Busy afternoon."

"Productive, I hope."

"Quite."

"She agreed to see you?"

"She made me tea," answered Gabriel. "And then she showed me a painting."

"Attribution?"

"Follower of Anthony van Dyck."

"Subject matter?"

"Portrait of an unknown woman. Late twenties or early thirties. Not terribly pretty."

"What was she wearing?"

"A gown of gold silk trimmed in white lace."

"Sounds like there might be a problem."

"Several, actually. Including the name of the gallery where her father purchased it."

"Do you think her mother was—"

"I do."

"Did you tell her?"

"I didn't see the point."

"What are your plans?"

"I need to go to Paris to have a word with an old friend."

"Do give him my best."

"Don't worry," said Gabriel. "I will."

12

Bordeaux—Paris

Gabriel slept poorly, awakened early, and set out for Bordeaux before it was properly light. A kilometer north of the village of Sainte-Croix-du-Mont, his headlamps picked out the gray-white stain of a spent safety flare. The tire marks appeared a few seconds later, two black slashes across the opposing lane.

He eased onto the grassy verge and surveyed his surroundings. On the right side of the road, columns of vines marched down the slope of a steep hill. On the left, nearer the river, there were vineyards as well, but the land was tabletop flat. And largely treeless, observed Gabriel, with the exception of a coppice of white-barked poplar toward which the tire marks led.

He fished an LED torch from the glove box and waited for a cargo truck to pass before climbing out and crossing to the opposite side of the road. He didn't venture much beyond the broken white line at the edge of the tarmac; it wasn't necessary. From his vantage point, the damage was plain to see.

Two of the poplars had been snapped by the force of the collision, and the sodden earth was strewn with cubes of shattered safety glass. Gabriel reckoned that Valerie Bérrangar must have been killed instantly by the force of the impact. Or perhaps she had remained conscious long enough to notice the gloved hand reaching through the broken window. Not to render assistance but to seize her phone. Gabriel dialed the number, hoping he might hear a death rattle from amid the trees, but once again the call went straight to voice mail.

Killing the connection, he turned and examined the parallel tire marks. They crossed the southbound lane at roughly a forty-five-degree angle. Yes, he thought, it was possible that Valerie Bérrangar had been distracted somehow and unwittingly swerved to the left, directly toward the only stand of trees in sight. But the more likely explanation was that her car had been forced off the road by the vehicle behind her.

A car approached from the north, slowed briefly, and continued on toward Sainte-Croix-du-Mont. Two minutes elapsed before another appeared, this time from the south. It was not a busy stretch of road. At three fifteen on a Monday afternoon, it would have been quiet as well. Even so, the associates of the man who had forced Valerie Bérrangar's car into the trees had probably taken steps to contain the traffic in both directions so there would be no witnesses. General Ferrari was right; inducing a fatal accident was not easily done. But the men who murdered Valerie Bérrangar knew what they were doing. After all, thought Gabriel, they were professionals. Of that, he was certain.

He crossed the road and slid behind the wheel of his rental car. The drive to the airport was thirty minutes. His flight to Paris departed promptly at nine, and at half past eleven, having entrusted his bag to the bell staff of the Bristol Hotel, he was walking up the rue de Miromesnil in the Eighth Arrondissement.

At the northern end of the street was a small shop called Antiquités Scientifiques. The sign in the window read OUVERT. The buzzer, when pressed, emitted an inhospitable howl. Several seconds elapsed with no invitation to enter. Finally the deadbolt snapped open with a thud, and Gabriel slipped inside.

On the morning of August 22, 1911, Louis Béroud arrived at the Musée du Louvre to resume work on a copy of a portrait of an Italian noblewoman, 77 by 53 centimeters, oil on poplar panel, that hung in the Salon Carré. The Louvre did not discourage the work of artists such as Béroud. In fact, it permitted them to store their paints and easels at the museum overnight. They were forbidden, however, to produce copies with the exact dimensions of the originals, as the European art market was awash with forgeries of Old Master paintings.

Formally attired in a black frock coat and striped trousers, Béroud strode into the Salon Carré that Tuesday morning only to discover that the portrait, Leonardo da Vinci's *Mona Lisa*, had been removed from its protective wood-and-glass case. He was disappointed but not unduly alarmed. Neither, for that matter, was Maximilien Alphonse Paupardin, the guard who kept watch over the Salon Carré and its priceless treasures, usually from atop a stool in the doorway. The Louvre was in the process of photographing its entire inventory of paintings and other objets d'art. Brigadier Paupardin was confident that Mona Lisa was merely having her picture taken.

But later that morning, after visiting the photography studio, a frantic Paupardin informed the Louvre's acting president that the *Mona Lisa* was missing. The gendarmes arrived at one o'clock and immediately sealed the museum. It would remain closed for the next week as the police scoured Paris for clues. Their investigation, such as it was, was a comedy of errors. Among the initial suspects were a brash young Spanish painter named Pablo Picasso and his friend, the poet and writer Guillaume Apollinaire.

Another was Vincenzo Peruggia, the Italian-born carpenter who had helped to construct the *Mona Lisa*'s protective case. But police cleared Peruggia of suspicion after a brief interview conducted in his Paris apartment. Which is where the *Mona Lisa* remained, hidden in a trunk in the bedroom, until 1913, when the humble woodworker attempted to sell the painting to a prominent art dealer in Florence. The dealer took it to the Uffizi Gallery, and Peruggia was promptly arrested. Convicted in an Italian courtroom of the greatest art crime in history, he received a one-year prison sentence but was set free after spending only seven months behind bars.

It was the remarkable tale of the *Mona Lisa*'s theft that inspired a restless Paris shopkeeper named Maurice Durand, in the drab winter of 1985, to steal his first painting—a small still life by Jean-Baptiste-Siméon Chardin that hung in a rarely visited corner of the Musée des Beaux-Arts in Strasbourg. Unlike Vincenzo Peruggia, Durand already had a buyer waiting, a disreputable collector who was in the market for a Chardin and wasn't worried about messy details such as provenance. Durand was well paid, the client was happy, and a lucrative career was born.

Two decades later, a fall through a skylight ended Durand's career as a professional art thief. He now operated solely as a broker in the process known as commissioned theft. Or, as Durand liked to describe it, he managed the acquisition of paintings that were not technically for sale. Working with a stable of Marseilles-based professional thieves, he was the hidden hand behind some of the most spectacular art heists of the twenty-first century. During the summer of 2010 alone, his men stole works by Rembrandt, Picasso, Caravaggio, and Van Gogh. With the exception of the Rembrandt, which hung in the National Gallery of Art in Washington, none of the paintings had resurfaced.

Durand ruled his global empire of art theft from Antiquités Scientifiques, which had been in his family for three generations. Its tastefully lit shelves were lined with antique microscopes, cameras, spectacles, barometers, surveyors, and globes, all meticulously arranged. So, too, was Maurice Durand. He wore a tailored suit, dark blue, and a striped dress shirt. His necktie was the color of gold leaf. His bald head was polished to a high gloss.

"I suppose it's true, after all," he said by way of greeting.

"What's that?" asked Gabriel.

"That men in your line of work never truly retire."

"Or yours, apparently."

Smiling, Durand lifted the lid of a varnished rectangular case. "Perhaps this might be of interest to you. An optician's trial lens kit. Turn of the century. Quite rare."

"Almost as rare as that watercolor you stole from the Musée Matisse a few months back. Or the lovely genre piece by Jan Steen you pinched from the Musée Fabre."

"I had nothing to do with the disappearance of either of those works."

"What about the sale?"

Durand closed the lid, soundlessly. "My associates and I acquired a number of valuable objects for you and your service over the years, including a remarkable terra-cotta hydria by the Amykos Painter. And then, of course, there was the job in Amsterdam. We caused quite a stir with that one, didn't we?"

"Which is why I have refrained from giving your name to the French authorities."

"What about General Cyclops, your friend from the Carabinieri?"

"He remains unaware of your identity. Or the identities of your associates in Marseilles."

"And what must I do to preserve this state of affairs?"

"You must provide me with information."

"About what?"

"Galerie Georges Fleury. It's on the rue—"

"I know where it is, Monsieur Allon."

"Are you in business with him?"

"Georges Fleury? Never. But I did foolishly agree to steal a painting from him once."

"What was it?"

"It was," said Durand, his expression darkening, "a disaster."

13

Rue de Miromesnil

Are you familiar with Pierre-Henri de Valenciennes?"

Gabriel sighed before answering. "Valenciennes was one of the most important landscape artists of the neoclassical period. He was among the earliest proponents of working *en plein air* rather than in a studio." He paused. "Shall I go on?"

"I meant no offense."

"None taken, Maurice."

They had retreated to Durand's cramped rear office. Gabriel was seated in the uncomfortable wooden armchair reserved for visitors; Durand, behind his spotless desk. The light of his antique lamp was reflected in his rimless spectacles, obscuring his watchful brown eyes.

"A number of years ago," he continued, "Galerie Georges Fleury exhibited a stunning landscape said to have been painted by Valenciennes in 1804. It depicted villagers dancing around classical ruins at dusk. Oil on canvas, sixty-six by ninety-eight centimeters. Immaculate condition, as Monsieur Fleury's paintings always are. A collector of considerable expertise and means whom we shall refer to as Monsieur Didier entered into negotiations to purchase the painting. But the talks broke down almost immediately because Monsieur Fleury refused to budge on the price."

"Which was?"

"Let's call it four hundred thousand."

"And how much was Monsieur Didier willing to pay you to steal it for him?"

"The rule of thumb is that a painting retains only ten percent of its value on the black market."

"Forty thousand is rather small beer for you."

"I told him so."

"How much did he offer?"

"Two hundred."

"And you accepted?"

"Unfortunately."

From the cabinet behind his desk Durand removed a bottle of calvados and two antique cut-glass tumblers. Nearly everything in the room was from another age, including the little black-and-white video monitor he used to keep watch on his front door.

He poured two glasses of the brandy and offered one to Gabriel.

"It's a bit early in the day for me."

"Nonsense," said Durand after consulting his wristwatch. "Besides, a little alcohol at midday is good for the blood."

"My blood is just fine, thank you."

"No lingering effects from that unpleasantness in Washington?"

"Only an abiding concern for the future of American democracy." Gabriel reluctantly accepted the brandy. "Who handled the job for you?"

"Your old friend René Monjean."

"Any complications?"

"Not with the robbery itself. The gallery's security system was rather outmoded."

"Surely you didn't take just the one painting."

"Of course not. René grabbed four others to cover our tracks."

"Anything good?"

"Pierre Révoil. Nicolas-André Monsiau." Durand shrugged. "A couple of portraits by Ingres."

"Five pictures is quite a haul. And yet I don't recall reading about the robbery in the newspapers."

"Evidently, Monsieur Fleury never reported it to the police."

"Unusual."

"I thought so."

"But you went ahead with the sale nevertheless."

"What choice did I have?"

"When did things go sideways?"

"About two months after Monsieur Didier took possession of the painting, he demanded a refund."

"Also unusual," said Gabriel. "At least in your line of work."

"Unheard of," murmured Durand.

"Why did he want his money back?"

"He claimed the Valenciennes wasn't a Valenciennes."

"He thought it was a later copy?"

"That's one way of putting it."

"And another?"

"Monsieur Didier was convinced the painting was a modern forgery."

Of course he was, thought Gabriel. A part of him had known it was leading to this from the moment he spotted the incongruous Flemish-style craquelure in the photograph of Julian's painting.

"How did you handle it?"

"I explained to Monsieur Didier that I had fulfilled my end of our arrangement and that he should take his complaints to Galerie Georges Fleury." Durand gave a faint smile over the rim of his glass. "Fortunately, he didn't take my suggestion."

"You returned his money?"

"Half of it," answered Durand. "It turned out to be a wise decision. I've done a great deal of business with him since."

Gabriel raised the glass of calvados to his lips for the first time. "You wouldn't happen to have it lying around, would you?"

"The fake Valenciennes?" Durand shook his head. "I burned it."

"And the four other paintings?"

"I sold them at a steep discount to a dealer in Montreal. They covered René's fee, but barely." He exhaled heavily. "It was a wash."

"All's well that ends well."

"Unless one is a paying customer of Galerie Georges Fleury."

"The phony Valenciennes wasn't a fluke?"

"*Non.* Apparently, selling forgeries is the gallery's business model. Don't get me wrong, Fleury sells plenty of genuine paintings. But that's not where he makes his money." Durand paused. "Or so I have been reliably told."

"By whom?"

"You have your sources, I have mine. And they have assured me that Fleury has been selling worthless fakes for years."

"I have a terrible feeling a friend of mine might have purchased one."

"He's a collector, this friend?"

"A dealer."

"Not Monsieur Isherwood?"

Gabriel hesitated, then nodded slowly.

"Why doesn't he simply return it and demand his money back?"

"He sold the painting to a litigious American."

"Is there any other kind?" Durand eyed a window shopper in the video monitor. "May I ask you one other question, Monsieur Allon?"

"If you insist."

Durand made a face. "What in God's name happened to your hand?"

After leaving Maurice Durand's shop, Gabriel walked south on the rue de Miromesnil to the rue la Boétie. He lingered for a moment outside the building at Number 19, then made his way along the elegant, gently curving street to Galerie Georges Fleury. Displayed in its window were three large oil paintings. Two were in the Rococo style. The third, a portrait of a young man by François Gérard, dated from the later period known as Neoclassicism.

Or so it appeared at first glance. But an inspection carried out by a trained professional—an art restorer, for example—might tell a different story. It could not be hurried, this appraisal. The restorer would have to take his time with each work in the gallery, engage in the time-honored tradition of connoisseurship. He might touch the paintings, examine their surfaces with a magnifying glass, even speak a few words to them in the hope they spoke to him. It would be advantageous if the gallery's owner—who was likely engaged in criminal conduct and therefore would be naturally vigilant—were not looking over his shoulder as he was conducting this ritual. Better still if he were distracted by the presence of someone else in the room.

But whom?

This was the question that Gabriel pondered as he made the short walk from the gallery to the Bristol. After checking into his room, he rang Chiara and described his quandary. She replied by immediately forwarding him a list of upcoming performances by the Orchestre de Chambre de Paris.

"Your girlfriend is in town all weekend. Perhaps she has a few minutes tomorrow afternoon to serve as your distraction."

"She's perfect. But are you sure you don't mind?"

"If you spend the weekend in Paris with a woman you were once madly in love with?"

"I was never in love with her."

"Please remind her of that fact the first chance you get."

"Don't worry," said Gabriel before the connection went dead. "I will."

14

Le Bristol Paris

She was staying at the Crillon, in the Leonard Bernstein suite. He was one of the few conductors, she added with a laugh, with whom she had never been romantically linked.

"Are you there now?"

"Actually, I interrupted my rehearsal to take your call. The entire Orchestre de Chambre de Paris is hanging on my every word."

"When will you be back at your hotel?"

"Not until four. But I have press interviews scheduled until six."

"My condolences."

"I plan on misbehaving terribly."

"How about a drink downstairs in Les Ambassadeurs when you're finished?"

"Let's have dinner instead."

"Dinner?"

"It's a meal that most people take in the early evening. Unless one is Spanish, of course. I'll ask the concierge to book us a quiet table for two at the most romantic restaurant in Paris. With any luck, the paparazzi will find us, and a *scandale* will ensue."

Before Gabriel could object, the connection was lost. He briefly considered alerting Chiara to his new dilemma but thought it unwise. Instead, he dialed the number for Valerie Bérrangar's missing phone. Once again the call went straight to her voice mail.

He rang off and scrolled through his contacts until he arrived at the entry for Yuval Gershon. Yuval was the director-general of Unit 8200, Israel's formidable signals intelligence service. Gabriel had not spoken to him—or any of his old colleagues, for that matter—since leaving Israel. It was a momentous step, one that would invite future contact, perhaps unwanted. Still, Gabriel reckoned it was worth the risk. If anyone could locate Madame Bérrangar's phone, it was Yuval and his hackers at the Unit.

He answered instantly, as though he had been anticipating Gabriel's call. Given the Unit's extraordinary capabilities, it was not beyond the realm of possibility.

"You miss me, don't you?"

"Almost as much as the hole in my chest."

"So why are you calling?"

"I have a problem only you can solve."

Yuval exhaled heavily into the phone. "What's the number?"

Gabriel recited it.

"And the problem?"

"The owner was murdered a few days ago. I have a feeling the killers were dumb enough to take her phone. I'd like you to find it for me."

"It won't be a problem if the device is still intact. But if they smashed it to pieces or dropped it into the Seine—"

"Why did you mention the Seine, Yuval?"

"Because you're calling from Paris."

"Bastard."

"I'll send up a flare when I have something. And have fun at dinner tonight."

"How did you know about dinner?"

"Anna Rolfe just sent you a text message. Shall I read it to you?"

"Why not?"

"Your reservation is at eight fifteen."

"Where?"

"She doesn't say. But it must be close to the Bristol, because she's picking you up at eight."

"I never mentioned that I was staying at the Bristol."

"It looks to me as though your room is on the third floor."

"The fourth," said Gabriel. "But who's counting?"

———

The first time Gabriel saw Anna Rolfe, she was standing on a stage in Brussels, delivering an electrifying performance of Tchaikovsky's Violin Concerto in D Major. He left the concert hall that night never imagining they might one day meet. But several years later—after the murder of Anna's father, the immensely wealthy Swiss banker Augustus Rolfe—they were formally introduced. On that occasion, Anna had offered her hand in greeting. Now, as Gabriel joined her in the back of a courtesy Mercedes-Maybach limousine, she threw her arms around his neck and pressed her lips against his cheek.

"Consider yourself my hostage," she said as the car drew away from the hotel. "This time escape is impossible."

"Where are you planning to take me?"

"Back to my suite at the Crillon, of course."

"I was promised dinner."

"A clever ruse on my part." Anna was casually attired in jeans, a cashmere sweater, and a car-length leather coat. Even so, there was no mistaking her for anyone other than the world's most famous violinist. "Did my publicist send you the new CD?"

"It arrived the day before yesterday."

"And?"

"A triumph."

"The reviewer from the *Times* said it displayed a newfound maturity." Anna frowned. "What do you think he meant by that?"

"It's a polite way of saying you're getting older."

"You wouldn't know it from the cover photograph. It's amazing what they can do with the click of a mouse these days. I look younger than Nicola Benedetti."

"You can be sure she idolized you when she was a child."

"I don't want to be anyone's *idol*. I just want to be thirty-three again."

"Whatever for?" Gabriel gazed out his window at the graceful Haussmann buildings lining the rue du Faubourg Saint-Honoré. "Where are we having dinner?"

"It's a surprise."

"I hate them."

"Yes," said Anna distantly. "I remember."

15

Chez Janou

The restaurant turned out to be Chez Janou, a bright and crowded bistro on the western fringes of the Marais. A low murmur passed through the dining room as they were escorted to their table. Anna took her time removing her coat and settling onto the red banquette. It was, thought Gabriel, a virtuoso performance.

When the commotion subsided, she leaned across the small wooden table and whispered, "I hope you're not disappointed it isn't more romantic."

"I'm relieved, actually."

"I was only joking, you know."

"Were you?"

"I got over you a long time ago, Gabriel."

"Two husbands ago, in fact."

"That was needlessly vindictive."

"Perhaps," said Gabriel. "But entirely accurate."

Both of Anna's marriages had been brief and unhappy, and both had ended with spectacular divorces. And then there was the string of disastrous affairs, always with rich and famous men. Gabriel had been the exception to Anna's pattern. He had survived her mood swings and episodes of personal recklessness longer than most—six months and fourteen days—and with the exception of a single shattered vase, their parting had been civil. It was true that he had never quite loved her, but he had cared for her a great deal and was pleased that after an interregnum of some twenty years they had renewed their friendship. Anna was a bit like Julian Isherwood. She definitely made life more interesting.

As usual, her perusal of the menu was hurried and her selections decisive. They threw Gabriel onto the defensive, for he had intended to order the same items. His fallback—ratatouille followed by liver and potatoes—produced a sneer of mild rebuke on the famous face of his dinner companion.

"Peasant," she hissed.

The waiter removed the cork from a bottle of Bordeaux and poured a small measure for Gabriel's approval. For all he knew, some of the grapes used to produce the wine had come from the vineyard north of Saint-Macaire where Valerie Bérrangar's life had ended. He sniffed, tasted, and with a nod instructed the waiter to fill their glasses.

"What shall we drink to?" asked Anna.

"Old friends."

"How dreadfully boring." Her lipstick left a smudge on the rim of the glass. She returned it to the tabletop and rotated it slowly between her thumb and forefinger, aware that the eyes of the room were upon her. "Do you ever wonder how our lives would have turned out if you hadn't walked out on me?"

"That's not how I would describe what happened."

"You tossed your meager possessions into a duffel bag and drove away from my villa in Portugal as fast as you could. And I did not receive so much as a single—"

"Please let's not do this again."

"Why not?"

"Because I can't change the past. Besides, if I hadn't left, you would have thrown me out sooner or later."

"Not you, Gabriel. You were a keeper."

"And what would I have done with myself while you were on tour?"

"You could have come with me and kept me out of all the trouble I got into."

"Followed you from city to city while you basked in the adulation of your adoring fans?"

She smiled. "That about sums it up."

"And how would you have explained me? Who would I have been?"

"I always adored Mario Delvecchio."

"Mario was a lie," said Gabriel. "Mario never was."

"But he did the most wonderful things to me in bed." She sighed and drank more of her wine. "You never told me your wife's name."

"It's Chiara."

"What does she look like?"

"A bit like Nicola Benedetti, but prettier."

"She's Italian, I take it."

"Venetian."

"Which would explain why you're living there again."

Gabriel nodded. "She's managing the city's largest restoration company. Eventually, I'll go to work for her."

"Eventually?"

"I'm on administrative leave until further notice."

"Because of what happened in Washington?"

"And other assorted traumas."

"There are worse places to recuperate than Venice."

"Much," agreed Gabriel.

"I think I'll schedule a performance there. A night of Brahms and Tartini at the Scuola Grande di San Rocco. I'll get a suite at that little hotel in San Marco, the Luna Baglioni, and stay there for a month or two. You can come by every afternoon and—"

"Behave, Anna."

"Will you at least introduce me to your family someday?"

"Don't you think that might be a bit awkward?"

"Not at all. In fact, I think your children might enjoy spending time with me. Despite my many faults and failings, all of which have been mercilessly chronicled in the tabloids, most people find me endlessly fascinating."

"Which is why I'd like to borrow you for an hour or two tomorrow."

"What did you have in mind?"

He told her.

"Is it really safe to visit an art gallery in Paris with you?"

"It was a long time ago, Anna."

"Another lifetime," she said. "But why me?"

"I need you to distract the owner while I take a careful look at his inventory."

"Shall I bring along my fiddle and perform a partita or two?"

"That won't be necessary. Just be your usual enchanting self."

"Eye candy?"

"Exactly."

She probed at the skin along her jawline. "I'm a bit old for that, don't you think?"

"You haven't changed a bit since—"

"The morning you walked out on me?" The waiter served their first course and withdrew. Anna lowered her eyes and said, "*Bon appétit.*"

16

Rue la Boétie

Gabriel rang the gallery at ten o'clock the following morning and, after a testy exchange with a male receptionist called Bruno, was connected to Monsieur Georges Fleury himself. Not surprisingly, the crooked French art dealer had never heard of anyone named Ludwig Ziegler.

"I advise a single client with a passion for Neoclassical paintings," Gabriel explained in German-accented French. "She happens to be in Paris for the weekend and would like to visit your gallery."

"Galerie Georges Fleury is not a tourist destination, Monsieur Ziegler. If your client wishes to see French paintings, I would suggest a visit to the Louvre instead."

"My client isn't here on holiday. She's performing this weekend at the Philharmonie de Paris."

"Is your client—"

"Yes."

Fleury's tone was suddenly more accommodating. "What time would Madame Rolfe like to stop by?"

"One o'clock this afternoon."

"I'm afraid I've already arranged to see another client at that time."

"Reschedule him. And tell Bruno to take a long lunch. I find him annoying, and so will Madame Rolfe. In case you were wondering, she drinks room-temperature mineral water. *Sans gaz*, with a slice of lemon. Not a wedge, Monsieur Fleury. A slice."

"Any particular brand of water?"

"Anything but Vittel. And no photographs or handshakes. For understandable reasons, Madame Rolfe never shakes hands before a performance."

Gabriel rang off, then dialed Anna's number. Her voice, when at last she answered, was heavy with sleep.

"What time is it?" she groaned.

"A few minutes after ten."

"In the *morning*?"

"Yes, Anna."

Swearing softly, she killed the connection. Madame Rolfe, Gabriel remembered, never rose before noon.

———————

Gabriel left the Bristol at half past twelve and walked beneath a leaden Parisian sky to the Crillon. It was one fifteen when Anna, in jeans and a zippered sweater, finally descended from her suite. Outside, they slid into the back of the Maybach for the short drive to Galerie Georges Fleury.

"Any last instructions?" she asked while appraising her face in the vanity mirror.

"Be charming, but difficult."

"Act naturally? Is that what you're saying?"

Anna glossed her heart-shaped lips as the car turned onto the rue la Boétie. A moment later it stopped outside the gallery. Its owner and namesake was waiting on the pavement like a doorman. His hands remained rigidly at his side as Anna emerged from the back of the limousine.

"Welcome to Galerie Georges Fleury, Madame Rolfe. It is truly an honor to meet you."

Anna acknowledged the art dealer's greeting with a regal nod. Unnerved, he thrust a hand toward Gabriel.

"And you must be Herr Ziegler."

"I must be," said Gabriel evenly.

Fleury regarded him for a moment through a pair of rimless spectacles. "Is it possible we've met somewhere before? At an auction, perhaps?"

"Madame Rolfe and I avoid them." Gabriel glanced at the gallery's heavy glass door. "Shall we go inside? It doesn't take long for her to attract a crowd."

Fleury used a handheld remote to unlock the door. In the vestibule, a bronze life-size bust of a young Greek or Roman man stood atop a plinth of black marble. Next to it was an unoccupied receptionist's desk.

"As you requested, Herr Ziegler, it's just the three of us."

"No hard feelings, I hope."

"None at all." Fleury placed the remote on the desk and escorted them into a high-ceilinged room with a dark wooden floor and walls of garnet red. "My main exhibition room. The better pictures are upstairs. If you wish, we can begin there."

"Madame Rolfe is in no hurry."

"Neither am I."

Dazzled, Fleury led his internationally renowned visitor on a laborious tour of the room's collection while Gabriel conducted an unchaperoned survey of his own. The first work to catch his connoisseur's eye was a large Rococo painting depicting a nude Venus and three young maidens. The inscription at the bottom of the canvas suggested the work had been executed by Nicolas Colombel in 1697. Gabriel doubted that was the case.

He placed a hand to his chin and tilted his head to one side. A moment passed before Fleury noticed his interest in the work and joined him before the canvas.

"I acquired it a few months ago."

"May I ask where?"

"An old private collection here in France."

"Dimensions?"

Fleury smiled. "You tell me, Monsieur Ziegler."

"One hundred and twelve by one hundred and forty-four centimeters." He paused, then added with a disarming smile, "Give or take a centimeter or two."

"Very close."

Only because Gabriel had deliberately misstated the painting's actual dimensions. Any fool could see that the work measured 114 by 148 centimeters.

"It's in remarkable condition," he said.

"I commissioned the restoration after purchasing it."

"May I see the conservator's report?"

"Now?"

"If you wouldn't mind."

When Fleury withdrew, Anna approached the painting. "It's beautiful."

"But too large to transport easily."

"You're not thinking about buying something, are you?"

"Not me," said Gabriel. "But you certainly are."

Before Anna could object, Fleury reappeared, empty-handed. "I'm afraid Bruno must have misfiled it. But if Madame Rolfe is interested in the painting, I can forward you a copy by email."

Gabriel produced his phone. "Would you mind if I photographed her standing next to it?"

"Of course not. In fact, I would be honored."

Anna inched closer to the painting and, turning, adopted the smile she wore when acknowledging the applause of a sold-out concert hall. Gabriel snapped the photograph, then moved to the neighboring painting.

"A follower of Canaletto," declared Fleury.

"A very good one."

"I thought so, too. I acquired it only last week."

"From where?"

"A private collection." The Frenchman treated Anna to a watery smile. "In Switzerland."

Gabriel leaned closer to the canvas. "How certain are you about the attribution?"

"Why do you ask?"

Because the painting, at just 56 by 78 centimeters, was easily transportable. Especially if it were to be removed from its stretcher. "Do you think Bruno mislaid the condition report for this one, too?"

"I'm afraid the painting is already spoken for."

"Is there no way Madame Rolfe can make a competitive bid?"

"I've already accepted the buyer's money."

"Is he a dealer or a collector?"

"Why do you ask?"

"Because if he's a dealer, I'd be interested in taking it off his hands."

"I can't reveal his identity. The terms of the sale are entirely private."

"Not for long," said Gabriel knowingly.

"What do you mean, monsieur?"

"Let's just say I get a funny feeling when I look at this painting." He snapped a photograph of it. "Perhaps you should show us the good pictures now, Monsieur Fleury."

17

Galerie Fleury

Fleury escorted them up a flight of stairs to the second-floor exhibition room. Here the walls were somber gray rather than red, and the paintings, by all appearances, were of a decidedly higher quality. There were several examples of Dutch and Flemish portraiture, including two works executed in the manner of Anthony van Dyck. There was also *A River Scene with Distant Windmills*, oil on canvas, 36 by 58 centimeters, bearing the distinctive initials of the Dutch Golden Age painter Aelbert Cuyp. Gabriel was doubtful the initials were authentic. In fact, after a moment of undisturbed reverie, he reached the conclusion, wholly unsupported by technical analysis, that the painting was a forgery.

"You have a very good eye," said Fleury from the opposite side of the room. He added a slice of lemon to Anna's mineral water and asked, "Something for you, Monsieur Ziegler?"

"The attribution for this painting would be nice."

"It has been firmly assigned by numerous experts to Cuyp himself."

"How do these experts explain the lack of a complete signature? After all, Cuyp generally signed the works he painted with his own hand and placed only his initials on paintings that were produced under his supervision."

"There are exceptions, as you know."

Which was indeed the case, thought Gabriel. "How's the provenance?"

"Lengthy and impeccable."

"Previous owner?"

"A collector of exceptional taste."

"French or Swiss?" asked Gabriel dryly.

"American, actually."

Fleury handed the glass of water to Anna and escorted her from painting to painting, leaving Gabriel free to carry out a second private inspection of the gallery's inventory. Eventually they all three convened before *A River Scene with Distant Windmills*, oil on canvas, 36 by 58 centimeters, by a forger of indisputable talent.

"Do you mind if I touch it?"

"I beg your pardon?"

"The painting," said Gabriel. "I'd like to touch it."

"Carefully," cautioned Fleury.

Gabriel placed the tip of his forefinger gently against the canvas and dragged it over the brushwork. "Did your man handle the cleaning?"

"It came to me in this condition."

"Are there paint losses?"

"Not extensive. But, yes, there is some abrading. Particularly in the sky."

"I assume the condition report contains photographs?"

"Several, monsieur."

Gabriel looked at Anna. "Does Madame Rolfe like it?"

"That depends on the price." She turned to Fleury. "What did you have in mind?"

"A million and a half."

"Come, come," said Gabriel. "Let's be realistic."

"How much would Madame Rolfe be willing to pay for it?"

"Are you asking me to negotiate with myself?"

"Not at all. I am merely offering you the opportunity to name your price."

Gabriel contemplated the worthless painting in silence.

"Well?" asked Fleury.

"Madame Rolfe will give you one million euros and not a euro more."

The art dealer smiled. "Sold."

———————

Downstairs in Fleury's office, Gabriel reviewed the condition report and provenance while Anna, a mobile phone pressed to her ear, transferred the sum of one million euros from her account at Credit Suisse to the gallery's account at Société Générale. The final sale price included the cost of the frame and shipping. Gabriel, however, declined both. Madame Rolfe, he said, did not care for the frame. As for the shipping, he intended to see to it personally.

"I should have the export license in hand by next Wednesday at the latest," said Fleury. "You can pick up the painting then."

"I'm afraid Wednesday won't do."

"Why not?"

"Because Madame Rolfe and I are taking the painting with us."

"*C'est impossible.* There is paperwork to submit and signatures to obtain."

"The paperwork and signatures are your problem. Besides, something tells me you know how to acquire an export license for a painting that has already left the country."

The dealer did not deny the accusation. "What about proper packaging?" he asked.

"Trust me, Monsieur Fleury. I know how to handle a painting."

"The gallery accepts absolutely no liability for any damage once the painting leaves these premises."

"But you *do* guarantee the attribution, along with the accuracy of the condition report and provenance."

"Yes, of course." Fleury handed Gabriel a copy of the certificate of authenticity, which declared the work to be firmly attributed to Aelbert Cuyp. "It says so right here."

The dealer placed the sales agreement before Anna and indicated the line where she should sign her name. After adding his own signature, he photocopied the document and inserted it into an envelope, along with copies of the provenance and condition report. The painting he covered in glassine paper and bubble wrap, which was more protection than it deserved. At three fifteen it was resting on the backseat of the Maybach as it drew to a stop outside the Bristol Hotel.

"I thought I was only supposed to be eye candy," said Anna.

"What's a million euros between friends?"

"A great deal of money."

"It will be back in your account by Monday afternoon at the latest."

"What a pity," she said. "I was hoping you might remain in my debt a little longer."

"And if I were?"

"I would ask you to come to my performance tonight. There's a gala reception afterward. All the beautiful people will be there."

"I thought you hated those things."

"With a passion. But if you were standing at my side, it might be tolerable."

"And how would you explain me, Anna? Who would I be?"

"How about Herr Ludwig Ziegler?" She frowned at the object lying on the seat between them. "The esteemed art adviser who just spent one million euros of my money for a worthless forgery."

Gabriel carried it upstairs to his room and removed the canvas from its stretcher. One hour later it was wedged into the overnight bag he wheeled across the cavernous ticket hall of the Gare du Nord. His journey through passport control proceeded without incident, and at five o'clock he boarded a Eurostar train bound for London. As the banlieues of northern Paris slid past his window, he reflected on the shifting fortunes of his career. Just four months earlier he had been the director-general of one of the world's most formidable intelligence services. Now, he thought, smiling, he had found a new line of work.

Art smuggler.

18

Jermyn Street

Not since the outbreak of the pandemic, when the art world had slipped into something approaching cardiac arrest, had Sarah Bancroft endured such a dreadful week. It began with Julian's calamitous visit to Bordeaux and concluded, late that afternoon, with the collapse of a potential sale—a case of cold feet on the buyer's part and hard-nosed determination on Sarah's not to sell the painting in question, *Adoration of the Magi* by Luca Cambiaso, at a loss. To make matters worse, her new husband had left London on a business trip. Because his trade was espionage, he could not say where he was going or when he might return. For all Sarah knew, it would be Midsummer Day before she laid eyes on him again.

Which explained why, after engaging the gallery's security system and locking the front door, she made straight for Wiltons and settled into her usual corner table at the bar. A perfect three-olive Belvedere martini, Saharan dry, materialized a moment later, delivered by a handsome young waiter in a blue blazer and red necktie. Perhaps, she thought as she raised the glass to her lips, all was not quite as bad as it seemed.

At once there was a burst of uproarious laughter. It was Julian who had provoked it. He was explaining the hideous purple-red bruise on his cheek to Oliver Dimbleby and Jeremy Crabbe, the head of the Old Master department of Bonhams. According to Julian's version of the story, the collision with the lamppost had taken place not in Bordeaux but in Kensington, and was the result of nothing more malicious than a misguided attempt to send a text message while walking.

Mobile phone in hand, Julian reenacted the fictitious incident, much to the delight of the other dealers, curators, and auctioneers lining the bar. For his reward, he was kissed by the crimson lips of the stunning former fashion model who now ran a thriving modern art gallery in King Street. Watching the performance from her corner table, Sarah sipped her martini and whispered, "Bitch."

The kiss was little consolation; Sarah could see that. Julian was mortified by his appearance and distraught over the suspicious death of the woman who had asked him to come to France. So, too, was Sarah. Moreover, she was concerned about the painting she had sold to Phillip Somerset, a man whose acquaintance she had made while working at the Museum of Modern Art in New York. Her old friend Gabriel Allon had agreed to look into the matter. As yet, he had delivered no update on the progress of his investigation.

Amelia March of *ARTnews* detached herself from the bar and approached Sarah's table. She was a slender woman of erect carriage, with short dark hair and the unblinking, too-wide eyes of an Apple emoji. It was Amelia, with Sarah's anonymous help, who had broken the news about *Portrait of an Unknown Woman*. Sarah now regretted having leaked the information. If she had kept her mouth shut, the rediscovery and sale of the painting would have remained shrouded in secrecy. And Madame Valerie Bérrangar, she thought, would still be alive.

"I heard a naughty rumor about you the other day," Amelia announced.

"Only one?" asked Sarah. "I'm disappointed."

She could only imagine the sort of gossip that occasionally reached Amelia's ever-vigilant ears. After all, Sarah was a former covert CIA operative whose husband had worked as a professional assassin before joining the Secret Intelligence Service. She had also served briefly as the art adviser to the crown prince of Saudi Arabia. Indeed, it was Sarah who had convinced His Majesty to plunk down $450 million on Leonardo da Vinci's *Salvator Mundi*, the highest price ever paid at auction for a work of art.

None of which Sarah wished to ever see in print. Therefore, she made no objection when Amelia sat down at her table uninvited. Sarah reckoned it was better to hear the reporter out and, if possible, use the opportunity to make a little mischief of her own. She was in that sort of mood.

"What is it this time?" she asked Amelia.

"I have been reliably told—"

"Oh, for heaven's sake."

"*Very* reliably told," Amelia continued, "that you are planning to move Isherwood Fine Arts from its longtime home in Mason's Yard to, how shall we say, a less secluded location."

"Untrue," declared Sarah.

"You looked at two potential sites in Cork Street last week."

But not for the reason Amelia suspected. It was Sarah's ambition to open a second gallery, one that specialized in contemporary art and would bear her name. She had yet to broach the topic with Julian and was keen that he not read about her plans in *ARTnews*.

"I can't possibly afford Cork Street," she demurred.

"You just sold a newly discovered Van Dyck for six and a half million pounds." Amelia lowered her voice. "Very hush-hush. Secret buyer. Mysterious source."

"Yes," said Sarah. "I think I read about that somewhere."

"I've been very good to you and Julian over the years," said Amelia. "And on numerous occasions, I have refrained from pursuing stories that might well have damaged the gallery's reputation."

"Such as?"

"Your exact role in the reemergence of that Artemisia, for a start."

Sarah sipped her drink but said nothing.

"Well?" probed Amelia.

"Isherwood Fine Arts will never leave Mason's Yard. Is now and ever shall be. World without end. Amen."

"Then why are you looking for a long-term lease in Cork Street?"

Because she wanted to cast a long shadow over the gallery owned by the former fashion model, who at that moment was whispering something into the ear of Simon Mendenhall, the mannequin-like chief auctioneer from Christie's.

"I swear to you," said Sarah, "as a friend and as a woman, that I will tell you when the time is right."

"You'll tell me *first*," insisted Amelia. "And in the meantime, you will give me something juicy."

"Have a quick look over your right shoulder."

Amelia did as Sarah suggested. "The lovely Miss Watson and sleazy Simon Mendenhall?"

"Torrid," said Sarah.

"I thought she was dating that actor."

"She's shagging sleazy Simon on the side."

As if on cue, there was another eruption of laughter from the opposite end of the bar, where Julian had just concluded an encore performance of the alleged incident in Kensington—this time for Nicky Lovegrove, art adviser to the vastly wealthy.

"Is that really how it happened?" asked Amelia.

"No," said Sarah, smiling sadly. "The lamppost attacked *him*."

––––––––––

After finishing her drink, Sarah wiped the smudge of lipstick from Julian's cheek and went into Jermyn Street. There were no taxis in sight, so she walked around the corner to Piccadilly and caught one there. As it bore her westward across London, she scrolled through the possibilities on Deliveroo, dithering between Indian and Thai. She ordered Italian instead and immediately regretted her choice. She had gained five pounds during the pandemic and another five after marrying Christopher. Despite thrice-weekly training runs on the footpaths of Hyde Park, the weight refused to budge.

As the taxi sped past the Royal Albert Hall, Sarah resolved to place herself on yet another diet. But not tonight; she was hungry enough to eat one of her Ferragamo pumps. After dinner, which she would consume while watching something mindless on television, she would crawl into her empty marital bed and remain there for the better part of the weekend, listening to "When Your Lover Has Gone" on repeat. Billie Holiday's classic 1956 recording, of course. When one was truly depressed, no other version would do.

She did her best Lady Day impersonation as the taxi turned into Queen's Gate Terrace and stopped opposite the elegant Georgian house at Number 18. It wasn't all theirs, only the luxurious maisonette on the lower two levels. Sarah was overjoyed to see a light burning downstairs in the kitchen. Environmentally conscious, she was certain she had not left it on by mistake that morning. The most plausible explanation was that her lover was not gone after all.

She paid off the driver and hurried down the steps to the maisonette's lower entrance. There she found the door ajar and the security system disengaged. Inside, lying on the kitchen island, was a canvas that had been removed from its stretcher—a riverscape with distant windmills, somewhere in the neighborhood of 40 by 60 centimeters, bearing what appeared to be the initials of the Dutch Golden Age painter Aelbert Cuyp.

Next to the painting was an envelope from Galerie Georges Fleury in Paris. And next to the envelope was an excellent bottle of Sancerre, from which Gabriel, wincing in pain, was attempting to extract the cork. Sarah closed the door and, laughing in spite of herself, shed her coat. It was, she thought, the perfect end to a perfectly dreadful week.

19

Queen's Gate Terrace

Sarah checked the status of her Deliveroo order and saw it was still open. "Tagliatelle with ragù or veal Milanese?"

"I wouldn't want to impose."

"My husband is away. I could use the company."

"In that case, I'll have the veal."

"Tagliatelle it is." Sarah placed the order, then looked down at the frameless, stretcherless canvas lying on her counter. "I'm sure there's a perfectly reasonable explanation for this. And for that swollen hand of yours as well."

"Where would you like me to begin?"

"Why not the hand?"

"I assaulted a plainclothes Carabinieri officer after meeting with Julian in Venice."

"And the painting?"

"I acquired it this afternoon at Galerie Georges Fleury."

"I can see that." Sarah tapped the envelope. "But how in the world did you pay for it?"

Gabriel removed the sales agreement from the envelope and pointed toward the practiced signature of the buyer.

"That was very generous of her," said Sarah.

"Generosity had nothing to do with it. She expects to be repaid in full."

"By whom?"

"You, of course."

"So the painting is mine? Is that what you're saying?"

"I suppose it is."

"How much did I spend on it?"

"One million euros."

"For that kind of money, I should have got a frame." Sarah tugged at the frayed corner of the canvas. "And a stretcher as well."

"The management of the Bristol Hotel might have found it odd if I had left an antique picture frame behind in my room."

"And the stretcher?"

"It's in a rubbish bin outside the Gare du Nord."

"Of course it is." Sarah sighed. "You should probably put it on a new one first thing in the morning to stabilize the image."

"If I do that, it won't fit in my carry-on luggage."

"Where are you planning to take it?"

"New York," said Gabriel. "And you're coming with me."

"Why?"

"Because that painting is a forgery. And I have a funny feeling the one you sold to Phillip Somerset for six and a half million pounds is a fake as well."

"Oh, hell," said Sarah. "I was afraid you were going to say that."

———

Gabriel drew his mobile phone and retrieved the photograph of the painting he had seen in Valerie Bérrangar's villa in Saint-André-du-Bois. *Portrait of an Unknown Woman*, oil on canvas, 115 by 92 centimeters, attributed to a follower of the Flemish Baroque painter Anthony van Dyck.

"That would explain the letter she wrote to Julian."

"Only partially."

"Meaning?"

"She called Georges Fleury first."

"Why?"

"She wanted to know whether her version of the painting was a valuable Van Dyck as well."

"And what did Monsieur Fleury tell her?"

"Given my limited experience with him, I can assure you it bore no resemblance to the truth. But whatever he said made her suspicious enough to contact the art crime unit of the Police Nationale."

Sarah swore softly as she pulled the cork from the bottle of Sancerre.

"Don't worry, I'm all but certain the police told Madame Bérrangar that they had no interest in pursuing the matter. Which is why she asked Julian to come to Bordeaux." Gabriel paused. "And why she is now dead."

"Was she—"

"Murdered?" Gabriel nodded. "And her killers took her mobile phone for good measure."

"Who were they?"

"I'm still working on that. I'm quite certain, however, that they were professionals."

Sarah poured two glasses of the wine and handed one to Gabriel. "What kind of art dealer hires professional assassins to kill someone in a dispute over a painting?"

"The kind who's involved in a lucrative criminal enterprise."

Sarah took up Gabriel's phone and enlarged the image. "Is Madame Bérrangar's painting a forgery, too?"

"In my opinion," replied Gabriel, "it is the work of a later follower of Van Dyck. Forty-eight hours ago, I told Valerie Bérrangar's daughter that I thought it was a copy of the painting you sold to Phillip Somerset. But I'm now convinced it's the other way around. Which would explain why the picture doesn't appear in Van Dyck's catalogue raisonné."

"The forger copied the follower?"

"In a manner of speaking, yes. And in the process, he made marked improvements. He's quite amazing. He truly paints like Anthony van Dyck. It's no wonder your five experts were deceived."

"How do you explain the paint losses and retouching that showed up when we examined the painting under ultraviolet light?"

"The forger artificially ages and damages his paintings. Then he restores them using modern pigments and medium in order to make them appear authentic."

Sarah glanced at the canvas lying on the countertop. "This one, too?"

"Absolutely."

Gabriel removed the painting's condition report from the envelope. Attached were three accompanying photographs. The first depicted the canvas in its present state: retouched, with a fresh coat of unsoiled varnish. The second photo, made with ultraviolet light, revealed the paint losses as an archipelago of small black islands. The last photograph presented the painting in its truest state, without retouching or varnish. The losses appeared as white blotches.

"It looks exactly like a four-hundred-year-old painting should look," said Gabriel. "I hate to admit it, but it's possible even I might have been fooled."

"Why weren't you?"

"Because I went into that gallery on the lookout for forgeries. And because I've been around paintings for a hundred years. I know the brushstrokes of the Old Masters like the lines around my eyes."

"With all due respect," replied Sarah, "that isn't good enough to prove the painting is a forgery."

"Which is why we're going to give it to Aiden Gallagher."

Gallagher was the founder of Equus Analytics, a high-tech art research firm that specialized in detecting forgeries. He sold his services to museums, dealers, collectors, auction houses, and, on occasion, to the Art Crime Team of the FBI. It was Aiden Gallagher, a decade earlier, who had proved that one of New York's most successful contemporary art galleries had sold nearly $80 million worth of fake paintings to unsuspecting buyers.

"His lab is in Westport, Connecticut," continued Gabriel. "If the forger made a technical mistake, Gallagher will find it."

"And while we're waiting for the results?"

"You'll arrange for me to have a look at the painting you sold to Phillip Somerset. If, as I suspect, it's a forgery—"

"Julian and I will be the laughingstocks of the art world."

No, thought Gabriel as he reached for his wineglass. If *Portrait of an Unknown Woman* turned out to be a forgery, Isherwood Fine Arts of Mason's Yard, purveyors of museum-quality Italian and Dutch Old Master paintings since 1968, would be ruined.

20

Westport

They passed through Heathrow security separately—Gabriel under his real name, with the forged Cuyp crammed into his carry-on—and reunited in the departure lounge. While waiting for the flight to be called, Sarah composed an email to Aiden Gallagher, informing him that Isherwood Fine Arts of London wished to hire Equus Analytics to conduct a technical evaluation of a painting. She did not identify the work in question, though she implied it was a matter of some urgency. She was scheduled to arrive in New York at noon and, barring a traffic disaster, could be in Westport by 3:00 p.m. at the latest. Could she deliver the painting to him then?

On board the plane, Sarah informed the flight attendant that she would require no food or drink during the eight-hour flight across the North Atlantic. Then she closed her eyes and did not open them again until the aircraft thudded onto the runway at John F. Kennedy International Airport. Armed with her American passport and Global Entry card, she glided through the rituals of the arrival process while Gabriel, his status reduced, spent an hour working his way through the maze of stanchions and retractable nylon restraints reserved for unwanted foreigners. His journey ended in a windowless room, where he was briefly questioned by a well-fed Customs and Border Protection officer.

"What brings you back to the United States, Director Allon?"

"Private research."

"Does the Agency know you're in the country?"

"They do now."

"How's your chest feeling?"

"Better than my hand."

"Anything in the bag?"

"A couple of firearms and a dead body."

The officer smiled. "Enjoy your stay."

A blue line directed Gabriel to baggage claim, where Sarah was pondering her mobile phone. "Aiden Gallagher," she said without looking up. "He's wondering whether it could wait until Monday. I told him it couldn't."

Just then her phone pinged with an incoming email.

"Well?"

"He wants a description of the painting."

Gabriel recited the particulars. "*A River Scene with Distant Windmills.* Oil on canvas. Thirty-six by fifty-eight centimeters. Currently attributed to Aelbert Cuyp."

Sarah sent the email. Gallagher's reply arrived two minutes later.

"He'll meet us in Westport at three."

Equus Analytics was located in an old redbrick building on Riverside Avenue near the overpass of the Connecticut Turnpike. Gabriel and Sarah arrived a few minutes after two o'clock in the back of an Uber SUV. They picked up coffee from a Dunkin' Donuts up the street and settled onto a bench along the sunlit bank of the Saugatuck. Fat white clouds flew across an otherwise spotless blue sky. Pleasure craft dozed like discarded playthings in their slips at a small marina.

"It almost looks like something Aelbert Cuyp might have painted," remarked Gabriel.

"Westport definitely has its charms. Especially on a day like this."

"Any regrets?"

"About leaving New York?" Sarah shook her head. "I think my story ended rather well, don't you?"

"That depends."

"On what?"

"Whether you're truly happy being married to Christopher."

"Deliriously so. Though I have to admit, my work at the gallery isn't quite as interesting as the jobs I used to do for you." She lifted her face toward the warmth of the sun. "Do you remember our trip to Saint-Barthélemy with Zizi al-Bakari?"

"How could I forget?"

"What about the summer we spent with Ivan and Elena Kharkov in Saint-Tropez? Or the day I shot that Russian assassin in Zurich?" Sarah checked the time on her phone. "It's nearly three. Let's go, shall we? I wouldn't want to keep him waiting."

They set out along Riverside Avenue and arrived at Equus Analytics as a black BMW 7 Series sedan was pulling into the parking lot. The man who emerged from the driver's seat had coal-black hair and blue eyes, and appeared much younger than his fifty-four years.

He extended a hand toward Sarah. "Miss Bancroft, I presume?"

"It's a pleasure to meet you, Dr. Gallagher. Thank you for seeing us on such short notice. And on a Saturday, at that."

"Not at all. Truth be told, I was planning to do a few hours' work before dinner." His accent, though faded, betrayed a Dublin childhood. He looked at Gabriel. "And you are?"

"Johannes Klemp," answered Gabriel, dredging up a name from his tangled past. "I work with Sarah at Isherwood Fine Arts."

"Did anyone ever tell you that you look a great deal like that Israeli who was shot on Inauguration Day? If I'm not mistaken, his name is Gabriel Allon."

"I get that a lot."

"I don't doubt it." Gallagher gave him a knowing smile before turning to Sarah. "That leaves the painting."

She nodded toward Gabriel's overnight bag.

"Ah," said Gallagher. "The plot thickens."

21

Equus

The locks on the outer door were museum grade, as were the security system and the equipment in Gallagher's laboratory. His inventory of high-tech gadgetry included an electron microscope, a shortwave infrared reflectography camera, and a Bruker M6 Jet-stream, a sophisticated spatial imaging device. Nevertheless, he began his analysis the old-fashioned way, by examining the painting with the naked eye under visible light.

"It seems to have survived the flight intact, but I'd like to put it on a stretcher as quickly as possible." He cast a reproachful glance in Gabriel's direction. "As long as Herr Klemp has no objections, of course."

"Perhaps you should refer to me by my real name," said Gabriel. "As for the stretcher, a standard fourteen-by-twenty-two should work well. I'd use a five-eighths setback for the canvas."

Gallagher's expression turned quizzical. "Are you a painter, Mr. Allon?"

Gabriel's answer was the same one he had given to Valerie Bérrangar's daughter seventy-two hours earlier, in the commune of Saint-André-du-Bois. Aiden Gallagher was similarly intrigued, though for a different reason.

"It turns out we have a great deal in common."

"I'm sorry to hear that," quipped Gabriel.

"Artistically, I mean. I trained to be a painter at the National College of Art and Design in Dublin before coming to America and enrolling at Columbia."

Where he had earned a PhD in art history and an MA in art conservation. While working on the restoration staff at the Metropolitan Museum of Art, he specialized in provenance research and, later, scientific detection of forgeries. He resigned from the Met in 2005 and founded Equus Analytics. The *Art Newspaper* had recently christened him "a rock star" with no equal in the field. Thus the new BMW 7 Series parked outside his office door.

He directed his gaze toward the painting. "Where was it acquired?"

"Gallery Georges Fleury in Paris," answered Gabriel.

"When?"

"Yesterday afternoon."

Gallagher looked up abruptly. "And you already suspect there's a problem?"

"No," said Gabriel. "I *know* there's a problem. The painting is a forgery."

"And how did you arrive at this conclusion?" asked Gallagher dubiously.

"Instinct."

"I'm afraid instinct isn't good enough, Mr. Allon." Gallagher contemplated the painting again. "How's the provenance?"

"A joke."

"And the condition report?"

"It's a real work of art."

Gabriel fished both documents from his briefcase and laid them on the table. Aiden Gallagher began his review with the provenance and ended with the three photos. The painting in its present form.

The painting under ultraviolet light. And the painting with the losses exposed.

"If it's a fake, the forger certainly knew what he was doing." Gallagher doused the overhead lights and examined the painting with an ultraviolet torch. The archipelago of black blotches corresponded with those in the photograph. "So far, so good." He switched on the overhead lights again and looked at Gabriel. "I assume you're familiar with Cuyp's work?"

"Very."

"Then you know his oeuvre has been plagued by confusion and misattribution for hundreds of years. He borrowed heavily from Jan van Goyen, and his followers borrowed heavily from him. One was Abraham van Calraet. Like Cuyp, he was from the Dutch town of Dordrecht. Because they shared the same initials, it can be difficult to tell the work of one from the other."

"Which is why a forger would choose a painter like Cuyp in the first place. Good forgers shrewdly select artists whose work has been subject to misattribution in the past. That way, when a new painting miraculously reemerges from a dusty European collection, the so-called art experts are more inclined to accept it as genuine."

"And if I conclude that the painting is the work of Aelbert Cuyp?"

"I'm confident you won't."

"Are you prepared to wager fifty thousand dollars?"

"Not me." Gabriel pointed at Sarah. "But she will."

"I require twenty-five thousand to begin an investigation. The rest is due upon delivery of my findings."

"How long will it take?" asked Sarah.

"Anywhere from a few weeks to a few months."

"Time is of the essence, Dr. Gallagher."

"When are you planning to return to London?"

"You tell me."

"I can have a preliminary report Monday afternoon. But there's a surcharge for rush jobs."

"How much?"

"Fifty thousand up front," said Gallagher. "Twenty-five thousand on delivery."

———————

After signing the release forms and handing over the check, Gabriel and Sarah hurried along Riverside Avenue to the Metro North station and purchased two tickets to Grand Central.

"The next train is at four twenty-six," said Sarah. "With any luck, we'll be sipping martinis at the Mandarin Oriental by six o'clock."

"I thought you preferred the Four Seasons."

"There was no room at the inn."

"Not even for you?"

"Trust me, I gave the head of reservations a piece of my mind."

"Where do you suppose Phillip Somerset is spending his weekend?"

"Knowing Phillip, he could be anywhere. Besides his town house on East Seventy-Fourth Street, he owns a ski lodge in Aspen, an estate on the East End of Long Island, and a large portion of Lake Placid in the Adirondacks. He flits between them on his Gulfstream."

"Not bad for a former bond trader from Lehman Brothers."

"You've obviously been reading up on him."

"You know me, Sarah. I've never been able to sleep on airplanes." Gabriel gave her a sideways glance. "What's the weather like in Lake Placid this time of year?"

"Miserable."

"What about Aspen?"

"No snow."

"That leaves Manhattan or Long Island."

"I'll call him first thing Monday."

"Get it over with. You'll feel better."

"Unless the Van Dyck turns out to be a forgery." Sarah opened a blank email and added Phillip Somerset's address. "What's the subject?"

"Catching up."

"Nice touch. Keep going."

"Tell him you're in New York unexpectedly. Ask him if he has a few minutes to spare."

"Should I mention the painting?"

"Under no circumstances."

"How should I describe you?"

"You're an art dealer who used to work for the CIA. I'm sure you'll think of something."

She completed the email as the train was drawing into the station. And at half past five, as they were climbing into a taxi outside Grand Central, Phillip Somerset rang her with his answer.

"Lindsay and I are having a few friends to lunch tomorrow at our place on Long Island. You're more than welcome to join us. And bring your friend," he suggested. "I'd love to meet him."

22

North Haven

Sarah declined Phillip's Somerset's offer of a car service and rented a premium European-made sedan instead. They collected it from a garage in Turtle Bay at half past ten the following morning and by noon were speeding through Suffolk County on the Long Island Expressway. To help pass the time, Sarah read aloud the quaint-sounding names of the towns and hamlets as they appeared on the faded green exit signs—first Commack, then Hauppauge, Ronkon-koma, and Patchogue. It was a silly game, she explained to Gabriel, that she had played as a child, when the Bancrofts had passed their summers in East Hampton with other rich Manhattan families like theirs.

"The new crowd is much richer than we were, and they're not ashamed to show it. Grotesque displays of wealth are now de rigueur." She tugged at the sleeve of the dark pantsuit that she had brought from London. "I only wish I'd had time to shop for something more appropriate."

"You look beautiful," said Gabriel, a hand balanced atop the steering wheel.

"But I'm not suitably attired for a weekend gathering at the North Haven estate of Phillip Somerset."

"How should one be dressed?"

"As expensively as possible." Sarah's phone chimed with an incoming text. "Speak of the devil."

"Have we been disinvited?"

"He's checking on our progress."

"Do you suppose he's contacting all his guests, or only you?"

"And just what are you implying?"

"That Phillip Somerset sounded inordinately pleased to hear from you yesterday."

"Our relationship is both personal and professional," admitted Sarah.

"How personal?"

"We were introduced by a mutual friend at MoMA's annual Party in the Garden fundraiser. Phillip was going through a messy divorce at the time. We dated for several months."

"Who ended it?"

"He did, if you must know."

"What on earth was he thinking?"

"I was in my late thirties at the time, and Phillip was looking for someone a bit younger. When he met lovely Lindsay Morgan, a yoga enthusiast and model twelve years my junior, he dropped me like an underperforming stock."

"And yet you remained invested in Masterpiece Art."

"How do you know that?"

"Lucky guess."

"I had already entrusted a small portion of my assets to Phillip before we began dating," said Sarah. "I saw no reason to demand a redemption simply because our relationship went awry."

"How small a portion?"

"Two million dollars."

"I see."

"I thought I made it clear the last time we were in New York that my father left me rather well off."

"You did," said Gabriel. "I only hope that Phillip has looked after your interests."

"My current balance is four point eight million dollars."

"Mazel tov."

"Compared to Phillip's other clients, I'm something of a pauper. He definitely has the Midas touch. That's why so many people in the art world are invested with him. The fund consistently delivers twenty-five-percent annual returns."

"How is that possible?"

"A magical proprietary trading strategy that Phillip guards jealously. Unlike other art funds, Masterpiece doesn't reveal the paintings in its inventory. Its book is entirely opaque. And quite large, apparently. Phillip currently controls one point two billion dollars' worth of art. He buys and sells paintings constantly and earns enormous profits on the churn."

"By churn, you mean volume and speed."

"And arbitrage, of course," replied Sarah. "Masterpiece operates exactly like a hedge fund. It has a million-dollar minimum for new investors, with a five-year lockup. The fee structure is the industry-standard two-and-twenty. A two percent management fee and a twenty percent cut of the profits."

"I suppose the firm is domiciled in the Cayman Islands."

"Aren't they all?" Sarah rolled her eyes. "I must admit, I do enjoy watching my account balance go up and up each year. But a part of me doesn't like to think of paintings as a commodity to be bought and sold like soybeans and oil futures."

"You'll have to get over that if you're going to make it as an art dealer. Most of the paintings purchased at auction will never be seen by the public again. They're locked away in bank vaults or in the Geneva Free Port."

"Or in a climate-controlled warehouse operated by Chelsea Fine Arts Storage. That's where Phillip told me to ship the Van Dyck." Sarah pointed toward the sign for exit 66. "Yaphank."

———————

The egg-shaped peninsula known as North Haven protrudes into Peconic Bay between Sag Harbor and Shelter Island. Phillip Somerset's weekend retreat, a thirty-thousand-square-foot acropolis of cedar and glass, stood on the eastern shore. His golden young wife greeted Gabriel and Sarah in the soaring entrance hall, dressed in a sleeveless linen pantsuit belted at her slender waist, her skin so smooth and flawless she looked like a filtered photograph on social media. When Gabriel introduced himself, he received a blank who-are-you stare in return, but Sarah's name Lindsay Somerset recognized instantly.

"You're the art dealer from London who sold my husband the Van Gogh."

"Van Dyck."

"I get them confused."

"It's a common mistake," Sarah assured her.

Lindsay Somerset turned to greet a new arrival, a prime-time television news anchor and his husband. Several more print and broadcast journalists were gathered in the luminous great room along with an assortment of hedge fund managers, painters, art dealers, fashion designers, models, actors, screenwriters, a renowned director of blockbuster motion pictures, an iconic musician who sang about the plight of Long Island's working classes, a progressive congresswoman from the Bronx, and a flock of young assistants from a New York publishing house. Evidently, it was a book party to which they had been invited.

"Carl Bernstein," whispered Sarah. "He was Bob Woodward's partner at the *Washington Post* during the Watergate scandal."

"Unlike you, Sarah, I was alive when Richard Nixon was president. I know who Carl Bernstein is."

"Would you like to meet him? He's right over there." Sarah snatched a glass of champagne from the tray of a passing waiter. "And there's Ina Garten. And that actor whose name I can never remember. The one who just got out of rehab."

"And there's a Rothko," said Gabriel quietly. "And a Basquiat. And a Pollock. And a Lichtenstein, a Diebenkorn, a Hirst, an Adler, a Prince, and a Warhol."

"You should see his town house on East Seventy-Fourth Street. It's like the Whitney in there."

"Not quite," said a baritone voice from behind them. "But you're welcome to visit anytime you like."

The voice belonged to Phillip Somerset. He greeted Sarah first—with a kiss on her cheek and a favorable remark about her appearance—before extending a sun-varnished hand toward Gabriel. He was a tall, physically fit specimen in his mid-fifties, with a boyish head of gray-blond hair and the confident, easy smile that comes naturally to the very rich. Strapped to his wrist was a colossal Richard Mille chronometer, a sporting model worn by wealthy men with pretensions of seamanship. His zippered cashmere sweater was vaguely maritime as well, as were his pale cotton trousers and electric-blue loafers. Indeed, everything about Phillip Somerset suggested that he had just stepped from the deck of a yacht.

Gabriel accepted the proffered hand and introduced himself, first name and last.

Phillip Somerset looked to Sarah for an explanation.

"He's an old friend," she said.

"And I thought I was going to spend the afternoon fending off questions about my trading strategy." Phillip Somerset released

Gabriel's hand. "What an unexpected surprise, Mr. Allon. To what do I owe the honor?"

"I was hoping to have a look at a painting."

"Well, you've certainly come to the right place. Is there anything in particular you'd like to see?"

"*Portrait of an Unknown Woman.*"

"By Anthony van Dyck?"

Gabriel smiled. "I certainly hope so."

———————

Phillip Somerset escorted Gabriel and Sarah up a flight of stairs and into a large, light-filled office with outsize computer monitors and a sweeping view of the whitecapped bay. A lengthy silence ensued as he regarded them speculatively from behind the no-man's-land of his half-acre desk. Then he looked directly at Sarah and said, "Perhaps you should tell me what this is all about."

Her answer was precise and lawyerly. "Isherwood Fine Arts has retained Mr. Allon to conduct a discreet inquiry into the circumstances surrounding the rediscovery of *Portrait of an Unknown Woman* and its sale to Masterpiece Art Ventures."

"Why was such an inquiry deemed necessary?"

"Late last week, the gallery received a letter expressing concerns over the transaction. The woman who sent it was killed in an auto accident near Bordeaux a few days later."

"Do the police suspect foul play?"

"No," answered Gabriel. "But I do."

"Why?"

"Her late husband purchased several paintings from the same gallery in Paris where Julian and Sarah acquired *Portrait of an Unknown Woman*. When I paid a visit to the gallery on Friday, I noticed three paintings that appeared to be forgeries. I purchased one of them and turned it over to Equus Analytics."

"Aiden Gallagher is the best in the business. I use him myself."

"He's hoping to have a preliminary report by tomorrow afternoon. But in the meantime—"

"You thought you'd have a look at the Van Dyck."

Gabriel nodded.

"I'd love to show it to you," said Phillip Somerset. "But I'm afraid it's not possible."

"May I ask why not?"

"Masterpiece Art Ventures sold it about three weeks ago. At a considerable profit, I might add."

"To whom?"

"I'm sorry, Mr. Allon. The transaction was private."

"Was there an intermediary?"

"One of the major auction houses."

"Did the house conduct a second review of the attribution?"

"The buyer insisted on one."

"And?"

"*Portrait of an Unknown Woman* was painted by Anthony van Dyck, almost certainly in his studio in Antwerp, sometime in the late sixteen thirties. Which means that, as far as Isherwood Fine Arts and Masterpiece Art Ventures are concerned, the matter is now closed."

"If you don't mind," said Sarah, "I'd like that in writing."

"Send me something tomorrow morning," replied Phillip Somerset. "I'll have a look."

23

Gallery 617

Early the following morning, Sarah rang her man at HSBC in London and instructed him to wire one million euros into the Credit Suisse account of the world's most famous violinist. Then she dialed Ronald Sumner-Lloyd, Julian's Berkeley Square solicitor, and together they drafted a letter shielding Isherwood Fine Arts against any and all future claims related to the sale of *Portrait of an Unknown Woman* by the Flemish Baroque painter Anthony van Dyck. Shortly before 9:00 a.m., she emailed the finished document to Phillip Somerset. He phoned her a few minutes later from his Sikorsky executive helicopter, which was bound from East Hampton to Manhattan.

"The language is rather aggressive, don't you think? Especially the clause regarding confidentiality."

"I have to look after our interests, Phillip. And if your sale goes sideways, I don't ever want to read the words Isherwood Fine Arts in the *New York Times*."

"I thought I made it clear that you have nothing to worry about."

"You also once assured me that you were interested in a long-term relationship."

"You're not still angry over that, are you?"

"I never was," lied Sarah. "Now do me a favor and sign the waiver."

"On one condition."

"What's that?"

"Tell me how you know Gabriel Allon."

"We met when I was working in Washington."

"That was a long time ago."

"Yes," said Sarah. "Lovely Lindsay must have been in elementary school at the time."

"She says you were rude to her."

"She doesn't know the difference between a Van Gogh and a Van Dyck."

"Once upon a time, neither did I," said Phillip before ringing off. "But look at me now."

———————

The document appeared in Sarah's in-box five minutes later, electronically signed and dated. She added her own signature and forwarded it to Julian and Ronnie in London. Then, after confirming two reservations for that evening's seven thirty British Airways flight to Heathrow, she rang Gabriel and told him that Isherwood Fine Arts was now legally and ethically in the clear.

"Which means that Julian and I get to keep our reputations, not to mention our six and a half million pounds. All in all," she said, "a rather fortunate turn of events."

"What are your plans for the rest of the morning?"

"First I'm going to pack my suitcase. Then I'm going to stare at my phone and wait for Aiden Gallagher of Equus Analytics to tell me that you needlessly spent a million euros of my money on *A River Scene with Distant Windmills*."

"How about a nice long walk instead?"

"A much better idea."

It was a perfect spring morning, bright and cloudless, with a mischievous wind blowing from the Hudson. They walked along West Fifty-Ninth Street to Fifth Avenue, then turned uptown.

"Where are you taking me?"

"The Metropolitan Museum of Art."

"Why?"

"Its collection includes several important paintings by Anthony van Dyck." Gabriel smiled. "Real ones."

Sarah rang a friend who worked in the Met's publicity department and requested two complimentary admission tickets. They were waiting at the information desk in the Great Hall. Upstairs, they made their way to Gallery 617, a room dedicated to Baroque portraiture. It contained four works by Van Dyck, including his iconic portrait of Henrietta Maria, wife of King Charles I. Gabriel snapped a photograph of the queen consort's face and showed it to Sarah.

"Craquelure," she said.

"Do you notice anything unusual about it?"

"No."

"Neither do I. It looks exactly like Van Dyck's craquelure should look. But now look at this one." It was the face of the unknown woman, the version that Julian and Sarah had sold to Phillip Somerset. "The craquelure pattern is different."

"It's slight," said Sarah. "But, yes, there's a difference."

"That's because the forger is using a chemical hardening agent to artificially age the painting. It produces four centuries' worth of craquelure in a matter of days. But it's not the right *kind* of craquelure."

"Two separate reviews have declared our *Portrait of an Unknown Woman* to be the work of Anthony van Dyck. Rome has spoken, Gabriel. The case is closed."

"But both reviews were based on expert opinion rather than science."

Sarah sighed in frustration. "Perhaps you're looking at this the wrong way."

"And what would be the right way?"

She gestured toward the portrait of Henrietta Maria. "Maybe that one is fake."

"It isn't."

"Are you sure about that?" Sarah led him into an adjoining gallery. "And what about that landscape over there? Are you absolutely certain that Claude Lorrain painted it? Or are you merely inclined to believe that because it's on display in the Metropolitan Museum of Art?"

"Your point?"

"My point," replied Sarah in a stage whisper, "is that no one really knows whether all the beautiful works of art hanging in the world's great museums are genuine or fakes. Least of all the learned curators and conservators employed by institutions such as this one. It's the dirty little secret they don't like to talk about. Oh, they do their utmost to guarantee the integrity of their collections. But the truth is, they get fooled all the time. By one estimate, at least twenty percent of the paintings in the National Gallery in London are misattributed works or outright forgeries. And I can assure you, the statistics for the private art market are much worse."

"Then perhaps we should do something about it."

"By putting Galerie Georges Fleury out of business?" Sarah shook her head slowly. "Bad idea, Gabriel."

"Why?"

"Because what starts in Paris won't stay in Paris. It will spread through the rest of the art world like a contagion. It will infect the auction houses, the dealers, the collectors, and the ordinary patrons of museums like the Met. No one, not even the most virtuous among us, will be spared its ravages."

"And if Aiden Gallagher tells us that the painting is a forgery?"

"We will pursue restitution quietly and then go our separate ways, never to speak of the matter again. Otherwise, we might shatter the illusion that all that glitters is actually gold."

"Glisters," said Gabriel.

Frowning, Sarah checked the time. "It is now officially afternoon."

They returned to the Mandarin Oriental and settled into the last empty table in the hotel's popular lobby bar. At two fifteen, as they were finishing their lunch, Sarah's phone shivered with an incoming call. It was from Equus Analytics.

"Maybe *you* should answer that," said Sarah.

Gabriel tapped the ACCEPT icon and lifted the device to his ear. "Thank you," he said after a moment. "But that won't be necessary. We're on our way now."

Sarah reclaimed her phone. "*What* won't be necessary?"

"Additional chemical analysis of the pigment."

"Why not?"

"Because Aiden Gallagher discovered several navy-blue polar fleece fibers embedded throughout the painting, including in places that had never been retouched. Since the fabric was invented in Massachusetts in 1979, it's safe to assume that Aelbert Cuyp wasn't wearing a fleece jacket or vest in the mid-seventeenth century. Which means—"

"Georges Fleury owes me a million euros."

Sarah switched their flights, then hurried upstairs to fetch her luggage. They would settle the matter quietly, she thought, and never speak of it again.

24

Galerie Fleury

The navigation application on Sarah's phone estimated the driving time from Columbus Circle to Westport, Connecticut, to be ninety minutes. But Gabriel, behind the wheel of their rented European sedan, managed to cover the distance in a little more than an hour. Aiden Gallagher's flashy BMW 7 Series was parked outside Equus Analytics, and *A River Scene with Distant Windmills*, adhered to a new stretcher, was lying on the examination table in the lab. Next to the painting was a two-page letter declaring the work to be a modern forgery. And next to the letter were three microscope photographs supporting Gallagher's conclusion.

"To be honest, I was a little surprised it was so cut-and-dried. Given the quality of his brushwork, I expected more of him." Gallagher pointed out the dark strands of polar fleece in the photographs. "It's a real amateur's mistake."

"Is there any other possible explanation for the presence of those fibers?" asked Gabriel.

"None whatsoever. That said, you should be prepared for Fleury to take great offense at my findings." Gallagher looked at Sarah. "In my experience, most art dealers become rather indignant when asked to part with a million euros."

"I'm quite confident Monsieur Fleury will see things our way. Especially when he reads your report."

"When are you planning to confront him?"

"We're leaving for Paris tonight. In fact," said Sarah, glancing at her watch, "we need to be on our way."

She made out a check for the final $25,000 of Gallagher's fee while Gabriel removed *A River Scene with Distant Windmills* from its stretcher and folded it into his carry-on bag. Their Air France flight commenced boarding at 6:45 p.m. At half past eight, they were over the East End of Long Island.

"There's North Haven," said Sarah, pointing out her window. "I actually think I can see Phillip's house."

"One wonders how he and Lindsay make do with only thirty thousand square feet."

"You should see the place in the Adirondacks." She lowered her voice. "I spent a long weekend there once."

"Kayaking and hiking?"

"Among other things. Phillip has lots of toys."

"He certainly didn't keep the Van Dyck for long."

"Some people flip houses. Phillip flips paintings."

Sarah accepted a glass of champagne from the flight attendant and insisted that Gabriel take one as well.

"What shall we drink to?" he asked.

"A disaster averted."

"I certainly hope so," said Gabriel, and left his glass untouched.

———

It was a few minutes after nine the following morning when the plane dropped from a cloudless sky and settled onto the runway of

Charles de Gaulle Airport. After clearing passport control and customs, Gabriel and Sarah climbed into a taxi and headed for the center of Paris. Their first stop was Brasserie L'Alsace on the Avenue des Champs-Élysées, where, at 10:45 a.m., Gabriel placed his first call to Galerie Georges Fleury. It went unanswered, as did his second. But the third time he tried the number, Bruno the receptionist came on the line. Posing once again as Ludwig Ziegler, art adviser to the renowned Swiss violinist Anna Rolfe, Gabriel demanded to speak to Monsieur Fleury at once.

"I'm sorry, but Monsieur Fleury is with another client."

"It is imperative that I see him immediately."

"May I ask what this is regarding?"

"*A River Scene with Distant Windmills.*"

"Perhaps I can be of help."

"I'm quite certain you can't."

The receptionist placed the call on hold. Two minutes passed before he came back on the line. "Monsieur Fleury will see you at two o'clock," he said, and the connection went dead.

Which left Gabriel and Sarah with three long hours to kill. They drank coffee at Brasserie L'Alsace until noon, then walked up the Champs-Élysées to Fouquet's for an unhurried lunch. Afterward, they crossed to the opposite side of the avenue and, with their luggage in tow, window-shopped their way to the rue la Boétie. It was two o'clock exactly when they arrived at Galerie Georges Fleury. Gabriel stretched his injured right hand toward the intercom, but the automatic lock snapped open before he could place his forefinger atop the call button. He heaved open the glass door and followed Sarah inside.

———

The vestibule was unoccupied save the bronze life-size bust of a young Greek or Roman man perched atop its plinth of black marble. Gabriel called out Fleury's name and, receiving no answer, led Sarah into the ground-floor exhibition room. It was likewise uninhabited. The large Rococo painting depicting a nude Venus and three young maidens was gone, as was the Venetian scene attributed to a follower of Canaletto. No new paintings hung in their place.

"Looks as though Monsieur Fleury is doing a brisk business," said Sarah.

"The missing paintings were both forgeries," answered Gabriel, and headed for Fleury's office. There he found the art dealer seated at his desk, his face tipped toward the ceiling, his mouth open. The wall behind him was spattered with still-damp blood and brain tissue, the result of two recent point-blank gunshot wounds to the center of his forehead. The younger man lying on the floor had also been shot at close range—twice in the chest and at least once in the head. Like Georges Fleury, he was quite obviously dead.

"Dear God," whispered Sarah from the open doorway.

Gabriel made no reply; his phone was ringing. It was Yuval Gershon, calling from his office at Unit 8200 headquarters outside Tel Aviv. He didn't bother with a greeting.

"Someone turned on the dead woman's phone about one thirty local time. We got inside a couple of minutes ago."

"Where is it?"

"The Eighth Arrondissement of Paris. The rue la Boétie."

"I'm in the same location."

"I know," said Yuval. "In fact, it looks to us as though you might be in the same room."

Gabriel rang off and located the number for Valerie Bérrangar's phone in his directory of recent calls. He started to dial, but stopped when his connoisseur's eye fell upon the aluminum-sided Tumi suitcase, 52 by 77 by 28 centimeters, standing in the corner of the cluttered office. It was possible that Monsieur Fleury had been planning to embark on a journey at the time of his death. But the more likely explanation was that the suitcase contained a bomb.

A bomb, thought Gabriel, that would be detonated with a call to Madame Bérrangar's phone.

He did not bother to explain any of this to Sarah. Instead, he seized her arm and pulled her through the exhibition room to the entrance of the gallery. The glass door was locked, and the remote was missing from the receptionist's desk. It was, Gabriel had to admit, a masterpiece of planning and execution. But then he would have expected nothing less. After all, they were professionals.

But even professionals, he thought suddenly, make mistakes. Theirs was the bronze life-size bust of a young Greek or Roman man perched atop its plinth of black marble. Gabriel raised the heavy object above his head and, ignoring the searing pain in his hand, hurled it against the glass door of Galerie Georges Fleury.

PART TWO

———

Underdrawing

25

Quai des Orfèvres

Perhaps not surprisingly, the French police assumed the worst when, at 2:01 p.m. on an otherwise pleasant spring afternoon, the elegant Eighth Arrondissement of Paris shook with the thunderclap of an explosion. The first units arrived at the scene moments later to find an Old Master art gallery engulfed in flames. Even so, the officers were encouraged by the fact that there appeared to be no large-scale loss of life of the sort associated with jihadist terrorist attacks. Indeed, at first glance, the only casualty appeared to be the life-size bronze bust of a young Greek or Roman man lying on the pavement, surrounded by blue-gray cubes of tempered glass. One veteran detective, after learning of the circumstances by which the weighty objet d'art exited the gallery, would declare it to be the first documented case in the annals of French crime that anyone had broken *out* of an art gallery.

The perpetrators of this most unusual act—a man of late middle age and an attractive fair-haired woman in her early forties—surrendered to police within minutes of the explosion. And at 2:45 p.m., after a series of hasty and incredulous phone calls between senior French intelligence and security officials, they were placed in the back of an unmarked Peugeot and delivered to 36 Quai des Orfèvres, the iconic headquarters of the Police Nationale's criminal division.

There they were separated and relieved of their personal effects. The woman's handbag and luggage contained nothing out of the ordinary, but her companion was in possession of several noteworthy items. They included a false German passport, an Israeli-made Solaris mobile phone, an Italian *permesso di soggiorno*, a painting without a frame or stretcher, documents from Galerie Georges Fleury and Equus Analytics, and a handwritten letter from a certain Valerie Bérrangar to Julian Isherwood, owner and sole proprietor of Isherwood Fine Arts, 7–8 Mason's Yard, St. James's, London.

At half past three, the items were arrayed upon the table of the interrogation room into which the man of late middle age was led. Also present was a sleek creature of about fifty clad in a banker's executive suit. Extending a hand cordially in greeting, he introduced himself as Jacques Ménard, commander of the Central Office for the Fight against Cultural Goods Trafficking. The man smiled as he lowered himself into his seat. It definitely sounded better in French.

Jacques Ménard opened the German passport. "Johannes Klemp?"

"A small man with a chip balanced precariously on his insignificant shoulder," said Gabriel. "Much loathed by hoteliers and restaurateurs from Copenhagen to Cairo."

"Do the Germans know you're abusing one of their passports?"

"The way I see it, allowing me to occasionally travel on one of their passports is the least the Germans can do."

Ménard took up the Solaris phone. "Is it as secure as they say?"

"I hope you didn't try to unlock it. I'll go blind reloading my contacts."

Ménard reached for the sales documents from Galerie Georges Fleury. "*The* Anna Rolfe?"

"She was in town last weekend. I borrowed her for a few hours."

"She has a fondness for Aelbert Cuyp?"

"It's not a Cuyp." Gabriel nudged the report from Equus Analytics across the tabletop. "It's a forgery. Which is why I purchased it in the first place."

"You can tell if a painting is a forgery merely by looking at it?"

"Can't you?"

"No," admitted Ménard. "I cannot. But perhaps we should begin here." He indicated the handwritten letter. "With Madame Bérrangar."

"Yes, let's," said Gabriel. "After all, if you had taken her complaint about *Portrait of an Unknown Woman* seriously, she'd still be alive."

"Madame Bérrangar was killed in a single-vehicle traffic accident."

"It wasn't an accident, Ménard. She was murdered."

"How do you know that?"

"Her phone."

"What about it?"

"The bombmaker used it to trigger the detonator."

"Perhaps we should start from the beginning," suggested Ménard.

Yes, agreed Gabriel. Perhaps they should.

Gabriel's account of his investigation into the provenance and authenticity of *Portrait of an Unknown Woman* was chronological in sequence and largely accurate in content. It commenced with Julian's star-crossed visit to Bordeaux and concluded with the destruction of Galerie Georges Fleury and the brutal murder of its owner and his assistant. Absent from Gabriel's briefing was any mention of his visit to a certain antiques shop on the rue de Miromesnil or the assistance he received from Yuval Gershon of Unit 8200. Nor did he divulge the name of the wealthy American art investor who had purchased *Portrait of an Unknown Woman* from Isherwood Fine Arts—only that the painting had since been resold to yet another unidentified buyer and that the matter had been resolved to the satisfaction of all the parties involved.

"Is it a Van Dyck or not?" asked Ménard.

"The auction house that brokered the sale says it is."

"So your investigation was a waste of time? Is that what you're saying?"

"The death of Valerie Bérrangar and the events of this afternoon would suggest otherwise." Gabriel looked down at the forgery. "As would this painting."

"Did you really expect Georges Fleury to return the money based on the findings of a single expert?"

"The expert in question is regarded as the best in the world. I was confident that I could convince Fleury to accept the findings and re-fund the money."

"You were planning to threaten him?"

"Me? Never."

Ménard smiled in spite of himself. "And you're sure Fleury was dead when you and Madame Bancroft arrived at the gallery?"

"Quite sure," answered Gabriel. "Bruno Gilbert, too."

"In that case, who let you in?"

"The assassin, of course. He unlocked the door using the keyless re-mote that usually rests on the receptionist's desk. Fortunately, he waited fifteen seconds too long before calling Valerie Bérrangar's phone."

"How do you—"

"It's not important how I know," interjected Gabriel. "All that matters is that you now have the evidence to link her murder to the bombing of the gallery."

"The phone's identification number and SIM card?"

Gabriel nodded.

"Only if they survived the detonation. Still, it was rather reckless on his part, don't you think?"

"Almost as reckless as leaving that bronze bust next to the door.

The man who hired him probably thought that I would be suspicious if it wasn't there. After all, I spotted three forgeries within a few minutes of setting foot in that gallery." Gabriel lowered his voice. "Which is why I had to die."

"Because you were a threat to a forgery ring?" asked Ménard skeptically.

"It's not a traditional ring. It's a sophisticated business enterprise that's flooding the art market with high-quality forgeries. And the man who's running it is making enough money to hire professionals to eliminate anyone who threatens him."

Ménard made a show of thought. "An interesting theory, Allon. But you have no proof."

"If you had listened to Valerie Bérrangar, you would have all the proof you need."

"I did listen to her," insisted Ménard. "But Fleury assured me there was nothing wrong with the painting he sold to Monsieur Isherwood, that it was simply a case of two copies of the same portrait."

"And you believed him?"

"Georges Fleury was a respected member of the Paris art community. My unit never received a single complaint about him."

"That's because the fakes he was selling were good enough to fool the best eyes in the art world. Based on what I've seen of the forger's work, he could hold his own among the Old Masters."

"From what I hear, you're not too bad yourself, Allon. One of the world's finest art restorers. At least that's the rumor."

"But I use my talent to heal existing paintings." Gabriel tapped the surface of the forgery. "This man is creating entirely new works that appear as though they were executed by some of the greatest artists who ever lived."

"Do you have any idea who he might be?"

"You're the detective, Ménard. I'm sure you'll be able to find him if you put your mind to it."

"And who are you these days, Allon?"

"I'm the director of the paintings department at the Tiepolo Restoration Company. And I'd like to go home now."

———

Ménard insisted on keeping the forged painting and the original copies of the documents, including Valerie Bérrangar's letter. Gabriel, who was in no position to make demands of his own, requested only anonymity—for himself and for Isherwood Fine Arts.

The French detective rubbed his jaw noncommittally. "You know how these things go, Allon. Criminal inquiries can be hard to control. But don't worry about the German passport. It will be our little secret."

By then it was approaching eight o'clock. Ménard escorted Gabriel downstairs to the courtyard, where Sarah waited in the backseat of the same unmarked Peugeot. It delivered them to the Gare du Nord in time to make the evening's last Eurostar to London.

"All in all," said Sarah, "a rather disastrous turn of events."

"It could have been worse."

"Much," she agreed. "But why is it that things always explode whenever I'm around you?"

"I just seem to rub certain people the wrong way."

"But not Jacques Ménard?"

"No," said Gabriel. "We got on famously."

"So much for handling the matter quietly. But I suppose that you got exactly what you wanted in the end."

"What's that?"

"A formal investigation by the French police."

"No one will be spared?"

"No one," said Sarah as she closed her eyes. "Not even you."

26

San Polo

For the remainder of that glorious April, as French police and prosecutors sifted through the ruins of Galerie Georges Fleury, the art world looked on in horror and held its collective breath. Those who knew Fleury well were guarded in their comments, in private and especially to the press. And those who had done business with him said little if anything at all. The director of the Musée d'Orsay called it the most unsettled month for the arts in France since the Germans entered Paris in June 1940. Several commentators criticized the remark as insensitive, but few took issue with its sentiment.

Because *l'affaire Fleury* included a bomb and two dead bodies, the serious crimes division of the Police Nationale—the so-called Central Directorate of the Judicial Police—controlled the investigation, with Jacques Ménard's art sleuths reduced to a supporting role. Veteran crime reporters immediately sensed that something was amiss, as their sources at the Quai des Orfèvres seemed incapable of answering even the most basic questions about the probe.

Did the *police judiciaire* have any leads on the bomber's current whereabouts?

If we did, came the terse reply from the Quai des Orfèvres, we would have arrested him by now.

Was it true that Fleury and his assistant were killed before the bomb exploded?

The Quai des Orfèvres was not in a position to say.

Was theft the motive?

The Quai des Orfèvres was pursuing several leads.

Were others involved?

The Quai des Orfèvres had ruled nothing out.

And what about the man of late middle age and the attractive fair-haired woman who were seen smashing their way out of the gallery seconds before the bomb detonated? Here again, the Quai des Orfèvres was at its most elusive. Yes, the police were aware of the eyewitness reports and were looking into them. For now, they would have nothing more to say on the matter, as it was part of an ongoing investigation.

Gradually, the press grew frustrated and sought out greener pastures. The flow of new revelations slowed to a trickle, then dried up entirely. Quietly the inhabitants of the art world breathed a collective sigh of relief. With their reputations and careers intact, they carried on as though nothing had happened.

Such was the case, to a lesser extent, for the man of late middle age. For several days after his return to Venice, he tried to spare his wife the details of his most recent brush with death. He revealed the truth while attempting, with limited success, to accurately reproduce her honey-and-gold-flecked irises on canvas. His task was made more difficult by the late-afternoon light falling across the underside of her left breast.

"You violated every possible rule of tradecraft," she admonished him. "The field officer always controls the environment. And he never allows the target to set the time of a meeting."

"I wasn't debriefing a deep-penetration agent in the backstreets of West Beirut. I was attempting to return a forged painting to a crooked art dealer in the Eighth Arrondissement of Paris."

"Will they try again?"

"To kill me? I can't imagine."

"Why not?"

"Because I've told the French everything I know. What would be the point?"

"What was the point of trying to kill you in the first place?"

"He's afraid of me."

"Who?"

"You really must stop talking." He loaded his brush and placed it against his canvas. "It changes the shape of your eyes when you open your mouth."

She seemed not to hear him. "Your daughter dreamed of your death while you were away. A terrible nightmare. And quite prophetic, as it turns out."

"Why?"

"You were lying on a sidewalk when you died."

"She must have been dreaming of Washington."

"Her dream was different."

"How so?"

"You had no arms or legs."

———

That evening Gabriel experienced the same dream. It was so vivid he didn't dare close his eyes again for fear of its return. Repairing to his studio, he completed the painting of Chiara in a few fevered hours of uninterrupted work. In the broad light of morning, she declared it the finest piece he had produced in years.

"It reminds me of a Modigliani."

"I'll take that as a compliment."

"You were inspired by him?"

"It's hard not to be."

"Could you paint one?"

"A Modigliani? Yes, of course."

"I like the one that fetched a hundred and seventy million at auction a few years ago."

The painting in question was *Reclining Nude*. Gabriel commenced work on it after dropping the children at school and completed it two days later while listening to Anna Rolfe's new CD. Then he produced a second version of the painting, with a change of perspective and a subtle rearrangement of the woman's pose. He signed it with Modigliani's distinctive signature, in the upper-right corner of the canvas.

"Obviously, your hand suffered no permanent damage," remarked Chiara.

"I painted it with my left."

"It's astonishing. It looks exactly like a Modigliani."

"It *is* a Modigliani. He just didn't paint it."

"Could it fool anyone?"

"Not with a modern canvas and stretcher. But if I found a canvas similar to the type he was using in Montmartre in 1917 and was able to concoct a convincing provenance . . ."

"You could bring it to market as a lost Modigliani?"

"Exactly."

"How much could you get for it?"

"A couple hundred, I'd say."

"Thousand?"

"Million." Gabriel placed a hand reflectively to his chin. "The question is, what should we do with it?"

"Burn it," said Chiara. "And don't ever paint another."

———

Chiara's directive to the contrary, Gabriel hung the two Modiglianis in their bedroom and then retreated once more to his quiet, unhurried life of semiretirement. He dropped the children at school at eight o'clock each morning and collected them again at half past three. He visited the Rialto Market to fetch the ingredients for the family's evening meal. He read dense books and listened to music on his new British sound system. And if he were so inclined, he painted. A Monet one day, a Cézanne the next, a stunning reinterpretation of Vincent's *Self-Portrait with Bandaged Ear* that, were it not for Gabriel's modern canvas and palette, would have set the art world ablaze.

He followed the news from Paris with mixed emotions. He was relieved that Quai des Orfèvres had seen fit to conceal his role in the affair and that his old friends Sarah Bancroft and Julian Isherwood had suffered no reputational damage. But when three additional weeks passed with no arrests—and no suggestion in the press that Galerie Georges Fleury had been flooding the market with paintings produced by one of the greatest art forgers in history—Gabriel reached the unsettling conclusion that a ministerial thumb had been laid upon the scales of French justice.

The arrival of the Bavaria C42 came as a welcome distraction. Gabriel took it on a pair of test runs in the sheltered waters of the *laguna*. Then, on the first Saturday of May, the Allon family sailed to Trieste for dinner. During their starlit return to Venice, Gabriel revealed that Sarah Bancroft had offered him a minor but lucrative commission. Chiara suggested he execute something original instead. He commenced work on a Picassoesque still life, then buried it beneath a version of Titian's *Portrait of Vincenzo Mosti*. Francesco Tiepolo declared it a masterpiece and advised Gabriel never to produce another.

He disagreed with Francesco's favorable assessment of the work—it was by no means a masterpiece, not by the mighty Titian's standards—so he cut the canvas from its stretcher and burned it. Next morning, after dropping the children at school, he repaired to Bar Dogale to consider how best to squander the remaining hours of his day. While he was consuming *un 'ombra*, a small glass of *vino bianco* taken by Venetians with their breakfast, a shadow fell across his table. It was cast by none other than Luca Rossetti of the Art Squad. His face bore only the faintest trace of the injuries he had suffered some six weeks earlier. He bore a message from Jacques Ménard of the Police Nationale.

"He was wondering whether you were free to come to Paris."

"When?"

"You're booked on the twelve forty Air France flight."

"Today?"

"Do you have something more pressing on your schedule, Allon?"

"That depends on whether Ménard intends to arrest me the minute I step off the plane."

"No such luck."

"In that case, why does he want to see me?"

"He wants to show you something."

"Did he say what it was?"

"No," said Rossetti. "But he said you might want to bring a gun."

27

Musée du Louvre

Jacques Ménard was waiting at the arrival gate at Charles de Gaulle when Gabriel emerged from the jetway, a bag over one shoulder, a 9mm Beretta pressing reassuringly against the base of his spine. After an expedited journey through passport control, they climbed into the back of an unmarked sedan and started toward the center of Paris. Ménard declined to disclose their destination.

"The last time someone surprised me in Paris, it didn't turn out so well."

"Don't worry, Allon. I think you'll actually enjoy this."

They followed the A1 past the Stade de France, then headed west on the boulevard Périphérique, Paris's high-speed ring road. Five minutes later, the Élysée Palace appeared before them.

"You should have warned me," said Gabriel. "I would have worn something appropriate."

Ménard smiled as his driver sped past the presidential palace, then turned left onto the Avenue des Champs-Élysées. Before reaching the Place de la Concorde, they dropped into a tunnel and followed the Quai des Tuileries to the Pont du Carrousel. A right turn would have taken them across the Seine to the Latin Quarter. They

turned to the left instead and, after passing beneath an ornate arch-
way, braked to a halt in the immense central courtyard of the world's
most famous museum.

"The Louvre?"

"Yes, of course. Where did you think I was taking you?"

"Somewhere a bit more dangerous."

"If it's danger you want," said Ménard, "we've definitely come to
the right place."

———————

A young woman with the elongated limbs of a Degas dancer
greeted Gabriel and Ménard outside I. M. Pei's iconic glass-and-steel
pyramid. Wordlessly she escorted them across the immense Cour
Napoléon and through a door reserved for museum staff. Two uni-
formed security guards waited on the other side. Neither seemed to
notice when Gabriel set off the magnetometer.

"This way, please," said the woman, and led them along a corridor
flooded with fluorescent light. After a walk of perhaps a half kilometer, they arrived at the entrance of the National Center for Research
and Restoration, the world's most scientifically advanced facility for
the conservation and authentication of art. Its inventory of cutting-
edge technology included an electrostatic particle accelerator that
allowed researchers to determine the chemical composition of an object without need of a potentially damaging sample.

The woman entered the passcode into the keypad, and Ménard led
Gabriel inside. The cathedral-like laboratory was gripped by an air of
sudden abandonment.

"I asked the director to close early so we could have a bit of privacy."

"To do what?"

"Look at a painting, Allon. What else?"

It was propped upon a laboratory easel, shrouded in black baize.

Ménard removed the cloth to reveal a full-length portrait of a nude Lucretia thrusting a dagger into the center of her chest.

"Lucas Cranach the Elder?" asked Gabriel.

"That's what it says on the placard."

"Where did it come from?"

"Where do you think?"

"Galerie Georges Fleury?"

"I always heard you were good, Allon."

"And where did Monsieur Fleury find it?"

"A very old and prominent French collection," answered Ménard dubiously. "When Fleury showed it to a curator at the Louvre, he said it was probably the work of a later follower of Cranach. The curator had other ideas and brought it here to the center for evaluation. I'm sure you can guess the rest."

"The most advanced facility for the restoration and authentication of paintings in the world declared it to be the work of Lucas Cranach the Elder rather than a later follower."

Ménard nodded. "But wait, it gets better."

"How is that possible?"

"Because the president of the Louvre declared it a national treasure and paid nine and a half million euros to ensure it remain in France permanently."

"And now he's wondering whether it's a Cranach or crap?"

"In so many words." Ménard switched on a standing halogen lamp. "Would you mind having a look at it?"

Gabriel went to the nearest stainless-steel utility cart and after a moment of searching found a professional-grade magnifier. He used it to scrutinize the brushwork and craquelure. Then he stepped away from the painting and placed a hand contemplatively to his chin.

"Well?" asked Ménard.

"It's the best Lucas Cranach the Elder I've ever seen."

"I'm relieved."

"Don't be," said Gabriel.

"Why not?"

"Because Lucas Cranach the Elder didn't paint it."

————————

How many more are there?"

"Three," answered Ménard. "They all emerged from Galerie Georges Fleury with a similar provenance and the same uncertain attribution. And the experts of the National Center for Research and Restoration, after careful evaluation, declared all three to be newly discovered works by the masters themselves."

"Anything good?"

"A Frans Hals, a Gentileschi, and the most delicious Van der Weyden you've ever laid eyes on."

"You're an admirer of Rogier?"

"Who isn't?"

"You'd be surprised."

They were sitting at a table at Café Marly, the Louvre's stylish restaurant. The declining sun had set fire to the glass panels of the pyramid. The light dazzled Gabriel's eyes.

"Are you formally trained?" he asked.

"As an art historian?" Ménard shook his head. "But four of my officers have advanced degrees from the Sorbonne. My background is in fraud and money laundering."

"Heaven knows, there's none of that in the art world."

Smiling, Ménard removed three photographs from a manila envelope—a Frans Hals, a Gentileschi, and an exquisite portrait by Rogier van der Weyden. "They were acquired by the Louvre over a ten-year period. The Van der Weyden and the Cranach were purchased during the tenure of the current president. The Frans Hals and Gentileschi were acquired on his recommendation when he was the director of the paintings department."

"Which means his fingerprints are on all four."

"Evidently, he and Monsieur Fleury were quite close." Lowering his voice, Ménard added, "Close enough so that rumors are swirling."

"Kickbacks?"

Ménard shrugged but said nothing.

"Is there any truth to it?"

"I wouldn't know. You see, the Central Office for the Fight against Cultural Goods Trafficking has been ordered not to investigate the matter."

"What happens if the four paintings turn out to be forgeries?"

"The world's most advanced facility for the conservation and authentication of art has determined that they are genuine. Therefore, absent a videotaped confession on the part of the forger, the Louvre will stand by its findings."

"In that case, why did you ask me to come to Paris?"

Ménard drew another photograph from the envelope and placed it on the table.

28

Café Marly

Nothing about the man depicted in the photograph suggested he belonged anywhere near an Old Master art gallery in the elegant Eighth Arrondissement of Paris. Not the logoless cap pulled low over his brow. Or the wraparound sunglasses covering his eyes. Or the false beard adhered to his face. And certainly not the aluminum-sided Tumi suitcase, 52 by 77 by 28 centimeters, that he was wheeling along the pavements of the rue la Boétie. He was sturdy in manufacture, compact in size, confident in demeanor. An athlete in his day, perhaps a former soldier. He wore a drab overcoat against the cool early-spring weather, and leather gloves—presumably so that he would leave no fingerprints on the handle of the suitcase or in the taxi that was pulling away from the curb.

The time stamp on the photo was 13:39:35. Jacques Ménard handed Gabriel a second image, captured at the same instant. "The first shot came from the camera at the *tabac* across the street. The second one is from the Monoprix a couple of doors down."

"Nothing from your surveillance cameras?"

"This is Paris, Allon. Not London. We have about two thousand cameras in high-traffic tourist areas and around sensitive government buildings. But there are gaps in our coverage. The man in the photograph exploited them."

"Where did he get into the taxi?"

"A little commune east of Paris, in the Seine-en-Marne *département*. My colleagues at the Quai des Orfèvres haven't been able to determine how he got there."

"Did they manage to find the driver?"

"He's an immigrant from the Côte d'Ivoire. He says the customer spoke French like a native and paid the fare in cash."

"He checks out?"

"The driver?" Ménard nodded. "No problem there."

Gabriel lowered his gaze to the second photograph. Same time stamp, slightly different angle. A bit like his reworking of Modigliani's *Reclining Nude*, he thought. "How long did he stay inside?"

Ménard drew two more photographs from the envelope. The first showed the man leaving the gallery at 13:43:34. The second showed him sitting at a table at Brasserie Baroche. It was located about forty meters from the gallery, at the corner of the rue la Boétie and the rue de Ponthieu. The time stamp was 13:59:46. The assassin was looking down at the object in his hand. It was the remote unlocking device he had removed from Bruno Gilbert's desk.

"You and Madame Bancroft approached the gallery from the opposite direction." Ménard produced a photograph of Gabriel and Sarah's arrival, as if to prove his point. "Otherwise, you would have walked right past him."

"Where did he go next?"

"A taxi to the Sixteenth. A nice long walk in the Bois de Boulogne. And then, *poof*, he disappeared."

"Very professional."

"Our explosives experts were quite impressed with his bomb."

"Were they able to identify the phone he used to trigger the detonation?"

"They say not."

"I'm certain that Valerie Bérrangar's phone was inside that gallery."

"My colleagues at the Quai des Orfèvres have their doubts about that. Furthermore, they are inclined to accept the conclusion of the local gendarmerie that Valerie Bérrangar died as the result of an unfortunate road accident."

"I'm glad we cleared that up. What else has the Quai des Orfèvres concluded?"

"That the two men who tried to steal Monsieur Isherwood's attaché case were probably ordinary thieves."

"What about the men who searched his room at the InterContinental?"

"According to the hotel's head of security, they don't exist."

"Did anyone bother to check the internal video?"

"Apparently, it was erased."

"By whom?"

"The Quai des Orfèvres can't say."

"What *can* it say?" asked Gabriel.

Ménard drew a breath before answering. "It is the conclusion of the Quai des Orfèvres that the murder of Georges Fleury and the destruction of his gallery were the result of an embezzlement scheme by Bruno Gilbert and the man with the suitcase."

"Is there a shred of evidence to support this nonsense?"

"A few hours before you and Madame Bancroft arrived at the gallery, someone transferred the entire balance of its accounts at Société Générale to the account of an anonymous shell company in the Channel Islands. The anonymous shell company then transferred it to the account of another anonymous shell company in the Bahamas, which in turn transferred it to the account of another anonymous shell company in the Cayman Islands. And then . . ."

"Poof?"

Ménard nodded.

"How much money are we talking about?"

"Twelve million euros. The Quai des Orfèvres is of the opinion the bomber wanted it all for himself."

"Clean and simple," said Gabriel. "And much more palatable than a scandal involving several million euros' worth of forgeries hanging on the walls of the world's most famous museum."

"Thirty-four million euros, to be exact. All of which had to be raised from outside sources. If it were to become public, the reputation of one of France's most treasured institutions would be severely tarnished."

"And we can't have that," said Gabriel.

"*Non*," agreed Ménard.

"But how do Sarah and I fit into this theory of theirs?"

"You and Madame Bancroft were never there, remember?"

Gabriel displayed the photograph of their arrival at the gallery. "And what happens if this becomes public?"

"Don't worry, Allon. No chance of that."

Gabriel placed the photograph atop the others. "How high does it go?"

"What's that?"

"The cover-up."

"Cover-up is an ugly word, Allon. So *américain*."

"*La conspiration du silence*."

"Much better."

"The director of the Police Nationale? The prefect?"

"Oh, no," said Ménard. "Much higher than that. The ministers of interior and culture are involved. Perhaps even *le Palais*."

"You disapprove?"

"I am a loyal servant of the French Republic. But I have a conscience as well."

"I'd listen to your conscience."

"You never violated yours?"

"I was an intelligence operative," said Gabriel without elaboration.

"And I am a senior Police Nationale officer who is obligated to follow the orders of my superiors to the letter."

"And if you were to disobey?"

"I would be terminated. *Avec la guillotine.*" Ménard inclined his head toward the west. "*A la Place de la Concorde.*"

"How about a leak to a friendly reporter at *Le Monde*?"

"A leak of what, exactly? A story about a London art dealer who purchased a forged Van Dyck portrait from a Parisian art gallery and then sold it to an American investor?"

"Perhaps the leak could be a bit narrower in scope."

"How narrow?"

"A Cranach, a Hals, a Gentileschi, and the most delicious Van der Weyden you've ever laid eyes on."

"The scandal would be immense." Ménard paused. "And it wouldn't accomplish our shared goal."

"What might that be?" asked Gabriel warily.

"Putting the forger out of business." Ménard nudged the photographs a few millimeters closer to Gabriel. "And while you're at it, you might want to track down the man who tried to kill you and Madame Bancroft."

"How am I supposed to do that?"

Ménard smiled. "You're the former intelligence operative, Allon. I'm sure you'll be able to find him if you put your mind to it."

————

What Jacques Ménard proposed next was *une petite collaboration*, the terms of which he outlined for Gabriel while walking along the footpaths of the Jardin des Tuileries. Theirs was to be an entirely secret relationship, with Ménard playing the role of case officer and

Gabriel acting as his informant and asset. It would be up to Ménard, and only Ménard, to determine how best to act upon their findings. If possible, he would resolve the situation quietly, without inflicting undue damage to the reputations of those who had been taken in.

"But if a few eggs need to be broken, well, so be it."

Gabriel made only a single demand in return, that Ménard make no attempt to observe his activities or monitor his movements. The Frenchman readily agreed to avert his eyes. He asked only that Gabriel avoid unnecessary violence, especially within the borders of the Republic.

"What if I'm able to find the man who tried to kill me?"

Ménard pulled his lips into a Gallic expression of indifference. "Do with him what you will. I'm not going to cry over a little spilled blood. Just make certain none of it splashes on me."

With that, the newfound partners went their separate ways— Ménard to the Quai des Orfèvres, Gabriel to the Gare de Lyon. As his train slithered from the station shortly after 5:00 p.m., he made two phone calls, one to his wife in Venice, the other to Sarah. Neither was pleased by his news or by his travel plans, Sarah especially. Nevertheless, after consulting with her husband on a separate line, she reluctantly agreed to Gabriel's request.

"How are you making the crossing?" she asked.

"The morning ferry from Marseilles."

"Peasant," she hissed, and rang off.

29

Ajaccio

At seven fifteen the following evening, Christopher Keller was seated at a waterfront café in the Corsican port of Ajaccio, an empty wineglass on the table before him, a freshly lit Marlboro burning between the first and second fingers of his sledgehammer right hand. He wore a pale gray suit by Richard Anderson of Savile Row, an open-neck white dress shirt, and handmade oxford shoes. His hair was sun-bleached, his skin was taut and dark, his eyes were bright blue. The notch in the center of his thick chin looked as though it had been cleaved with a chisel. His mouth seemed permanently fixed in an ironic half-smile.

His waitress had presumed him to be a European from the mainland and had greeted him accordingly, with apathy bordering on contempt. But when he addressed her in fluent *corsu*, in the dialect of one from the northwestern corner of the island, she warmed to him instantly. They conversed in the Corsican way—about family and foreigners and the damage left by the springtime winds—and when he finished his first glass of rosé, she placed another before him without bothering to ask whether he wanted it.

It had done him no good, the second glass of wine, and neither had the cigarette, the fourth since his arrival at the café. It was a habit he had acquired while living under deep cover in Catholic West Belfast during one of the nastier periods of the Troubles. He now served in a clandestine operations unit of the Secret Intelligence Service sometimes referred to, incorrectly, as the Increment. His visit to Corsica, however, was entirely private in nature. A friend required the assistance of a man for whom Christopher had once worked—a certain Don Anton Orsati, patriarch of one of the island's most notorious families. As the friend's situation involved an attempt to kill Christopher's wife, he was only too happy to oblige him.

Just then the prow of an arriving Corsica Linea ferry nosed into the inner harbor, past the ramparts of the ancient citadel. Christopher slid a twenty-euro banknote beneath the empty wineglass and crossed the Quai de la République to the car park opposite the port's modern terminal. Behind the wheel of his battered Renault hatchback, he watched as the newly arrived passengers came spilling down the steps. Luggage-laden tourists. Returning Corsicans. Mainland French. A man of medium height and build dressed in a well-tailored Italian sport coat and gabardine trousers.

He tossed his overnight bag into the back of the Renault and dropped into the passenger seat. His emerald-green eyes stared with reproach at the cigarette burning in the ashtray.

"Must you?" he asked wearily.

"Yes," said Christopher as he started the engine. "I'm afraid I must."

———

They crossed the bony ridge of hills north of Ajaccio, then followed the twisting road down to the Golfu di Liscia. The waves somersaulting onto the small crescent beach were unusually large, driven by an approaching *maestral*. It was how the Corsicans referred to the violent, unwelcome wind that blew in winter and springtime from the valleys of the Rhône.

"You arrived in the nick of time," said Christopher, his elbow protruding from the open window. "If you'd waited another day, you would have had the ferry ride from hell."

"It was bad enough as it was."

"Why didn't you fly from Paris?"

Gabriel removed the Beretta from its resting place at the small of his back and laid it on the center console.

"It's good to know that some things don't change." Christopher gave Gabriel a sideways glance. "You need a haircut. Otherwise, you're looking quite well for a man of your advanced age."

"It's the new me."

"What was wrong with the old you?"

"I had a bit of excess baggage I needed to lose."

"You and me both." Christopher turned his head to watch the waves rolling in from the west. "But at this moment, I am suddenly reminded of the man I used to be."

"The director of northern European sales for the Orsati Olive Oil Company?"

"Something like that."

"Does His Holiness know that you're back on the island?"

"We're expected for dinner. As you might imagine, excitement is high."

"Perhaps you should go alone."

"The last person who declined an invitation to dine with Don Anton Orsati is somewhere out there." Christopher gestured toward the waters of the Mediterranean. "In a concrete coffin."

"Has he forgiven me for stealing you away from him?"

"He blames the British. As for forgiveness, Don Orsati is unfamiliar with the word."

"I'm not in a terribly forgiving mood myself," said Gabriel quietly.

"How do you think I feel?"

"Would you like to see a photograph of the man who tried to murder your wife?"

"Not while I'm driving," said Christopher. "I'm liable to kill us both."

———————

By the time they reached the town of Porto, the sun was an orange disk balanced atop the dark rim of the sea. Christopher headed inland along a road lined with laricio pine and started the long climb into the mountains. The air smelled of the *macchia*, the dense undergrowth of gorse, briar, rockrose, rosemary, and lavender that covered much of the island's interior. The Corsicans seasoned their foods with the *macchia*, heated their homes with it in winter, and took refuge in it during times of war and vendetta. It had no eyes, went one often-repeated Corsican proverb, but the *macchia* saw everything.

They passed through the hamlets of Chidazzu and Marignana and arrived in the village of the Orsatis a few minutes after ten o'clock. It had been there, or so it was said, since the time of the Vandals, when people from the coasts took to the hills for safety. Beyond it, in a small valley of olive groves that produced the island's finest oil, was the don's sprawling estate. Two heavily armed men stood watch at the entrance. They touched their distinctive Corsican caps respectfully as Christopher turned through the gate.

Several more bodyguards stood like statuary in the floodlit forecourt of the palatial villa. Gabriel left his Beretta in the Renault and followed Christopher up a flight of stone steps to Don Orsati's office. Entering, they found him seated at a large oaken table, before an open leather-bound ledger. As usual, he was wearing a bleached white shirt, loose-fitting cotton trousers, and a pair of dusty leather sandals that looked as though they had been purchased at the local outdoor market. At his elbow was a decorative bottle of Orsati olive oil—olive oil being the legitimate front through which the don laundered the profits of death.

Laboriously he rose to his feet. He was a large man by Corsican standards, well over six feet and broad through the back and shoulders, with coal-black hair, a dense mustache, and the brown-streaked eyes of a canine. They settled first on Christopher, inhospitably. He addressed him in *corsu*.

"I accept your apology."

"For what?"

"The wedding," answered the don. "Never in my life have I been insulted. And from you of all people."

"My new employers might have found it odd if you had been there."

"How do you explain your eight-million-pound flat in Kensington?"

"It's a maisonette, actually. And it cost me eight and a half."

"All of which you earned working for me." The don frowned. "Did you at least receive my wedding gift?"

"The fifty thousand pounds' worth of Baccarat crystal? I sent you a rather lengthy handwritten note of gratitude."

Don Orsati turned to Gabriel and in French said, "I assume *you* were in attendance."

"Only because they needed someone to give away the bride."

"Is it true she's an American?"

"Barely."

"What does that mean?"

"She spent most of her childhood in England and France."

"Is that supposed to make me feel better?"

"At least she's not Italian," said Gabriel knowingly.

"At the end of many disasters," said Don Orsati, reciting a Corsican proverb, "there is always an Italian. But your lovely wife is definitely the exception to the rule."

"I'm confident you'll feel the same about Sarah."

"She's intelligent?"

"She has a PhD from Harvard."

"Attractive?"

"Stunningly beautiful."

"Is she good to her mother?"

"When they're on speaking terms."

Don Orsati looked at Christopher in horror. "What kind of woman doesn't speak to her mother?"

"They've had their ups and downs."

"I'd like to have a word with her about this as soon as possible."

"We're hoping to spend a week or two on the island this summer."

"He who lives on hope dies on shit."

"How eloquent, Don Orsati."

"Our proverbs," he said gravely, "are sacred and correct."

"And there's one for every occasion."

Don Orsati laid a granite hand gently upon Christopher's cheek. "Only the spoon knows the pot's sorrows."

"Mistakes are made even by priests at the altar."

"Better to have little than nothing."

"But he who has nothing will not eat."

"Shall we?" asked Don Orsati.

"Perhaps we should discuss our mutual friend's problem first," suggested Christopher.

"This business with the art gallery in Paris?"

"Yes."

"Is it true your beautiful American wife was involved?"

"I'm afraid so."

"In that case," said Don Orsati, "you have a problem, too."

30

Villa Orsati

Gabriel laid two photographs on Don Orsati's desk. Same time stamp, slightly different angle. The don contemplated them as though they were Old Master paintings. He was a connoisseur of death and the men who dispensed it for a living.

"Do you recognize him?"

"I'm not sure his own mother would recognize him in that ridiculous disguise." The don glanced up at Christopher. "You would have never been caught dead looking like that."

"Never," he agreed. "One has to maintain certain standards."

Smiling, Don Orsati returned his gaze to the photographs. "Is there anything you can tell me about him?"

"The taxi driver said he spoke French like a native," answered Gabriel.

"The driver would have said the same about Christopher." The don's eyes narrowed. "He looks like a former soldier to me."

"I thought so, too. He certainly seems to know his way around explosive devices."

"Unless someone else built it for him. There are many fine bomb makers in this business of ours." Orsati once again turned to Christopher. "Wouldn't you agree?"

"Not as many as there used to be. But let's not dwell on the past."

"Perhaps we should," said Gabriel. Then he added quietly, "Just for a moment or two."

The don bunched his hands beneath his chin. "Is there something you wish to ask me?"

"There was a similar incident in Paris about twenty years ago. The gallery was owned by a Swiss dealer who was trading in paintings looted by the Nazis during the war. The bomb was delivered by a former British commando who—"

"I remember it well," interjected Don Orsati.

"As do I."

"And now you're wondering whether the man in these photographs works for my organization."

"I suppose I am."

Orsati's expression darkened. "You may rest assured, my old friend, that any man who offered me money to kill you would not leave this island alive."

"It's possible they thought I was someone else."

"With all due respect, I doubt that. For a man of the secret world, you have a rather famous face." Don Orsati looked at Christopher and exhaled heavily. "As for the former British commando, his fair hair, blue eyes, perfect English, and elite military training allowed him to fulfill contracts that were far beyond the skill level of my Corsican-born *taddunaghiu*. Needless to say, my business has suffered as a result of his decision to return home."

"Because you've turned down job offers where the risk of exposure was too high?"

"More than I can count." Orsati tapped the cover of his leather-bound ledger of death. "And my profits have fallen sharply as a result.

Oh, don't get me wrong. I still get plenty of criminal and vengeance work. But my higher-profile clients have gone elsewhere."

"Anywhere in particular?"

"An exclusive new organization that offers white-glove concierge service to the sort of men who travel in private aircraft and dress like Christopher."

"Wealthy businessmen?"

"That's the rumor. This organization specializes in accidents and apparent suicides, the sort of thing the Orsati Olive Oil Company never bothered with. It is said that they're quite accomplished when it comes to staging crime scenes, perhaps because they employ several former police officers. They are also rumored to possess certain technical capabilities."

"Phone and computer hacking?"

The don shrugged his heavy shoulders. "This is your area of expertise. Not mine."

"Does this organization have a name?"

"If it does, I am not aware of it." Orsati looked down at the photographs. "The more important question is, who might have retained the services of this organization to kill you?"

"The leader of a sophisticated forgery network."

"Paintings?"

Gabriel nodded.

"He must be making a great deal of money."

"Thirty-four million euros from the Louvre alone."

"Perhaps I'm in the wrong line of work."

"I've often thought the same about myself, Don Orsati."

"What *is* your business these days?" he asked.

"I'm the director of the paintings department at the Tiepolo Restoration Company." Gabriel paused. "Currently on loan to the Police Nationale."

"A complicating factor, to say the least." Orsati made a face. "But please tell me how I can be of assistance to you and your friends from the French police."

"I'd like you to find the man in those photographs."

"And if I can?"

"I'll ask him a simple question."

"The name of the man who hired him to kill you?"

"You know what they say about assassinations, Don Orsati. The important thing is not who fired the shot but who paid for the bullet."

"Who was it who said that?" asked the don, intrigued.

"Eric Ambler."

"Wise words indeed. But in all likelihood, the man who tried to kill you in Paris doesn't know the client's name."

"Perhaps not, but he'll certainly be able to point me in the right direction. If nothing else he can provide valuable information on your competitor." Gabriel lowered his voice. "I would think that would be of interest to you, Don Orsati."

"One hand washes the other, and both hands wash the face."

"A very old Jewish proverb."

The don gave a dismissive wave of his enormous hand. "I'll put these photographs into circulation first thing in the morning. In the meantime, you and Christopher can spend a few days relaxing here on the island."

"Nothing like going on holiday with a man who once tried to kill you."

"If Christopher had actually *tried* to kill you, you would be dead."

"Just like the man who paid for the bullet," remarked Gabriel.

"Did Eric Ambler really say that about assassinations?"

"It's a line from *A Coffin for Dimitrios*."

"Interesting," said the don. "I never knew that Ambler was Corsican."

———————

The distinctive scent of the *macchia* rose from the sumptuous feast that awaited them downstairs in Don Orsati's garden. They did not remain there long. Indeed, not five minutes after they sat down, the first knife-edged blast of the *maestral* arrived from the northwest. With the help of the don's bodyguards, they beat a hasty retreat to the dining room, and the meal resumed, though now it was accompanied by the howl and scrape of the much-despised intruder from across the sea.

It was after midnight when Don Orsati finally tossed his napkin onto the table, signaling that the evening had reached its end. Rising, Gabriel thanked the don for his hospitality and asked him to conduct his search with discretion. The don replied that he would use only his most trusted operatives. He was confident of a successful resolution.

"If it is your wish, I'll have my men bring him back here to Corsica. That way you won't have to get your hands dirty."

"It's never bothered me before. Besides," said Gabriel with a glance in Christopher's direction, "I have him."

"Christopher is a respectable English spy now. A man of distinction who resides at one of London's poshest addresses. He couldn't possibly get mixed up in a nasty business like this."

With that, Gabriel and Christopher went into the windblown night and climbed into the Renault. Leaving the estate, they headed eastward into the next valley. Christopher's secluded villa stood at the end of a dirt-and-gravel track lined on both sides by high walls of *macchia*. When the car's headlamps fell upon three ancient olive trees, he lifted his foot from the throttle and leaned anxiously over the steering wheel.

"Surely it's dead by now," said Gabriel.

"We'll know in a minute."

"You didn't ask the don?"

"And spoil an otherwise delightful evening?"

Just then a horned domestic goat, perhaps two hundred and fifty pounds in weight, emerged from the *macchia* and established itself in the center of the track. It had the markings of a palomino and a red beard, and was scarred from old battles. Its eyes shone defiantly in the glare of the headlamps.

"It has to be a different goat."

"No," answered Christopher as he applied the brakes. "Same bloody goat."

"Careful," said Gabriel. "I think it heard you."

The enormous goat, like the three ancient olive trees, belonged to Don Casabianca. It regarded the track as its private property and demanded tribute from those who traveled it. For Christopher, an Englishman with no Corsican blood in his veins, it harbored a particular resentment.

"Perhaps you could have a word with him on my behalf," he suggested.

"Our last conversation didn't go terribly well."

"What did you say to him?"

"It's possible I insulted his ancestry."

"On Corsica? What were you thinking?" Christopher inched the car forward, but the goat lowered its head and stood its ground. A tap of the horn was no more effective. "You won't mention any of this to Sarah, will you?"

"I wouldn't dream of it," vowed Gabriel.

Christopher slipped the car into PARK and exhaled heavily. Then he flung open his door and charged the goat in his bespoke Richard Anderson suit, flailing his arms like a madman. The tactic usually resulted in an immediate capitulation. But on this night, the first night of a *maestral*, the animal fought gamely for a minute or two before finally fleeing into the *macchia*. Fortunately, Gabriel captured the entire confrontation on video, which he immediately dispatched to Sarah in London. All in all, he thought, it was a fine start to their holiday on Corsica.

31

Haute-Corse

The villa had a red tile roof, a large blue swimming pool, and a broad terrace that received the sun in the morning and in the afternoon was shaded by laricio pine. When Gabriel rose the following morning, the granite paving stones were strewn with tree limbs and other assorted flora. In the well-appointed kitchen, he found Christopher, in hiking boots and a waterproof anorak, preparing café au lait on a butane camp stove. A local newscast issued from a battery-powered radio.

"We lost power around three a.m. The winds reached eighty miles per hour last night. They say it's the worst springtime *maestral* in living memory."

"Was there any mention of an incident involving an Englishman and an elderly goat?"

"Not yet. But thanks to you, it's all anyone's talking about in London." Christopher handed Gabriel a bowl of coffee. "Did you manage to get any sleep?"

"Not a wink. You?"

"I'm a combat veteran. I can sleep through anything."

"How long will it last?"

"Three days. Maybe four."

"I guess that rules out windsurfing."

"But not a hike up Monte Rotondo. Care to join me?"

"As tempting as that sounds," said Gabriel, "I think I'll spend the morning in front of a fire with a good book."

He carried his coffee into the comfortably furnished sitting room. Several hundred volumes of fiction and history lined the shelves, and upon the walls hung a modest collection of modern and Impressionist paintings. The most valuable piece was a Provençal landscape by Monet, which Christopher, through an intermediary, had acquired at Christie's in Paris. On that morning, however, Gabriel's eye was caught by the painting hanging next to it—another landscape, this one by Paul Cézanne.

He took down the painting and removed it from the frame. The stretcher appeared similar to those used by Cézanne in the mid-1880s, as did the canvas itself. There was no signature—not unusual, as Cézanne only signed works he considered truly finished—and the varnish was the color of nicotine. Otherwise, the painting appeared to be in good condition.

And yet . . .

Gabriel propped the painting in a rhombus of brilliant morning sunlight streaming through the French doors, then snapped a magnified detail image with his phone. With thumb and forefinger, he enlarged the photograph further and examined the brushwork. His reverie was so complete he failed to notice that Christopher, a gifted surveillance artist, had stolen into the room.

"May I ask what you're doing?"

"Looking for something to read," said Gabriel absently.

Christopher took down Ben McIntyre's biography of Kim Philby. "You might find this more interesting."

"Though somewhat incomplete." Gabriel looked down at the painting again.

"Is there a problem?"

"Where did you purchase it?"

"A gallery in Nice."

"Does the gallery have a name?"

"Galerie Edmond Toussaint."

"Did you seek the opinion of a professional?"

"Monsieur Toussaint gave me a certificate of authentication."

"May I see it? The provenance as well."

Christopher went upstairs to his study. Returning, he handed Gabriel a large business envelope, then slung a nylon rucksack over his powerful right shoulder.

"Last chance."

"Enjoy," said Gabriel as a gust of wind rattled the French doors. "And do give my best to your little caprine friend."

Steeling himself, Christopher went out and climbed into the Renault. A moment later Gabriel heard the blare of a car horn, followed by shouted threats of unspeakable violence. Laughing, he removed the contents of the envelope.

"Idiot," he said after a moment, to no one but himself.

———

The *maestral* eased around eleven, but by late afternoon it was blowing hard enough to loosen several tiles from Christopher's roof. He returned home at dusk and proudly displayed for Gabriel the 136-kilometer-per-hour wind reading he had taken on Monte Rotondo's northern face. Gabriel reciprocated by disclosing his concerns over the authenticity of the Cézanne, a painting that Christopher had purchased under a false French identity while working as a professional assassin.

"Thus leaving you with no legal recourse. Or moral recourse, for that matter."

"Perhaps one or two of the don's most terrifying men should have a word with Monsieur Toussaint on my behalf."

"Perhaps," countered Gabriel, "you should forget I ever said any-thing, and let it go."

The wind blew without relent the following day and the day after that as well. Gabriel sheltered in place at the villa while Christopher flung himself against two more mountains—first Renoso, then d'Oro, where his pocket anemometer recorded the winds at 141 kilometers per hour. That evening they dined at Villa Orsati. Over coffee, the don acknowledged that his operatives had no leads on the identity or whereabouts of the man who had carried the bomb into Galerie Georges Fleury. He then chastised Christopher over the tenor and tone of his recent confrontations with Don Casabianca's goat.

"He called me this morning. He's very upset."

"The don or the goat?"

"It's no laughing matter, Christopher."

"How does Don Casabianca even know that things have taken a turn for the worse?"

"The news has spread like wildfire."

"I certainly didn't mention it to anyone."

"It must have been the *macchia*," said Gabriel, and repeated the ancient proverb regarding the ability of the aromatic vegetation to see everything. At this, the don nodded his head solemnly in agreement. It was, he concluded, the only possible explanation.

The wind raged for the remainder of that night, but by dawn it was a memory. Gabriel spent the morning helping Christopher repair the damage to the roof and clear the debris from the terrace and the pool. Then, in late afternoon, he drove into the village. It was a cluster of sandstone-colored cottages huddled around the bell tower of a church, before which lay a dusty square. Several men in newly pressed white shirts were playing a closely fought game of *pétanque*. Once they might have regarded Gabriel with suspicion—or pointed at him in the Corsican way, with their first and fourth fingers, to ward off the effects of the *occhju*, the evil eye. Now they greeted him warmly, as he was known throughout the village as a friend of Don Orsati and the Englishman named Christopher, who, thank goodness, had returned to the island after a prolonged absence.

"Is it true he's married?" asked one of the men.

"That's the rumor."

"Has he killed that goat?" asked another.

"Not yet. But it's only a matter of time."

"Perhaps you can talk some sense into him."

"I've tried. But I'm afraid they've reached the point of no return."

The men insisted that Gabriel join the game, as they were in need of another player. Declining, he repaired to the café in the far corner of the square for a glass of Corsican rosé. As the church bells tolled five o'clock, a young child, a girl of seven or eight, knocked on the door of the crooked little house next to the rectory. It opened a few inches, and a small pale hand appeared, clutching a slip of blue paper. The young girl carried it to the café and placed it on Gabriel's table. She bore an uncanny resemblance to Irene.

"What is your name?" he asked.

"Danielle."

Of course it was, he thought. "Would you like an ice cream?"

The child sat down and pushed the blue slip of paper across the tabletop. "Aren't you going to read it?"

"I don't need to."

"Why not?"

"I know what it says."

"How?"

"I have powers, too."

"Not like hers," said the child.

No, agreed Gabriel. Not like hers.

32

Haute-Corse

The hand the old woman offered Gabriel in greeting was warm and weightless. He held it gently, as though it were a cage bird.

"You've been hiding from me," she said.

"Not from you," he answered. "From the *maestral*."

"I've always liked the wind." Confidingly she added, "It's good for business."

The old woman was a *signadora*. The Corsicans believed that she possessed the power to heal those infected by the *occhju*. Gabriel had once suspected that she was nothing more than a conjurer and a clever teller of fortunes, but that was no longer the case.

She placed her hand against his cheek. "You're burning with fever."

"You always say that."

"That's because you always feel as though you are on fire." Her hand moved to his upper chest. The left side, slightly above his heart. "This is where the madwoman's bullet entered you."

"Did Christopher tell you that?"

"I haven't spoken to Christopher since his return." She lifted the front of Gabriel's dress shirt and examined the scar. "You were dead for several minutes, were you not?"

"Two or three."

She frowned. "Why do you bother trying to lie to me?"

"Because I prefer not to dwell on the fact that I was dead for ten minutes." Gabriel held up the blue slip of paper. "Where did you find that child?"

"Danielle? Why do you ask?"

"She reminds me of someone."

"Your daughter?"

"How is possible that you know what she looks like?"

"Perhaps you're merely seeing what you want to see."

"Don't speak to me in riddles."

"You named the child Irene after your mother. Every time she looks at you, you see your mother's face and the numbers that were written on her arm in the camp named for the trees."

"Someday you're going to have to show me how you do that."

"It is a gift from God." She released the front of his shirt and contemplated him with her bottomless black eyes. The face in which they were set was as white as baker's flour. "You are suffering from the *occhju*. It is as plain as day."

"I must have contracted it from Don Casabianca's goat."

"He is a demon."

"Tell me about it."

"I'm not joking. The animal is possessed. Stay away from it."

The *signadora* drew him into the parlor of her tiny home. On the small circular table was a candle, a shallow plate of water, and a vessel of olive oil. They were the tools of her trade. She lit the candle and sat down in her usual place. Gabriel, after a moment's hesitation, joined her.

"There's no such thing as the evil eye, you know. It's just a superstition that was prevalent among the ancient people of the Mediterranean."

"You are an ancient person of the Mediterranean as well."

"As ancient as it gets," he agreed.

"You were born in the Galilee, not far from the town where Jesus lived. Most of your ancestors were killed by the Romans during the siege of Jerusalem, but a few survived and made their way to Europe." She nudged the vessel of olive oil across the tabletop. "Proceed."

Gabriel returned the vessel to the woman's side of the table. "You first."

"You want me to prove that it's not a trick?"

"Yes."

The old woman dipped her forefinger into the oil. Then she held it over the plate and allowed three drops to fall into the water. They coalesced into a single gobbet.

"Now you."

Gabriel performed the same ritual. This time the oil shattered into a thousand droplets, and soon there was no trace of it.

"*Occhju*," whispered the old woman.

"Magic and misdirection," said Gabriel in reply.

Smiling, she asked, "How's your hand?"

"Which one?"

"The one you injured when you attacked the man who works for the one-eyed creature."

"He shouldn't have followed me."

"Make your peace with him," said the *signadora*. "He will help you find the woman."

"What woman?"

"The Spanish woman."

"I'm looking for a man."

"The one who tried to kill you in the art gallery?"

"Yes."

"Don Orsati hasn't been able to find him. But don't worry, the

Spanish woman will lead you to the one you seek. Don Orsati knows of her."

"How?"

"It is not in my power to tell you that."

Without another word, the *signadora* took hold of Gabriel's hand and engaged in the familiar ritual. She recited the words of an ancient Corsican prayer. She wept as the evil passed from his body into hers. She closed her eyes and fell into a deep sleep. When at last she awoke, she instructed Gabriel to repeat the trial of the oil and the water. This time the oil coalesced into a single drop.

"Now you," he said.

The old woman sighed and did as he asked. The oil shattered.

"Just like the door of the art gallery," she said. "Don't worry, the *occhju* won't stay within me for long."

Gabriel laid several banknotes on the table. "Is there anything else you can tell me?"

"Paint four pictures," said the old woman. "And she will come for you."

"Is that all?"

"No," she said. "You didn't contract the *occhju* from Don Casabianca's goat."

———

Upon his return to the villa, Gabriel informed Christopher that Don Orsati's inquiries would bear no fruit and that Don Casabianca's goat was the devil incarnate. Christopher questioned the accuracy of neither assertion, as both had come from the mouth of the *signadora*. He nevertheless advised against telling the don to preemptively break off his search. It was far better, he said, to allow the wheel to spin until the ball had dropped.

"Unless the wheel continues to spin for another week or two."

"Trust me, it won't."

"There's more, I'm afraid."

Gabriel explained the old woman's prophecy regarding the Spanish woman.

"Did she say how the don knows her?"

"She said it wasn't in her power to tell me."

"Or so she claimed. It's her version of 'no comment.'"

"Did you ever run across a Spanish woman when you were working for the don?"

"One or two," said Christopher beneath his breath.

"How should we raise it with him?"

"With the utmost care. His Holiness doesn't like anyone rummaging through his past. Especially the *signadora*."

And so it was that two nights later, while seated beneath a cloud-draped moon in the garden of Villa Orsati, Gabriel feigned incredulity when told that the don's operatives had failed to locate the man who had delivered the expertly constructed bomb to Galerie Fleury. Then, after a moment or two of companionable silence, he cautiously asked Don Orsati whether he had ever encountered a Spanish woman who might have ties to the criminal art world.

The don's brown-streaked eyes narrowed with suspicion. "When did you speak to her?"

"The Spanish woman?"

"The *signadora*."

"I thought the *macchia* sees all."

"Do you want to know about the Spanish woman or not?"

"It was two days ago," admitted Gabriel.

"I suppose she also knew that I wouldn't be able to find the man you're looking for."

"I wanted to tell you, but Christopher said it would be a mistake."

"Did he?" Don Orsati glared at Christopher before turning once more to Gabriel. "Several years ago, perhaps five or six, a woman came to see me. She was from Roussillon, up in the Lubéron. Late thirties, quite composed. One had the impression she was comfortable in the presence of criminals."

"Name?"

"Françoise Vionnet."

"Real?"

Don Orsati nodded.

"What was her story?"

"The man she lived with disappeared one afternoon while walking in the countryside outside Aix-en-Provence. The police found his body a few weeks later near Mont Ventoux. He'd been shot twice in the back of the head."

"Vengeance was required?"

The don nodded.

"I assume you agreed to provide it."

"Money doesn't come from singing, my friend." It was one of the don's most cherished Corsican proverbs and the unofficial slogan of the Orsati Olive Oil Company. "Money is earned by accepting and then fulfilling contracts."

"What was the name on this one?"

"Miranda Álvarez. The Vionnet woman was confident it was an alias. She was able to give us a physical description and a profession, but little else."

"Why don't we start with her appearance."

"Tall, dark hair, very beautiful."

"Age?"

"At the time, she was in her mid-thirties."

"And her profession?"

"She was an art dealer."

"Based where?"

"Maybe Barcelona." The don shrugged his heavy shoulders. "Maybe Madrid."

"That isn't much to go on."

"I've accepted contracts based on less, provided the client agrees to confirm the target's identity once the target is located."

"Thus avoiding needless bloodshed."

"In a business like mine," said Don Orsati, "mistakes are permanent."

"I take it you were never able to find her."

The don shook his head. "Françoise Vionnet begged me to continue looking, but I told her there was no point. I refunded her money, excluding the deposit and the expenses for the search, and we went our separate ways."

"Did she ever tell you why her partner was murdered?"

"Apparently, it was a business dispute."

"He was an art dealer as well?"

"A painter, actually. Not a successful one, mind you. But she spoke highly of his work."

"Do you happen to remember his name?"

"Lucien Marchand."

"And where might Christopher and I find Françoise Vionnet?"

"The Chemin de Joucas in Roussillon. If you like, I can get you the address."

"If it's not too much trouble."

"Not at all."

It was upstairs in his office, said Don Orsati. In his leather-bound ledger of death.

33

Le Lubéron

The next mainland-bound car ferry departed Ajaccio at half past eight the following evening and arrived in Marseilles shortly after dawn. Gabriel and Christopher, having passed the night in adjoining cabins, rolled into the port in a rented Peugeot and made their way to the A7 Autoroute. They headed north through Salon-de-Provence to Cavaillon, then followed a caravan of tour buses into the Lubéron. The honey-colored houses of Gordes, perched on a limestone hilltop overlooking the valley, sparkled in the crystalline morning light.

"That's where Marc Chagall used to live," said Christopher.

"In an old girls' school on the rue de la Fontaine Basse. He and his wife, Bella, were reluctant to leave after the German invasion. They finally fled to the United States in 1941 with the help of the journalist and academic Varian Fry and the Emergency Rescue Committee."

"I was just trying to make conversation."

"Perhaps we should enjoy the scenery instead."

Christopher lit a Marlboro. "Have you given any thought to how you're going to make your approach?"

"To Françoise Vionnet? I thought I'd start with *bonjour* and hope for the best."

"How cunning."

"Maybe I'll tell her I was sent by a mystical Corsican woman who cured me of the *occhju*. Or better yet, I'll say that I'm a friend of the Corsican organized crime figure she hired to kill a Spanish art dealer."

"That should win her over."

"How much do you suppose the don charged her?" asked Gabriel.

"For a job like that? Not much."

"What does that mean?"

"Maybe a hundred thousand."

"How much was the contract on my life?"

"Seven figures."

"I'm flattered. And Anna?"

"You two were part of a package deal."

"Is there a discount for that sort of thing?"

"The don is unfamiliar with that word as well. But it warms my heart that you two have rekindled your relationship after all these years."

"There was no kindling involved. And we don't have a relationship."

"Did you or did you not borrow a million euros from her to buy that fake Cuyp riverscape?"

"The money was repaid three days later."

"By my wife," said Christopher. "As for your approach to the aforementioned Françoise, I suggest you fly a false flag. In my experience, respectable residents of the Lubéron don't hand over briefcases filled with cash to someone like His Holiness Don Anton Orsati."

"Are you suggesting that Françoise Vionnet and Lucien Marchand, an unknown painter with no established sales record, might have been involved in a criminal enterprise of some sort?"

"I'd bet my Cézanne on it, too."

"You don't own a Cézanne."

They rounded a bend in the road, and the Lubéron Valley revealed itself as a patchwork quilt of vineyards and orchards and fields ablaze with wildflowers. The brick-colored buildings of Roussillon's ancient center occupied a ridge of ocher-rich clay on the southern rim. Christopher approached the village along the narrow Chemin de Joucas and eased onto the grassy verge at the point where the slope of the hill met the valley floor. On one side of the road was newly plowed cropland. On the other, partially hidden from view behind an unkempt wall of vegetation, was a small single-level villa. From somewhere came the muted baritone bark of a large dog.

"But of course," murmured Gabriel.

"Better a canine than a caprine."

"Caprines don't bite."

"Wherever did you get an idea like that?" asked Christopher, and turned into the drive. Instantly a barrel-shaped dog with the jaws of a Rottweiler shot from the front door. Next there appeared a languorous barefoot girl in her early twenties. She wore leggings and a wrinkled cotton pullover. Her light brown hair swung long and loose in the Provençal light.

"She's too young," said Gabriel.

"What about that one?" asked Christopher as an older version of the girl emerged from the villa.

"She looks like a Françoise to me."

"I agree. But how are you going to play it?"

"I'm going to wait for one of them to get that dog under control."

"And then?"

"I thought I'd start with *bonjour* and hope for the best."

"Brilliant," said Christopher.

———

By the time Gabriel opened his door and extended his hand, he was once again, in aspect and accent, Ludwig Ziegler of Berlin. But this version of Herr Ziegler was not an art adviser with a single famous client. He was a runner—a dealer without a gallery or inventory—who specialized in finding works by undervalued contemporary painters and bringing them to market. He claimed to have heard about Lucien Marchand through a contact and was intrigued by the terrible story of his disappearance and death. He introduced Christopher as Benjamin Reckless, his London representative.

"Reckless?" asked Françoise Vionnet skeptically.

"It's an old English name," explained Christopher.

"You speak French like a native."

"My mother was French."

In the villa's rustic kitchen, they all four gathered around a pot of tar-black coffee and a pitcher of steamed milk. Françoise Vionnet and the barefoot girl each lit a cigarette from the same packet of Gitanes. They had the same drowsy, heavy-lidded eyes. Beneath the girl's were puffy half-moons of unlined flesh.

"Her name is Chloé," said Françoise Vionnet, as though the girl were incapable of speech. "Her father was a struggling sculptor from Lacoste who walked out on us not long after she was born. Fortunately, Lucien agreed to take us in. We were hardly a traditional family, but we were happy. Chloé was seventeen when Lucien was murdered. His death was very hard on her. He was the only father she ever knew."

The girl yawned and stretched elaborately and then withdrew. A moment later came the sound of a slender female body entering the water of a swimming pool. Frowning, Françoise Vionnet crushed out her cigarette.

"You must excuse my daughter's behavior. I wanted to move to Paris after Lucien's death, but Chloé refused to leave the Lubéron. It was a terrible mistake to raise her here."

"It's very beautiful," said Gabriel in Herr Ziegler's German-accented French.

"*Oui*," said Françoise Vionnet. "The tourists and rich foreigners adore Provence. Especially the English," she added, glancing at Christopher. "But for girls like Chloé who lack a university education or ambition, the Lubéron can be a trap with no escape. She spends her summers waiting tables at a restaurant in the *centre ville* and her winters working at a hotel in Chamonix."

"And you?" asked Gabriel.

She shrugged. "I make do with the modest estate that Lucien was able to leave me."

"You were married?"

"A civil solidarity pact. The French equivalent of a common-law marriage. Chloé and I inherited the villa after Lucien was murdered. And his paintings, of course." She rose suddenly. "Would you like to see some of them?"

"I'd love nothing more."

They filed into the sitting room. Several unframed paintings—Surrealist, Cubist, Abstract Expressionist—hung on the walls. They lacked originality but were competently executed.

"Where was he trained?" asked Gabriel.

"Beaux-Arts de Paris."

"It shows."

"Lucien was an excellent draftsman," said Françoise Vionnet. "But unfortunately he was never terribly successful. He made ends meet painting copies."

"I beg your pardon?"

"Lucien painted copies of Impressionist paintings and sold them in the gift shops of the Lubéron. He also worked for a company that sold hand-painted copies online. He was paid more for those, but not much. Maybe twenty-five euros. He produced them very quickly. He could paint a Monet in fifteen or twenty minutes."

"Do you happen to have one?"

"*Non*. Lucien found the work very embarrassing. Once the paintings were dry, he delivered them to his clients."

Outside, the girl extracted herself from the pool and stretched her body on a chaise longue. Whether she was clothed or not Gabriel could not say, for he was contemplating what was clearly the finest painting in the room. It bore a distinct resemblance to a work called *Les Amoureux aux Coquelicots*, by the French-Russian artist who had lived for a time on the rue de la Fontaine Basse in Gordes. Not an exact copy, more a pastiche. The original was signed in the bottom-right corner. Lucien Marchand's version had no signature at all.

"He was a great admirer of Chagall," said Françoise Vionnet.

"As am I. And if I didn't know better, I would have thought that Chagall painted it himself." Gabriel paused. "Or perhaps that was the point."

"Lucien painted his Chagalls purely for pleasure. That's why there's no signature."

"I'm prepared to make you a generous offer for it."

"I'm afraid it's not for sale, Monsieur Ziegler."

"May I ask why not?"

"Sentimental reasons. It was the last painting Lucien completed."

"Forgive me, Madame Vionnet. But I can't recall the date of his death."

"It was the seventeenth of September."

"Five years ago?"

"*Oui.*"

"That's odd."

"Why, monsieur?"

"Because this painting appears much older than that. In fact, it looks to me as though it was painted in the late nineteen forties."

"Lucien used special techniques to make his paintings appear older than they really were."

Gabriel took down the painting from the wall and turned it over. The canvas was at least a half-century old, as was the stretcher. The upper horizontal bar was stamped with a *6* and an *F*. On the center bar were the remnants of an old adhesive sticker.

"And did Lucien have special techniques for aging his canvases and stretchers as well? Or did he have a ready supplier of worthless old paintings?"

Françoise Vionnet regarded Gabriel calmly with her heavy-lidded eyes. "Get out of my house," she said through gritted teeth. "Or I'll sic the dog on you."

"If that dog comes anywhere near me, I'm going to shoot it. And then I'm going to call the French police and tell them that you and your daughter are living off the money that Lucien Marchand earned forging paintings."

Her full lips curled into a slight smile. Evidently, she didn't frighten easily. "Who are you?"

"You wouldn't believe me if I told you."

She looked at Christopher. "And him?"

"He's anything but reckless."

"What do you want?"

"I want you to help me find the woman who called herself Miranda Álvarez. I'd also like you to give me any additional forgeries you have lying around, along with a complete list of every fake painting Lucien ever sold."

"That's impossible."

"Why?"

"There are far too many."

"Who handled them?"

"Lucien sold most of his forgeries to a dealer in Nice."

"Does the dealer have a name?"

"Edmond Toussaint."

Gabriel looked at Christopher. "I guess that settles that."

34

Roussillon

"Why didn't you simply tell me the truth from the beginning, Monsieur Allon?"

"I was afraid you would skip the pleasantries and go straight to the part about setting the dog on me."

"Would you have really shot it?"

"*Non*," replied Gabriel. "Mr. Reckless would have shot it for me."

Françoise Vionnet eyed Christopher down her freshly lit Gitane, then nodded her head slowly in agreement. They had returned to the table in the rustic kitchen, though now it was a chilled bottle of Bandol rosé around which they were gathered.

"How much of the original story was true?" asked Gabriel.

"Most of it."

"Where did the fiction begin?"

"Chloé doesn't spend the winter in Chamonix."

"Where does she go?"

"Saint-Barthélemy."

"Does she work there?"

"Chloé?" She made a face. "Not a day in her life. We have a villa in Lorient."

"Lucien must have painted a lot of twenty-five-euro copies to afford a place like that."

"He never stopped painting them, you know. He needed some form of legitimate income."

"When did the fakes start?"

"A couple of years after Chloé and I moved in."

"It was your idea?"

"More or less."

"Which is it?"

"It was obvious that Lucien's copies were very good," she answered. "One day I asked him whether he thought he could fool anyone. A week later he showed me his first forgery. A reworking of *Place du village* by the French Cubist Georges Valmier."

"What did you do with it?"

She took it to Paris and hung it on the wall of a friend's chic apartment in the Sixth. Then she rang one of the auction houses—which one, she refused to say—and the auction house sent over a so-called expert to have a look at it. The expert asked a couple of questions about the painting's provenance, declared it authentic, and gave Françoise forty thousand euros. She gave two thousand to her chic friend from Paris and the rest to Lucien. They used part of the money to enlarge the villa's swimming pool and renovate the little outbuilding that Lucien used as his atelier. The rest they deposited in a bank account at Credit Suisse in Geneva.

"As for the reworking of *Place du village* by Georges Valmier, it recently sold for nine hundred thousand dollars at auction in New York. Which means the auction house made more in fees and commissions than Lucien was paid for his original painting. Who is the criminal, Monsieur Allon? Did the auction house *really* not realize that it was selling a fake? How is this possible?"

She sold several more forgeries to the same Paris auction house—all lesser-known Cubists and Surrealists, all for five figures—and in the winter of 2004 she sold a Matisse to Galerie Edmond Toussaint. The dealer purchased a second Matisse from Françoise a few months later, followed in short order by a Gauguin, a Monet, and a Cézanne landscape of Mont Sainte-Victoire. It was then that Toussaint informed Françoise that all five of the paintings she had brought him were forgeries.

"Which is why he had purchased them in the first place," said Gabriel.

"*Oui*. Monsieur Toussaint wanted an exclusive arrangement. No more independent sales through the Paris auction houses or other dealers. He said it was far too risky. He promised to take very good care of Lucien financially."

"Did he?"

"Lucien had no complaints."

"How much money did he earn?"

"Over the lifetime of the deal?" Françoise Vionnet shrugged. "Six or seven million."

"Spare me," said Gabriel.

"Maybe it was in the neighborhood of thirty million."

"Which side of the neighborhood? The north or the south?"

"The north," said Françoise Vionnet. "Definitely the north."

"And Monsieur Toussaint? What was his take?"

"Two hundred million, at least."

"So Lucien got screwed."

"That's what the Spanish woman told him."

"Miranda Álvarez?"

"That's what she called herself."

"Where did you meet with her?"

"Here in Roussillon. She sat in the same chair where you're sitting now."

"She was a dealer?"

"Of some sort. She was quite guarded in how she described herself."

"What did she want?"

"She wanted Lucien to work for her instead of Toussaint."

"How did she know that Lucien was forging paintings?"

"She refused to say. But it was obvious she knew her way around the dirty side of the business. She said Toussaint was selling more forgeries than the art market could absorb, that it was only a matter of time before Lucien and I were arrested. She said she was part of a sophisticated network that knew how to sell forgeries without getting caught. She promised to pay us twice what Toussaint was paying us."

"How did Lucien react?"

"He was intrigued."

"And you?"

"Less so."

"But you agreed to consider her offer?"

"I asked her to come back in three days."

"And when she did?"

"I told her we had a deal. She gave us a million euros in cash and said she would be in touch."

"When did the deal fall apart?"

"After I told Toussaint that we were leaving him."

"How much did he pay you to stay?"

"Two million."

"I assume you banked the million the Spanish woman gave you."

"*Oui*. And six months later Lucien was dead. He was working on another Cézanne when he was killed. The police never found it."

"I don't suppose you told them that Lucien was an art forger or that he had recently received a visit from a mysterious Spanish woman who called herself Miranda Álvarez."

"If I had, I would have implicated myself."

"How did you explain the thirty million at Credit Suisse in Geneva?"

"It was thirty-four million at the time," admitted Françoise Vionnet. "And the police never discovered it."

"What about the villa in Saint-Barthélemy?"

"It's owned by a shell company registered in the Bahamas. Chloé and I keep a low profile here in the Lubéron. But when we go to the island . . ."

"You live well on the proceeds of Lucien's forgeries."

She lit another Gitane but said nothing.

"How many are left?" asked Gabriel.

"Fakes?" She blew a stream of smoke toward the ceiling. "Only the Chagall. The others are all gone."

Gabriel laid his phone on the table. "How many, Françoise?"

———————

Outside, Chloé was stretched like a Modigliani nude across the sunbaked paving stones next to the pool. "If only someone would pay her for doing that," said her mother judgmentally. "Chloé would be the richest woman in France."

"You were a front woman for a forger," said Gabriel. "You didn't exactly set a good example."

She led them along a gravel footpath toward Lucien's atelier. It was a small building, ocher in color, with a tile roof. The door was secured with a padlock, as were the wooden shutters.

"Someone tried to break in not long after Lucien was murdered. That's when I got the dog."

She unlocked the door and led Gabriel and Christopher inside. The dank air smelled of canvas and dust and linseed oil. Beneath an overhead skylight stood an ancient studio easel and a cluttered old worktable with shelves and drawers for supplies. The paintings were leaning against the walls, perhaps twenty to a row.

"Is this all of them?" asked Gabriel.

Françoise Vionnet nodded.

"No warehouse or storage unit somewhere?"

"*Non*. Everything is here."

She walked over to the nearest queue of paintings and leafed through them as though they were vinyl record albums. Reluctantly she extracted one and displayed it for Gabriel.

"Fernand Léger."

"You have a good eye, Monsieur Allon."

She moved to the next row. From it she unearthed a pastiche of *Houses at L'Estaque* by Georges Braque. The next row of paintings produced a Picasso and another Léger.

"Surely the police searched this place after the murder," said Gabriel.

"Yes, of course. But fortunately they sent Inspector Clouseau." She removed another painting, a version of *Composition in Blue* by Roger Bissière. "I've always liked this one. Do I really have to give it up?"

"Keep going."

The next painting was a Matisse. It was followed by a Monet, a Cézanne, a Dufy, and, finally, by a second Chagall.

"Is that all of them?"

She nodded.

"Do you know what's going to happen if I find any more?"

Sighing, she produced two additional paintings—a second Matisse and a stunning André Derain. Twelve in all, with an estimated market value of more than €200 million. Gabriel photographed them with his phone, along with the Chagall in the sitting room. Then he removed all thirteen canvases from their stretchers and piled them on the grate. Christopher handed over his gold Dunhill lighter.

"Please don't," said Françoise Vionnet.

"Would you rather I give them to the French police?" Gabriel ignited the lighter and touched the flame to the canvases. "I suppose you'll have to make do with the thirty-four million."

"There's only twenty-five left."

"And you can keep it so long as you never tell anyone that I was here."

Françoise Vionnet saw Gabriel and Christopher to the door and waited until they were nearly inside the Renault before unleashing the dog. They made their escape without resort to violence.

"Tell me something," said Christopher as they sped across the picturesque valley. "When did you realize that you were going to do that Herr Ziegler routine?"

"It came to me while you were needlessly lecturing me about the likelihood that Françoise Vionnet might have been Lucien's front woman."

"I have to say, it was one of your better performances. You did, however, make one serious tactical mistake."

"What's that?"

"You burned the bloody evidence."

"Not all of it."

"The Cézanne?"

"Idiot," murmured Gabriel.

35

Le Train Bleu

They jettisoned the rented Peugeot in Marseilles and caught the two o'clock TGV from the Gare Saint-Charles to Paris. An hour before they were due to arrive, Gabriel dialed the number for Antiquités Scientifiques on the rue de Miromesnil. Receiving no answer, he checked the time, then rang a nearby shop that sold antique glassware and figurines. Its proprietor, a woman named Angélique Brossard, seemed slightly out of breath when she picked up the phone. She offered no expression of surprise or evasiveness when Gabriel asked to speak to Maurice Durand. Their longtime *cinq à sept* was one of the worst-kept secrets in the Eighth Arrondissement.

"Enjoying yourself?" asked Gabriel when Durand came on the line.

"I was," answered the Frenchman. "I hope this is important."

"I was wondering whether you might be free for a drink at, say, half past five."

"I believe I'm having open-heart surgery then. Let me check my schedule."

"Meet me at Le Train Bleu."

"If you insist."

The iconic Paris restaurant, with its garish gilded mirrors and painted ceilings, overlooked the ticket hall of the Gare de Lyon. At five thirty Maurice Durand was seated in a plush royal-blue chair in the lounge area before an open bottle of champagne. Rising, he hesitantly shook Christopher's hand.

"If it isn't my old friend Monsieur Bartholomew. Still caring for widows and orphans, or have you managed to find honest work?" Durand turned to Gabriel. "And what brings you back to Paris, Monsieur Allon? Another bombing in the works?" He smiled. "That's certainly *one* way to put a dirty gallery out of business."

Gabriel sat down and handed Durand his mobile phone. The diminutive Frenchman slipped on a pair of gold half-moon reading glasses and contemplated the screen. "A rather interesting reinterpretation of Braque's *Houses at L'Estaque.*"

"Swipe to the next one."

Durand did as he was told. "Roger Bissière."

"Keep going."

Durand dragged the tip of his forefinger horizontally across the screen and smiled. "I've always had a soft spot for Fernand Léger. He was one of my first."

"How about the next one?"

"My old friend Picasso. Quite a good one, in fact."

"The Chagalls are better. The Monet, the Cézanne, and the two Matisses aren't bad, either."

"Where did you find them?"

"In Roussillon," answered Gabriel. "In the atelier of a failed painter named—"

"Lucien Marchand?"

"You knew him?"

"Lucien and I weren't acquainted, but I knew of his work."

"How?"

"We both did business with the same gallery in Nice."

"Galerie Edmond Toussaint?"

"*Oui.* Quite possibly the dirtiest art gallery in France, if not the Western world. Only a fool would buy a painting there."

Gabriel exchanged a glance with Christopher before returning his gaze to Durand. "I thought you dealt directly with collectors."

"For the most part. But I occasionally filled special orders for Monsieur Toussaint. He did a brisk trade in stolen art, but Lucien Marchand was his golden goose."

"Which is why Toussaint fought so hard to keep Lucien when the front woman from a rival forgery network tried to steal him away."

Durand smiled at Gabriel over the rim of his champagne glass. "You're getting rather good at this, Monsieur Allon. Soon you will no longer require my help."

"Who is she, Maurice?"

"Miranda Álvarez? That depends on whom you ask. Apparently, she's something of a chameleon. They say she lives in a remote village in the Pyrenees. They also say that she and the forger are lovers or perhaps even husband and wife. But this is only a rumor."

"Who are *they*?"

"People who toil in the dirty end of the art trade."

"People like you, you mean?"

Durand was silent.

"Is the forger Spanish, too?"

"That is the assumption. But, again, this is only speculation. Unlike some forgers who crave notoriety, this man is very serious about his privacy. The woman is said to be one of only two people who know his identity."

"And the other?"

"The man who runs the business side of the network. Think of them as an unholy trinity."

"What's the Spanish woman's role?"

"She oversees the delivery of the paintings to the galleries where they are sold. Most are midmarket pieces that quietly generate enormous amounts of cash. But every few months, another so-called lost master magically reappears."

"How many galleries are there?"

"I couldn't say."

"Try."

"One hears rumors about a gallery in Berlin and another in Brussels. One also hears rumors of a recent expansion into Asia and the Middle East."

"One wonders," said Gabriel pointedly, "why you didn't disclose any of this information during our last conversation."

"Perhaps if you had told me that you intended to purchase a painting from Galerie Fleury, I might have been more forthcoming." Durand smiled. "*A River Scene with Distant Windmills*. Definitely *not* by the Dutch Golden Age painter Aelbert Cuyp."

"How do you know about the sale?"

"Fleury was discreet in some matters, less so in others. He boasted of the sale to several of his competitors, despite the fact that he allowed Madame Rolfe's art adviser to remove the painting from France without an export license."

"He had no suspicions about me?"

"Apparently not."

"Then why was I targeted for assassination when I returned to the gallery four days later?"

"Perhaps you should ask the man who delivered the bomb."

Gabriel handed the Frenchman his phone a second time. "Do you recognize him?"

"Fortunately, no."

"I believe he murdered a woman in Bordeaux not long ago."

"The Bérrangar woman?"

Gabriel exhaled heavily. "Is there anything you *don't* know, Maurice?"

"Information is the key to my longevity, Monsieur Allon. And yours, I imagine." Durand looked down at the phone. "How else to explain the fact that you are in possession of this photograph?"

"It was given to me by the head of the Police Nationale's art crime unit."

"Jacques Ménard?"

Gabriel nodded.

"And what exactly is the nature of your relationship?"

"It's a bit like ours."

"Coercive and abusive?"

"Discreet and unofficial."

"Is he aware of our past collaboration?"

"*Non.*"

"I'm relieved." Durand returned the phone. "That said, I think this should be our last meeting for the foreseeable future."

"I'm afraid that's not possible."

"Why not?"

"Because I have an assignment for you."

"The names of those galleries in Berlin and Brussels?"

"If you wouldn't mind."

Durand removed his spectacles and rose. "Tell me something, Monsieur Allon. What happened to those paintings you found in Lucien's workshop?"

"Up in smoke."

"The Picasso?"

"All of them."

"A pity," said Durand with a sigh. "I could have found a good home for them."

———

At half past ten the following morning, while seated at the Louvre's Café Marly, Gabriel delivered his first report to Jacques Ménard. The briefing was thorough and complete, though evasive when it came to sources and methods. Like Christopher Keller, who occupied a nearby table, Ménard found fault with Gabriel's decision to destroy the forgeries he had discovered in Lucien Marchand's studio in Roussillon. Nevertheless, the French art detective was impressed by the scope of his informant's findings.

"I have to admit, it all makes a great deal of sense." Ménard gestured toward the gleaming glass-and-steel structure in the Cour Napoléon. "The criminal art world is a bit like *la pyramide*. There are tens of thousands of people involved in the illicit market, but it's controlled by a few major players at the top." He paused. "And it's obvious that you're acquainted with at least one or two of them."

"Aren't you?"

"*Oui*. Just not the right ones, apparently. Your ability to gather this much information so quickly is most embarrassing."

"Edmond Toussaint never popped up on your radar?"

Ménard shook his head. "And neither did Lucien Marchand. I don't care what sort of promises you made to the Vionnet woman. I'm going to open a case against her and seize those assets, including the villa in the Lubéron."

"First things first, Ménard."

"I'm afraid nothing has changed," said the Frenchman. "My hands remain tied."

"Then I suppose you'll have to force the issue."

"How?"

"By turning over my findings to one of your European partners."

"Which one?"

"Since we're looking for a Spanish woman who might or might not reside in a remote village in the Pyrenees, I would think the Guardia Civil might be the most logical choice."

"I don't trust them."

"I'm sure they feel the same about you."

"They do."

"How about the British?"

"Scotland Yard dismantled its Art and Antiquities Squad a few years ago. They treat art theft and fraud like any other property or financial crime."

"Then I suppose that leaves the Italians."

"They're the best in the business," conceded Ménard. "But what's the Italian connection?"

"At the moment, there isn't one. But I'm sure General Ferrari and I will think of something."

"He speaks very highly of you, the general."

"As well he should. I helped him crack an antiquities-smuggling ring a few years ago. I also helped him find a missing altarpiece."

"Not the Caravaggio?"

Gabriel nodded.

"The white whale," whispered Ménard. "How did you find it?"

"I hired a gang of French art thieves to steal *Sunflowers* from the Van Gogh Museum in Amsterdam. Then I painted a copy of it in a safe flat overlooking the Pont Marie and sold it for twenty-five million euros to a Syrian named Sam in a warehouse outside Paris." Gabriel lowered his voice. "All without your knowledge."

Jacques Ménard's face turned the color of the tablecloth. "You're not going to steal any paintings this time, are you?"

"*Non*. But I might forge a few."

"How many?"

Gabriel smiled. "Four, I think."

36

Mason's Yard

Lately, it had occurred to Oliver Dimbleby that he was a very lucky man indeed. Yes, his gallery had endured its ups and downs—the Great Recession had been a rather close shave—but somehow the hand of fate had always interceded to save him from ruin. The same was true of his personal life, which was, by universal acclaim, the untidiest in the London art world. Despite his advancing years and ever-increasing girth, Oliver had encountered no shortage of willing partners. He was, after all, a glorified salesman—a man of immense charm and charisma who, as he was fond of saying, could sell sand to a Saudi. He was not, however, a womanizer. Or so he told himself each time he awoke with a strange body on the other side of his bed. Oliver loved women. *All* women. And therein lay the root of his problem.

Tonight he had nothing on his schedule other than a well-deserved drink—and perhaps a few laughs at Julian Isherwood's expense—at Wiltons. To reach his destination he merely had to turn to the left after leaving his gallery and walk one hundred and fourteen paces along the spotless pavements of Bury Street. His journey took him past the premises of a dozen competitors, including the mighty

P. & D. Colnaghi & Co., the world's oldest commercial art gallery. Next door was the flagship store of Turnbull & Asser, where Oliver's deficit spending was approaching American levels.

Entering Wiltons, he was pleased to see Sarah Bancroft sitting alone at her usual table. He procured a glass of Pouilly-Fumé at the bar and joined her. The unexpected warmth of her smile nearly stopped his heart.

"Oliver," she purred. "What a pleasant surprise."

"Do you mean that?"

"Why wouldn't I?"

"Because I've always had the distinct impression that you find me repulsive."

"Don't be silly. I positively adore you."

"So there's hope for me yet?"

She raised her left hand and displayed a three-carat diamond ring and accompanying wedding band. "Still married, I'm afraid."

"Any chance of a divorce?"

"Not at the moment."

"In that case," said Oliver with a dramatic sigh, "I suppose I'll have to settle for being your sexual plaything."

"You have plenty of those already. Besides, my husband might not approve."

"Peter Marlowe? The professional assassin?"

"He's a business consultant," said Sarah.

"I think I liked him better when he was a contract killer."

"So did I."

Just then the door swung open and in came Simon Mendenhall and Olivia Watson.

"Did you hear the rumor about those two?" whispered Sarah.

"The one about their torrid affair? Jeremy Crabbe may have mentioned it. Or perhaps it was Nicky Lovegrove. It's on everyone's lips."

"A shame, that."

"I only wish they were saying the same about us." Smiling wolfishly, Oliver drank from his wineglass. "Sell anything lately?"

"A couple of Leonardos and a Giorgione. You?"

"Truth be told, I'm in a bit of a slump."

"Not you, Ollie?"

"Hard to believe, I know."

"How's your cash flow?"

"A bit like a leaky faucet."

"What about the five million I slipped you under the table on the Artemisia deal?"

"Are you referring to the newly discovered painting that I sold for a record price to a Swiss venture capitalist, only to find myself embroiled in a scandal involving the finances of the Russian president?"

"But it was great fun, wasn't it?"

"I enjoyed the five million. The rest of it I could have lived without."

"Fiddlesticks, Oliver. There's nothing you love more than being the center of attention. Especially when beautiful women are involved." Sarah paused. "Spanish women, in particular."

"Wherever did you hear a thing like that?"

"I happen to know that you've been carrying a secret torch for Penélope Cruz for years."

"Nicky," murmured Oliver.

"It was Jeremy who told me."

Oliver regarded Sarah for a moment. "Why do I get the feeling I'm being recruited for something?"

"Perhaps because you are."

"Is it naughty?"

"Extremely."

"In that case," said Oliver, "I'm all ears."

"Not here."

"My place or yours?"

Sarah smiled. "Mine, Ollie."

————

They slipped out of Wiltons unnoticed and walked along Duke Street to the passageway that led to Mason's Yard. Isherwood Fine Arts was located in the northeast corner of the quadrangle, in three floors of a sagging warehouse once owned by Fortnum & Mason. Parked outside was a silver Bentley Continental. Its gleaming hood was warm to Oliver's touch.

"Isn't this your husband's car?" he asked, but Sarah only smiled and unlocked the gallery's door.

Inside, they climbed a flight of carpeted stairs, then rode the cramped lift to Julian's upper exhibition room. In the half-light Oliver could make out two silhouetted figures. One was contemplating *Baptism of Christ* by Paris Bordone. The other was contemplating Oliver. He wore a dark single-breasted suit, Savile Row, perhaps Richard Anderson. His hair was sun-bleached. His eyes were bright blue.

"Hullo, Oliver," he drawled. Then, almost as an afterthought, he added, "I'm Peter Marlowe."

"The hit man?"

"Former hit man," he said with an ironic smile. "I'm a wildly successful business consultant now. That's why I drive a Bentley and have a wife who looks like Sarah."

"I never laid so much as a finger on her."

"Of course you didn't."

He placed a hand on Oliver's shoulder and guided him toward the Bordone. The man standing before the canvas turned slowly. His green eyes seemed to glow in the faint light.

"Mario Delvecchio!" exclaimed Oliver. "As I live and breathe! Or is it Gabriel Allon? I often can't tell them apart." Receiving no an-swer, he looked at the man he knew as Peter Marlowe, then at Sarah. At least, he thought that was her name. At that moment he wasn't certain of the ground beneath his feet. "The retired chief of Israeli in-telligence, a former hit man, and a beautiful American woman who may or may not have worked for the CIA. What could you possibly want with tubby Oliver Dimbleby?"

It was the retired Israeli spymaster who answered. "Your bottom-less reservoir of charm, your ability to talk your way out of almost anything, and your reputation for cutting the occasional corner."

"Me?" Oliver feigned righteous indignation. "I resent the implica-tion. And if it's a dirty dealer you want, Roddy Hutchinson is most definitely your man."

"Roddy lacks your star power. I need someone who can move the needle."

"For what?"

"I'd like you to sell a few paintings for me."

"Anything good?"

"A Titian, a Tintoretto, and a Veronese."

"What's the source?"

"An old European collection."

"And the subject matter?"

"I'll let you know the minute I finish painting them."

————

The first challenge for any art forger is the acquisition of canvases and stretchers of appropriate age, dimensions, and condition. When executing his copy of Vincent's *Sunflowers*, Gabriel had purchased a third-tier Impressionist streetscape from a small gallery near the Jardin du Luxembourg. He had no need to resort to such methods now. He merely had to ride the lift down to Julian's storerooms, which were crammed with an apocalyptic inventory of what was affectionately known in the trade as dead stock. He selected six minor Venetian School works from the sixteenth century—follower of so-and-so, manner of such-and-such, workshop of what's-his-name—and asked Sarah to express-ship them to his apartment in San Polo.

"Why six instead of only three?"

"I need two spares in the event of a disaster."

"And the other one?"

"I'm planning to leave a Gentileschi with my front man in Florence."

"Silly me," said Sarah. "But how are we going to explain the missing paintings to Julian?"

"With any luck, he won't notice."

Sarah instructed the shippers to arrive no later than nine the following morning and advised Julian to take the day off. Nevertheless, he wandered into Mason's Yard at his usual time, a quarter past twelve, as the crated paintings were being loaded into a Ford Transit van. The tragicomedy that followed included yet another collision with an inanimate object. This time it was Sarah's shredder, into which Julian, in a spasm of self-pity, attempted to insert himself.

Gabriel did not witness the incident, for he was in the back of a taxi bound from Fiumicino Airport toward Rome's Piazza di Sant'Ignazio. Upon arrival he took a table at Le Cave, one of his favorite restaurants in the *centro storico*. It was located a few steps from the ornate yellow-and-white palazzo that served as the headquarters of the Art Squad.

The palazzo's door swung open at half past one, and General Cesare Ferrari emerged in his bemedaled blue-and-gold uniform. He crossed the gray cobbles of the square and without uttering a word of greeting sat down at Gabriel's table. Instantly the waiter delivered a frigid bottle of Frascati and a plate of fried *arancini*.

"Why doesn't that happen when I arrive at restaurants?" asked Gabriel.

"I'm sure it's only the uniform." The general plucked one of the risotto balls from the plate. "Shouldn't you be in Venice with your wife and children?"

"Probably. But I needed to have a word with you first."

"About what?"

"I'm thinking about embarking on a life of crime, and I was wondering whether you would be interested in a piece of the action."

"What sort of misdeed are you contemplating this time?"

"Art forgery."

"Well, you certainly have the talent for it," said the general. "But what would be my end?"

"A high-profile case that will shake the art world to its core and ensure that the generous funding and personnel levels of the Art Squad remain unchanged for years to come."

"Has a crime been committed on Italian soil?"

"Not yet," said Gabriel with a smile. "But soon."

37

Bridge of Sighs

Umberto Conti, universally regarded as the greatest art restorer of the twentieth century, had bequeathed to Francesco Tiepolo a magical ring of keys that could open any door in Venice. Over drinks at Harry's Bar, Francesco entrusted them to Gabriel. Late that evening he slipped into the Scuola Grande di San Rocco and spent two hours in solitary communion with some of Tintoretto's greatest works. Then he breached the defenses of the neighboring Frari church and stood transfixed before Titian's magisterial *Assumption of the Virgin*. In the deep silence of the cavernous nave, he recalled the words Umberto had spoken to him when he was a broken, gray-haired boy of twenty-five.

Only a man with a damaged canvas of his own can be a truly great restorer . . .

Umberto would not have approved of his gifted pupil's newest commission. And neither, for that matter, did Francesco. Nevertheless, he agreed to serve as a consultant to the project. He was, after all, one of the world's foremost authorities on the Venetian School painters. If Gabriel could fool Francesco Tiepolo, he could fool anyone.

Francesco likewise agreed to accompany Gabriel during his nocturnal Venetian wanderings, if only to prevent another mishap like the one involving poor Capitano Rossetti. They stole into churches and *scuole*, roamed the Accademia and the Museo Correr, and even stormed the Doge's Palace. While peering through the stone-barred windows of the Bridge of Sighs, Francesco summarized the difficulty of the task ahead.

"Four different works by four of the greatest painters in history. Only a madman would attempt such a thing."

"If he can do it, so can I."

"The forger?"

Gabriel nodded.

"It's not a competition, you know."

"Of course it is. I have to prove to them that I would be a worthy addition to the network. Otherwise, they won't make a play for me."

"Is that why you allowed yourself to be dragged into this? For the challenge?"

"Wherever did you get the idea that this was going to be a challenge for me?"

"You don't lack for confidence, do you?"

"Neither does he."

"You're all the same, you art forgers. You all have something to prove. He's probably a failed painter who's taking his revenge on the art world by fooling the connoisseurs and the collectors."

"The connoisseurs and collectors," said Gabriel, "haven't seen anything yet."

He spent his days in his studio with his monographs and catalogues raisonnés and photographs from past restorations, including several that he had conducted for Francesco. Together, after much debate, some of it conducted with raised voices, they settled on the subject matter and iconography for the four forgeries. Gabriel produced a series of preparatory sketches, then turned the sketches into four swiftly executed rehearsal paintings. Francesco declared the Gentile-schi, a reworking of *Danaë and the Shower of Gold*, to be the finest of the lot, with Veronese's *Susanna in the Bath* a close second. Gabriel agreed with Francesco's assessment of the Gentileschi, though he was fond of his reinterpretation of Tintoretto's *Bacchus, Venus, and Ariadne*. His Titian, a pastiche of *The Lovers*, wasn't bad, either, though he thought the brushwork was a touch tentative.

"How can one *not* be tentative when one is forging a Titian?"

"It's a dead giveaway, Francesco. I have to *become* Titian. Otherwise, we're sunk."

"What are you going to do with that one?"

"Cremation. The others, too."

"Have you taken leave of your senses?"

"Clearly."

Early the following morning, Gabriel uncrated one of the paintings he had pillaged from Julian's storerooms, an early sixteenth-century Venetian School devotional piece of no value and little merit. Even so, he felt a stab of guilt as he scraped the unknown artist's work from the canvas and covered it in gesso and an *imprimatura* of lead white with traces of lampblack and yellow ocher. Next he executed his underdrawing—with a brush, the way *he* would have done it—and meticulously prepared his palette. Lead white, genuine ultramarine, madder lake, burnt sienna, malachite, yellow ocher, red ocher, orpiment, ivory black. Before commencing work, he once again reflected on the shifting fortunes of his career. He was no longer the leader of a powerful intelligence service or even one of the world's finest art restorers.

He was the sun amidst small stars.

He was Titian.

———

For the better part of the next week, Chiara and the children saw little of him. On the rare occasions he emerged from his studio, he was on edge and preoccupied, not at all himself. Only once did he accept an invitation to join Chiara for lunch. His hands left smudges of paint across her breasts and abdomen.

"I feel like I just made love to another man."

"You did."

"Who are you?"

"Come with me. I'll show you."

Wrapped in a bedsheet, Chiara followed him into the studio and stood before the canvas. At length she whispered, "You're a freak."

"Do you like it?"

"It's absolutely—"

"Amazing, I think."

"I see a touch of Giorgione in it."

"That's because I was still under his influence when I painted it in 1510."

"Who will you be next?"

Jacobo Robusti, the artist known as Tintoretto, was a learned and unsmiling man who rarely set foot outside Venice and allowed few visitors to enter his workspace. If there was one consolation, he was among the swiftest painters in the republic. Gabriel completed his version of *Bacchus, Venus, and Ariadne* in half the time it took him to finish *The Lovers*. Chiara nevertheless declared it superior to the Titian in every respect, as did Francesco.

"I'm afraid your wife is right. You truly are a freak."

Next Gabriel assumed the personality and remarkable palette of Paolo Veronese. *Susanna in the Bath* required the largest of the six canvases he had acquired from Isherwood Fine Arts and several additional days to complete—in large part because Gabriel intentionally damaged the work and then restored it. Luca Rossetti visited him three times during the painting's execution. Brush in hand, Gabriel lectured the young Carabinieri officer on the artistic merits and fraudulent pedigrees of his four forged masterpieces. Rossetti in turn briefed Gabriel on the preparations for their forthcoming operation. They included the acquisition of two properties—an isolated villa for the reclusive forger and an apartment in Florence for his front man.

"It's on the south side of the Arno, on the Lungarno Torrigiani. We've loaded it up with paintings and antiquities from the Art Squad's evidence room. It definitely looks like the home of an art dealer."

"And the villa?"

"Your friend the Holy Father called Count Gasparri. It's all arranged."

"How soon can you settle into the apartment and assume your new identity?"

"As soon as you say I'm ready."

"Are you?"

"I know my lines," answered Rossetti. "And I know more about the Venetian School painters than I ever thought possible."

"What was Veronese's name when he was young?" inquired Gabriel.

"Paolo Spezapreda."

"And why was that?"

"His father was a stonecutter. It was traditional for children to be named after their father's occupation."

"Why did he start calling himself Paolo Caliari?"

"His mother was the illegitimate child of a nobleman called Antonio Caliari. Young Paolo thought it was better to be named for a nobleman than a stonecutter."

"Not bad." Gabriel drew his Beretta from the waistband of his trousers. "But will you be able to recite your lines so confidently if someone points one of these at your head?"

"I grew up in Naples," said Rossetti. "Most of my childhood friends are now in the Camorra. I'm not going to fall to pieces if someone starts waving a gun around."

"I heard a rumor that an elderly Venetian School painter gave you a good thrashing the other night in San Polo."

"The elderly painter attacked me without warning."

"That's the way it works in the real world. Criminals don't often announce their intentions before resorting to violence." Gabriel returned the gun to the small of his back and contemplated the towering canvas. "What do you think, Signore Calvi?"

"You have to darken the garments of the two elders. Otherwise, I won't be able to convince Oliver Dimbleby that it was painted in the late sixteenth century."

"Oliver Dimbleby," said Gabriel, "will be the least of your problems."

By the time he commenced work on the Gentileschi, he was so exhausted he could scarcely hold a brush. Fortunately, Chiara agreed to pose for him, as the artist he was attempting to impersonate preferred the Caravaggesque method of painting directly from live models. He gave his Danaë Chiara's body and facial features, but turned his wife's dark hair to gold and her olive skin to luminous alabaster. Most of their sessions necessarily included an intermezzo in the bedroom—a hurried one, for Gabriel's time was limited. The end result of their collaboration was a painting of astonishing beauty and veiled eroticism. It was, they both agreed, the finest of the four works.

Like the other three paintings, it was unmarred by craquelure, a sure sign it was a modern forgery and not the work of an Old Master. The solution was a large professional oven. General Ferrari obtained one from the seized inventory of a Mafia-owned kitchen supplies firm and delivered it to the mainland warehouse of the Tiepolo Restoration Company. After removing the four paintings from their stretchers, Gabriel baked them for three hours at 220 degrees Fahrenheit. Then, with Francesco's help, he dragged the paintings over the edge of a rectangular work table, first vertically, then horizontally. The result was a fine network of Italianate surface cracks.

That evening, alone in his studio, Gabriel covered the paintings with varnish. And in the morning, when the varnish was dry, he photographed them with a tripod-mounted Nikon. He hung the

Titian and the Tintoretto in the sitting room of the apartment, surrendered the Gentileschi to General Ferrari, and shipped the Veronese to Sarah Bancroft in London. The photos he emailed directly to Oliver Dimbleby, owner and sole proprietor of Dimbleby Fine Arts of Bury Street, upon whose rounded shoulders the entire venture rested. Shortly before midnight one of the images appeared on the website of *ARTnews*, beneath the byline of Amelia March. Gabriel read the exclusive story to his dark-haired, olive-complected Danaë. She made love to him in a shower of gold.

38

Kurfürstendamm

The article was purportedly based on a single source who wished to remain anonymous. Even this was misleading, as it was Sarah Bancroft who had provided the initial tip and Oliver Dimbleby who had supplied the off-the-record confirmation and the photograph—thus making it, in point of fact, a two-source story.

The work in question was said to be 92 centimeters in height and 74 in width. That much, at least, was accurate. It was not, however, a lost work of the Late Renaissance painter known as Titian, and there had been no quiet sale to a prominent collector who wished to remain unidentified. Truth be told, there was no buyer, prominent or otherwise, and no money had changed hands. As for the painting, it was now hanging in a glorious *piano nobile* overlooking the Grand Canal in Venice, much to the delight of the wife and two young children of the newly minted art forger who had produced it.

The dealers, curators, and auctioneers of the London art world greeted the news with astonishment and no small amount of jealousy. After all, Oliver was still basking in the glow of his last coup. In the salerooms and watering holes of St. James's and Mayfair, questions were raised, usually in conspiratorial whispers. Did this new Titian have a proper provenance, or did it fall off the back of a truck? Was tubby Oliver absolutely certain of the attribution? Did others more learned than he concur? And what exactly was his role in the transaction? Had he actually *sold* the painting to his unnamed buyer? Or had he merely acted as a middleman and pocketed a lucrative commission in the process?

For three interminable days, Oliver refused to either confirm or deny that he handled the work in question. Finally he released a brief corroboratory statement that was scarcely more illuminating than Amelia March's original story. It contained only two new pieces of information, that the painting had emerged from an old European collection and had been examined by no fewer than four leading Venetian School experts. All four agreed, without qualifications or conditions, that the canvas had been executed by Titian himself and not by a member of his workshop or a later follower.

That evening Oliver walked the one hundred and fourteen paces from his gallery to the bar at Wiltons and in keeping with neighborhood tradition promptly ordered six bottles of champagne. Much was made of the fact that it was Taittinger Comtes Blanc de Blanc, the most expensive on the list. Still, all those in attendance would later remark that Oliver seemed subdued for a man who had just pulled off one of the art world's biggest coups in years. He refused to divulge the price the Titian had fetched and feigned deafness when Jeremy Crabbe pressed him for additional details on the painting's provenance. Sometime around eight he pulled Nicky Lovegrove aside for a heart-to-heart, which gave rise to speculation that Oliver's unidentified buyer was one of Nicky's superrich clients. Nicky swore it wasn't so, but Oliver cagily declined comment. Then, after kissing the proffered cheek of Sarah Bancroft, he waddled into Jermyn Street and was gone.

It emerged the following day, in a lengthy article in the *Art Newspaper*, that the unidentified buyer had made a takeaway offer for the Titian after being granted an exclusive viewing at Oliver's gallery. According to the *Independent*, the offer was £25 million. Niles Dunham, an Old Master specialist from the National Gallery, denied a report that he had authenticated the painting on Oliver's behalf. Curiously, so did every other connoisseur of Italian School painting in the United Kingdom.

But it was the photograph of the painting that raised the most eyebrows, at least among the backbiting world of St. James's. For many years Oliver had utilized the services of the same fine art photographer—the renowned Prudence Cuming of Dover Street. But not, as it turned out, for his newly discovered Titian. Perhaps even more suspicious was his claim that he had taken the photograph himself. All were in agreement that Oliver could handle a tumbler of good whisky, or a shapely backside, but not a camera.

And yet no one, not even the unscrupulous Roddy Hutchinson, suspected Oliver of wrongdoing. Indeed, the general consensus was that he was guilty of nothing more serious than protecting the identity of his source, a common practice among art dealers. The logical conclusion was that it was only a matter of time before another noteworthy picture emerged from the same European collection.

When the inevitable finally happened, it was once again Amelia March of *ARTnews* who broke the story. This time the work in question was *Bacchus, Venus, and Ariadne* by the Venetian painter Tintoretto—deeply private sale, price unavailable upon request. Just ten days later, to absolutely no one's surprise, Dimbleby Fine Arts announced its newest offering: *Susanna in the Bath*, oil on canvas, 194 by 194 centimeters, by Paolo Veronese. The gallery retained Prudence Cuming of Dover Street to make the photograph. The art world swooned.

———

With the exception, that is, of the powerful director of the Uffizi Gallery in Florence, who found the sudden appearance of three Italian Old Master paintings suspicious, to say the least. He rang General Ferrari of the Art Squad and demanded an immediate investigation. Surely, he shouted down the line to Rome, the canvases had been smuggled out of Italy in violation of the country's draconian Cultural Heritage Code. The general promised to look into the matter, though his fingers were firmly crossed at the time. Needless to say, he did not inform the director that the paintings in question were all modern fakes and that he himself was operating in league with the forger.

The forger's phantom front man—a collector and occasional dealer who called himself Alessandro Calvi—was currently living in an art-filled apartment within sight of the Uffizi, on the Lungarno Torrigiani. As it happened, General Ferrari had occasion to ring this disreputable character two days later on an unrelated matter. It concerned a piece of information the forger had received from a well-placed informant in Paris, an art thief and antiques dealer named Maurice Durand.

"Galerie Konrad Hassler. It's located on the Kurfürstendamm in Berlin. There's a coffeehouse on the opposite side of the street. Your associate will meet you there tomorrow afternoon at three."

And so it was that the phantom front man, whose real name was Capitano Luca Rossetti, left the luxury apartment on the Arno early the following morning and rode in a taxi to Florence Airport. His tailored Italian suit was new and expensive, as were his handmade shoes and his soft-sided leather attaché case. The watch on his wrist was a Patek Philippe. Like his collection of art and antiquities, it was borrowed from the evidence rooms of the Carabinieri.

Rossetti's travel itinerary included a stopover in Zurich, and it was approaching three o'clock when he arrived at the coffeehouse on the Kurfürstendamm. Gabriel was seated at a table outside, in the dappled shade of a plane tree. He ordered two coffees from the waitress in rapid German before handing a manila envelope to Rossetti.

Inside were two photographs. The first depicted three unframed paintings displayed side by side against the wall of an artist's workshop—a Titian, a Tintoretto, and a Veronese. The second was a high-resolution image of *Danaë and the Shower of Gold*, purportedly by Orazio Gentileschi. Rossetti knew the work well. At present, it was hanging on the wall of the apartment in Florence.

"When is he expecting me?"

"Three thirty. He's under the impression that your name is Giovanni Rinaldi and that you are from Milano."

"How do you want me to play it?"

"I'd like you to present Herr Hassler with a unique opportunity to acquire a lost masterwork. I would also like you to make it clear that you are the source of the three paintings that have resurfaced in London."

"Do I tell him they're forgeries?"

"You won't have to. He'll get the idea when he sees the photos."

"Why am I coming to him?"

"Because you're looking for a second distributor for your merchandise and you've heard rumors that he's less than honest."

"How do you suppose he'll react?"

"He'll either make you an offer or throw you out of his gallery. I'm betting on the latter. Make sure you leave behind the photo of the Gentileschi on your way out the door."

"What happens if he calls the police?"

"Criminals don't call the police, Rossetti. In fact, they do their best to avoid them."

The Carabinieri officer lowered his gaze to the photograph.

"When was he born?" asked Gabriel quietly.

"Fifteen sixty-three."

"What was his name?"

"Orazio Lomi."

"What sort of work did his father do?"

"He was a Florentine goldsmith."

"Who was Gentileschi?"

"An uncle he lived with when he moved to Rome."

"Where did he paint *Danaë and the Shower of Gold*?"

"Probably in Genoa."

"Where did I paint my version?"

"None of your fucking business."

––––––––––

Capitano Luca Rossetti left the coffeehouse at 3:27 p.m. and crossed to the opposite side of the elegant tree-lined boulevard. Gabriel tensed as the young Carabinieri officer reached his right hand toward the intercom of Galerie Konrad Hassler. Fifteen seconds elapsed, long enough for the dealer to have a good long look at his visitor. Then Rossetti leaned on the glass door and disappeared from view.

Five minutes later Gabriel's phone shivered with an incoming call. It was General Ferrari.

"Nothing exploded, did it?"

"Not yet."

"Let me know the minute he walks out of there," said the general, and rang off.

Gabriel returned the phone to the tabletop and directed his gaze toward the gallery. By now the introductions had been made and the two men had withdrawn to the dealer's office for a bit of privacy. A photograph had been placed on his desk. Perhaps two. When viewed together, the images made it clear that a talented new forger had stepped onto the stage of the illicit art market. Which was exactly the message that Gabriel wished to send.

Just then his phone pulsed with another call. "What's going on in there?" asked General Ferrari.

"Hold on, I'll run across the road and check."

This time it was Gabriel who killed the connection. Two minutes later the door of the gallery opened, and out stepped Rossetti, followed by a well-dressed man with iron-gray hair and a crimson face. A few final words were exchanged, and fingers were pointed in anger. Then Rossetti ducked into a taxi and was gone, leaving the crimson-faced man alone on the pavement. He looked left and right along the boulevard before returning to the gallery.

Message delivered, thought Gabriel.

He dialed Rossetti's number.

"Looks as though you two really hit it off."

"It went exactly the way you said it would."

"Where's the photograph?"

"It's possible that in my rush to get out of the gallery I might have left it on his desk."

"How long before he sends it to our girl?"

"Not long," said Rossetti.

39

Queen's Gate Terrace

For the remainder of that week, the phone at Dimbleby Fine Arts rang nearly without cease. Cordelia Blake, Oliver's long-suffering receptionist, served as the first line of defense. Those with names she recognized—longtime clients or representatives of prominent museums—she transferred directly to Oliver's line. Those of lesser repute were asked to leave a detailed message and were given no assurance their inquiry would receive a reply. It was Mr. Dimbleby's ambition, Cordelia explained, to find a suitable home for the Veronese. He had no intention of selling the painting to just anyone.

Unbeknownst to Cordelia, Oliver delivered each of her pink message slips to Sarah Bancroft in Mason's Yard, and Sarah in turn forwarded the names and numbers to Gabriel in Venice. By the close of business on that Friday, Dimbleby Fine Arts had received more than two hundred requests to view the forged Veronese—from the directors of the world's greatest museums, from representatives of prominent collectors, and from a multitude of journalists, art dealers, and learned connoisseurs of the Italian Old Masters. With the exception of a curator from the J. Paul Getty Museum in Los Angeles, none of the names on the list was Spanish in origin, and none of the callback numbers began with a Spanish country code. Forty-two women wished to see the painting, all of whom were well-known figures in the art world.

One of the women was a reporter from the London bureau of the *New York Times*. With Gabriel's approval, Oliver allowed her to see the painting the following Monday, and by Wednesday evening her story and accompanying photographs were the talk of the art world. The result was another avalanche of calls to Dimbleby Fine Arts. Twenty-two of the new callers were women. None of their names or callback numbers were Spanish in origin. And none, according to Cordelia Blake, spoke with a Spanish accent.

Gabriel feared the worst, that the forgery network's front woman had no intention of attending the party he had so meticulously planned in her honor. Nevertheless, he instructed Oliver to prepare a schedule for the viewings. They were to last for one week only. The price band would be set at £15 million to £20 million, which would separate the wheat from the chaff. Oliver was to make it clear that he reserved the right not to sell to the highest bidder.

"And make sure you dim the lights in your exhibition room," added Gabriel. "Otherwise, one of your eagle-eyed clients might notice that your newly discovered Veronese is a forgery."

"Not a chance. On the surface, at least, it looks like Veronese painted it in the sixteenth century."

"He did paint it, Oliver. I just happened to be holding the brush at the time."

Gabriel spent Saturday sailing the Adriatic with Chiara and the children, and on Sunday, the day before the viewings were to begin, he flew to London. Upon arrival he headed for Christopher and Sarah's maisonette in Queen's Gate Terrace. There, arrayed on the granite-topped kitchen island, he found a surveillance photograph from Heathrow Airport, a scan of a Spanish passport, and a printout of a guest registration from the Lanesborough Hotel.

Smiling, Sarah handed him a glass of Bollinger Special Cuvée. "Tagliatelle with ragù or veal Milanese?"

————

She was tall and slender, with the square shoulders of a swimmer, narrow hips, and long legs. The pantsuit she wore was dark and businesslike, but the daring neckline of her white blouse revealed the fine curve of her delicate upturned breasts. Her hair was nearly black and hung long and straight down the center of her back. Even in the unflattering light of Heathrow's Terminal 5, it shone like a newly varnished painting.

Her name, according to the passport, was Magdalena Navarro. She was thirty-nine and a resident of Madrid. She had arrived at Heathrow aboard Iberia Flight 7459 and had dialed Dimbleby Fine Arts at 3:07 p.m. from her room phone at the Lanesborough. The call had bounced automatically to Oliver's mobile. After listening to the message, he had rung Sarah, who had prevailed upon her husband, an officer of Her Majesty's Secret Intelligence Service, to have an off-the-record peek at the Spanish woman's particulars. He had done so with the approval of his director-general.

"It took our brethren at MI5 all of twenty minutes to pull together the file."

"Did they have a look at her recent travel?"

"It seems she's a frequent visitor to France, Belgium, and Germany. She also spends a fair amount of time in Hong Kong and Tokyo."

Christopher ignited a Marlboro and exhaled a cloud of smoke toward the ceiling of his elegantly decorated drawing room. He wore a pair of fitted chinos and a costly cashmere pullover. Sarah was more casually attired, in stretch jeans and a Harvard sweatshirt. She plucked a cigarette from Christopher's packet and quickly lit it before Gabriel could object.

"Any other interesting travel?" he asked.

"She goes to New York about once a month. Apparently, she lived there for a few years in the mid-aughts."

"Credit card?"

"A corporate American Express. The company has a fuzzy Liechtenstein registry. She seems to use it only for foreign travel."

"Which would help to conceal the real location of her home in Spain." Gabriel turned to Sarah. "How did she describe herself in the message?"

"She says she's a broker. But she doesn't have a website or an entry on LinkedIn, and neither Oliver nor Julian has ever heard of her."

"Sounds like she's our girl."

"Yes," agreed Sarah. "The question is, how long do we make her wait?"

"Long enough to create the impression that she is of absolutely no consequence."

"And then?"

"She'll have to convince Oliver to let her see the painting."

"Could be dangerous," said Sarah.

"He'll be fine."

"It's not Oliver I'm worried about."

Gabriel smiled. "All's fair in love and forgery."

40

Dimbleby Fine Arts

The director of the National Gallery arrived at Dimbleby Fine Arts at ten the following morning, accompanied by the infallible Niles Dunham and three other curators who specialized in Italian Old Masters. They sniffed, poked, prodded, kicked the tires, and examined the canvas under ultraviolet light. No one questioned the authenticity of the work, only the provenance.

"An old European collection? It's a bit gossamer, Oliver. That said, I must have it."

"Then I suggest you make me an offer."

"I won't get caught up in a bidding war."

"Of course you will."

"Who's next at bat?"

"The Getty."

"You wouldn't dare."

"I will if the price is right."

"Scoundrel."

"Flattery will get you nowhere."

"See you at Wiltons tonight?"

"Unless I get a better offer."

The delegation from the Getty arrived at eleven. They were young and suntanned and loaded with cash. They made a takeaway offer of £25 million, £5 million above the top end of the estimated price band. Oliver turned them down flat.

"We won't be back," they vowed.

"I have a feeling you will."

"How can you tell?"

"Because I see that look in your eyes."

It was noon when Oliver ushered the Gettys into Bury Street. Cordelia handed him a stack of telephone messages on her way to lunch. He leafed through them quickly before ringing Sarah.

"She's called twice this morning."

"Wonderful news."

"Perhaps we should put her out of her misery."

"Actually, we'd like you to play hard to get a little longer."

"Hard to get isn't my usual modus operandi."

"I've noticed, Ollie."

The afternoon session was a reprise of the morning. The delegation from the Metropolitan Museum of Art was smitten, their counterparts from Boston head over heels. The director of the Art Gallery of Ontario, a Veronese expert himself, was practically speechless.

"How much do you want for it?" he managed to say.

"I've got twenty-five from the Getty."

"They're heathens."

"But rich."

"I might be able to do twenty."

"A novel negotiating tactic."

"Please, Oliver. Don't make me beg."

"Match the Getty's offer, and it's yours."

"Is that a promise?"

"You have my solemn word."

Which is how the first day of viewings ended, with one final untruth. Oliver showed the Ontario delegation out of the gallery and collected the newest telephone messages from Cordelia's desk.

Magdalena Navarro had called at four fifteen.

"She sounded rather annoyed," said Cordelia.

"With good reason."

"Who do you suppose she represents?"

"Someone with enough money to put her up at the Lanesborough."

Cordelia collected her belongings and went out. Alone, Oliver reached for the telephone and dialed Sarah.

"How was your afternoon?" she asked.

"I have a bidding war on my hands for a painting I can't sell. Otherwise, nothing much happened."

"How many times did she call?"

"Only once."

"Perhaps she's losing interest."

"All the more reason I should call her and get it over with."

"Let's discuss it at Wiltons. I feel a martini coming on."

Oliver hung up the phone and engaged in the familiar ritual of putting his gallery to bed for the night. He lowered the internal security screens over the windows. He engaged the alarm. He placed a baize-cloth cover over *Susanna in the Bath*, oil on canvas, 194 by 194 centimeters, by Gabriel Allon.

Outside, Oliver triple-locked his door and set off along Bury Street. It should have been a triumphal march. He was, after all, the toast of the art world, the dealer who had stumbled upon a long-hidden collection of lost masters. Never mind that all of the paintings were forgeries. Oliver assured himself that his actions were in service of a noble cause. If nothing else, it would make for a good story one day.

Crossing Ryder Street, he became conscious of the fact that someone was walking behind him. Someone wearing a pair of well-made pumps, he thought, with stiletto heels. He paused outside the Colnaghi gallery and cast a leftward glance along the pavement.

Tall, slender, expensively attired, lustrous black hair hanging over the front of one shoulder.

Dangerously attractive.

Much to Oliver's surprise, the woman joined him and fixed her wide dark eyes on the Old Master painting displayed in the window. "Bartolomeo Cavarozzi," she said in faintly accented English. "He was an early follower of Caravaggio who spent two years working in Spain, where he was much admired. If I'm not mistaken, he painted this picture after his return to Rome in 1619."

"Who in the world *are* you?" asked Oliver.

The woman turned to him and smiled. "I'm Magdalena Navarro, Mr. Dimbleby. And I've been trying to reach you all day."

———

Wiltons was overrun with American and Canadian museum curators, all divided into opposing camps. Sarah shook the hand of the Austrian-born director of the Met, then shouldered her way to the bar, where she endured a wait of ten minutes for her martini. The cocktail-party din was so deafening that for a moment she didn't realize her phone was ringing. It was Oliver calling from his mobile.

"Are you in this madhouse somewhere?" she asked.

"Change in plan, I'm afraid. We'll have to do it another time."

"What are you talking about?"

"Yes, tomorrow evening would be fine. Cordelia will call you in the morning and make the arrangements."

And with that, the call went dead.

Sarah quickly dialed Gabriel. "I could be wrong," she said, "but I believe our girl just made her next move."

41

Piccadilly

Where are you taking me?"

"Somewhere I can have you all to myself."

"Not the Lanesborough?"

"No, Mr. Dimbleby." She gave him a look of contrived reproach. "Not on our first date."

They were walking along Piccadilly into the blinding light of the sun. It was one of those perfect early-summer evenings in London, cool and soft, a gentle breeze. The woman's intoxicating scent reminded Oliver of the south of Spain. Orange blossom and jasmine and a hint of manzanilla. Twice the back of her hand brushed against his. Her touch was electric.

She slowed to a stop outside Hide. It was one of London's costliest restaurants, a temple of gastronomic and social excess beloved by Russian billionaires, Emirati princes, and, evidently, beautiful Spanish art criminals.

"I'm not quite posh enough for this place," protested Oliver.

"The art world is at your feet tonight, Mr. Dimbleby. You are, without a doubt, the poshest man in London."

They made quite an entrance—the corpulent, pink-cheeked art

dealer and the tall, elegantly dressed woman with shimmering black hair. She led him down a swirling oaken staircase to the dimly lit bar. A secluded candlelit table awaited them.

"I'm impressed," said Oliver.

"My butler at the Lanesborough arranged it."

"Do you stay there often?"

"Only when a certain client of mine is footing the bill."

"A client who's interested in acquiring the Veronese?"

"Let's not rush things, Mr. Dimbleby." She leaned into the warm light of the candle. "We Spaniards like to take our time."

The front of her blouse had fallen open, exposing the inner curve of a pear-shaped breast. "Is it as nice as they say?" blurted Oliver.

"What's that, Mr. Dimbleby?"

"The Lanesborough."

"You've never been?"

"Only the restaurant."

"I have a suite overlooking Hyde Park. The view is quite lovely."

So was Oliver's. He nevertheless forced himself to lower his gaze to the cocktail menu. "What do you recommend?"

"The concoction they call the Currant Affairs is life-changing."

Oliver read the ingredients. "Bruno Paillard champagne with Ketel One vodka, red currant, and guava?"

"Don't mock it until you try it."

"I generally drink my champagne and vodka separately."

"They have an extraordinary sherry selection."

"A much better idea."

She summoned the waiter with a raised eyebrow and ordered a bottle of Cuatro Palmas Amontillado.

"Have you been to Spain, Mr. Dimbleby?"

"Many times."

"Business or pleasure?"

"A little of both."

"I'm from Seville originally," she informed him. "But these days I live mostly in Madrid."

"Your English is quite extraordinary."

"I attended a special art history program at Oxford for a year." She was interrupted by the reappearance of the waiter. After an elaborate presentation of the wine, he poured two glasses and withdrew. She raised hers a fraction of an inch. "Cheers, Mr. Dimbleby. I hope you enjoy it."

"You must call me Oliver."

"I couldn't."

"I insist," he said, and drank some of the wine.

"What do you think?"

"It's ambrosia. I only hope that your client is picking up the check."

"He is."

"Does he have a name?"

"Several, in fact."

"He's a spy, your client?"

"He is a member of an aristocratic family. His name is rather cumbersome, to say the least."

"Is he Spanish like you?"

"Perhaps."

Oliver sighed heavily before returning his glass to the tabletop.

"Forgive me, Mr. Dimbleby, but my client is an extremely wealthy man who does not want the world to know the true scale of his art collection. I cannot reveal his identity."

"In that case, perhaps we should discuss yours."

"As I explained to your assistant, I'm a broker."

"How is it that I've never heard of you?"

"I prefer to operate in the shadows." She paused. "As do you, it seems."

"Bury Street is hardly the shadows."

"But you have been, how shall we say, less than forthcoming about the origin of the Veronese. Not to mention the Titian and the Tintoretto."

"You don't know much about the art trade, do you?"

"Actually, I know a great deal, as does my client. He is a sophisticated and shrewd collector. Until he falls in love with a painting, that is. When that happens, money is no object."

"I take it he has a crush on my Veronese?"

"It was love at first sight."

"I already have two bids of twenty-five million."

"My client will match any offer you receive. Pending a thorough examination of the canvas and provenance on my part, of course."

"And if I were to sell it to him? What would he do with it?"

"It would be displayed prominently in one of his many homes."

"Will he agree to lend it for exhibitions?"

"Never."

"I admire your honesty."

She smiled but said nothing.

"How long are you planning to stay in London?"

"I'm scheduled to return to Madrid tomorrow evening."

"A pity."

"Why?"

"Because I might have an opening in my schedule on Wednesday afternoon. Thursday, at the latest."

"How about now instead?"

"Sorry, but my gallery is buttoned up for the night. Besides, it's been a long day, and I'm exhausted."

"A pity," she said playfully. "Because I was hoping you would have dinner with me at the Lanesborough."

"Tempting," said Oliver. "But not on our first date."

On the pavements of Piccadilly, Oliver offered the Spanish woman his hand in farewell but received a kiss instead. Not two Iberian air pecks but a single warm and breathy display of affection that landed near his right ear and lingered long after the woman had set off toward Hyde Park Corner and her hotel. The evening was made complete by the seductive final glance she gave him over one shoulder. *Silly boy*, she was saying. *Silly, silly boy.*

He turned in the opposite direction and, feeling slightly inebriated, fished his phone from the breast pocket of his suit jacket. He had received several calls and text messages since he had checked it last, none from Sarah. Curiously, her name and number had vanished from his directory of recent calls. Nor was there any record of a Sarah Bancroft in his contacts. Julian's numbers were likewise missing, as was the entry for Isherwood Fine Arts.

Just then the phone pulsed with an incoming call. Oliver didn't recognize the number. He tapped the ACCEPT icon and raised the device to his ear.

"Your car and driver are waiting for you in Bolton Street," said a male voice, and the connection went dead.

Oliver returned the phone to his pocket and continued on his present easterly heading. Bolton Street was a few paces ahead on the left. He rounded the corner and spotted a silver Bentley Continental idling curbside. Seated behind the wheel was Sarah's husband. Oliver lowered his rotund form into the passenger seat. A moment later they were headed west along Piccadilly.

"Is your name really Peter Marlowe?"

"Why wouldn't it be?"

"Sounds made up."

"So does Oliver Dimbleby." Smiling, he pointed out the tall woman with shimmering black hair walking past the entrance of the Athenaeum. "There's our girl."

"I never laid so much as a finger on her."

"It's probably better not to mix work and play, wouldn't you agree?"

"No," said Oliver as the beautiful Spanish woman disappeared from view. "I most certainly would not."

42

Queen's Gate Terrace

As part of his retirement package from the Office, Gabriel had been given a personal copy of the Israeli cell phone hacking malware known as Proteus. The program's most insidious feature was that it required no blunder on the part of the target—no unwise software update or click of an innocent-looking photograph or advertisement. All Gabriel had to do was enter the target's phone number into the Proteus application on his laptop, and within minutes the device would be under his complete control. He could read the target's emails and text messages, review the target's Internet browsing history and telephone metadata, and monitor the target's physical movements with the GPS location services. Perhaps most important, he could activate the phone's microphone and camera and thus turn the device into a full-time instrument of surveillance.

He had protectively installed Proteus on Oliver Dimbleby's Samsung Galaxy after his recruitment but had allowed the malware to remain dormant until 5:42 that afternoon. With the click of his laptop's trackpad—an action he undertook while drinking tea in Sarah and Christopher's kitchen in Queen's Gate Terrace—he established that his missing operative was at that moment walking westward along Piccadilly, accompanied by a sultry-voiced woman who spoke fluent English with a Spanish accent. Sarah hurried home from Wiltons in time to hear the final minutes of their conversation in the trendy bar of Hive.

"She's a worthy opponent, our Magdalena. And not to be taken lightly."

"All the more reason we need to keep tubby Oliver on a very short leash."

To that end, Gabriel dispatched Christopher to Mayfair to corral his wayward asset. It was approaching seven thirty when they arrived at the maisonette. The after-action debriefing, such as it was, began with an awkward admission on Gabriel's part.

Oliver frowned. "That would explain why Sarah and Julian vanished from my contacts."

"I deleted them as a precautionary measure after you agreed to have drinks with that woman without giving us any warning."

"I'm afraid she didn't leave me much of a choice."

"Why?"

"Because she's nearly six feet tall and shockingly beautiful. What's more, she seems to have left Madrid without packing a brassiere." Oliver looked at Sarah. "I think I'll have that drink now."

"The Currant Affairs or the Tropic Thunder?"

"Whisky, if you have it."

Christopher opened a cabinet and took down a bottle of Johnnie Walker Black Label and a pair of cut-glass tumblers. He filled one of the glasses with two fingers of whisky and sent it across the kitchen island toward Oliver.

"Baccarat," he said approvingly. "Maybe you're a wildly successful business consultant after all." He turned to Gabriel. "Isn't Proteus the software that the Saudi crown prince used to spy on that journalist he murdered?"

"The journalist's name was Omar Nawwaf. And, yes, the Israeli prime minister approved the sale of Proteus to the Saudis over my strenuous objections. In the hands of a repressive government, the malware can be a dangerous weapon of surveillance and blackmail. Imagine how something like this might be used to silence a meddlesome journalist or prodemocracy advocate."

Gabriel clicked the software's PLAY icon.

"Because she's nearly six feet tall and shockingly beautiful. What's more, she seems to have left Madrid without packing a brassiere."

Gabriel paused the recording.

"Dear God," murmured Oliver.

"Or how about this?" Gabriel clicked PLAY again.

"How is it that I've never heard of you?"

"I prefer to operate in the shadows. As do you, it seems."

"Bury Street is hardly the shadows."

Gabriel clicked PAUSE.

"Aren't you going to play the part where I turned down a night of incredible sex in a suite at the Lanesborough?"

"I believe the offer was dinner."

"You need to get out more, Mr. Allon."

He closed the laptop.

"What now?" asked Oliver.

"At some point late tomorrow afternoon, you will invite her to see the painting on Wednesday at six p.m. You will also ask her for the number of her mobile phone. She will no doubt refuse to give it to you."

"And when she arrives at my gallery on Wednesday evening?"

"She won't."

"Why not?"

"Because you're going to call her Wednesday afternoon and reschedule the appointment for eight p.m. on Thursday."

"Why would I do that?"

"To let her know that she is the furthest thing from your mind."

"If only it were true," said Oliver. "But why so late?"

"I don't want Cordelia Blake to be around when you show her the painting." Gabriel lowered his voice. "It might spoil the mood."

"Is she really interested in buying it?"

"Not at all. She just wants to have a look at it before it disappears."

"And if she likes what she sees?"

"After examining the provenance, she will ask you to reveal the identity of the man who sold it to you. You, of course, will refuse, leaving her no choice but to extract the information by some other means."

"Music to my ears."

"It's possible she might try to seduce you," said Gabriel. "But don't be disappointed if she threatens to destroy you instead."

"I can assure you, she won't be the first."

Gabriel tapped a few keys on the laptop. "I just added a new name to your contacts. Alessandro Calvi. Mobile phone number only."

"Who is he?"

"My front man in Florence. Call him at that number in the Spanish woman's presence. Signore Calvi will take care of the rest."

———

The front man, whose real name was Luca Rossetti, left Florence at ten o'clock the following morning and headed south on the E35 Autostrada. The car beneath him was a Maserati Quattroporte sedan. Like the Patek Philippe timepiece on his wrist, it was the property of the Arma dei Carabinieri, Rossetti's employer.

He arrived at his destination, Rome's Fiumicino Airport, at half past one. Another hour elapsed before Gabriel finally emerged from the door of Terminal 3. He tossed his overnight bag in the trunk and dropped into the passenger seat.

"I was starting to get worried about you," said Rossetti as he accelerated away from the curb.

"I spent almost as much time trying to get through passport control as I did flying from London." Gabriel looked around the interior of the luxury automobile. "Nice sled."

"It belonged to a heroin trafficker from the Camorra."

"A childhood friend of yours?"

"I knew his younger brother. They're both down in Palermo now, in Pagliarelli Prison."

Rossetti turned onto the A90, Rome's high-speed orbital motorway, and headed north. He took his eyes off the road long enough to glance at the surveillance photograph that Gabriel had placed in his hand.

"What's her name?"

"According to her passport and credit cards, it's Magdalena Navarro. She made a move on Oliver Dimbleby last night."

"How did he hold up?"

"As well as could be expected." Gabriel reclaimed the photograph. "You're next."

"When?"

"Thursday night. A quick phone call only. I want you to give her a time and a place and then hang up before she can ask any questions."

"What's the time?"

"Nine p.m. on Friday."

"And the place?"

"Beneath the *arcone* in the Piazza della Repubblica. You won't have any difficulty spotting her." Gabriel slipped the photograph into his briefcase. "What year did he go to England?"

"Who?"

"Orazio Gentileschi."

"He traveled from Paris to Rome in 1626."

"Was Artemisia with him?"

"No. Only his three sons."

"When did he return to Italy?"

"He never did. He died in London in 1639."

"Where is he buried?"

Rossetti hesitated.

"The Queen's Chapel of Somerset House." Gabriel frowned. "Does this sled of yours go any faster? I'd like to get to Umbria while it's still light."

Rossetti put his foot to the floor.

"Better," said Gabriel. "You're a criminal now, Signore Calvi. Don't drive like a cop."

43

Villa dei Fiori

The Villa dei Fiori, a thousand-acre estate located between the Tiber and Nera Rivers, had been in the possession of the Gasparri family since the days when Umbria was still ruled by the popes. There was a large and lucrative cattle operation, an equestrian center that bred some of the finest jumpers in all of Italy, and a flock of playful goats kept solely for entertainment value. Its olive groves produced some of Umbria's best oil, and its small vineyard contributed several hundred kilos of grapes each year to the local cooperative. Sunflowers shone in its fields.

The villa itself stood at the end of a dusty drive shaded by towering umbrella pine. In the eleventh century, it had been a monastery. There was still a small chapel and, in the walled interior courtyard, the remains of an oven where the brothers had baked their daily bread. At the base of the house was a large blue swimming pool, and adjacent to the pool was a trellised garden where rosemary and lavender grew along walls of Etruscan stone.

The current Count Gasparri, a faded Roman nobleman with close ties to the Holy See, did not rent Villa dei Fiori or allow friends and relatives to borrow it. Indeed, the last unaccompanied guests of the property had been the morose art restorer from the Vatican Museums and his beautiful Venetian-born wife, an experience the four-member staff would not soon forget. They were surprised, then, to learn that Count Gasparri had agreed to lend the villa to an un-named acquaintance for a stay of indeterminate length. Yes, said the count, it was likely his unnamed acquaintance would have guests of his own. No, he would not require the services of the household staff, as he was intensely private by nature and wished not to be disturbed.

Accordingly, two members of the staff—Anna the fabled cook, and Margherita the temperamental housekeeper—departed Villa dei Fiori early on Tuesday morning for a brief and unexpected holiday. Two other employees, however, remained at their posts: Isabella, the ethereal half Swede who ran the equestrian center; and Carlos, the Argentinian cowboy who cared for the cattle and the crops. Both took note of the unmarked blue-black Fiat Ducato van that came bumping up the drive shortly before noon. The two occupants un-loaded their cargo with the swiftness of thieves stashing stolen loot. The plunder included two large metal crates of the sort used by tour-ing rock musicians, provisions enough to feed a small army, and, curi-ously, a professional-grade studio easel and a large blank canvas.

No, thought Isabella. It wasn't possible. Not after all these years.

The van soon departed, and a tense calm returned to the villa. It was shattered at 3:42 p.m. by the appalling roar of a Maserati engine. A moment later the car streaked past the equestrian center in a cloud of powdery dust. Even so, Isabella managed to catch a brief glimpse of the passenger. His most distinguishing feature was the swath of gray hair—like a smudge of ash—at his right temple.

It was a coincidence, Isabella assured herself. It couldn't possibly be the same man.

The Maserati's engine note faded to a dull drone as the sedan sped toward the villa through the twin rows of umbrella pine. It stopped outside the walls of the ancient courtyard, and the man with gray temples emerged. Medium height, noted Isabella with mounting dread. Slender as a cyclist.

He collected an overnight bag from the backseat and spoke a few parting words to the driver. Then he slung the bag over his shoulder—like a soldier, thought Isabella—and walked a few paces across the drive toward the gate of the courtyard. The same forward slump to the shoulders. The same slight outward bend to the legs.

"Dear God," whispered Isabella as the Maserati shot past her in a blur. It was true, after all.

The restorer had returned to Villa dei Fiori.

———

Next morning he settled into his familiar routine. He led himself on a forced march around the property. He went for a vigorous swim in the pool. He leafed through a book about the Flemish Baroque painter Anthony van Dyck while sitting in the shade of the trellised garden. Carlos and Isabella watched over him from afar. His mood, they observed, was much improved. It was as though a great burden had been lifted from his shoulders. Carlos declared that he was a changed man, but Isabella went even further. He was not a changed man, she said. He was a new man entirely.

His work habits, however, were as disciplined as ever. Wednesday's labors before the easel began after a spartan lunch and continued late into the night. In his previous incarnation, he had listened to music while he worked. But now he seemed to be engrossed in a dreadful play on the radio, something that sounded like the output of a butt-dialed mobile phone. The program featured a roguishly charming London art dealer called Oliver and his plucky assistant, Cordelia. Of that much, at least, Isabella was certain. The rest of it was a disjointed hodgepodge of traffic noise, toilet flushes, one-sided phone calls, and bursts of barroom laughter.

The episode that aired Thursday morning featured a conversation between Oliver and Cordelia over a seemingly trivial scheduling matter—a visit to the gallery by a woman called Magdalena Navarro. At the conclusion of the program, the restorer set off on a punishing hike around the estate. And Isabella, in contravention of Count Gasparri's strict instructions, set off toward the now undefended villa. She entered through the kitchen and made her way to the great room, which the restorer had once again converted into an artist's atelier.

The canvas rested on the easel, shimmering with a recent application of oil-based paint. It was a three-quarter-length portrait of a woman wearing a gown of gold silk trimmed in white lace. Isabella, who had studied art history before devoting her life to horses, recognized the style as Van Dyck's. The woman's face was not yet complete, only her hair, which was almost black. Lampblack, thought Isabella, with a magnificent sheen of lead white with touches of lapis lazuli and vermilion.

His pigments and oils were arrayed on a nearby table. Isabella knew better than to touch anything, as he left behind hidden telltales to alert him to intruders. His Winsor & Newton Series 7 sable-hair brush lay on his palette. Like the painting, it was damp. Next to it was a slumbering laptop. The device was connected to a pair of Bose speakers. Better to hear the travails of Oliver and Cordelia, thought Isabella.

She turned to the unfinished painting once more. He had made a remarkable amount of progress in so short a time. But why was he *painting* a painting and not restoring one? And where was his model? The answer, thought Isabella, was that he had no need of one. She remembered the remarkable painting that had flowed from his hand after he had suffered the terrible injury to his eye—*Two Children on a Beach*, in the style of Mary Cassatt. He had finished it in a handful of marathon sessions, with only his memory to guide him.

"What do you think of it so far?" he asked calmly.

Isabella swung round and laid a hand over her heart. Somehow she managed not to scream.

He took a step forward. "What are you doing in here?"

"Count Gasparri asked me to check on you."

"In that case, why did you come when you knew I was out?" He contemplated his pigments and oils. "You didn't touch anything, did you?"

"Of course not. I was just wondering what you were working on."

"Is that all? Or were you also wondering why I returned to this place after all these years?"

"That, too," Isabella conceded.

He took another step forward. "Do you know who I am?"

"Until a moment ago, I thought you were an art restorer who sometimes worked at the Vatican Museums."

"And you no longer believe that to be the case?"

"No," she said after a moment. "I do not."

A silence fell between them.

"Forgive me," said Isabella, and started toward the door.

"Wait," he called out.

She stopped and turned slowly to face him. The greenness of his eyes was unsettling. "Yes, Signore Allon?"

"You never told me what you thought of the painting."

"It's quite extraordinary. But who is she?"

"I'm not sure yet."

"When will you know?"

"Soon, I hope." He took up his palette and brush, and opened the laptop.

"What's it called?" asked Isabella.

"*Portrait of an Unknown Woman.*"

"Not the painting. The program about Oliver and Cordelia."

He looked up suddenly.

"You've been playing it quite loudly. The sound carries well in the countryside."

"I hope it didn't disturb you."

"Not at all," said Isabella, and turned to go.

"Your phone," he said suddenly.

She stopped. "What about it?"

"Please leave it behind. And bring me your laptop and the keys to your car. Tell Carlos to bring me his devices as well. No phone calls or emails until further notice. And no leaving the estate."

Isabella switched off her phone and laid it on the table, next to the open laptop. As she slipped from the villa, she heard roguish Oliver tell someone named Nicky that his client would have to increase his offer to £30 million if he wanted the Veronese. Nicky called Oliver a thief, then asked whether he was free for a drink that evening. Oliver said he wasn't.

"What's her name?"

"Magdalena Navarro."

"Spanish?"

"I'm afraid so."

"What does she look like?"

"A bit like Penélope Cruz, but prettier."

44

Dimbleby Fine Arts

It was Sarah Bancroft, from a table at Franco's Italian restaurant in Jermyn Street, who spotted her first—the tall, slender woman with almost black hair, dressed in a shortish skirt and a formfitting white top. She rounded the corner into Bury Street and instantly caught the attention of Simon Mendenhall, who was leaving Christie's after an interminable senior staff meeting. Simon being Simon, he paused to have a look at the woman's backside and was aghast to see her make a beeline for Dimbleby Fine Arts. Simon in turn made a beeline for Wiltons and informed all those present, including the dealer of contemporary art with whom he was rumored to be having a torrid affair, that Oliver's hot streak continued unabated.

At eight o'clock precisely, the raven-haired woman rang the gallery's bell. Oliver waited until she rang it a second time before rising from his Eames desk chair and unlocking the door. Stepping across the threshold, she pressed her lips suggestively against his cheek. During their weeklong game of cat and mouse, Oliver had sidestepped two offers of dinner and a thinly veiled sexual proposition. Only heaven knew what the next few minutes might bring.

He closed the door and locked it tightly. "Would you like a drink?"

"I'd love one."

"Whisky or whisky?"

"Whisky would be perfect."

Oliver led her through the half-light to his office and filled two tumblers with scotch.

"Blue Label," she remarked.

"I keep it for special occasions."

"What are we celebrating?"

"The impending record-shattering sale of *Susanna in the Bath* by Paolo Veronese."

"Where does the bidding stand?"

"As of this evening, I have two firm offers of thirty."

"Museums?"

"One museum," answered Oliver. "One private."

"I have a feeling that both of your bidders are going to be disappointed."

"The museum's offer is final. The collector made a killing during the pandemic and has money to burn."

"So does my client. He's anxious to hear from me."

"Then perhaps we shouldn't keep your client waiting any longer."

They carried their drinks to the gallery's rear exhibition room. The large painting was propped on a pair of baize-covered display easels. The tableau was only faintly visible in the semidarkness.

Oliver reached for the dimmer switch. As Susanna and the two elders emerged from the gloom, the woman raised a hand to her mouth and murmured something in Spanish.

"Translation?" asked Oliver.

"It wouldn't survive." She approached the painting slowly, as though trying not to disturb the three figures. "It's no wonder you have the entire art world at your feet, Mr. Dimbleby. It's a masterwork painted by an artist at the height of his powers."

"I believe those were the very words I used to describe it in the press release."

"Were they?" She reached into her handbag.

"No photographs, please."

She produced a small ultraviolet torch. "Would you mind switching off the lights for a moment?"

Oliver reached for the dimmer again and returned the room to darkness. The woman played the purple-blue beam of the torch over the surface of the painting.

"The losses are rather extensive."

"The *losses*," replied Oliver, "are exactly what one would expect to find in a four-hundred-and-fifty-year-old Venetian School painting."

"Who handled the restoration for you?"

"It came to me in this condition."

"How fortunate," she said, and switched off the ultraviolet torch.

Oliver allowed the darkness to linger for a moment before slowly bringing up the room lights. The woman was now holding a rectangular LED magnifier. She used it to examine the exposed flesh of Susanna's neck and shoulder, followed by the vermilion-colored robe she was clutching to her breasts.

"The brushwork is quite visible," she said. "Not only in the garments but the skin as well."

"Veronese became more overtly painterly in his brushwork later in his career," explained Oliver. "This work reflects the change from his earlier style."

She returned the magnifier to her handbag and stepped away from the painting. A minute passed. Then another.

Oliver cleared his throat gently.

"I heard that," she said.

"I don't mean to rush things, but it's rather late."

"Do you have a moment to show me the provenance?"

Oliver ushered the woman back to his office. There he drew a copy of the provenance from a locked file drawer and laid it on the desk. The woman reviewed it with justifiable skepticism.

"An old European collection?"

"Very old," replied Oliver. "And very private."

The woman pushed the provenance across the desktop. "I must know the identity of the previous owner, Mr. Dimbleby."

"The previous owner, like your client, insists on anonymity."

"Are you in direct contact with him?"

"Her," said Oliver. "And the answer is no. I deal with her representative."

"A lawyer? A dealer?"

"I'm sorry, but I can't reveal the representative's name or characterize his connection to the collection. Especially to a competitor." Oliver lowered his voice. "Even one as attractive as you."

She gave him a coquettish pout. "Is there really nothing I can do to change your mind?"

"I'm afraid not."

The woman sighed. "And if I were to offer you, say, thirty-five million pounds for your Veronese?"

"My answer would be the same."

She tapped the provenance with the tip of her forefinger. "Are none of your other potential buyers concerned about the flimsiness of the painting's chain of ownership?"

"Not at all."

"How can that be?"

"Because it doesn't matter where the painting came from. The work speaks for itself."

"It certainly spoke to me. In fact, it was rather talkative."

"And what did it say?"

She leaned forward across the desk and looked directly into his eyes. "It said that Paolo Veronese didn't paint it."

"Nonsense."

"Is it, Mr. Dimbleby?"

"I have spent the last four days showing that painting to the leading Old Master experts from the world's most respected museums. And not one of them has questioned the authenticity of the work."

"That's because none of those experts know about the man who visited Galerie Konrad Hassler in Berlin a few days after you announced the rediscovery of your so-called Veronese. This man showed Herr Hassler a photograph of the so-called Veronese side by side with the so-called Titian and the so-called Tintoretto. The photograph was taken in the studio of the art forger who painted them."

"That's not possible."

"I'm afraid it is."

"He assured me that the paintings were genuine."

"Signore Rinaldi?"

"Never heard of him," swore Oliver, truthfully.

"That's the name he used when he visited Galerie Hassler. Giovanni Rinaldi."

"I know him by a different name."

"And what name is that?"

Oliver made no reply.

"He deceived you, Mr. Dimbleby. Or perhaps you simply wanted to be deceived. Whatever the case, you are now in a very precarious situation. But don't worry, it will be our little secret." She paused. "For a small fee, of course."

"How small?"

"Half of the final sales price of the Veronese."

Oliver uncharacteristically chose the high road. "I couldn't possibly sell the picture after what you've told me."

"If you withdraw the painting now, you will be forced to return the millions of pounds you accepted for the Titian and the Tintoretto. And then ..."

"I'll be ruined."

She handed Oliver a sheet of stationery from the Lanesborough. "I would like you to wire fifteen million pounds into that account first thing tomorrow morning. If the money doesn't appear by the close of business, I will telephone that reporter from the *New York Times* and tell her the truth about your so-called Veronese."

"You're a cheap blackmailer."

"And you, Mr. Dimbleby, don't know as much about the art world as you think you do."

He looked down at the account number. "You will receive the money *after* the sale of my Veronese. Which, I might add, is a genuine Veronese and not a fake."

"I insist on immediate payment."

"You can't have it."

"In that case," said the woman, "I will require a security deposit."

"How much?"

"Not money, Mr. Dimbleby. A name."

Oliver hesitated, then said, "Alessandro Calvi."

"And where does Signore Calvi live?"

"Florence."

"Please call Signore Calvi from your mobile phone. I'd like to have a word with him."

———

It was half past eight when Oliver showed her into Bury Street. She offered him a hand in farewell. And when he refused it, she placed her mouth close to his ear and warned him of the professional humiliation he would suffer if he failed to send her the money as promised.

"Dinner at the Lanesborough?" he asked as she set off toward Jermyn Street.

"Some other time," she said over her shoulder, and was gone.

Inside the gallery, Oliver returned to his office. The scent of orange blossom and jasmine hung in the air. On the desk were two unfinished glasses of Johnnie Walker Blue Label whisky, a fictitious provenance for a fake painting by Paolo Veronese, and a sheet of stationery from the Lanesborough Hotel. Oliver returned the provenance to the file drawer. The sheet of stationery he photographed with his phone.

It rang a moment later. "Bravo!" said the voice at the other end of the connection. "I couldn't have done it better myself."

45

Firenze

General Ferrari arrived at Villa dei Fiori at two the following afternoon. He was accompanied by four tactical officers and two technicians. The tactical officers conducted a site survey of the villa and the grounds while the techs turned the dining room into an op center. The general, in a business suit and open-necked dress shirt, sat in the great room with Gabriel and watched him paint.

"Your girl arrived in Florence shortly before noon."

"How did she manage that?"

"A chartered Dassault Falcon from London City Airport. The Four Seasons sent a car for her. She's there now."

"Doing what?"

"Our surveillance capabilities inside the hotel are limited. But we'll keep an eye on her if she decides to do a bit of sightseeing. And we'll definitely have a couple of teams in the Piazza della Repubblica at nine o'clock."

"If she spots them, we're dead."

"This might come as a surprise to you, my friend, but the Arma dei Carabinieri has done this a time or two. Without your help," the general added. "The minute she purchases that painting, we'll have the grounds to arrest her on numerous art fraud and conspiracy charges. She will be staring down the barrel of a very long sentence in an Italian prison for women. Not a pleasant prospect for a frequent guest of the Lanesborough Hotel in London."

"I don't want her in a prison cell," said Gabriel. "I want her on the opposite side of an interrogation table, telling us everything she knows."

"As do I. But I am obligated under Italian law to provide her with an attorney if she desires one. If I do not, anything she says will be inadmissible at trial."

"What does Italian law say about art restorers taking part in interrogations?"

"Not surprisingly, Italian law is silent on that question. If, however, she were to consent to the restorer's presence, it might be permissible."

Gabriel stepped away from the canvas and appraised his work. "Perhaps the portrait will influence her thinking."

"I wouldn't count on it. In fact, it might be a good idea to put her in handcuffs before you let her see it."

"Please don't," said Gabriel as he loaded his brush. "I wouldn't want to spoil the surprise."

———

She spent the afternoon at the pool and at 6:00 p.m. headed upstairs to her suite to shower and dress. She chose her clothing with care. Pale blue stretch jeans. A loose-fitting white blouse. Flat-soled suede moccasins. Her face was aglow from the Tuscan sun and required little makeup. Her raven hair she wound into a bun, with a few stray tendrils along her neck. Attractive, she thought as she evaluated her appearance in the mirror, but serious. There would be no flirtation tonight. No fun and games of the sort she had played with the art dealer in London. The man she was meeting in the Piazza della Repubblica could not be seduced or tricked into doing her bidding. She had seen a video of his visit to Galerie Hassler in Berlin. He was young, good-looking, athletically built. A dangerous man, she reckoned. A professional.

Downstairs, she crossed the lobby and stepped through the hotel's unassuming entrance into the Borgo Pinti. The midday crowds had retreated from the city, as had the heat. She stopped for a coffee at Caffè Michelangelo, then walked through the cool twilight to the Piazza della Repubblica. Its dominant architectural feature was the towering triumphal arch on the western flank. She arrived there, as instructed, at nine o'clock exactly. The Piaggio motor scooter drew alongside her a minute later.

She recognized the man at the helm.

Young, good-looking, athletically built.

Wordlessly he moved to the back of the saddle. Magdalena mounted the bike and asked for a destination.

"The Lungarno Torrigiani. It's on the—"

"I know where it is," she said, and executed a flawless U-turn in the narrow street. As she sped toward the river, his strong hands moved over the small of her back, her hips, her crotch, the inside of her thighs, her breasts. There was nothing sexual in his touch. He was merely searching her for a concealed weapon.

He was a professional, she thought. Fortunately, she was a professional, too.

———

The call arrived at Villa dei Fiori at 9:03 p.m. It was from one of the Carabinieri surveillance artists in the Piazza della Repubblica. The woman had appeared at the rendezvous point as instructed. She and Rossetti were now bound for the apartment. General Ferrari quickly relayed the information to Gabriel, who was still at his easel. He carefully wiped the paint from his brush and headed to the make-shift op center to watch the next act. The Oliver Dimbleby show had been a smashing success. Now it was Alessandro Calvi's turn in the spotlight. One mistake, thought Gabriel, and they were dead.

46

Lungarno Torrigiani

The building was the color of burnt sienna, with a balustrade running along the length of the second floor. The apartment was on the third. In the darkened entrance hall, Rossetti relieved the woman of her Hermès Birkin handbag and emptied the contents onto the kitchen counter. Her possessions included an ultraviolet torch, a professional-grade LED magnifier, and a disposable Samsung phone. The device was powered off. The SIM card had been removed.

Rossetti opened her passport. "Is your name really Magdalena Navarro?"

"Is yours really Alessandro Calvi?"

He unsnapped her Cartier wallet and checked the credit cards and the Spanish driver's permit. All bore the name Magdalena Navarro. The cash compartment contained about three thousand euros and a hundred unspent British pounds. In the zippered compartment Rossetti found a few receipts, all from her visit to London. Otherwise, the wallet and bag were unusually free of pocket litter.

He returned her belongings to the bag, leaving a single item on the counter. It was a photograph of *Danaë and the Shower of Gold* by Gabriel Allon. "Where did you get this?" he asked.

"I happened to be in Berlin not long ago and had lunch with an old friend. He told me an interesting story about a recent visitor to his art gallery. Evidently, this visitor tried to sell my friend the painting in that photograph. He said it came from the same private collection as the pictures that have caused such a sensation in London. He showed my friend a photograph of those paintings as well. Three paintings, one photo. My friend found that odd, to say the least."

"The photograph was taken by my restorer."

"In my experience, art restorers make the best forgers. Wouldn't you agree?"

"That sounds like a question a cop would ask."

"I'm not a police officer, Signore Calvi. I am an art broker who connects buyers and sellers and lives off the scraps."

"Lives quite well, from what I hear."

He led her into the apartment's large sitting room. Three tall casement windows, open to the evening air, overlooked the domes and campanili of Florence. The woman, however, had eyes only for the paintings hanging on the walls.

"You have extraordinary taste."

"The apartment doubles as my saleroom."

She pointed out an exquisite terra-cotta Etruscan amphora. "You also deal in antiquities, I see."

"It's a major part of my business. Chinese billionaires love Greek and Etruscan pottery."

She trailed a forefinger along the curve of the vessel. "This piece is quite lovely. But tell me something, Signore Calvi. Is it a forgery like those three paintings you sold to Mr. Dimbleby? Or is it merely looted?"

"The paintings I sold to Dimbleby were examined by the most prominent Italian Old Master experts in London. And no one questioned the attribution."

"That's because your forger is the world's greatest living Old Master painter."

"There's no such thing as a *living* Old Master."

"Of course there is. I should know. You see, I work for one. He, too, can fool the experts. But your forger is far more talented than mine. That Veronese is a masterpiece. I nearly fainted when I saw it."

"I thought you said you were a broker."

"I *am* a broker. But the paintings I represent simply happen to be forgeries."

"So you're a front man? Is that what you're saying?"

"*You* are a front man, Signore Calvi. As you well know, I am in fact a woman."

"Why are you in Florence?"

"Because I'd like to make you and your forger an offer."

"What sort of offer?"

"Show me the Gentileschi," said the woman. "And then I'll explain everything."

———

Rossetti led her into the adjoining room and switched on the lights. She stared at the painting in silence, as though she had been struck mute.

"Shall I bring you the magnifier and ultraviolet torch?" asked Rossetti after a moment.

"That won't be necessary. The painting is . . ."

"Incandescent?"

"Incendiary," whispered the woman. "But also quite dangerous."

"Is that so?"

"Oliver Dimbleby behaved recklessly by bringing those three pictures to market from your so-called old European collection. Already there are whispers in certain corners of the art world that the paintings might be forgeries. And then you compounded the mistake with your conduct at Galerie Hassler. It is only a matter of time before your ruse unravels. And when it does, there will be collateral casualties."

"You?"

She nodded. "The market for museum-quality Old Masters is a small one, Signore Calvi. There are only so many good pictures and so many collectors and museums who are willing to pay millions for them. Two major Old Master forgery rings cannot compete against one another and survive. One will inevitably collapse. And it will take the other one down with it."

"What's the alternative?"

"I am prepared to offer you and your partner the protection of a proven distribution network, one that will guarantee a steady stream of income for many years to come."

"I don't need your network."

"Your behavior in Berlin would suggest otherwise. The painting in the next room is worth thirty million if handled properly. And yet you were willing to let Herr Hassler have it for a mere two million."

"And if I were to entrust it to you?"

"I would sell it in a way that favors long-term security over short-term financial gain."

"I didn't hear a price."

"Five million," said the woman. "But I would insist on meeting with your forger in his studio before payment."

"Ten million," countered Rossetti. "And you will wire the money into my account before meeting with my forger."

"When would such a meeting take place?"

Rossetti pondered his Patek Phillipe wristwatch. "Shortly after midnight, I imagine. Provided, of course, that you have more than three thousand euros hidden in that Cartier wallet of yours."

"Where do you do your banking, Signore Calvi?"

"Banca Monte dei Paschi di Siena."

"I need the account and routing numbers."

"I'll bring you your phone."

———

She entered the number manually and from memory. The first time she dialed, she received no answer and rang off without leaving a message. The second attempt met with the same result. Call number three, however, found its intended target.

She addressed the person at the other end of the call in excellent English. There was no exchange of pleasantries, only the swift execution of a wire transfer of €10 million to an account at the world's oldest bank. Email confirmation arrived a few minutes after the call was concluded. With her thumb concealing the sender's name, she showed it to Rossetti. Then she carried the phone to the nearest window and hurled it into the black waters of the Arno.

"Where are we going?" she asked.

"A little town in southern Umbria."

"Not by motor scooter, I hope."

The Maserati was parked outside the building. Rossetti behaved himself in town but let it rip when they hit the Autostrada. He waited until they reached Orvieto before informing his forger—with a phone call placed in speaker mode on the car's Bluetooth system— that he was coming to see him on an important matter. His forger expressed disappointment at the intrusion on his privacy, as he was hoping to complete a painting that evening.

"Can't it wait until morning?"

"I'm afraid not. Besides, I have some good news."

"Speaking of news, have you seen the *Times*? Oliver Dimbleby announced that he sold the Veronese to a private collector. Thirty-five million. At least that's the rumor."

And with that, the call went dead.

"He doesn't sound pleased," said the Spanish woman.

"With good reason."

"It wasn't a consignment deal?"

"Straight sale."

"How much did Dimbleby pay you for it?"

"Three million."

"And the new painting?" asked the woman.

"It's a Van Dyck."

"Really? What's the subject matter?"

"I wouldn't want to spoil the surprise," said Rossetti, and put his foot to the floor.

––––––––––

Shortly before midnight Isabella was awakened from a pleasant dream by the frenzied barking of the dogs. Usually, the culprit was one of the wild boars that dwelled in the surrounding woods. But on that evening the source of the commotion was the two men traipsing across the moonlit pasture. They were part of a large all-male party of guests who had arrived that afternoon. Isabella was of the opinion that the *guests* were not guests at all, but were in fact police officers. How else to explain the fact that two of them were now strolling the pasture by moonlight, each armed with a compact submachine gun?

Eventually the dogs fell silent, and Isabella returned to her bed, only to be awakened a second time, at 12:37 a.m. Now the culprit was the wretched Maserati sports car. The same car, she thought, that had delivered the restorer to Villa dei Fiori earlier that week. It shot past her bedroom window in a blur and raced up the tree-lined drive toward the villa. Two figures emerged into the moonlit forecourt. One was an athletically built man, perhaps another police officer. The other was a tall, raven-haired woman.

It was the woman who entered the villa first, with the man a step behind. The shrieking began a few seconds later, a terrible anguished wailing, like the cry of a wounded animal. Surely it had something to do with the painting. *Portrait of an Unknown Woman* . . . Perhaps she had been mistaken, thought Isabella as she covered her ears. Perhaps Signore Allon was the same man after all.

PART THREE

———

Pentimento

47

Villa dei Fiori

She did not surrender without a fight, but then they had not expected she would. Luca Rossetti attempted to subdue her first and was soon the target of a ferocious counterattack, leaving Gabriel no choice but to abandon his defense of the painting and come to his newfound friend's aid. He was joined a few seconds later by two of the tactical officers, who burst into the room with guns drawn like characters in a French farce. Next the techs entered the fray, and Gabriel wisely withdrew to safer ground to observe the end stages of the contest. It was Rossetti, with blood flowing from one nostril, who applied the handcuffs. Gabriel found the metallic crunch of the locking mechanism to be a most satisfying sound.

Only then did General Ferrari step unhurriedly onto the stage. After determining to his satisfaction that the suspect had not been injured, he commenced a review of the evidence against her. It included a €10 million wire transfer to the Banca Monte dei Paschi di Siena as well as the suspect's admission, preserved on video, that she was a key player in an international forgery network. At present, the Carabinieri were attempting to determine the origin of the payment. They were likewise working to identify the last three phone numbers dialed from the disposable Samsung now lying on the bottom of the Arno River. Neither task, said the general, would prove difficult.

But even without the information, he continued, there was sufficient evidence under Italian law to hand the suspect over to a magistrate for an immediate trial. Because she had been caught in flagrante delicto engaging in art fraud and related financial crimes, the outcome of such a proceeding would not be in doubt. She would likely receive a lengthy sentence in one of Italy's prisons for women, which, regrettably, were among Western Europe's worst.

"Upon your release, you will be extradited to France, where you will undoubtedly face charges for your role in the murders of Valerie Bérrangar, Georges Fleury, and Bruno Gilbert. I'm sure Spanish prosecutors will think of something with which to charge you as well. Suffice it to say, you will be an elderly pensioner by the time you are a free woman again. Unless, of course, you accept the lifeline that I am about to offer you."

Under the terms of the deal, the suspect would receive no prison time for her offenses related to the evening's sting operation in Florence. In exchange, she would provide the Carabinieri with the names of the other members of her network, a complete inventory of the forgeries now in circulation, and, of course, the identity of the forger himself. Any attempt at evasion or deception on the suspect's part would result in the withdrawal of the agreement and immediate incarceration. A second offer of immunity would be unlikely.

They had expected a declaration of innocence, but she made none. Nor did she request a lawyer or demand that General Ferrari put his cooperation agreement in writing. Instead, she looked at Gabriel and posed a single question.

"How did you find me, Mr. Allon?"

"I painted four pictures," he replied. "And you walked straight into my arms."

At which point the mêlée resumed. Capitano Luca Rossetti was the only casualty.

————————

She began by clearing up any lingering questions as to the authenticity of her identity. Yes, she assured them, her name was in fact Magdalena Navarro. And, yes, she had been born and raised in the Andalusian city of Seville. Her father was a dealer of Spanish Old Master paintings and antique furniture. His gallery was located near the Plaza Virgen de los Reyes, a few paces from the entrance of the Doña Maria Hotel. It catered to Seville's wealthiest inhabitants, those of noble birth and inherited wealth. The Navarro clan were not members of that rarefied social stratum, but the gallery had given Magdalena a glimpse of the life led by those for whom money was of no concern.

The gallery had also instilled in her a love of art—Spanish art, in particular. She revered Diego Velázquez and Francisco de Goya, but Picasso was her obsession. She imitated his drawings as a young child and at the age of twelve produced a near-perfect copy of *Two Girls Reading*. She began her formal training soon after, at a private art school in Seville, and upon completing her secondary education she entered the Barcelona Academy of Art. Much to the dismay of her classmates, she sold her first canvases while still a student. An important writer from a Barcelona culture magazine predicted that one day Magdalena Navarro would be Spain's most famous female painter.

"When I graduated in 2004, two prominent art galleries offered to show my work. One was in Barcelona, the other in Madrid. Needless to say, they were quite surprised when I turned them down."

They had placed her in a straight-backed chair in the great room's main seating area. Her feet were flat upon the terra-cotta tiles of the floor; her hands were cuffed behind her back. General Ferrari was seated directly opposite, with Rossetti at his side and a tripod-mounted video camera over his shoulder. Gabriel was contemplating the L-shaped tear, 15 by 23 centimeters, in the lower left corner of *Portrait of an Unknown Woman*.

"Why would you do that?" he asked.

"Turn down a chance to show my work at the tender age of twenty-one? Because I had no interest in being the most famous female artist in Spain."

"Spain was too small for a talent like yours?"

"I thought so at the time."

"Where did you go?"

She arrived in New York in the autumn of 2005 and settled into a one-room apartment on Avenue C, in the Alphabet City section of Lower Manhattan. The apartment was soon filled with newly completed paintings, none of which she was able to sell. The money she had brought with her from Spain quickly ran out. Her father sent what he could, but it was never enough.

A year after her arrival in New York, she could no longer afford painting supplies and was facing eviction. She found work waiting tables at El Pote Español in Murray Hill and at Katz's Delicatessen on East Houston Street. Before long she was working sixty hours a week, which left her too exhausted to paint.

Depressed, she started drinking too much and discovered she had a taste for cocaine. She fell into a relationship with her dealer, a handsome Dominican of Spanish descent named Hector Martínez, and was soon acting as a courier and delivery girl in his network. Many of her regular customers were Wall Street traders who were making fortunes selling derivatives and mortgage-backed securities, the complex investment instruments that in three years' time would leave the global economy on the brink of collapse.

"And then, of course, there were the rock musicians, screenwriters, Broadway producers, painters, sculptors, and gallery owners. As strange as it might sound, being a cocaine dealer in New York was a good career move. Anyone who was anyone was using. And everyone knew my name."

The money she earned dealing drugs allowed Magdalena to stop waiting tables and resume painting. She gave one of her canvases to a Chelsea art dealer with a thousand-dollar-a-week cocaine habit. Rather than keep the painting for himself, the dealer sold it to a client for $50,000. He gave half of the proceeds to Magdalena, but refused to divulge the buyer's name.

"Did he tell you why?" asked Gabriel.

"He said the client insisted on anonymity. But he was also concerned I would cut him out of the picture."

"Why would he suspect a thing like that?"

"I was the daughter of an art dealer. I knew how the business worked."

The Chelsea art dealer bought two more canvases from Magdalena and immediately sold both works to the same anonymous client. The dealer then informed Magdalena that the anonymous client was a wealthy investor who admired her work greatly and was interested in becoming her patron.

"But only if I stopped dealing cocaine."

"I assume you agreed."

"I dropped my pager down a sewer on West Twenty-Fifth Street and never made another delivery."

And her new patron, she continued, lived up to his end of the deal. Indeed, during the summer of 2008, he purchased four additional paintings through the auspices of the same Chelsea gallery. Magdalena earned more than $100,000 from the sales. Fearful of losing her patron's financial support, she made no attempt to discover his identity. But on a frigid morning in mid-December, she was awakened by a phone call from a woman claiming to be her patron's secretary.

"She wanted to know whether I was free for dinner that evening. When I said that I was, she said a limousine would collect me at my apartment at four p.m."

"Why so early?"

"My anonymous patron was planning to take me to Le Cirque. He wanted to make certain that I had something appropriate to wear."

The limousine arrived as promised and delivered Magdalena to Bergdorf Goodman, where a personal shopper named Clarissa selected $20,000 worth of clothing and jewelry, including a gold Cartier wristwatch. Then she escorted Magdalena to the store's exclusive hair salon for a cut and blow-dry.

Le Cirque was located a few blocks away, in the Palace Hotel. Magdalena arrived at eight o'clock and was immediately shown to a table in the center of the iconic dining room. In her mind she had sketched an image of her patron as a well-preserved blazer-wearing septuagenarian from Park Avenue. But the man who awaited her was tall and blond and forty-five at most. Rising, he offered Magdalena his hand and at long last introduced himself.

His name, he said, was Phillip Somerset.

48

Villa dei Fiori

Admittedly, it was the last name in the world that Gabriel had expected to come out of Magdalena Navarro's mouth. An experienced interrogator, he offered no expression of surprise or incredulity. Instead, he turned to General Ferrari and Luca Rossetti, to whom the name meant nothing, and recited a redacted version of Phillip Somerset's curriculum vitae. Former bond trader at Lehman Brothers. Founder and chief executive officer of Masterpiece Art Ventures, an art-based hedge fund that routinely returned profits of 25 percent to its investors. It was clear the general suspected there was more to the story. Nevertheless, he permitted Gabriel to resume questioning the suspect. He began by asking Magdalena to describe her evening at what was once Manhattan's most celebrated restaurant.

"The food was awful. And the decor!" She rolled her beautiful dark eyes.

"What about your dinner date?"

"Our conversation was cordial and businesslike. There was nothing romantic about the evening."

"Why the fancy dress and Cartier watch?"

"They were a demonstration of his power to transform my life. The entire evening was a piece of performance art."

"You were impressed by him?"

"Quite the opposite, actually. I thought he was a cross between Jay Gatsby and Bud Fox. He was pretending to be something he wasn't."

"And what was that?"

"A man of extraordinary wealth and sophistication. A Medici-like patron of the arts."

"But Phillip *was* wealthy."

"Not as wealthy as he claimed to be. And he didn't know the first thing about art. Phillip gravitated toward the art world because that's where the money was."

"Why did he gravitate to you?"

"I was young and beautiful and talented, with an exotic name and Hispanic heritage. He said he was going to turn me into a billion-dollar global brand. He promised to make me rich beyond my wildest dreams."

"Was any of it true?"

"Only the part about making me rich."

Phillip acquired Magdalena's paintings almost as quickly as she could finish them and deposited the money in an account at Masterpiece Art Ventures. The balance soon exceeded $2 million. She left her studio apartment in Alphabet City and settled into a brownstone on West Eleventh Street. Phillip retained ownership of the property but allowed her to live there rent-free. He visited often.

"To see your latest paintings?"

"No," she answered. "To see me."

"You were lovers?"

"Love had very little to do with what took place between us, Mr. Allon. It was a bit like our dinner at Le Cirque."

"Awful?"

"Cordial and businesslike."

Occasionally Phillip took her to a Broadway performance or a gallery opening. But for the most part he kept her hidden from view in the brownstone, where she spent her days painting, like Rumpelstiltskin's daughter at her spinning wheel. He assured her that he was arranging a splashy exhibition of her work, one that would turn her into the hottest artist in New York. But when the promised exhibition never materialized, she accused Phillip of deceiving her.

"How did he react?"

"He took me to a loft in Hell's Kitchen, just off Ninth Avenue."

"What was in the loft?"

"Paintings."

"Were any of them genuine?"

"No," said Magdalena. "Not a single one."

————

They were, however, works of breathtaking beauty and quality, executed by a forger of immense talent and technical skill. He had not copied existing paintings. Instead, he had cleverly imitated the style of an Old Master artist to create a picture that could be passed off as newly rediscovered. All of the canvases, stretchers, and frames were appropriate to their period and school, as were the pigments. Which meant that none of the paintings could ever be exposed as forgeries by a scientific evaluation.

"Did Phillip tell you the forger's name that night?"

"Of course not. Phillip has never told me his name."

"You don't really expect us to believe that, do you?"

"Why would he tell me such a thing? Besides, the forger's name wasn't relevant to what Phillip wanted me to do."

"Which was?"

"Sell the paintings, of course."

"But why you?"

"Why *not* me? I was a trained art historian and a former drug dealer who knew how to walk into a room with a quarter-ounce of cocaine and walk out with the money. I was also the daughter of an art dealer from Seville."

"A perfect point of entry for the European market."

"And a perfect place to take a few forged paintings out for a test drive," she added.

"But why would a wildly successful businessman like Phillip Somerset want to get mixed up in art fraud?"

"You tell me, Mr. Allon."

"Because the businessman wasn't so wildly successful after all."

Magdalena nodded in agreement. "Masterpiece Art Ventures was a bust from the beginning. Even when art prices were soaring, Phillip was never able get the trading formula right. He needed some sure bets to show his investors a profit."

"And you agreed to this scheme?"

"Not at first."

"What changed your mind?"

"Another two million dollars in my account at Masterpiece Art Ventures."

Magdalena returned to Seville a month later and took delivery of the first six paintings from New York. The shipping documents described them as Old Master works of minimal value, all produced by later followers or imitators of the masters themselves. But when Magdalena offered them for sale at her father's gallery, she inflated the attributions to "circle of" or "workshop of," which increased the value of the works substantially. Within a few weeks, all six paintings had been snatched up by her father's wealthy Seville clientele. Magdalena gave him a 10 percent cut of the profits and transferred the rest of the money to Masterpiece Art Ventures through an account in Liechtenstein.

"How much?"

"A million and a half." Magdalena shrugged. "Chump change."

After the initial test run, the paintings began arriving from New York at a steady clip. There were too many to sell through the gallery, so Magdalena established herself as a Madrid-based runner. She sold one of the canvases—a biblical scene purportedly by the Venetian painter Andrea Celesti—to Spain's most prominent Old Master dealer, who in turn sold it to a museum in the American Midwest.

"Where it hangs to this day."

But Phillip soon discovered that it was far easier for Magdalena to simply *sell* the paintings back to Masterpiece Art Ventures—at wildly inflated prices, with no actual money changing hands. He then moved the works in and out of Masterpiece's portfolio through private phantom sales of his own, using an array of corporate shell entities. Each time a painting supposedly changed hands, it increased in value.

"By the end of 2010, Masterpiece Art Ventures claimed to control more than four hundred million dollars' worth of art. But a significant percentage of those paintings were worthless fakes, the value of which had been artificially inflated with fictitious sales."

But Phillip was not content with the scale of the operation, she continued. He wanted to show explosive growth in the value of Masterpiece's portfolio and higher earnings for his investors. Meeting that goal required the introduction of additional paintings to the market. Until then they had limited themselves primarily to middle-tier works, but Phillip was eager to raise the stakes. The current distribution network wouldn't do; he wanted a premier gallery in a major art world hub. Magdalena found such a gallery in Paris, on the rue la Boétie.

"Galerie Georges Fleury."

Magdalena nodded.

"How did you know that Monsieur Fleury would be interested in going into business with you?"

"He acquired a painting from my father once and conveniently forgot to pay for it. Even by the reduced standards of the art world, Monsieur Fleury was an unscrupulous worm."

"How did you play it with him?"

"Straight up."

"He had no qualms about selling forgeries?"

"None whatsoever. But he insisted on subjecting one of our pictures to scientific analysis before agreeing to handle them."

"What did you give him?"

"A Frans Hals portrait. And do you know what Monsieur Fleury did with it?"

"He showed it to the future president of the Louvre. And the future president of the Louvre gave it to the National Center for Research and Restoration, which affirmed its authenticity. And now the forged Frans Hals portrait is part of the Louvre's permanent collection, along with a Gentileschi, a Cranach, and the most delicious little Van der Weyden you've ever laid eyes on."

"Not the outcome Phillip expected. But quite an accomplishment nonetheless."

"How many fakes did the two of you move through Galerie Fleury?"

"Somewhere between two and three hundred."

"How was Fleury compensated?"

"The first sales were consignment deals."

"And after that?"

"Phillip purchased the gallery through an anonymous shell corporation in 2014. For all intents and purposes, Monsieur Fleury was an employee of Masterpiece Art Ventures."

"When did Galerie Hassler in Berlin come under your control?"

"The following year."

"I'm told you have a distribution point in Brussels."

"Galerie Gilles Raymond on the rue de la Concorde."

"Am I missing any?"

"Hong Kong, Tokyo, and Dubai. And all of it flows into the coffers of Masterpiece Art Ventures."

"The greatest scam in the history of the art world," said Gabriel. "And it might well have gone on forever if Phillip hadn't purchased *Portrait of an Unknown Woman* from Isherwood Fine Arts of London."

"It was your friend Sarah Bancroft's fault," said Magdalena. "If she hadn't bragged about the sale to that reporter from *ARTnews*, the Frenchwoman would have never known about it."

Which brought them, at half past two in the morning, to Madame Valerie Bérrangar.

49

Villa dei Fiori

The first time Magdalena heard Valerie Bérrangar's name, she was in her usual suite at the Pierre Hotel in New York. It was a cold and rainy afternoon in mid-March. A frustrated Phillip was lying next to her, annoyed that she had interrupted their lovemaking to take a phone call. It was from Georges Fleury in Paris.

"What were you doing in New York?" asked Gabriel.

"I pop over at least once a month to discuss the sort of things that can't be put in an email or encrypted text."

"Do you and Phillip always end up in bed?"

"That part of our relationship has never changed. Even during his brief infatuation with your friend Sarah Bancroft, Phillip was sleeping with me on the side."

"Does his wife know about the two of you?"

"Lindsay doesn't have a clue. About much of anything."

With General Ferrari's approval, Rossetti had removed the restraints from her wrists. Her long hands were folded atop her right leg, which was crossed over her left. Her dark eyes tracked Gabriel as he slowly paced the perimeter of the room.

"I imagine Monsieur Fleury was rather nervous that afternoon in mid-March," he said.

"Panic stricken. A French policeman named Jacques Ménard had come to the gallery unannounced to question Fleury about *Portrait of an Unknown Woman*. He was afraid the entire house of cards was about to collapse."

"Why did he contact you and not Phillip?"

"I'm in charge of sales and distribution. Phillip owns the galleries, but he keeps the dealers at arm's length. Unless there's a problem, of course."

"Like Valerie Bérrangar?"

"Yes."

"What did Phillip do?"

"He made a phone call."

"To whom?"

"A man who makes his problems go away."

"Does this man have a name?"

"If he does, I'm not aware of it."

"Is he American?"

"I wouldn't know."

"What *do* you know?"

"That he is a former intelligence officer who has a network of skilled professionals at his disposal. They hacked into Madame Bérrangar's mobile phone and laptop, and broke into her villa in Saint-André-du-Bois. That's when they discovered the entry in her desk calendar. And the painting, of course."

"*Portrait of an Unknown Woman*, oil on canvas, one hundred and fifteen by ninety-two centimeters, attributed to a follower of the Flemish Baroque painter Anthony van Dyck."

"It was a dreadful mistake on Fleury's part," said Magdalena. "He should have told me that he had handled the original version of the painting. The truth is, it was so long ago it slipped his mind."

"How did the forger produce his copy?"

"Apparently, he used a photograph he found in an old exhibition catalogue. It was a minor picture produced by a nameless artist working in Van Dyck's style. The forger simply executed a more skillful version of it and, voilà, a lost Van Dyck suddenly reappeared after centuries in hiding."

"At the same Paris gallery where Valerie Bérrangar's husband purchased the original version thirty-four years earlier."

"The scenario wasn't out of the question, but it was suspicious, to say the least. If the French art squad had opened an investigation . . ."

"You would have been arrested. And Phillip Somerset's forgery-and-fraud empire would have unraveled in spectacular fashion."

"With disastrous consequences for the entire art world. Fortunes would have been lost and countless reputations ruined. Emergency measures had to be taken to contain the damage."

"Eliminate Madame Bérrangar," said Gabriel. "And find out what, if anything, she had told Julian Isherwood and his partner, Sarah Bancroft."

"I had nothing to do with the Bérrangar woman's death. It was Phillip who arranged everything."

"A single-car accident on an empty stretch of road." Gabriel paused. "Problem solved."

"Or so it appeared. But less than a week after her death, you and Sarah Bancroft showed up at Phillip's estate on Long Island."

"He told us that he had sold *Portrait of an Unknown Woman*. He also said that a second review of the attribution had determined that the painting was in fact a genuine Van Dyck."

"Neither of which was true."

"But why did he purchase his own forgery in the first place?"

"I explained that to you earlier."

"Explain it again."

"First of all," said Magdalena, "Masterpiece Art Ventures didn't actually pay six and a half million pounds for *Portrait of an Unknown Woman.*"

"Because Isherwood Fine Arts unwittingly purchased it from Masterpiece Art Ventures for three million euros."

"Correct."

"Nevertheless, Phillip handed over a substantial amount of money for a worthless painting."

"But it was other people's money. And the painting is far from worthless to a man like Phillip. He can use it as collateral to obtain bank loans and then sell it to another art investor for much more than he paid for it."

"And by routing the original sale through Isherwood Fine Arts," added Gabriel, "Phillip gave himself plausible deniability if it was ever discovered to be a forgery. After all, it was Sarah who sold the forgery to *him*. And it was Julian, a well-respected expert in Dutch and Flemish Old Masters, who concluded that the picture was painted by Anthony van Dyck and not by a later follower."

"Julian Isherwood's blessing increased the painting's value significantly."

"Where is it now?"

"Chelsea Fine Arts Storage."

"I suppose Phillip owns that, too."

"Phillip controls the entire physical infrastructure of the network, including Chelsea. And he was afraid that you and Sarah were going to bring it all down."

"What did he do?"

"He made another phone call."

"To whom?"

"Me."

————

With a small portion of the money that Magdalena had earned working for Phillip Somerset and Masterpiece Art Ventures, she had purchased a luxurious apartment on the Calle de Castelló in the Salamanca district of Madrid. Her circle of friends included artists, writers, musicians, and fashion designers who knew nothing of the true nature of her work. Like most young Spaniards, they usually ate dinner around ten and then headed off to a nightclub. Consequently, Magdalena was still sleeping when Phillip rang her at one o'clock on a Monday afternoon and told her to clean up the mess at Galerie Fleury.

"What sort of cleanup did he have in mind?"

"Destroy the forgeries in the gallery's inventory and, if necessary, return the million euros that you and the violinist paid for *A River Scene with Distant Windmills*."

"I was right about it being a forgery?"

She nodded. "Evidently, you told Phillip that you had given it to Aiden Gallagher for scientific analysis. Phillip was convinced that Aiden would be able to tell it was a fake."

"Because Aiden is the best in the business."

"The final word," said Magdalena.

"And when you heard the gallery had been bombed?"

"I knew that Phillip had once again misled me." She paused. "And that he had made a dreadful mistake."

For three weeks, she continued, she remained a prisoner of her apartment in Madrid. She followed the news from Paris obsessively, chewed her nails to the quick, painted a Picassoesque self-portrait, and drank far too much. Her suitcases stood in the entrance hall. One of them contained a million euros in cash.

"Where were you planning to go?"

"Marrakesh."

"Leaving your father to face the music for your crimes?"

"My father did nothing wrong."

"I doubt the Spanish police would have seen it that way," said Gabriel. "But please go on."

She instructed the network's remaining galleries to freeze all sales of forged paintings and reduced her telephone-and-text contact with Phillip to a bare minimum. But in late April, he summoned her to New York and told her to open the spigot.

"One of his largest investors had requested a forty-five-million-dollar redemption. The kind of redemption that leaves a mark on the balance sheet. Masterpiece needed to replenish its cash reserves in a hurry."

And so the forgeries flowed into the market, and the money flowed into Phillip's accounts in the Cayman Islands. By June the bombing of Galerie Fleury had receded from the headlines, and the eyes of the art world were on London, where Dimbleby Fine Arts was preparing to exhibit a newly discovered version of *Susanna in the Bath* by Paolo Veronese. The painting had purportedly emerged from the same unidentified European collection that had previously produced a Titian and a Tintoretto. But Magdalena knew what the rest of the art world did not, that all three paintings were forgeries.

"Because the forger's front man," said Gabriel, "made quite a scene at Galerie Hassler in Berlin."

Magdalena looked at Rossetti. "I was suspicious about those paintings even before your front man tried to sell the Gentileschi to Herr Hassler."

"Why?"

"I know a provenance trap when I see one, Mr. Allon. Yours wasn't terribly clever or original. Still, I wasn't surprised by the reaction of the art world. It's the secret of our success."

"What's that?"

"The gullibility of collectors and so-called experts and connoisseurs.

The art world desperately wants to believe that there are lost masterpieces just waiting to be rediscovered. Phillip and I make dreams come true." She managed a smile. "As do you, Mr. Allon. Your Veronese took my breath away, but the Gentileschi was to die for."

"You had to have it?"

"No," she answered "I had to have *you*."

"Because the market for museum-quality Old Masters is small? Because two major Old Master forgery rings cannot compete against one another and survive?"

"And because Phillip's forger is unable to supply enough painting to meet the demands of my distribution network," said Magdalena. "And because, for all his talent, he cannot hold a candle to you."

"In that case, I accept your offer."

"What offer?"

"To join the team at Masterpiece Art Ventures." Gabriel switched off the video camera. "Let's take a walk, shall we, Magdalena? There are one or two details we need to finalize before you call Phillip and give him the good news."

50

Villa dei Fiori

They made their way down the gentle slope of the drive, beneath the canopy of the umbrella pine. The first brushstrokes of dawn lay over the hills to the east, but overhead the stars shone brightly. The air was cool and still, not a breath of movement. It smelled of orange blossom and jasmine and the cigarette that Magdalena had charmed from Luca Rossetti.

"Where did you learn to paint like that?" she asked.

"In the womb."

"Your mother was an artist?"

"And my grandfather. He was a disciple of Max Beckmann."

"What was his name?"

"Viktor Frankel."

"I know your grandfather's work," said Magdalena. "But good genes alone can't explain talent like yours. If I didn't know better, I would have guessed that you were an apprentice in Titian's workshop."

"It's true that I served my apprenticeship in Venice, but it was with a famous restorer named Umberto Conti."

"And you were no doubt Signore Conti's finest pupil."

"I suppose I have a knack for it."

"Restoring paintings?"

"Not just paintings. People, too. I'm trying to decide whether you're worth the effort." He gave her a sideways glance. "I have a terrible feeling you're beyond repair."

"The damage is self-inflicted, I'm afraid."

"Not all of it. Phillip targeted you for recruitment. He groomed you. Preyed on your vulnerabilities. Got you hooked. I know his techniques. I've used them a time or two myself."

"Are you using them now?"

"A little," he admitted.

She turned away and expelled a slender stream of smoke. "And what if I told you that I willingly stepped into the trap Phillip set for me?"

"Because you wanted the money?"

"It certainly wasn't for the sex."

"How much is there?"

"In addition to the million euros in the suitcase in my apartment?" She lifted her gaze skyward. "I have another four or five scattered around Europe, but the bulk of my money is invested in Masterpiece Art Ventures."

"Current balance?"

"Maybe fifty-five."

"Million?"

"It's a fraction of what I deserve. If it wasn't for me, there wouldn't be a Masterpiece Art Ventures."

"It's not exactly a résumé enhancer, Magdalena."

"How many people can say they built a multibillion-dollar global forgery network?"

"Or brought one down," said Gabriel quietly.

She frowned. "How did you find me, Mr. Allon? The truth, this time."

"Your attempt to recruit Lucien Marchand gave me valuable insight into the way you ran your operation."

Magdalena took a final pull at the cigarette and with a flick of her long forefinger sent the ember arcing into the darkness. "And how is Françoise these days? Still living in Roussillon? Or has she settled permanently in Lucien's villa on Saint-Barthélemy?"

"Why did you try to hire him?"

"Phillip wanted to expand our inventory to include Impressionist and postwar works. His forger wasn't capable of it, so he asked me to find someone who was. I made Lucien a generous offer, which he accepted."

"Along with one million euros in cash."

She made no reply.

"Is that why you had him murdered? A lousy million euros?"

"I'm sales and distribution, Mr. Allon. Phillip deals with problems."

"Why was Lucien a problem?"

"Do I really need to explain that to you?"

"After Lucien and Françoise accepted the money and then reneged on the deal, Phillip was concerned that they posed a threat to you and Masterpiece Art Ventures."

Magdalena nodded. "Françoise is lucky that Phillip didn't have her killed, too. She was the real brains behind that network. Lucien was the brush and Toussaint the cash register, but Françoise was the glue that kept it together." She slowed to a stop before a small shrine to the Virgin Mary, one of several scattered about the estate. "Where in the world are we?"

"The villa was once a monastery. The current owner is quite close to the Vatican."

"As are you. Or so they say." She made the sign of the cross and set off again.

"Are you a believer?" asked Gabriel.

"Like ninety percent of my fellow Spaniards, I no longer attend Mass, and it has been more than twenty years since I last set foot in a confessional. But, yes, Mr. Allon. I remain a believer."

"Do you believe in absolution as well?"

"That depends on how many Hail Marys you intend to make me recite."

"If you help me take down Phillip Somerset," said Gabriel, "your sins will be forgiven."

"All of them?"

"A few years ago, I met a woman who ran a modern art gallery in Saint-Tropez. It was a money-laundering front for her boyfriend's narcotics empire. I got her out of the situation cleanly. Now she's a successful dealer in London."

"Somehow I doubt there's an art gallery in my future," said Magdalena. "But what did you have in mind?"

"A final face-to-face meeting with Phillip in New York next week."

"About the newest member of the team at Masterpiece Art Ventures?"

"Exactly."

"I imagine he's quite anxious to have a look at your Gentileschi."

"Which is why you're going to overnight it to Chelsea Fine Arts Storage."

"I hope your front man is covering the shipping costs."

"I'm afraid it wasn't included in the hammer price."

"I guess ten million euros doesn't go as far as it used to. But how are we going to get the painting through Italian customs?"

"I believe we're covered on that score." Gabriel handed her a mobile phone. "This call is being recorded for quality assurance. If you try to pass a message to him, I'll hand you over to General Ferrari and wave goodbye."

She dialed the number and raised the phone to her ear. "Hello, Lindsay. It's Magdalena. I'm sorry to be calling at such a dreadful hour, but I'm afraid it's rather urgent. I promise not to keep Phillip long."

51

Villa dei Fiori

Rossetti drove Magdalena back to Florence to collect her belongings from the Four Seasons and settle the enormous bill. By noon they had returned to Villa dei Fiori, and Magdalena, in sunglasses and a stunning white two-piece swimsuit, was stretched upon a chaise longue by the pool, a glass of chilled Orvieto wine in her hand. General Ferrari observed her disapprovingly from the shade of the trellised garden.

"Is there anything the staff of the Hotel Carabinieri can do to make her stay more comfortable?" he asked Gabriel.

"What would you have me do? Confine her to her room until we leave for New York?"

"Surely this place has a dungeon. After all, it was built in the eleventh century."

"I believe Count Gasparri converted it into his wine cellar."

Ferrari sighed but said nothing.

"Has the Art Squad never cut a deal with a thief or a fence to get to the next step of the ladder?"

"We do it all the time. And more often than not, the thief or the fence tells us only part of the story." The general paused. "Just like that beautiful creature lying comfortably next to the swimming pool. She's smarter than you realize. And quite dangerous."

"I'm a former intelligence officer, Cesare. I know how to handle an asset."

"She's not an asset, my friend. She is a criminal and a confidence artist who has millions of dollars stashed around the world and access to private airplanes."

"At least she doesn't have tattoos," remarked Gabriel.

"Her one and only redeeming quality. But I assure you, she is not to be trusted."

"I have enough leverage to keep her in line, including her videotaped confession."

"Ah, yes. A tragic tale about a once promising artist who was lured into a life of crime by the evil and manipulative Phillip Somerset. You realize, I hope, that perhaps half of it is true."

"Which half?"

"I haven't a clue. But I find it difficult to believe that she doesn't know the name of the forger."

"It's entirely plausible that Phillip kept it from her."

"Perhaps. But it is also entirely plausible that she was the one who took Phillip to that loft in Hell's Kitchen, and that the forger is now lying in the Umbrian sun with a drink in her hand."

"She doesn't have the training to paint Old Masters."

"So she says. But if I were you, I would revisit the matter."

"I'll boil her in suntan oil after lunch."

"Why don't you let me take her back to Rome instead? She can tell her tragic tale to the FBI legal attaché at the embassy. A prize like Magdalena would do wonders for my standing in Washington. Besides, it's an American problem now. Let the Americans handle it."

"And do you know what the FBI legal attaché will do?" asked Gabriel. "He'll call his superior at FBI headquarters. And his superior will call the assistant director, who will call the director, who will walk across Pennsylvania Avenue to the Justice Department. DOJ will assign the case to the US attorney for the Southern District of New York, and the US attorney will spend months gathering evidence before arresting Phillip and shutting down his company."

"The wheels of justice turn slowly."

"Which is why I'm going to deal with Phillip myself. By the time I'm finished, Masterpiece Art Ventures will be a smoldering ruin. The Feds will have no choice but to immediately make arrests and seize assets."

"A fait accompli?"

Gabriel smiled. "It definitely sounds better in French."

———————

General Ferrari and the rest of the Carabinieri team departed Villa dei Fiori at two that afternoon. A unit from the Amelia station kept watch over the gate, but otherwise Gabriel and Magdalena were alone. She slept through the afternoon and insisted on preparing a proper Spanish dinner of tapas and a potato omelet. They ate outside on the villa's terrace, in the cool evening air. Magdalena's personal mobile phone lay between them, flaring with incoming message traffic and silenced phone calls, mainly from her circle of friends in Madrid.

"No man in your life?" asked Gabriel.

"Only Phillip, I'm afraid."

"Are you in love with him?"

"God, no."

"Are you sure about that?"

"Why do you ask?"

"Because it is my intention to leave you alone in his presence for several hours in New York next week. And I want to know whether you intend to live up to our agreement or run away with him."

"Don't worry, Mr. Allon. I'll get you everything you need to take Phillip down."

He asked where the meeting would take place.

"That's up to Phillip," said Magdalena. "Sometimes we meet at Masterpiece's office on East Fifty-Third Street. But usually we get together at the town house on East Seventy-Fourth. It doubles as Masterpiece's gallery. That's where Phillip receives potential investors and buyers."

"How does he handle the sales?"

"He prefers to deal directly with clients to avoid scrutiny and commissions. But if the client insists on an intermediary, he routes the sales through another dealer or one of the auction houses."

"How many other people work for the firm?"

"Three young female art experts and Kenny Vaughan. Kenny used to work with Phillip at Lehman Brothers. He's in it up to his eyeballs."

"What about the women?"

"They think the sun rises and sets on Phillip and that I'm a broker who buys and sells paintings on his behalf in Europe."

"General Ferrari is convinced that you're the forger."

"Me?" She laughed. "A Picasso, maybe. But not an Old Master. I don't have talent like yours."

Gabriel read late into the night and was relieved to find Magdalena still in her bed when he rose the following morning. After loading the *automatico* with Illy and San Benedetto, he unleased Proteus on Phillip's personal smartphone, and within minutes the device was under his control. A scalable map depicted its current location and elevation: the eastern shore of an egg-shaped peninsula, twelve feet above sea level.

Gabriel downloaded Phillip's data onto his laptop and spent the remainder of the morning wandering the digital debris of one of the greatest scam artists in history. It was half past twelve when Magdalena finally appeared. She wandered into the kitchen and emerged a moment later with a bowl of milky coffee. She drank it in silence, her eyes unblinking.

"Not a morning person?" asked Gabriel.

"Opposite of a morning person. A night stalker."

"Is the night stalker ready to do some work?"

"If you insist," she said, and carried her coffee to the pool.

Gabriel followed her outside with the laptop. "What were the first six paintings you sold through your father's gallery?"

"It was a thousand years ago," she groaned.

"The exact amount of time you'll spend in an Italian prison if you don't start talking."

———

She recited the artist, tableau, and dimensions of each work, along with the name of the buyer and the price it had fetched. Next she listed the particulars of more than one hundred paintings that had passed through her brokerage in Madrid during the first year of the scheme. Most of the paintings she had simply sold back to Masterpiece Art Ventures. Phillip had then inflated their value with additional phantom sales before unloading the paintings onto unsuspecting buyers and cashing in on his investment. He also used the works as collateral to secure massive art-backed loans, money he used to acquire legitimate art and pay handsome returns to his investors.

"The loans," said Magdalena, "are the key to everything. Without leverage, Phillip and Kenny Vaughan wouldn't be able to make it work."

"So in addition to selling forged paintings, Phillip is committing bank fraud?"

"On a daily basis."

"Where does he do his banking?"

"Mainly, he deals with Ellis Gray at JPMorgan Chase. But he also has a relationship with Bank of America."

"How much debt is he carrying?"

"I'm not sure even Phillip knows the answer to that."

"Who does?"

"Kenny Vaughan."

The next ground they covered was Magdalena's expansion into bricks-and-mortar retailing, beginning with her partnership with Galerie Georges Fleury of Paris and concluding with the recent acquisition by Masterpiece Art Ventures of galleries in Hong Kong, Tokyo, and Dubai. The total number of forged paintings the network had unleashed on the art market exceeded five hundred, with a paper valuation of more than $1.7 billion—far too many works for Magdalena to recall accurately. She was certain, however, that a significant percentage had passed through Masterpiece's opaque portfolio.

"How many does he currently control?"

"That's impossible to say. Phillip doesn't even reveal the genuine paintings in his possession, let alone the forgeries. His most valuable pictures are in his Manhattan and Long Island homes. The rest are in the warehouse on East Ninety-First Street. It's the equivalent of his trading book."

"Can you get inside?"

"Not without Phillip's approval. But a directory of the warehouse's current contents would tell you everything you need to know."

Over lunch, Gabriel logged into Magdalena's ProtonMail account and forwarded several years' worth of encrypted emails to his own address. Next they reviewed her personal finances, including her account at Masterpiece Art Ventures. Her balance was $56,245,539.

"Don't even think about trying to make a withdrawal," Gabriel warned her.

"My next redemption window isn't until September. I couldn't if I tried."

"I'm sure Phillip would make an exception in your case."

"Actually, he's quite strict when it comes to redemptions. He and Kenny fly rather close to the sun. If a handful of major investors were to simultaneously withdraw their funds, he would have to sell some of his inventory or secure another loan."

"Using a painting as collateral?"

"The art-backed loans," repeated Magdalena, "are the key to everything."

Gabriel downloaded Magdalena's account statements, then checked the tracking information for *Danaë and the Shower of Gold*. The painting was currently westbound over the Atlantic. It would spend the night in the air cargo center at Kennedy International and was scheduled to reach its final destination, Chelsea Fine Arts Storage, no later than noon on Monday.

A search of the flights from Rome to New York produced several options. "How do you feel about the ten a.m. Delta into JFK?" asked Gabriel.

"That would require awakening several hours before noon."

"You can sleep on the plane."

"I never sleep on planes." Magdalena reached for the laptop. "Can I pay for your ticket?"

"Phillip might find that suspicious."

"At least let me give you some miles."

"I have plenty."

"How many have you got?"

"The moon and back."

"I've got more." She booked their seats. "That leaves the hotel. Is the Pierre all right?"

"I'm afraid Sarah prefers the Four Seasons."

"Please tell me she's not coming with us."

"I need someone to keep an eye on you when I'm not around."

Magdalena reserved her usual suite at the Pierre and with a childlike frown returned to her chaise longue next to the pool. Her wounds, thought Gabriel, were definitely self-inflicted. Still, she was by no means beyond repair. After all, if a former contract killer like Christopher Keller was salvageable, then surely Magdalena was as well.

For the moment, she was merely a means to an end. All Gabriel required now was a reporter to turn her remarkable story into a weapon that would reduce Masterpiece Art Ventures to rubble. A reporter who was familiar with the worlds of finance and art. Perhaps one who had investigated Masterpiece in the past.

Only a single candidate fit the profile. Fortunately, the number for her cell phone was in Phillip Somerset's contacts. Gabriel dialed it and introduced himself. Not with a work name, or one he plucked from thin air, but his real name.

"Yeah, right," she said, and hung up the phone.

52

Rotten Row

The next call Gabriel placed that afternoon was to Sarah Bancroft. It found her on Rotten Row in Hyde Park, where she was attempting to dislodge the ten pounds that had settled astride her hips. The news from Italy came as a shock, so much so that she asked Gabriel to repeat it, just to make certain she hadn't misunderstood him. It was no less astounding the second time. Masterpiece Art Ventures, the art-based hedge fund where a portion of Sarah's inheritance was invested, was a $1.2 billion fraud propped up by the sale and collateralization of forged paintings. Furthermore, it seemed that Magdalena Navarro, she of the shimmering black hair and elongated body, had been sleeping with Phillip the entire time he had dated Sarah. For that reason alone, she leapt at the chance to travel to New York to take part in his destruction. Even if it meant staying at the Pierre.

"Shall I bring along Mr. Marlowe? I find that he comes in rather handy in situations like these."

"As do I. But I have another job in mind for him."

"Nothing dangerous, I hope."

"I'm afraid so."

Sarah left for New York early the following morning and arrived at JFK at midday. A Nissan Pathfinder awaited her at Hertz. She killed an hour in the cell phone lot and at two fifteen made her way to Terminal 1. Gabriel emerged a moment later, accompanied by the woman whom Sarah had last seen walking along the pavements of Jermyn Street.

Now, as then, she was wearing a shortish skirt and a formfitting white top. Gabriel loaded their bags into the rear storage compartment and slid into the backseat. Magdalena climbed into the passenger seat, bringing with her the scent of orange blossom and jasmine. She crossed one long leg over the other and smiled. Sarah slipped the Nissan into DRIVE and set out for Manhattan.

The Pierre Hotel stood at the corner of East Sixty-First Street and Fifth Avenue. Magdalena entered the ornate lobby alone and was received by the hotel's management as though she were returning royalty. Her suite, with its sweeping views of Central Park, was located on the twentieth floor. Gabriel and Sarah had been assigned adjoining rooms on the opposite side of the corridor. Like Magdalena, they checked in pseudonymously and instructed the woman at Reception to block all outside calls.

Upstairs, all three convened in the sitting room of Magdalena's suite. She opened a complimentary bottle of Taittinger champagne while Gabriel connected his laptop to the hotel's Wi-Fi network and logged in to Proteus. It appeared that Phillip had decided to remain in North Haven rather than return to the city. Gabriel increased the volume on the feed from the microphone and heard the clatter of a keyboard. The output from the camera was a rectangle of solid black.

Gabriel handed Magdalena her phone. "Let him know that

you've arrived and would like to see him as soon as possible. And remember—"

"This call is being recorded for quality assurance."

Gabriel carried the laptop into the bedroom and closed the heavy internal door. Phillip answered Magdalena's call instantly. "How about one o'clock tomorrow afternoon?" he asked. "We'll have lunch."

"Will Lindsay be joining us?"

"Unfortunately, she's spending the week on the island."

"Lucky you."

"I'll send a car," said Phillip, and the connection went dead.

Gabriel listened to a minute or two of typing before returning to the sitting room. "Now the Gentileschi," he said to Magdalena.

The number for the warehouse was in her contacts. She tapped the screen and lifted the phone to her ear.

"Hello, Anthony. It's Magdalena Navarro calling. Did the painting arrive from Florence as scheduled? . . . Wonderful. Send it to Mr. Somerset's residence tomorrow morning . . . Yes, the town house, please. Place it on the easel in the gallery. And make certain it arrives no later than noon."

Magdalena killed the connection and surrendered her phone to Gabriel.

"Your wallet and passport as well."

She removed them from her Hermès Birkin handbag and handed them over.

"I need to run an errand, which means that you and Sarah will have a chance to get to know one another better. But don't worry," said Gabriel as he stepped into the corridor. "I won't be long."

Sarah chained the door behind him and returned to the sitting room. Magdalena was adding champagne to her glass. At length Sarah asked, "Is it true that Phillip was sleeping with you the entire time he was seeing me?"

"Only when I was in New York."

"Ah, that's a relief."

"If you must know," said Magdalena, "he was only using you."

"For what?"

"Introductions to rich benefactors of the Museum of Modern Art."

"And to think I gave him two million dollars to invest."

"What's your current balance?"

"Four and a half. You?"

"Fifty-six point two."

Sarah smiled without parting her lips. "I guess you were better in bed than I was."

53

Literary Walk

In the spring of 2017, *Vanity Fair* magazine published an investigative profile titled "The Great Somerset." Twelve thousand words in length, the article chronicled its subject's rise from a working-class town in northeastern Pennsylvania to the pinnacle of Wall Street and the art world. No corner of his personal life escaped scrutiny: the instability of his childhood home, his youthful athletic prowess, his brief but meteoric career at Lehman Brothers, his ugly divorce, his peculiar penchant for secrecy. A source described only as a former friend said he had a dark side. An old colleague went further, suggesting he was a sociopath and a malignant narcissist. Both sources agreed that he was hiding something.

The article was written by Evelyn Buchanan, an award-winning reporter whose work for *Vanity Fair* had served as the intellectual property for two Hollywood films and a Netflix limited series. At present, she was seated on a bench along Central Park's Literary Walk. Robert Burns, feather pen in hand, eyes skyward in search of inspiration, loomed over her right shoulder. On the opposite side of the footpath, a sketch artist sat waiting for a subject.

Evelyn Buchanan was waiting, too. Not for a subject but a source.

He had called her without warning the previous day—from where he refused to say. No, he had assured her, it was not a practical joke; he was in fact the man he claimed to be. He was coming to New York on an unpublicized visit and wished to meet with her. She was to tell no one that he had been in touch. He promised that she would not be disappointed.

"But national security isn't my beat," Evelyn protested.

"The matter I wish to discuss is related to the financial world and the art market."

"Can you be a bit more specific?"

"The Great Somerset," he said, and rang off.

It was an intriguing clue, all the more so because of the source. He had attended a book party at Phillip's showy North Haven estate that spring. Or so claimed Ina Garten, who insisted he'd had a hot little blonde on his arm. Evelyn, who had attended the same party, had found the prospect laughable. Now she had to admit it was possible after all. How else to explain why a man like Gabriel Allon would be interested in a creep like Phillip Somerset?

Evelyn checked the time. It was one minute before five o'clock. One minute before the world's most famous retired spy had promised to appear. The walkway was crowded with tourists, spandex-clad joggers, and Upper East Side nannies pushing strollers laden with the tycoons of tomorrow. But there was no one who looked as though he might be Gabriel Allon. Indeed, the only possible candidate was a man of medium height and build who was pondering the placard at the foot of the Walter Scott statue.

At the stroke of five o'clock, he crossed the walkway and sat down on Evelyn's bench. "Please go away," she said quietly. "My husband will be back any minute, and he has anger-management issues."

"I thought I made it clear that you were to come alone."

Evelyn turned with a start. Then, regaining her composure, she stared straight ahead. "Who was the blonde?"

"I beg your pardon?"

"The woman you brought to Carl Bernstein's book party."

"She used to work at MoMA. Now she's an art dealer in London. I was helping her with a problem."

"What sort of problem?"

"The Great Somerset."

"You obviously read my article," said Evelyn.

"Several times."

"Why?"

"As you might imagine, the ability to read between the lines is an essential skill for an intelligence officer. Is the information accurate, or is my adversary trying to deceive me? Is my agent overstating his case, or is he playing it too safe? Has my source, for one reason or another, left critical information out of his report?"

"And when you finished reading my story about Phillip?"

"I had the nagging sense that you knew more about him than you shared with your readers."

"Much more," she admitted.

"Why wasn't the material included in the piece?"

"You first, Mr. Allon. Why Phillip Somerset, of all people?"

"Masterpiece Art Ventures is a fraud. And I'd like you to be the one to break the story."

"What have you got for me?"

"A whistleblower."

"An employee of the company?"

"Close enough."

"What does that mean?"

"It means that I'm going to impose some rather strict ground rules in order to protect the whistleblower's identity and to conceal my role in this matter."

"And if I refuse to accept those ground rules?"

"I'll find someone who will. And you and your magazine will be playing catch-up when Masterpiece crashes and burns."

"In that case, I'll listen to what you and your whistleblower have to say." She paused. "But only if you tell me where you got the number for my cell phone."

"I found it in Phillip's contacts."

Evelyn Buchanan smiled. "Ask a silly question."

54

Central Park

How did you find her?"

"She was arrested in Italy last weekend after purchasing a forged Gentileschi from an undercover Carabinieri officer. I was a consultant to the Italian investigation."

"A consultant?" asked Evelyn dubiously.

"It's possible I might have painted the Gentileschi for them."

"A fake forgery painted by Gabriel Allon? This story is getting better by the minute."

They were moving at an unhurried pace along the footpaths of Central Park. For the moment, Evelyn's notepad was tucked safely into her Chanel handbag. She was a petite woman of perhaps fifty, with short, dark hair and oversize tortoiseshell glasses. They were her trademark, the spectacles, like her razor-sharp prose, acerbic wit, and ruthless competitive streak.

"Where's the painting now?" she asked.

"A warehouse on East Ninety-First Street."

"Chelsea Fine Arts Storage?"

"That's the one."

"I remember when Phillip acquired it. I have to say, it made no sense to me at the time. Why would a tycoon like Phillip Somerset want to own a small-time art services company like Chelsea?"

"Because the tycoon needed the ability to ship and store forged paintings, no questions asked. He's flooded the art market with hundreds of fake paintings, including four that have ended up in the Louvre. But the best part of the story is that—"

"Phillip is using forged paintings as collateral to obtain massive bank loans."

"How did you know?"

"An educated guess." Evelyn smiled. "Did I mention that my husband works for Millennium Management. It's one of the world's largest hedge funds. Before that, he was a prosecutor in the US attorney's office for the Southern District of New York. When I was working on the profile of Phillip, Tom took a hard look at—"

"Your husband is named Tom Buchanan?"

"Do you want to hear the rest of the story or not?"

"Please."

"When Tom analyzed Masterpiece's annual returns, he was quite impressed. Envious, actually."

"Because Masterpiece had outperformed Millennium?"

"Easily. Tom being Tom, he started doing some digging."

"And?"

"He was convinced that Phillip was using borrowed money and money from new investors to pay off his old investors. In short, Tom believes that Phillip Somerset is the Bernie Madoff of the art world."

"He's running a Ponzi scheme?"

"Correct."

"How close did you get to proving it?"

"Not close enough for my editors. But Phillip definitely knew that I was on to him."

"How?"

"He employs a man named Leonard Silk to watch his back. Silk is retired CIA. When he left the Agency, he opened a one-man private security firm here in New York. He called me when I was working on my profile and threatened legal action if the piece alleged wrongdoing of any kind. I also received messages from a man who somehow knew that I liked to take long walks in the park. He warned me to be careful. He said bad things happen to women who walk alone in New York City."

"How subtle."

"Leonard Silk doesn't waste time on subtlety. That's Phillip's department. He was incredibly charming during our interviews. It's no wonder your whistleblower agreed to work for him."

"Actually, she saw through Phillip from the beginning."

"What was the original connection?"

"Drugs. When she couldn't sell any of her paintings here in New York, she earned a living dealing cocaine. Many of her clients were Wall Street types."

"Phillip snorted a mountain of blow back when he was at Lehman Brothers," said Evelyn. "It was just one of the reasons why they fired him. Even by Wall Street standards, he was out of control."

"Your article said he left Lehman on good terms."

"That was the public version of the story, but it isn't true. Phillip was practically frog-marched out of the building, and a do-not-resuscitate order went out on the street. When no one else would hire him, he started a hedge fund called Somerset Asset Management. And when the hedge fund collapsed, he hit upon a novel idea."

"He gravitated to the art world," said Gabriel. "Because that's where the money was."

Evelyn nodded. "Phillip started turning up at gallery openings and museum fundraisers, always with a beautiful woman on his arm and a pocketful of business cards. You have to hand it to him. The art-based hedge fund was an intriguing idea. Prices for blue-chip art were rising faster than equities or any other asset class. How could he possibly go wrong?"

"It never worked. That's why he started loading up his book with forged paintings."

They had arrived at Grand Army Plaza. "You never mentioned your whistleblower's name," said Evelyn.

"Magdalena Navarro."

"Where is she now?"

Gabriel glanced toward the Pierre Hotel. "It's her New York address. She has fifty-six million dollars invested in Masterpiece Art Ventures, all of which she earned selling forgeries for Phillip."

"So she says. But I can't accuse Phillip Somerset of the greatest art fraud in history based solely on the word of a former drug dealer. I need proof that he's knowingly selling forged paintings."

"What if you were able to hear it directly from Phillip's mouth?"

"Do you have a recording?"

"The conversation hasn't happened yet."

"When will it?"

"Tomorrow afternoon at one o'clock."

"What's on the agenda?"

"Me."

———

They threaded their way through the gridlocked traffic along Fifth Avenue and came whirling through the Pierre's revolving door, into the refrigerated cool of the lobby. Upstairs, Gabriel knocked softly on the door of Magdalena's suite. Sarah confirmed his identity before opening the door.

"How's the prisoner?" he asked.

"The prisoner is resting in her room." Sarah offered Evelyn her hand, then turned to Gabriel. "Do we need to clarify the ground rules before we begin?"

"Ms. Buchanan has agreed that your name and the name of your highly regarded gallery in London will not appear in her copy. She will describe you only as an art world insider." Gabriel glanced at Evelyn. "Isn't that correct, Ms. Buchanan?"

"And how will I describe *you*?"

"This story isn't about me. It's about Phillip Somerset and Masterpiece Art Ventures. Any information that I provide is for background purposes only. You may not quote me directly. Nor are you to say where this interview is taking place."

"An undisclosed location?"

"I'll let you choose the words, Ms. Buchanan. I'm not the writer."

"You're just the consultant to the Italian police who painted a fake forgery?"

"Exactly."

"In that case, perhaps it's time for me to meet the prisoner."

Gabriel knocked on the door of the bedroom, and a moment later out stepped Magdalena.

"My goodness," said Evelyn Buchanan. "This story is getting better by the minute."

55

Pierre Hotel

They went through it once from the beginning. And then they went through it a second time, just to make certain of the relevant facts and dates. Magdalena's childhood in Seville. Her formal training as an artist in Barcelona. The years she spent dealing cocaine in New York. Her introduction to Phillip Somerset at Le Cirque. Her role in building and maintaining the most lucrative and sophisticated art-and-financial fraud scheme in history. There were no discrepancies between the version of the story she revealed under interrogation in Umbria and the one she recounted for Evelyn Buchanan of *Vanity Fair*. If anything, thought Gabriel, the Pierre Hotel edition was even more captivating. So, too, was the subject herself. She came across as cosmopolitan and sophisticated and, most important, credible. Never once did she lose her composure, even when the questions turned personal.

"Why would someone with your talent become a drug dealer?"

"At first, I did it because I needed the money. And then I discovered that I enjoyed it."

"You were good at it?"

"Very."

"Are there similarities between selling drugs and forgeries?"

"More than you realize. For some people, art is like a drug. They *have* to have it. Phillip and I simply catered to their addiction."

There was a gaping hole in Magdalena's account—namely, the precise set of circumstances by which she had ended up in Italian custody. Evelyn pressed Gabriel for details, but he refused to budge from his original statement. Magdalena had been arrested after purchasing a forged Gentileschi in Florence. The painting was now in an art storage warehouse on East Ninety-First Street. In the morning it would be moved to the gallery of Phillip Somerset's town house on East Seventy-Fourth Street. And at 1:00 p.m. it would be the subject of a conversation that would provide Evelyn with all the ammunition she needed to expose Masterpiece Art Ventures as a fraud.

"Will Magdalena be wearing a wire?"

"Her phone will be acting as a transmitter. Phillip's phone is also compromised."

"I don't suppose he gave his consent to being hacked."

"I didn't ask for it."

At nine o'clock they took a break for dinner. Sarah arranged for a round of martinis to be sent up from the bar while Magdalena ordered room service from Perrine, the hotel's acclaimed restaurant. At Gabriel's suggestion, Evelyn invited her husband to join them. He arrived as the waiters were rolling the table into the suite. Tom Buchanan was affable and erudite, the very opposite of the wellborn polo player who had lived grandly on the shoreline of East Egg and fretted about the decline of the white race.

Evelyn swore her husband to secrecy, then gave him a detailed briefing on the remarkable story that had landed in her lap earlier that afternoon. Tom Buchanan took out his anger on his Caesar salad.

"Leave it to Phillip Somerset to come up with something like this. Still, one has to admire his ingenuity. He spotted a weakness and cleverly took advantage of it."

"What weakness is that?" asked Gabriel.

"The art market is totally unregulated. Prices are arbitrary, quality control is virtually nonexistent, and most paintings change hands under conditions of total secrecy. All of which makes it the perfect environment for fraud. Phillip took it to the extreme, of course."

"How is it possible that no one noticed?"

"For the same reason no one noticed that mortgage-backed securities and collateralized debt obligations were about to take down the global economy."

"Everyone is making too much money?"

Tom nodded. "And not just Phillip's investors. His bankers, too. And they're all going to suffer enormous losses when Evelyn's story appears. Nevertheless, I approve of your methods. Waiting for the Feds to act isn't an option. That said, I wish you could give my wife an incriminating document or two."

"You mean the inner-office memo in which Phillip spells out his plan to create and maintain the largest art fraud in history?"

"Point taken, Mr. Allon. But what about the documents stored in that warehouse on East Ninety-First Street?"

"Phillip's current inventory?"

"Exactly. If Magdalena can say with absolute certainty that he has forged paintings on his book, it would be devastating."

"Is the former federal prosecutor suggesting that I clandestinely acquire a comprehensive list of paintings contained in that property?"

"I wouldn't dream of it. But if you do, you should definitely give it to my wife."

Gabriel smiled. "Any other advice, counselor?"

"If I were you, I'd think about putting a bit of pressure on Phillip's finances."

"By encouraging a handful of his important investors to take redemptions, you mean?"

"It sounds to me as though you already have a plan in place," said Tom.

"There's a man in London named Nicholas Lovegrove. Nicky's one of the most sought-after art advisers in the world. Several of his clients are invested with Phillip."

"We hedge fund types get very suspicious when investors pull their money. Therefore, it needs to be handled with discretion."

"Don't worry," said Sarah. "We art dealer types are nothing if not discreet."

56

Galerie Watson

The destruction of Masterpiece Art Ventures commenced the following morning at 10:45 a.m. London time—5:45 a.m. in New York—when Christopher Keller presented himself at Galerie Olivia Watson in King Street. The small placard in the window read BY APPOINTMENT ONLY. Christopher hadn't made one, wagering that a surprise attack would prove more successful. He pressed the call button and, wincing, awaited a response.

"Well, well," breathed a sultry female voice. "Look what the cat left on my doorstep. If it isn't my dear friend Mr. Bancroft."

"It's Marlowe, remember? Now open the door."

"Sorry, but I'm all tied up at the moment."

"Untie yourself and let me in."

"I *do* love it when you beg, darling. Hold on, I can't quite seem to reach the button for the damn lock."

Several additional seconds elapsed before the deadbolt thumped and the door yielded to Christopher's touch. Inside, he found Olivia seated at a sleek black writing table in the gallery's main exhibition room. She had arranged herself with care, as though posing for an invisible camera. As usual, her chin was turned slightly to the left, the right side of her face being the one that the photographers and advertisers had preferred. Christopher had never had a favorite. Olivia was a work of art, regardless of the vantage point.

Rising, she stepped from behind the table, crossed one ankle over the other, and placed a hand on her hip. She was clad in a fashionably cut jacket and matching slim-fitting trousers, suitably summer in color and weight.

"Marks and Spencer?" asked Christopher.

"It's a little something that Giorgio threw together for me." She lifted her chin a few degrees and stared at Christopher down the straight lines of her nose. "What brings you to my corner of the neighborhood?"

"A mutual friend needs a favor."

"Which friend is that?"

"The one who cleaned up your dreadful past and allowed you to open a respectable gallery here in St. James's." Christopher paused. "A gallery filled with paintings that were purchased with your boyfriend's drug money."

"Our mutual friend performed a similar service for you, as I recall." Olivia folded her arms. "Does your adorable American wife know what you used to do for a living?"

"My adorable American wife is none of your concern."

"Is it true she used to work for the CIA?"

"Wherever did you hear a thing like that?"

"Neighborhood gossip. There's also a nasty rumor going round that I'm involved in a flaming shag-fest with Simon Mendenhall."

"I thought you were dating a pop star."

"Colin is an actor," said Olivia. "And he's currently starring in the hottest play in the West End."

"Are you two serious?"

"Quite."

"So why are you shagging sleazy Simon on the side?"

"The rumor was started by your wife," said Olivia evenly.

"I find that difficult to believe."

"She also whispers the word *bitch* every time she sees me in Wiltons."

Christopher smiled in spite of himself.

"I'm glad you think it's funny." Olivia scrutinized his clothing. "Who's dressing you these days?"

"Dicky."

"Nice."

"I'll tell him you said so."

"I'd rather you tell your adorable American wife to cease and desist." Olivia shook her head slowly. "Honestly, I can't imagine why she would stoop to something so low."

"She's a bit jealous, that's all."

"If anyone has a right to be jealous, it's me. After all, Sarah's the one who ended up with you."

"Come now, Olivia. You don't really mean that. I was just a comfortable place for you to lay your head while you found your footing here in London. Now you're dating a pop star and your gallery is all the rage."

"All because of our mutual friend?"

Christopher made no reply.

"I thought he retired," said Olivia.

"It's a private matter involving a man named Phillip Somerset."

"*The* Phillip Somerset?"

"Friend of yours?"

"I sat next to Phillip and his wife at Christie's postwar and contemporary evening sale in New York a couple of years ago. The wife did some modeling before she hit the jackpot with Phillip. Laura is her name. Or is it Linda?"

"Lindsay."

"Yes, that's it. She's quite young and unspeakably stupid. Phillip struck me as a real operator. He asked whether I wanted to invest in his fund. I told him I wasn't in his league."

"Wise move on your part."

"Is there a problem?"

"Phillip is a bit like your old boyfriend. Shiny on the outside, dirty underneath. What's more, there's a rumor going around New York that his finances are rather shaky."

"Another rumor?"

"This one happens to be true. Our mutual friend would like you to whisper it into the ear of a prominent London art adviser whose client list includes some of the richest collectors in the world."

"How do you want me to play it?"

"A casual aside over an otherwise pleasant and businesslike lunch."

"When?"

"Today."

She glanced at her watch. "But it's nearly eleven. Surely Nicky has a lunch date already."

"Something tells me he'll break it."

Olivia reached for her mobile. "I'll do it on one condition."

"I'll have a word with her," said Christopher.

"Thank you." Olivia dialed and raised the phone to her ear. "Hello, Nicky. It's Olivia Watson calling. I know it's terribly short notice, but I was wondering whether you happened to be free for lunch today . . . The Wolseley at one? See you then, Nicky."

57

The Wolseley

And so it began, with an apparently offhand remark, made over a costly lunch in one of Mayfair's finer dining rooms. The midday clatter of cutlery was such that Nicky leaned forward over his dressed Dorset crab appetizer and asked Olivia to repeat her statement. She did so in a confessional murmur, with the addition of a don't-quote-me-on-this disclaimer. The time was half past one o'clock. Or so claimed Julian Isherwood, who was dining well at a nearby table and noticed the ashen expression wash over Nicky's face. Julian's tubby tablemate didn't see a thing, for he was making a run at young Tessa, the newest addition to the Wolseley's waitstaff.

Nicky pressed Olivia to reveal the name of her source. And when she refused, he begged her pardon and immediately dialed Sterling Dunbar, a wealthy Manhattan real estate developer who bought paintings by the ton, always with Nicky looking over one shoulder. Sterling had been one of the first major investors in Masterpiece Art Ventures.

"Do you know my current balance?" he sniffed.

"I'm sure it's considerably larger than mine."

"A hundred and fifty million, a fivefold increase over my initial investment. Phillip assures me the fund is rock solid. Truth be told, I'm thinking about giving him another hundred."

The reactionary industrialist Max van Egan had parked $250 million at Masterpiece. He told Nicky he wasn't going anywhere. Simon Levinson—of the retailing Levinsons—was also inclined to stay put. But Ainsley Cabot, a collector of exceptional taste but only eight-figure wealth, heeded Nicky's advice. He rang Phillip at 9:15 a.m. Eastern time, as Phillip was stepping from his Sikorsky at the East Thirty-Fourth Street Heliport.

"How much?" he shouted over the whine of the rotors.

"All of it."

"Once you're out, there's no getting back in again. Do you understand me, Ainsley?"

"Spare me the bravado, Phillip, and send me my money."

Buffy Lowell reached Phillip at 9:24 a.m. as he was rolling up Third Avenue in his chauffeured Mercedes. Livingston Ford caught him eight minutes later, as he was crawling crosstown on East Seventy-Second Street. Livingston had $50 million in the fund and wanted out.

"You're going to regret this," warned Phillip.

"That's what my third wife told me, and I've never been happier."

"I'd like you to consider only a partial redemption."

"Are you suggesting there isn't enough cash in the till?"

"The money isn't sitting in an account at Citibank. I'll have to unload several paintings to make you whole."

"In that case, Phillip, I suggest you start unloading."

Which was how a seemingly offhand remark—made forty-five minutes earlier over a costly lunch in London—blew a $100 million hole in Masterpiece Art Ventures. The firm's founder, however, knew nothing of what had transpired. Desperate for information, he conducted a pair of hasty Internet searches—one for his own name, the other for the name of his firm. Neither unearthed anything that would explain why three of his largest investors had suddenly fled his fund. A search of social media likewise produced nothing damaging. Finally, at 9:42 a.m., he tapped the icon for Telegram, the encrypted cloud-based messaging system, and opened an existing secret chat thread.

I'm bleeding to death, he typed. Find out why.

———

When Phillip Somerset purchased his town house on East Seventy-Fourth Street in 2014, $30 million was considered a great deal of money. He had obtained the loan from his banker at JPMorgan Chase using several forged paintings as collateral, just one of the ways he had waved a magic wand and turned swaths of worthless canvas into gold. Several additional forgeries adorned the interior of the mansion, all to impress prospective investors and confer upon Phillip a patina of extraordinary wealth and sophistication. They were the elite of the art world, his investors. The ones with more money than sense. Phillip was a fraud and a clever forgery himself, but his investors were the fools who had made the elaborate scheme possible. And Magdalena, he thought suddenly. It would have never worked without her.

He entered the mansion's ground-floor foyer and was greeted by Tyler Briggs, his chief of security. Tyler was an Iraq War veteran. He wore a dark suit over a gym-hardened body.

"How was the ride in from the island, Mr. Somerset?"

"Better than the drive from the heliport."

Phillip's phone was ringing again. It was Scooter Eastman, a $20 million investor.

"Any scheduled deliveries today?" asked Tyler.

"A painting is supposed to arrive from the warehouse any minute."

"Clients?"

"Not today. But Ms. Navarro is supposed to drop by around one. Send her up to my office when she arrives."

Phillip dispatched Scooter Eastman's call to his voice mail and mounted the staircase. Soledad and Gustavo Ramírez, the Peruvian couple who ran his household, were waiting on the second-floor landing. Phillip absently returned their greetings while eyeing his phone. It was Rosamond Pierce. Midnight-blue blood. Ten million invested in Masterpiece Art Ventures.

"I'll be having lunch at home today. Ms. Navarro will be joining me. Seafood Cobb salads, please. One thirty or so."

"Yes, Mr. Somerset," replied the Ramírezes in unison.

Upstairs in his office, he listened to the new voice mails. Scooter Eastman and Rosamond Pierce both wanted out. In the span of thirty minutes, he had lost $135 million in investment money. Redemptions of that scale would threaten the most ethically run hedge fund. For a fund like Masterpiece Art Ventures, they were cataclysmic.

He relayed the news to Kenny Vaughan, the firm's chief investment officer, during their usual ten o'clock video call.

"Are you fucking kidding me?"

"I wish."

"A hundred and thirty-five million is going to hurt, Phillip."

"How long before we start to feel the pain?"

"Livingston Ford, Scooter Eastman, and Rosamond Pierce are all eligible for redemptions this month."

"Eighty million?"

"More like eighty-five."

"How much cash do we have on hand?"

"Fiftyish. Maybe."

"I could dump the Pollock."

"You owe JPMorgan sixty-five against the Pollock. Selling it isn't an option."

"How much do you need to make it work, Kenny?"

"Eighty-five would be nice."

"Be reasonable."

"Is there any chance you can lay your hands on forty?"

Phillip went to the window and watched two men in matching blue coveralls maneuvering a large rectangular crate from the back of a Chelsea Fine Arts Storage delivery truck.

"Yeah, Kenny. I think I might."

58

Pierre Hotel

Evelyn Buchanan arrived at the Pierre at half past twelve. Upstairs in Magdalena's suite, she informed Gabriel that her editors had signed off on an outline of her story. It would appear on *Vanity Fair*'s website immediately upon completion and would be included in the next print edition as well. The magazine's publicity department was putting in place a plan for a social media blitz. The *New York Times*, *Wall Street Journal*, Reuters, Bloomberg News, and CNBC had been alerted that a major story with far-reaching financial implications was forthcoming.

"Which means it will go viral within minutes of appearing on our site. There's no way Phillip will be able to contain the damage. He'll be dead before he knows what hit him."

"How soon can you publish?"

"If today goes as promised, I can have it ready by tonight."

"At the rate Phillip is going, he might not survive that long."

"Redemptions?"

"A hundred and thirty-five million and counting."

"He must be reeling."

"See for yourself."

Gabriel played a recording of Phillip's video call with Kenny Vaughan.

"How much cash do we have on hand?"

"Fiftyish. Maybe."

"I could dump the Pollock."

"You owe JPMorgan sixty-five against the Pollock. Selling it isn't an option."

Gabriel paused the recording.

"Do you realize what you have?" asked Evelyn.

"It gets better."

Gabriel clicked PLAY.

"How much do you need to make it work, Kenny?"

"Eighty-five would be nice."

"Be reasonable."

"Is there any chance you can lay your hands on forty?"

"Yeah, Kenny. I think I might."

Gabriel clicked PAUSE.

"Where is he going to get the money?"

"Unclear. But the timing would suggest he's thinking about putting my Gentileschi into play."

"If he does that—"

"We'll have irrefutable evidence that Phillip is engaged in bank fraud."

Just then the bedroom door opened and Magdalena emerged, wearing white stretch trousers, a loose-fitting blouse, and stiletto-heeled pumps.

Gabriel handed over her phone. "Keep it with you at all times. And whatever you do—"

"Where would I go without a passport, Mr. Allon? Staten Island?"

She dropped the phone into her handbag and went out. Her intoxicating scent lingered in the room after she had gone.

"Does she ever wear a bra?" asked Evelyn.

"Evidently, she forgot to pack one."

Gabriel switched the feed on the Proteus software from Phillip's device to Magdalena's. Then he rang Sarah, who was downstairs in the rented Nissan SUV.

"Don't worry," she said. "I won't let her out of my sight."

———

Two minutes later Sarah watched as Magdalena emerged from the East Sixty-First Street door of the Pierre and slid into the back of Phillip's waiting Mercedes S-Class limousine. The driver made three consecutive left turns and headed uptown on Madison Avenue. Sarah followed directly behind it—a violation of basic vehicle surveillance techniques, but a necessary one. The traffic was bumper-to-bumper, and Sarah had no backup other than the phone in Magdalena's handbag.

The traffic thinned at East Sixty-Sixth Street, and the Mercedes accelerated. Sarah was forced to run a pair of red lights to keep from losing it, but at East Seventy-Fifth Street she had no choice but to stop. When at last the light changed to green, the Mercedes was nowhere in sight. Two more left turns brought Sarah to the door of Phillip's town house on East Seventy-Fourth Street.

No Mercedes.

No sign of Magdalena.

Sarah drove to the end of the block and found a spot along the curb. Then she snatched up her phone and dialed Gabriel at the Pierre. "Please tell me she's inside that house."

"She's on her way upstairs."

Sarah killed the connection and smiled. Enjoy it while you can, she thought.

———

Tyler Briggs had instructed Magdalena to proceed directly to Phillip's fourth-floor office. Instead, she had taken a detour to the gallery.

The Gentileschi was propped on a display easel. Magdalena snapped a photograph of the work with her mobile phone. Then she took two wide-angle shots that left little doubt as to the painting's current location—a room that had been described in great detail in an unflattering *Vanity Fair* profile written by the woman who was at that moment sitting in Magdalena's suite at the Pierre.

She realized suddenly that Tyler was watching her from the gallery's doorway. He must have spotted her on one of the security cameras. She reacted with the studied calm of a drug dealer.

"Extraordinary, isn't it?"

"If you say so, Ms. Navarro."

"You don't appreciate art, Tyler?"

"To be honest, I don't know much about it."

"Has Mr. Somerset seen it yet?"

"You would have to ask Mr. Somerset. In fact, he's probably wondering where you are."

Magdalena made her way upstairs. The door to Phillip's office was open. He was sitting at his desk with a phone to his ear and a palm pressed to his forehead.

"You're making a big mistake," he snapped, then killed the call.

A frigid silence settled over the room.

"Who's making a mistake?" asked Magdalena.

"Warren Ridgefield. He's one of our investors. Unfortunately, several others are making the same mistake."

"Is there anything I can do to help?"

Phillip took her by the hand and smiled.

59

Upper East Side

Phillip's shower was twice the size of the kitchen in Magdalena's old apartment in Alphabet City, an aquatic wonderland of marble and glass, the shower for the man who had everything. Magdalena could never recall which of the many brushed-chrome handles performed which function. She turned one and was blasted by water cannon on all sides. Frantically she tried another and was caressed by a gentle tropical cascade. She washed herself with Phillip's male-scented soap, dried herself with one of Phillip's monogrammed towels, and then contemplated her nude form in Phillip's gilt-framed mirror. She found the image unappealing and sorely in need of restoration. Portrait of a drug dealer, she thought. Portrait of a thief.

Portrait of an unknown woman . . .

In the master bedroom there was no sign of Phillip other than the stain he had left on the sheet. Their lovemaking had bordered on rape and had been accompanied by the constant tolling and chiming of his mobile phone. Magdalena's was tucked in her Hermès handbag, which lay at the foot of the bed, along with the clothing Phillip had ripped from her body. Aware that others were listening, she had endured his assault in muted silence. Her ravenous lover, however, had been in fine voice.

Dressed, she took up her handbag and went in search of him. She found him downstairs in the gallery, standing before the forged Gentileschi. He was wearing the expression of curatorial refinement he always donned for the benefit of his guileless investors. Phillip Somerset, patron of the arts. To Magdalena he would always be the uncultured philistine whom she had first encountered that night at Le Cirque. Bud Fox with a dash of Jay Gatsby. A forgery, she thought. And quite an obvious one at that.

"How good is it?" he asked finally.

"Better than the version at the Getty."

"Price?"

"All things being equal . . . thirty million."

"I need to unload it."

"I would advise against that, Phillip."

"Why?"

"Because the painting came from the same source as the ones that were sold by Oliver Dimbleby in London. If another picture emerges from the same so-called old European collection, it will raise red flags. The painting needs an entirely new provenance and sufficient time to cool off. We might also want to take the attribution down a notch or two."

"Attributed to Gentileschi?"

"Maybe circle of Gentileschi. Or even a follower."

"I'd be lucky to get a million for it."

"I didn't buy a painting in Florence, Phillip. I bought the greatest art forger in history. He'll pay dividends for years to come. Put the Gentileschi on ice in the warehouse and be patient."

Phillip stared at his phone. "I'm afraid patience is a virtue I can't afford at the moment."

"Who is it now?"

"Harriet Grant."

"What's going on?"

"I haven't a clue."

———

They ate their seafood Cobb salads at the table in the kitchen, with CNBC playing softly in the background. Magdalena drank Sancerre with hers, but Phillip, parched from his bedroom exertions, guzzled iced tea. His phone lay faceup at his elbow, silenced but aglow with incoming message traffic.

"You never told me his name," he said.

"I'm afraid I can't."

"Why not?"

"Parity, I suppose. You have your forger, and now I have mine."

"But you acquired your forger with ten million dollars of my money."

"You wouldn't have any money if it wasn't for me, Phillip. Besides, I went to a great deal of trouble to find him. I think I'll keep him all to myself."

He laid down his cutlery and eyed her without expression.

"Delvecchio," she said with a sigh. "Mario Delvecchio."

"What's his story?"

"The usual one. A failed painter who takes his revenge on the art world with a palette and a brush. He lives in an isolated villa in southern Umbria. He's extraordinarily well educated and trained. And quite beautiful, I must say. We became lovers during my stay. Unlike you, he's familiar with female pleasure centers."

"Is there something else I can do for you?"

"I'd love some more of this Sancerre."

Phillip signaled Señora Ramírez. "Does your lover have any other finished works lying around?"

"None that I'm inclined to introduce to the market at this time.

I've asked him to cool it on the masterpieces for a while and concentrate on mid-level works that I can move under the radar."

"What are we going to do about his partner? This Alessandro Calvi fellow?"

"Now that Mario and I are sleeping together, I think I can convince him to part company with Signore Calvi."

"You're joking, right?"

"You know there's no one but you, Phillip." She patted the back of his hand reassuringly. "The truth is, I'm more worried about he who shall not be named than I am about Signore Calvi."

"Let me worry about him."

"How will he feel about having an Old Master stablemate?"

"I never promised him exclusivity."

Magdalena raised her wineglass to her lips. "Where have I heard that one before?"

Phillip adopted a new expression—caring friend and sexual partner. It was even less authentic than Phillip the intellectual and art world sophisticate. "What's got into you?" he asked.

"Besides you, you mean?" Magdalena laughed quietly at her own witticism. "I suppose I've just been thinking about my future, that's all."

"Your future is assured."

"Is it really?"

"Have you checked your balance lately? You could retire tomorrow and spend the rest of your life lying on a beach in Ibiza."

"And if I did?"

Phillip made no reply; he was staring at his phone again.

"Who is it now?"

"Nicky Lovegrove." He sent the call to voice mail. "Several of his clients are trying to cash out of my fund."

"My money is in that fund. *All* of it."

"Your money is safe."

"You also once assured me that you were going to turn me into a

Spanish Damien Hirst. But it was nothing more than a clever ploy on your part to put a little cash in my pocket."

"It wasn't a little cash, as I recall."

"Where are they?" asked Magdalena suddenly.

"The paintings?"

She nodded.

"They're in the warehouse."

"I'd like them back."

"You can't have them."

"Why not?"

"Because they belong to me. And so do you, Magdalena. Never forget that."

His phone flared.

"Not another one."

"No. It's only Lindsay."

Magdalena smiled. "Do give her my best."

———————

After speaking briefly to his wife and bidding farewell to his business partner and mistress, Phillip Somerset returned to his office and rang Ellis Gray, head of art-based lending at JPMorgan Chase. Phillip and Ellis had bumped into one another in Sag Harbor over the weekend, rendering foreplay unnecessary. Phillip said he needed a bit of cash. Ellis, who had made millions dealing with Masterpiece Art Ventures, merely asked for the number Phillip had in mind and a description of the painting he intended to use as collateral.

"The number is forty million."

"And the painting?"

Phillip answered.

"A *Gentileschi* Gentileschi?" asked Ellis.

"It's newly discovered. I'm planning to keep it under wraps for a year or two before putting it on the market."

"How's the attribution?"

"Bulletproof."

"And the provenance?"

"On the thin side."

"Where did you purchase it?"

"A Spanish dealer. That's all I can say."

Ellis Gray, who made his living lending money against paintings, was well acquainted with the opacity of the art world. Nevertheless, he was not prepared to fork over $40 million of JPMorgan Chase's money on a picture without a past, even for a client as important and reliable as Phillip Somerset.

"Not without a full scientific evaluation," added Ellis. "Send it to Aiden Gallagher up in Westport. If Aiden says it's kosher, I'll expedite the loan."

Phillip killed the connection. Then he video-called Kenny Vaughan and told him that no emergency infusion of cash was in the offing.

"We might have to consider suspending redemptions."

"We can't. You have to make it work."

"I'll light a few candles and see what I can do."

Phillip dumped Kenny and accepted another call.

It was Allegra Hughes.

Allegra wanted out.

60

Pierre Hotel

Gabriel had made the request of Yuval Gershon early that morning. Yes, he realized it was an imposition and not altogether legal, as he had no official standing. And, no, he could not state with any degree of certainty that it would be the last time. It seemed he had become the first port of call for anyone with a problem, be they adulterous British prime ministers, supreme Roman pontiffs, or London art dealers. His current investigation, as was often the case, had included an attempt on his life. Yuval Gershon, of course, knew this. In fact, were it not for Yuval's timely intercession, the attempt might well have proven successful.

He gave the job to a new kid. It was no matter; in a field like theirs, the new kids were frequently better than the old hands. This one was an artist in the truest sense of the word. He made his first move at ten fifteen Eastern time, and by half past two he owned the place—the place being a Manhattan-based concern called Chelsea Fine Arts Storage.

As instructed, the kid headed straight for the database: insurance records, tax documents, personnel files, a dispatch log with a year's worth of pickups and deliveries, a master list of the paintings stored in a secure, climate-controlled warehouse on East Ninety-First Street near York Avenue. There were 789 paintings in all. Each entry included the name of the work, the artist, the support, the dimensions, the date of execution, the estimated value, the current owner, and the painting's exact location in the warehouse, by floor and rack number.

Six hundred and fifteen of the paintings were said to be owned directly by Masterpiece Art Ventures—which also happened to own Chelsea Fine Arts Storage. The remaining works were controlled by corporate shell companies with the sort of three-letter uppercase abbreviations beloved by asset concealers and kleptocrats the world over. The most recent arrival was *Danaë and the Shower of Gold*, purportedly by Orazio Gentileschi. The stated value of the work was $30 million, which was approximately $30 million more than what it was actually worth. As yet, the work was uninsured.

The warehouse also contained sixteen canvases by a once promising Spanish artist named Magdalena Navarro. At three fifteen that afternoon—following an incriminating luncheon with one Phillip Somerset, founder and CEO of Masterpiece Art Ventures—she returned to the Pierre Hotel. Upstairs in her suite she immediately surrendered her phone to Gabriel. He gave her a list of 789 paintings, and they went to work.

———

They fell into a predictable if altogether depressing rhythm. Magdalena would cast her eye down the list and call out when she spotted a painting she knew to be a forgery. Then, with Sarah and Evelyn Buchanan taking careful notes, she would recite the date and circumstances by which the work had found its way into the inventory of Masterpiece Art Ventures. The overwhelming majority of the canvases had been acquired through phantom sales conducted within Magdalena's distribution network, which meant no actual money had changed hands. But several had been routed through reputable dealers to provide Phillip with plausible deniability in the event the authenticity of the works was ever called into question.

Notably absent from the directory was Sir Anthony van Dyck's *Portrait of an Unknown Woman*, oil on canvas, 115 by 92 centimeters, which Masterpiece had recently purchased from Isherwood Fine Arts. According to the dispatch logs, the painting was moved to Sotheby's in New York in mid-April.

"A week after the bombing in Paris," Gabriel pointed out.

"Phillip must have unloaded it," replied Magdalena. "Which means some unsuspecting collector is now the proud owner of a worthless painting."

"I'll have a word with Sotheby's tomorrow morning."

"A quiet word," cautioned Sarah.

"Somehow," said Gabriel with a glance at Evelyn, "I don't think that's going to be an option."

By 5:00 p.m. they had twice scoured the list from top to bottom. The final tally was a breathtaking 227 forgeries with a declared valuation of more than $300 million, or 25 percent of Masterpiece's purported assets under management. When combined with the rest of the evidence that Gabriel and Magdalena had acquired in New York—including a recording of an attempt by Phillip Somerset to obtain an art-backed loan from JPMorgan Chase using a forged painting as collateral—it was irrefutable proof that Masterpiece Art Ventures was a criminal enterprise run by one of the greatest financial con artists in history.

At the conclusion of the review, Evelyn rang her editor at *Vanity Fair*'s Fulton Street headquarters and told him to expect her finished draft no later than 9:00 p.m. Then she sat down at her laptop and began to write.

"At some point," she informed Gabriel, "I'll have to ask Phillip for a comment."

Fortunately, they knew how to reach him. According to Proteus, his phone was presently near the corner of Fifth Avenue and East Seventy-Fourth Street, 134 feet above sea level. There were six missed calls, three new voice mails, and twenty-two unread text messages. The camera was staring at the ceiling. The microphone was listening to nothing at all. The damn thing was just sitting there, thought Gabriel. Like a paperweight with a digital pulse.

61

Sutton Place

Leonard Silk was well acquainted with the dark side of human nature. His clients, all of whom were sufficiently wealthy to afford his services, were a rogues' gallery of fraudsters, schemers, scammers, larcenists, embezzlers, insider traders, philanderers, and sexual deviants of every stripe. Silk never sat in judgment of them, for Silk was not without sin himself. He dwelled in a proverbial house of glass. He did not make a habit of throwing stones.

Silk's fall from grace had occurred in the late 1980s while he was serving in the CIA's station in Bogotá. Recently divorced, his personal finances under duress, he had entered into a lucrative partnership with the Medellín cocaine cartel. Silk had supplied the drug lords with valuable intelligence on DEA and Colombian efforts to penetrate their organization. In return, the drug lords had supplied Silk with money—$20 million in cash, all of it derived from selling cocaine in the country he was sworn to defend.

Somehow Silk managed to extricate himself from the relationship with both his ill-gotten fortune and his life, and retired from the Agency just days before the attacks of 9/11. He used a portion of the funds to purchase a luxury Sutton Place apartment. And in the winter of 2002, while his old colleagues were fighting the opening battle of the global war on terrorism, Silk went into business as a security consultant and private investigator. In a deliberate play on words, he called his one-man firm Integrity Security Solutions.

Silk offered his clients the usual array of advisory services but derived most of his income through illicit activities such as corporate espionage, computer hacking, blackmail, sabotage, and a product he euphemistically referred to as "reputational defense." He was renowned for his ability to make problems go away, or, whenever possible, to prevent problems from arising in the first place. He also possessed the capability, as a last resort, to make "problems" suffer fatal auto accidents or drug overdoses, or vanish without a trace. He had no operatives on his payroll. Instead, he hired freelance professionals as needed. Two recent operations had taken place in France, where Silk was well connected. Both had been carried out at the behest of the same client.

At 9:42 that morning, the client had asked Silk to ascertain why several investors had requested multimillion-dollar redemptions from his art-based hedge fund. With a few phone calls to his network of paid or coerced informants, Silk had discovered a possible explanation. It was not the sort of matter he liked to discuss over the phone, so he summoned his driver and headed uptown. Arriving at the client's residence on East Seventy-Fourth Street, Silk saw two workmen maneuvering a crated painting into the back of a delivery truck. A security man named Tyler Briggs was observing their efforts from the open doorway.

"Where's your boss?" asked Silk.

"Upstairs in his office."

"Is he alone?"

"He is now. He had company earlier."

"Anyone interesting?"

Briggs ushered Silk into the mansion's security control room. The art-filled residence was protected by an array of high-resolution cameras. At present, one was trained on Silk's client. He was sitting at his desk, a phone to his ear. He looked unwell.

Briggs sat down at a computer and wordlessly entered a few keystrokes. A moment later a tall, dark-haired woman appeared on one of the video screens. She was standing before a painting in the gallery. A Gentileschi, thought Silk. Quite stunning, but almost certainly a forgery.

"Why is she photographing it?"

"I didn't ask."

"Where did she go next?"

The security man played the recording.

"That's quite enough," said Silk after a moment.

The image froze.

"Walk upstairs to Mr. Somerset's office and quietly tell him to meet me in the garden."

The security man rose and started toward the door.

"One more thing, Tyler."

"Yes, Mr. Silk?"

"Tell Mr. Somerset to leave his phone behind."

————

Silk followed a corridor toward the back of the town house—past the wine cellar, the movie theater, and the yoga studio—and emerged into the walled garden. It was shaded by a large tree in midsummer leaf and overlooked on the north and east by elderly apartment buildings. Decorator outdoor furnishings stood forlornly on the spotless stonework. The splashing of the Italianate fountain silenced the rush of afternoon traffic on Fifth Avenue.

Five minutes elapsed before Phillip Somerset finally appeared. As usual, he was nautically attired. They sat down in a pair of low-slung wicker chairs. Silk delivered his findings without preamble or pleasantries. He was a busy man, and Phillip Somerset was in serious trouble.

"How bad is it going to be?"

"My sources haven't been able to uncover anything regarding the content."

"Isn't that exactly the sort of information I pay you for, Leonard?"

"The magazine's publicity department has contacted every business news desk in the city. They wouldn't have done that unless she had something big."

"Is it fatal?"

"Could be."

"And you're sure the story is about me?"

Silk nodded.

"Is the FBI involved?"

"My sources say not."

"So where is it coming from? And why did several of my investors choose today of all days to flee the fund?"

"It's possible that rumors are swirling in the art world about a damaging story in the works. But the more likely explanation is that you are under a coordinated attack by a determined and resourceful adversary."

"Any candidates?"

"Only one."

Silk didn't speak the name; it wasn't necessary. He had opposed targeting a man like Gabriel Allon but had relented when Phillip offered him a payment of $10 million. Silk had given a substantial portion of that money to a French organization known only as the Groupe, the same organization that had handled the Valerie Bérrangar job. He had also supplied the Groupe detailed information regarding Allon's travel plans—specifically, his intention to pay a visit to an art gallery on the rue la Boétie in Paris. Even so, the Israeli and his friend Sarah Bancroft had managed to escape the gallery alive.

"You assured me that Allon was no longer an issue," said Phillip.

"The video of Ms. Navarro's arrival here earlier this afternoon would suggest otherwise."

Phillip frowned. "Is Tyler Briggs on your payroll or mine, Leonard?"

Silk ignored the question. "She took several photographs of the painting that was on display in the gallery. Close-ups and wide shots. Looked to me as though she was trying to establish its location."

Phillip's expression darkened, but he said nothing.

"Did the two of you discuss business after you were finished in the bedroom?"

"In detail," answered Phillip.

"Was your phone with you?"

"Yes, of course."

"Where was hers?"

"I assume it was in her handbag."

"It was probably recording every word you said. You should assume your phone is probably compromised, too."

Phillip swore softly.

"I'm afraid to ask."

"I had two rather candid calls with Kenny Vaughan. I also tried to obtain an art-backed loan from Ellis Gray of JPMorgan Chase."

"Because several of your largest investors just happened to withdraw from your fund on the very day that Ms. Navarro was in your home taking pictures of a painting."

Phillip clambered to his feet.

"Sit down," said Silk calmly. "You're not going anywhere near her."

"You work for *me*, Leonard."

"Which is not something I'd like the FBI to know. Or Gabriel Allon, for that matter. Therefore, you will do exactly what I tell you to do."

Phillip managed a smile. "Did you just threaten me?"

"Only amateurs make threats. And I'm no amateur."

Phillip lowered himself into his chair.

"Where is she staying?" asked Silk.

"Her usual suite at the Pierre."

"I think I'll check in on her. In the meantime, I'd like you to go upstairs and pack a bag."

"Where am I going?"

"To be determined."

"If I leave the country now—"

"Your remaining investors will head for the lifeboats, and your fund will collapse within hours. The question is, do you want to be in New York when that happens? Or would you rather be lying on a beach with Lindsay?"

Phillip gave no answer.

"How much cash is on hand?" asked Silk.

"Not much."

"In that case, now might be a good time for you to settle your bill with Integrity Security Solutions." Silk handed over a phone. "Your outstanding balance is fifteen million."

"Rather steep, don't you think?"

"Now is not the time to quibble over money, Phillip. I'm the only thing standing between you and a cell in the Metropolitan Correctional Center."

Phillip dialed Kenny Vaughn and instructed him to wire $15 million into Silk's account at Oceanic Bank and Trust Ltd. in Nassau. "I know, Kenny. Just do whatever you need to do."

Phillip killed the call and tried to return the phone.

"Keep it," said Silk. "Leave your personal phone on the desk connected to a charger and go to your place on the island. Don't make a move until you hear from me."

62

Pierre Hotel

During the thirteen-block ride from Phillip Somerset's town house to the Pierre Hotel, Leonard Silk made a series of hurried phone calls. The first was to Executive Jet Services at MacArthur Airport on Long Island; the second, to a man who had run guns to the Contras and cocaine for the cartels. Lastly, Silk called an old friend from the Agency named Martin Roth. Marty was a supplier of cyber-and-surveillance specialists and, if circumstances warranted, muscle and firepower. His private security business was based in a warehouse in Greenpoint. Silk was a regular customer.

"When do you need them?" asked Marty.

"Twenty minutes ago."

"The traffic in Midtown is a bitch. And I'm stretched pretty thin as it is."

"Do what you can," said Silk as his Escalade drew to a stop outside the Pierre's Fifth Avenue entrance. "My client will be grateful. And so will I."

Inside, the hostess in the Two E Bar & Lounge greeted Silk by name and showed him to a corner table. A glass of single malt appeared a moment later, followed soon after by Ray Bennett, a retired NYPD detective who now served as the Pierre's director of security. Nothing happened inside the hotel's walls that escaped Bennett's notice, which is why Silk paid him a substantial monthly retainer.

Bennett wasn't alone. There were others like him at every high-end hotel in town, all feeding Silk a steady stream of dirt, most of it accompanied by receipts and security video. Information about the private lives of reporters was a priority. Bennett had once given Silk the means to kill a *New York* magazine exposé about one of his most important clients. Silk had rewarded his asset with a $25,000 bonus, enough to take the financial sting out of his divorce settlement and pay for his kid's tuition at Holy Rosary.

Hotel regulations forbade Bennett to sit down with a customer, so he remained on his feet while Silk made his request. "There's a woman staying in a suite on the twentieth floor. She's acquainted with an important client of mine. The client is concerned she might be in danger."

"What's her name?"

"She checked in under Miranda Álvarez. Her real name is—"

"Magdalena Navarro. She's a regular."

"Have you noticed anything unusual?"

"Unless I'm mistaken, she's only set foot outside the hotel once since she arrived."

"What's she been doing with herself?"

"She had a dinner party last night."

"Really? With whom?"

"Her friends from across the hall. They checked in at the same time. False names. Just like Ms. Navarro."

"I need their real names," said Silk.

"How badly?"

"Ten thousand."

"Twenty."

"Done," said Silk.

———

Ray Bennett returned to his office, closed the door, and sat down at his computer. As director of security, he had unlimited access to guest information, regardless of their demands for privacy. He called Leonard Silk a moment later and read him the names.

"Sarah Bancroft and Gabriel Allon."

Bennett's iPhone pinged with a text message.

"Look at the photograph I just sent you," said Silk.

Bennett enlarged the image.

"Recognize her?"

"She's that reporter from *Vanity Fair*."

"Has she been in Ms. Navarro's suite?"

"I believe she's there now."

"Thanks, Ray. The check's in the mail."

The connection died.

Bennett looked at the two names on his computer screen. One of them was familiar. *Gabriel Allon* . . . Bennett was certain he had seen it before. But where?

Google gave him the answer.

"Shit," he said softly.

———

Outside, Leonard Silk slid into the back of his Escalade and dialed the burner phone he had given to Phillip.

"Did you speak to her?" he asked.

"I couldn't. She's rather busy at the moment."

"Doing what?"

"Telling Evelyn Buchanan everything she knows about Masterpiece

Art Ventures. Gabriel Allon and your friend Sarah Bancroft are with her. It's over, Phillip. Your charter leaves MacArthur at ten fifteen. Don't be late."

"Maybe I should take the Gulfstream instead."

"The point of this operation is to get you and Lindsay out of the country without leaving any footprints. When you arrive in Miami, a car will run you down to Key West. By the time the sun rises, you'll be halfway to the Yucatán Peninsula."

"What about you, Leonard?"

"That depends on whether you ever mentioned my name to your friend from Seville."

"Don't worry, she can't implicate you in anything."

Silk heard a chorus of car horns through the phone. "Why aren't you on the chopper yet?"

"Second Avenue is jammed."

"You won't have to worry about traffic where you're going."

Silk hung up the phone and lifted his gaze toward the upper floors of the hotel. *She can't implicate you* . . . Perhaps not, but Silk wasn't prepared to take that chance.

He rang Ray Bennett.

"I have another assignment, if you're interested."

"I'm listening."

Silk explained.

"How much?" asked Bennett.

"Fifty thousand."

"To go up against a man like Gabriel Allon? Get real, Leonard."

"How about seventy-five?"

"A hundred."

"Done," said Silk.

63

North Haven

Alone in the vast, empty house in North Haven, Lindsay Somerset sat in a simple cross-legged pose, her hands resting lightly on her knees. The floor-to-ceiling window before her overlooked the copper waters of Peconic Bay. Ordinarily the panorama filled her with a sense of contentment, but not now. She could find no inner peace, no *shanti*.

Her phone lay on the floor next to her mat, silenced, aglow with an incoming call. She didn't recognize the number, so she tapped DECLINE. Instantly the phone rang a second time, and once again Lindsay terminated the call. After two additional attempts to fend off the intruder, she lifted the device angrily to her ear.

"What the hell do you want?"

"I was hoping to have a word with my wife."

"Sorry, Phillip. I didn't recognize the number. Whose phone are you using?"

"I'll explain when I get there."

"I thought you were staying in the city tonight."

"Change in plan. We're scheduled to land at East Hampton at six forty-five."

"Wonderful news. Shall I make a dinner reservation?"

"I don't think I can face the mob scene tonight. Let's pick up something on the way home."

"Lulu?"

"Perfect."

"Any requests?"

"Surprise me."

"Is something wrong, Phillip? You sound down."

"Rough day. That's all."

Lindsay hung up the phone and, rising, pulled on a pair of Nike and a Lululemon half-zip hoodie. Then she headed downstairs to the great room. *Rothko, Pollock, Warhol, Basquiat, Lichtenstein, Diebenkorn...* Nearly a half-billion dollars' worth of paintings, all controlled by Masterpiece Art Ventures. Phillip had carefully shielded Lindsay from the company's affairs, and her knowledge of how it functioned was limited to the basics. Phillip purchased paintings shrewdly and sold them at an immense profit. He kept a portion of those profits for himself and passed the rest on to his investors. Banks were eager to lend him capital because he never missed a payment and used his inventory as collateral. The loans allowed him to buy still more art, which produced still greater returns for his investors. Most saw the paper valuation of their accounts double in just three years. Few ever withdrew their money. Masterpiece was too sweet a deal.

Lindsay contemplated the Basquiat. She had been at Phillip's side the night he purchased it at Christie's for $75 million. In fact, it was their first real date. Afterward, he had taken her to Bar SixtyFive at the Rainbow Room to celebrate the acquisition with his employees. They were a small team—three ponytailed young women with sensible shoes and Ivy League educations, and a guy named Kenny Vaughan who had worked with Phillip at Lehman Brothers. There was also a tall, beautiful Spanish woman named Magdalena Navarro. Phillip said she worked as a scout and broker for Masterpiece in Europe.

"Are you still sleeping with her?" Lindsay had asked during the drive to Phillip's town house.

"With Magdalena? Not anymore."

Lindsay posed the same question when Phillip proposed marriage—and when he insisted that she sign a prenuptial agreement guaranteeing her a payment of $10 million were they ever to divorce. In neither instance did she believe Phillip's denial. More troubling was her deeply held conviction that her husband and Magdalena remained lovers to this day. The sexual bond they shared was obvious in their every gesture and expression. Lindsay wasn't blind. And she wasn't as dumb as they thought she was.

I'll explain when I get there...

The sensation of disharmony returned. Whether it was their marriage or Phillip's business, Lindsay could not say. But something was amiss, off-kilter. She was certain of it.

Outside, she climbed behind the wheel of her white Range Rover and headed up the drive. As she passed the staff cottage, a security guard gave her a perfunctory wave and opened the gate. She turned left into Actors Colony Road, then dialed Lulu Kitchen & Bar in Sag Harbor. She greeted the hostess by name and placed her order: fried calamari, grilled octopus, two Bibb lettuce salads, grilled halibut, and a skirt steak. Phillip's credit card was on file, so there was no discussion of payment or even the size of the bill.

"Is seven fifteen all right, Mrs. Somerset? We're a bit busy tonight."

"Seven would be better."

She followed Route 114 down the length of the peninsula and into downtown Sag Harbor. The airport lay about four miles south of the village, on Daniels Hole Road. Once owned and operated by the town of East Hampton, it was now a fully private airfield that catered to people like the Somersets of North Haven. Phillip's Sikorsky was dropping from the clear evening sky as Lindsay turned through the entrance. The security guard allowed her to drive onto the tarmac, thus sparing Mr. Somerset the indignity of having to walk to the parking lot.

He settled into the passenger seat of the Range Rover while the ground staff loaded two large aluminum-sided Rimowa suitcases into the back. Both bags appeared to be unusually heavy.

"Dumbbells?" asked Lindsay as she kissed Phillip's lips.

"One contains two million dollars in cash. The other is filled with five-hundred-gram gold ingots."

"Why?"

"Because I'm not the man you think I am," said Phillip. "And I'm in trouble."

64

Pierre Hotel

Shortly before taking over day-to-day management of Isherwood Fine Arts, Sarah Bancroft had endured a brutal interrogation at the hands of a senior Russian intelligence officer, during which she was threatened with a deadly radiological toxin. Watching Evelyn Buchanan write her article was only slightly less torturous. Sarah offered guidance where she could, but mainly she kept her head down and tried to stay out of the line of fire, most of which was directed at Gabriel. No, he said time and time again, he had no desire to see his name included in the story. Ground rules were ground rules. There was no going back at the last minute.

"In that case," said Evelyn, "I have a few more questions I'd like to ask Magdalena."

"About what?"

"Oliver Dimbleby."

"Who?"

"Magdalena mentioned his name when she and Phillip were discussing your Gentileschi."

"Did she? I wasn't listening at the time."

"She also implied that all those newly discovered paintings were forgeries."

"That's because they were."

"Who painted them?"

"Who do you think?"

"Why?"

"To lure Magdalena into the open."

"Did anyone actually *buy* them?"

"Goodness, no. That would have been unethical."

"Please tell me the rest of the story."

"Finish the one in front of you, Evelyn. Your editor is expecting your first draft at nine o'clock."

By half past six Sarah could take no more. Rising, she announced her intention to go downstairs for a proper Belvedere martini. Magdalena requested permission to join her.

"Permission denied."

"If I was going to flee, I would have done it this afternoon while I was with Phillip. Besides, we had a deal, Mr. Allon."

She had a point. "One drink only," he said. "And no phone or passport."

"Two drinks," countered Sarah. Then she turned to Magdalena. "I'll meet you at the elevators in five minutes."

"Ten would be better."

Sarah headed to her room to freshen up. Magdalena did the same, leaving Gabriel alone with Evelyn.

"I'd like to ask you a few more questions."

"I'm sure you would," replied Gabriel absently. Then he checked the feed from Phillip Somerset's phone. The device had not moved in more than three hours. Fourteen missed calls, eight new voice mails, thirty-seven unread text messages.

No images.

No audio.

No Phillip.

When it was over, there was near-universal agreement that it was all Christopher's fault. He rang Sarah from London as she was entering her room and kept her on the phone while she stripped off her wrinkled clothing and changed into something more appropriate. Putting her hair and makeup in order proved more of a challenge than she had imagined it would, placing her at the elevators two minutes behind schedule. Arriving, she breathed a sigh of relief. It seemed her new friend from Spain was running late as well.

But when three additional minutes elapsed with no sign of Magdalena, Sarah grew anxious. Her fear of impending disaster worsened when a press of the call button produced a glowing light but no carriage. Frantic, she snatched up the receiver of the house phone, explained her plight to the hotel operator, and was assured she would momentarily be lobby bound.

At last a carriage appeared. It stopped on a half-dozen floors, collecting a menagerie of annoyed hotel guests, before finally reaching the lobby. Sarah made straight for the bar, but Magdalena was nowhere to be found. She asked a waiter whether he had seen a tall, black-haired woman, approximately forty years old, quite beautiful. Unfortunately, said the waiter, he had not.

Sarah received a similar answer from the girl at Reception. And from the dark-suited security man standing nearby. And from the porters and valets at both of the hotel's entrances.

Finally she dialed Gabriel's number. "Please tell me that Magdalena is still upstairs with you."

"She left fifteen minutes ago."

Sarah's shouted obscenity reverberated through the Pierre's grand lobby. She had turned her back on Magdalena. And now she was gone.

65

Midtown

Magdalena had recognized the man who greeted her elevator. She saw him each time she stayed at the Pierre. He was the hotel's head of security. A big guy with an Irish face and an outer boroughs accent. In her previous life, Magdalena would have avoided a man like him. It was obvious the guy was a cop. Retired, sure. But a cop all the same.

On that evening, however, the former police officer whose name Magdalena did not know had presented himself as her guardian. Quietly, his voice calm and assured, he had asked Magdalena whether she was expecting any visitors. And when she replied that she wasn't, he informed her that he had noticed two men loitering outside her suite earlier that afternoon. The same two men, he explained, were now drinking club soda in the lobby bar. It was his considered opinion that both were federal law enforcement agents.

"FBI?"

"Probably. And I think there might be a couple more outside."

"Can you get me out of here?"

"That depends on what you've done."

"I trusted someone I shouldn't have."

"I've done that once or twice myself." He looked her up and down. "Do you need anything from your suite?"

"I can't go back."

"Why not?"

"Because the man I trusted is there now."

With that, he took her by the arm and led her through a doorway. It opened onto a hallway lined with small offices, which in turn gave onto the hotel's loading bay. A black Escalade idled curbside on East Sixty-First Street.

"He's waiting for another guest. It's yours if you want it."

"I don't have any way to pay him."

"I know the driver. I'll take care of it."

The big former cop with an Irish face escorted Magdalena across the sidewalk and opened the rear driver's-side door. Seated in the back was a gray man in a gray suit. The former cop forced Magdalena inside and slammed the door. The Escalade lurched forward and made a left turn onto Fifth Avenue.

The gray man in the gray suit watched Magdalena without expression as she clawed at the door latch. Finally she capitulated and turned to face him. "Who are you?"

"I'm the man who makes Phillip's problems go away," he answered. "And you, Ms. Navarro, are a problem."

———————

The driver had a neck like a fire hydrant and stubble-length hair. At the corner of East Fifty-Ninth Street and Park Avenue, Magdalena politely asked him to unlock her door. Receiving no response, she appealed to the gray man in the gray suit, who told her to shut her mouth. Furious, she tried to gouge his eyes from their sockets. Her attack ended when he seized her right wrist and twisted it to the breaking point.

"Are you finished?"

"Yes."

He increased the pain. "Are you sure?"

"I promise."

He reduced the pressure, but only slightly. "Why are you in New York?"

"I was arrested."

"Where?"

"Italy."

"How is Allon involved?"

"He was working with the Italian police."

"I assume you made a deal?"

"Doesn't everyone?"

"What were the terms?"

"He promised me that I wouldn't face charges if I helped him take down Phillip."

"And you fell for this nonsense?"

"He gave me his word."

"He used you, Ms. Navarro. And you can be sure that he was planning to hand you over to the FBI the minute he no longer needed you."

Magdalena tore her wrist from his grasp and retreated to the edge of the seat. They were inching across the intersection of East Fifty-Ninth Street and Third Avenue. On the other side of her blacked-out window was a traffic officer, arm raised. If Magdalena were successful in getting the officer's attention, she might extricate herself from her current circumstances. But she would also set in motion a chain of events that would lead inevitably to her incarceration. It was better, she reasoned, to take her chances with the solver of Phillip's problems.

"How much does Allon know?" he asked.

"Everything."

"And the reporter?"

"More than enough."

"When will the article appear?"

"Later tonight. Masterpiece will be toast by the morning."

"Will the story include my name?"

"How could it? I don't know your name."

"Phillip never whispered it into your ear while you were—"

"Fuck you, you bastard."

The blow came without warning, a lightning-fast backhand. Magdalena tasted blood.

"How chivalrous. There's nothing quite so attractive as a man who strikes a defenseless woman."

His phone rang before he could pose another question. He raised the device to his ear and listened in silence. Finally he said, "Thanks, Marty. Let me know if Allon makes a move." Then he returned the phone to his coat pocket and looked at Magdalena. "Evidently, Evelyn Buchanan's computer is about to have a serious malfunction."

"It won't stop the article."

"Perhaps not. But it will give you and Phillip plenty of time to get out of the country before the FBI issues warrants for your arrest."

"I'm not going anywhere with him."

"The alternative is a shallow grave in the Adirondacks."

Magdalena said nothing.

"Wise choice, Ms. Navarro."

66

Sag Harbor

Lindsay insisted on stopping in downtown Sag Harbor to pick up the food at Lulu. Phillip thought it an act of madness, like the suicide who slips into her wedding gown before swallowing an overdose of sleeping tablets. Now, as he stood at the end of the restaurant's handsome bar awaiting their order, he was relieved to have a moment to himself.

The din of the room was pleasant and midsummer in volume. Phillip's present circumstances notwithstanding, it had been a good day on Wall Street. Money had been made. He shook a few of the better hands, rubbed a couple of important shoulders, and acknowledged the discreet nod of a respected collector who had recently purchased a painting from Masterpiece Art Ventures for $4.5 million. In a few hours' time, the collector would learn that the painting was doubtless a forgery. In an attempt to conceal his embarrassment over being duped, he would assure his closest friends and business associates that he had always known that Phillip Somerset was a con artist and swindler. The collector would likely receive no restitution, as the available assets of Masterpiece Art Ventures would be limited and the line of claimants long. The talented Mr. Somerset would be unable to offer assistance to the authorities, for his whereabouts would be unknown. Lulu Kitchen & Bar on Main Street in Sag Harbor would be among the last places anyone would recall laying eyes on him.

He felt a hand on his elbow and, turning, found himself gazing into the terrier-like eyes of Edgar Malone. Edgar lived well on the fortune left to him by his grandfather, a substantial portion of which he had unwisely entrusted to Masterpiece Art Ventures.

"I hear you lost several investors today," he announced.

"All of whom profited handsomely from their association with my fund."

"Should I be worried?"

"Do I look worried to you, Edgar?"

"You don't. That said, I'd like to take some of my money off the table."

"Sleep on it. Call me in the morning with your decision."

The hostess informed Phillip that his order was delayed and offered him a glass of complimentary wine as recompense, as he was a valued customer and a prominent member of East End society—at least for a few more hours. He declined the glass of wine but accepted an incoming call to his burner phone.

"Send your helicopter back to Manhattan immediately," said Leonard Silk.

"Why?"

"To pick up the final member of your traveling party."

"Anyone I know?"

"Call your crew," said Silk. "Get that bird back to Manhattan."

———

Five minutes later, bags in hand, Phillip stepped from the restaurant's doorway into the warm evening air. He placed the food in the back of the Range Rover and settled into the passenger seat. Lindsay reversed out of the space without so much as a glance in the rearview mirror. Tires screeched, a horn blared. Phillip supposed it would one day be a part of the lore surrounding his disappearance— the near-collision on Main Street in Sag Harbor. Much would be made of the fact that Lindsay had been the one behind the wheel.

She jammed the transmission into DRIVE, and the Range Rover shot forward. "Explain how it worked," she demanded.

"There isn't time. Besides, you couldn't possibly understand."

"Because I'm not smart enough?"

Phillip reached for her, but she recoiled. She was driving dangerously fast.

"Tell me!" she screamed.

"In the beginning, it was a way to generate the extra cash that I needed to show a profit to my investors. But as time went on, buying and selling forgeries became my business model. If I had stopped, the fund would have collapsed."

"Because your so-called fund was nothing but a glorified Ponzi scheme?"

"No, Lindsay. It was a real Ponzi scheme. And a very lucrative one at that."

And it would have gone on forever, thought Phillip, if it wasn't for a Frenchwoman named Valerie Bérrangar. She wrote a letter to Julian Isherwood about *Portrait of an Unknown Woman*. And Isherwood asked none other than the great Gabriel Allon to investigate. Phillip might have been able to outwit the FBI, but Allon was a far more formidable adversary—a gifted art restorer who also happened to be a retired intelligence officer. What were the odds? It had been a mistake to let him leave New York alive.

Lindsay ignored the stop sign at the end of Main Street and swerved onto Route 114. Phillip seized his armrest as they flew across the narrow two-lane bridge separating Sag Harbor from North Haven.

"You really need to slow down."

"I thought you have a plane to catch."

"We both do." Phillip released his death grip on the armrest. "It leaves from MacArthur at ten fifteen."

"Bound for where?"

"Miami."

"I know I'm not as smart as you are, Phillip, but I'm fairly certain Miami is part of the United States."

"It's only the first stop."

"And after Miami?"

"A beautiful home overlooking the ocean in Ecuador."

"I thought rich criminals like you and Bobby Axelrod went to Switzerland to avoid arrest."

"Only in the movies, Lindsay. We'll have new identities and plenty of money. No one will ever find us."

She laughed bitterly. "I'm not going anywhere with you, Phillip."

"Do you know what will happen if you stay behind? The minute the fund collapses, the FBI will seize the houses and the paintings and freeze all the bank accounts. You'll be an outcast. Your life will be ruined. And no one will ever believe that you didn't know your husband was a criminal."

"They will if I turn you in."

Phillip unplugged Lindsay's phone from its charger and slipped it into his coat pocket.

"Surely you didn't do this all on your own," she said.

"Kenny Vaughan was the one who made the numbers work."

"What about Magdalena?"

"She ran sales and distribution."

"Where is she now?"

"On her way to the Thirty-Fourth Street Heliport."

Lindsay pressed the accelerator to the floor.

"If you don't slow down," said Phillip, "you're going to kill someone."

"Maybe I'll kill *you*."

"Not if I kill you first, Lindsay."

67

Pierre Hotel

When Magdalena left her suite on the twentieth floor of the Pierre Hotel for the last time, she was clad in the same dark pantsuit she had been wearing the night she plucked Oliver Dimbleby from the pavements of Bury Street in London. She had her Spanish driver's permit and a single twenty-dollar bill, but no phone or passport. And no handbag, either. It was lying at the foot of her unmade bed, next to a Spanish-language copy of *Love in the Time of Cholera*. It was, in Gabriel's opinion, the clearest evidence of her intent. Of his many female friends and acquaintances, not one would take flight without a purse. Therefore, he was confident that there was some other explanation for Magdalena's sudden disappearance. An explanation that in all likelihood involved Phillip Somerset and Leonard Silk.

Whatever had happened, the hotel's surveillance cameras had been watching. Gabriel rang Yuval Gershon, explained the situation, and asked him to have a look at the recordings. Yuval suggested that Gabriel have a word with hotel security instead.

"I have a terrible feeling hotel security was involved."

"What makes you think that?"

"The elevators mysteriously froze around the time she went missing."

"Describe her."

"Tall, long dark hair, dark pantsuit, no handbag."

"It looks to me as though you're on the nineteenth floor."

"Twentieth, Yuval."

"I'll get back to you when I have something."

Gabriel rang off. Sarah was anxiously pacing the room. Evelyn Buchanan was staring at her laptop with the shocked expression of someone who had just witnessed a murder.

"Is something wrong?" asked Gabriel.

"My article just disappeared from my screen." Evelyn dragged a forefinger across her trackpad. "And my documents folder is empty. All of my work, including my notes and the transcript of my interview with Magdalena, is gone."

Gabriel quickly disconnected his computer from the hotel's Wi-Fi network and instructed Evelyn to do the same. "How long will it take you to retype the piece?"

"It's not a matter of simply retyping it. I have to rewrite it from beginning to end. Five thousand words. Entirely from memory."

"Then I suggest you get started." Gabriel snatched up his phone and looked at Sarah. "Double-lock the door, and don't open it for anyone but me."

He went into the corridor without another word and headed for the elevators. An empty carriage appeared at once. He rode it down to the lobby and left the hotel via the Fifth Avenue entrance.

Outside, the sun had dropped below the trees of Central Park, but the twilight was abundant. Gabriel turned to the left and then made another left onto East Sixtieth Street. As he passed the entrance of the fabled Metropolitan Club, the private playground of New York's financial elite, he spotted two men sitting in a parked Suburban. Both were wearing earpieces. The one behind the wheel noticed Gabriel first. He said something to his partner, who turned his head to have a look at the legend as well.

The legend rounded the corner onto Madison Avenue and walked to East Sixty-First Street. The second team was parked directly opposite the Pierre's delivery entrance. They were three in number—the third member being the hacker who had penetrated the Pierre's Wi-Fi network and sucked the documents off Evelyn's laptop.

Gabriel was tempted to ask the hacker to return the purloined material. Instead, he crossed Fifth Avenue and entered Central Park. There he sat down on a bench and waited for his phone to ring, wondering, not for the first time, how his life had come to this.

Though Gabriel did not know it, Magdalena was at that moment pondering the same question. She was seated not on a park bench but in the back of a luxury SUV, next to a man who a few minutes earlier had threatened to kill her if she did not agree to flee the country with the financier whose art-based hedge fund she had exposed as a fraud. She had been given no information regarding their destination, though her lack of a passport suggested that their journey would be unconventional. It would begin, apparently, with a helicopter flight, as they were parked beneath the FDR Drive, near the pale-gray, boxlike terminal of the East Thirty-Fourth Street Heliport.

Magdalena glanced at her wristwatch, the Cartier tank that Clarissa the personal shopper had chosen for her at Bergdorf Goodman that frigid December afternoon in 2008. What a waste, she thought suddenly, these costly trinkets. Art was all that mattered—art and books and music. And family, of course. It had been a mistake to involve her father in Phillip's fraud. Still, she was confident he would not be prosecuted. Art criminals never received the punishment they deserved. It was one of the reasons there was so much art crime.

A second SUV drew up beside them, and Tyler Briggs emerged from the passenger seat. Evidently, Magdalena would have a chaperone on the first leg of her journey into exile, lest she misbehave on board the aircraft and endanger the crew. She was considering one final act of insurrection before leaving Manhattan, a parting gesture to avenge her split and swollen lip.

Her seatmate was looking down at his phone. "Your ride is about to land," he informed her.

"Where am I going?"

"East Hampton."

"In time for dinner, I hope."

"It's only the first stop."

"And then?"

"Somewhere you'll be able to use that Spanish of yours."

"How's yours?"

"Fluent, actually."

"In that case, you won't have any trouble understanding what I'm about to tell you."

Calmly, she recited the crudest, vilest Spanish insult she could bring herself to repeat. The gray man in the gray suit only smiled. "Phillip always said you have quite a mouth on you."

This time it was Magdalena who lashed out without warning. Her blow opened a small cut in the corner of his eye. He wiped away the blood with a linen pocket square.

"Get on the helicopter, Ms. Navarro. Otherwise, there's a shallow grave in your future."

"Yours, too, I imagine."

Tyler Briggs opened Magdalena's door and escorted her to the waiting Sikorsky. Five minutes later they were headed across the East

River. Before them stretched the working-class neighborhoods of Queens and the suburbs of Nassau and Suffolk counties. That slender riotous island, thought Magdalena.

She checked her Cartier. It was 7:50 p.m. At least she thought it was. The damn watch kept lousy time.

68

Pierre Hotel

Ray Bennett, the Pierre Hotel's head of security, was roughly the same size as Capitano Luca Rossetti. Well over six feet tall, at least 225 pounds. Most of that weight remained in reasonably good shape for a man of his age, which was mid-fifties. His hair was metallic gray and well groomed, his face was wide and square. It was a face, thought Gabriel, that had been made to take a punch. He asked its owner whether it would be possible for them to have a word in private. Ray Bennett said he preferred to speak in the lobby.

"That would be a mistake on your part, Mr. Bennett."

"And why is that, sir?"

"Because your colleagues will hear what I have to say to you."

Bennett contemplated Gabriel with a pair of all-seeing cop's eyes. "What's this about?"

"A missing guest."

"Name?"

"Not here."

Bennett led Gabriel through a doorway behind Reception and down a corridor to his office. He left the door open. Gabriel closed it soundlessly and turned to face the larger man.

"Where is she?"

"Who?"

Gabriel delivered a lightning-strike blow to Bennett's larynx, then raised a knee to his exposed groin, just to keep things sporting. After all, Gabriel was the smaller and older of the two combatants. A generous point spread was in order.

"You were standing at the elevator when she came downstairs. You told her something that put her mind at ease and escorted her to the delivery entrance. A black Escalade was waiting outside. You forced her into the backseat."

Bennett made no reply. He wasn't capable of one.

"I have a feeling I know who put you up to it, Ray. Nevertheless, I'd like to hear you say his name."

"*S-s-s-s-s-s* . . ."

"Sorry, but I didn't catch that."

"*S-s-s-s-s-s* . . ."

"Leonard Silk? Is that what you're trying to tell me?"

Bennett nodded vigorously.

"How much did he pay you?"

"*H-h-h-h-h* . . ."

"I beg your pardon?"

"*H-h-h-h-h* . . ."

Gabriel patted the front of Bennett's suit jacket and found his phone. It was an iPhone 13 Pro. He waved it before Bennett's face, and he was in. The same New York–based cellular number appeared three times in his RECENTS. One incoming, two outgoing. The last call was approximately an hour earlier, at 6:41 p.m. It was outgoing.

Gabriel showed the number to Ray Bennett. "Is this Silk?"

Bennett nodded.

Gabriel snapped a photograph of the screen with his Solaris. Then he handed Bennett the receiver of his desk phone. "Tell the valet to bring Ms. Bancroft's car to the Fifth Avenue entrance. Not the East Sixty-First Street doorway. Fifth Avenue."

Bennett pressed the speed-dial button and emitted an incomprehensible croak into the mouthpiece.

"Bancroft," said Gabriel slowly. "I know you can do it, Ray."

Upstairs on the twentieth floor, Gabriel forwarded Leonard Silk's phone number to Yuval Gershon before cramming his belongings into his overnight bag. In the room next door, Sarah packed with equal haste. Then she hurried across the hall and stuffed Magdalena's clothing and toiletries into her costly Louis Vuitton carry-on. At the writing desk, Evelyn Buchanan hammered away at her laptop without pause, oblivious, or so it seemed, to the commotion around her.

At 7:40 p.m. the phone in Sarah's room rang. It was the valet calling to say that Ms. Bancroft's car was waiting, as requested, outside the hotel's Fifth Avenue entrance. Evelyn Buchanan shoved her laptop into her bag and followed Gabriel and Sarah into the elevator. Downstairs in the lobby, there was no sign of Ray Bennett. Sarah informed the young woman at Reception that she and Mr. Allon were checking out earlier than expected.

"Is there a problem?" the woman inquired.

"Change in plans," lied Sarah effortlessly, and declined the woman's offer of a printed receipt.

A bellman relieved them of their luggage and loaded it into the Nissan Pathfinder. Evelyn Buchanan crawled into the backseat and immediately removed her laptop. Sarah settled into the passenger seat; Gabriel, behind the wheel. As he sped through the intersection of Fifth Avenue and East Sixtieth Street, he turned his head to the right, hiding his face from the two men sitting in the Suburban outside the Metropolitan Club. They made no attempt to follow them.

"Is kidnapping complimentary at the Pierre?" asked Sarah. "Or is there an extra charge?"

Gabriel laughed quietly.

"Where do you suppose she is?"

"I have a terrible feeling she's about to leave the country, whether she wants to or not."

"With Phillip?"

"Who else?"

"She doesn't have a passport."

"Maybe she won't need one where they're going."

"Phillip keeps his Gulfstream at Teterboro," said Sarah.

"He's too smart to use his own plane. He'll leave on a charter that someone has booked on his behalf." Gabriel paused. "Someone like Leonard Silk."

"Perhaps we should telephone Mr. Silk and ask him where his client is headed."

"I rather doubt that Mr. Silk would prove receptive to our advances."

"In that case," said Sarah, "we should probably contact the FBI."

"Could get ugly."

"For Magdalena?"

"And me."

"Better than the alternative, though."

"The FBI can't arrest Phillip without a warrant. And they can't obtain a warrant based on my say-so alone. They need credible evidence of criminal wrongdoing."

"They'll have it soon enough." Sarah glanced over her shoulder at Evelyn Buchanan, who was typing furiously on her laptop. Then she turned and gazed down the length of Fifth Avenue. "I hope you realize that none of this would have happened if we'd stayed at the Four Seasons."

"Lesson learned."

"And I never got my martini."

"We'll get you a martini after we stop Phillip from fleeing the country."

"I certainly hope so," said Sarah.

Not surprisingly, Ray Bennett chose not to inform Leonard Silk that the number for his personal mobile phone had fallen into the hands of the world's most famous retired spy. Consequently, Silk took no action to protect his device from attack. It came as he was headed uptown on First Avenue—a stealth zero-click invasion carried out by the Israeli-made malware known as Proteus. Like countless other victims before him, including numerous heads of state, Silk was unaware his device had been compromised.

Within minutes the phone was spewing a geyser of valuable information. Of immediate interest to Yuval Gershon were the GPS location data and the call history. On his own initiative, Gershon attacked a second device before calling Gabriel. It was eight fifteen in New York. Gabriel was barreling along Broadway through Lower Manhattan. The two men spoke in Hebrew to ensure that nothing was lost in translation.

"He left the Pierre at six forty-four. By the way, that was the exact time Ray Bennett led your girl out the service door. Something tells me it wasn't a coincidence."

"Where did he go?"

"East Thirty-Fourth Street Heliport. He was there until seven fifty-two."

"Where is he now?"

"Back in his apartment on Sutton Place. Number fourteen, in case you're wondering. Sixteenth floor, if I had to guess."

"Any interesting calls?"

"Executive Jet Services. It's a charter company based at MacArthur Airport on Long Island."

"I know where MacArthur is, Yuval."

"Do you know when Silk made the calls?"

"Maybe you should tell me."

"The first call was at four twenty-three this afternoon. He called again about twenty minutes ago."

"Sounds to me as if someone is planning to take a trip."

"Someone is. Silk called him twice. The last call was around seven o'clock. I lit him up a few minutes ago. There's no data on the phone, which means it's probably a burner. But I was able to get a fix on his location."

"Where is he?"

"The eastern shore of the North Haven Peninsula."

"Twelve feet above sea level?"

"How did you guess?"

"Message me if he so much as twitches."

Gabriel rang off and looked at Sarah.

"What did he say?" she asked.

"He said that we should probably charter a helicopter."

Sarah dialed.

———

The offices of *Vanity Fair* magazine were located on the twenty-fifth floor of One World Trade Center. Gabriel dropped Evelyn Buchanan on West Street near the 9/11 memorial, then followed the Battery Park Underpass to the Downtown Manhattan Heliport. He squeezed the Nissan into an empty space in the small staff parking lot, gave the attendant $500 in cash to keep the vehicle for the night, and led Sarah into the terminal. Their chartered Bell 407 waited at the end of the L-shaped pier. It departed at 9:10 p.m. and raced eastward, into the cooling twilight.

69

North Haven

The Somersets of North Haven were owners of his-and-hers Range Rovers. Phillip's was a fully loaded 2022, black, tan interior. With the help of a security guard, he placed five aluminum-sided suitcases by Rimowa of Madison Avenue into the spacious rear storage compartment. Two of the suitcases contained cash; two, gold ingots. The largest was filled with clothing, toiletries, and a few personal mementos—including a collection of luxury wristwatches valued at $12 million.

Inside the house, Phillip found Lindsay where he had left her, seated at the island in the kitchen, the food properly plated and arrayed before her. She had lit candles, poured wine, touched nothing. The air smelled of lilies and grilled octopus. It turned Phillip's stomach. He checked the display screen of the hardline phone. Lindsay had made no calls during his brief absence.

"Shall I pack a bag for you?" he asked.

She stared silently into an emptiness of Phillip's making. She had not spoken a word since his ill-advised threat of violence. It was Lindsay who had drawn her sword first, but it had been reckless of Phillip to respond in kind. Almost as reckless, he thought, as divulging the name of the country where he planned to take refuge.

"You won't tell them where I am, will you?"

"The first chance I get." She gave him a counterfeit smile. "But not tonight, Phillip. I've decided it would be best if you simply disappeared. That way, I'll never have to look at your face again or, heaven forbid, visit you in prison."

Phillip returned to his office and executed a series of wire transfers, all designed to leave little if no trace of the money's final destination. Taken together, they had the effect of draining every cent from the accounts of Masterpiece Art Ventures. There was nothing left. Nothing but the real estate, the toys, the debt, and the paintings. The genuine works in the company's inventory were worth at least $700 million, but all were leveraged to the hilt. Perhaps Christie's would hold a special evening sale to auction the works off. *The Somerset Collection . . .* It had a certain ring to it, he had to admit.

Rising, he went to his window and for the last time surveyed his realm. The bay. His boat. His manicured garden. His blue swimming pool. He realized suddenly he hadn't used it once all summer.

A green light flared on the multiline desk phone. Phillip snatched up the receiver and heard Lindsay abruptly hang up downstairs. Evidently, she was still entertaining thoughts of turning him in. He switched lines and dialed East Hampton Airport. Mike Knox, the regular evening head of flight operations, answered.

"Your helicopter arrived about twenty minutes ago, Mr. Somerset. The passengers decided to stay on board."

"Any other inbound birds?"

"A Blade, a couple of privates, and a Zip Aviation charter from downtown."

"What's the ETA on the charter?"

"Twenty-five minutes or so."

"Is my helicopter fueled?"

"Finishing now."

"Thanks, Mike. I'm on my way."

Phillip hung up the phone and opened the bottom drawer of his desk. It was where he kept his unregistered firearm.

Not if I kill you first, Lindsay . . .

It would certainly guarantee a clean departure, he thought. But it would also saddle him with eternal infamy. If the truth be told, a part of him was actually looking forward to exile. Keeping the Ponzi scheme up and running all these years had been exhausting; he was sorely in need of a vacation. And now it seemed he would have beautiful Magdalena to keep his bed warm, at least until the storm blew over and it was safe for her to return to Spain.

Or perhaps not, Phillip thought suddenly. Perhaps they would live out their lives together in hiding. He imagined a Ripley-like existence, with Magdalena playing the role of Héloïse Plisson. With the passage of time, he might come to be viewed in a more favorable light—as an alluring figure of mystery, a villain protagonist. Putting a bullet into Lindsay would spoil that. The whole of the Upper East Side would be rooting for his death.

He closed the drawer, deleted his documents and emails, and emptied his digital trash. Downstairs, he returned Lindsay's phone. She stared through him as though he were made of glass. "Leave" was all she said.

————

The Blade commuter helicopter arrived at East Hampton Airport at ten minutes past nine o'clock. Six passengers, Manhattanites all, spilled onto the tarmac and, after collecting their luggage, traipsed off toward the terminal. Magdalena watched them from the window of the Sikorsky. Tyler Briggs sat in the opposing seat, legs spread, crotch on full display. Magdalena calculated the odds of delivering a debilitating strike and then snatching the phone from his hand. They were reasonable, she reckoned, but retribution would likely be swift and severe. Tyler was ex-military, and Magdalena was already damaged from her skirmishes with the gray eminence. She'd had quite enough excitement for one evening. Better to ask nicely.

"May I borrow your phone for a moment, Tyler?"

"No."

"I just want to check a website."

"The answer is still no."

"Will you please check it for me, please? It's *Vanity Fair.*"

"The magazine?"

"Haven't you heard? They're about to publish a story about your boss. By tomorrow morning, the town house will be surrounded by camera crews and reporters. Who knows? If you play your cards right, you might be able to earn a little extra money. But I beg of you, don't sell those naughty videos you've saved on your computer. My poor mother will never get over it."

"Mr. Somerset ordered us to wipe the system this afternoon."

"That was wise of him. Now be a love, Tyler, and check the website for me. It's *Vanity Fair.* I can spell it for you, if that helps."

The phone rang before he could reply. "Yes, Mr. Somerset," he said after a moment. "No, Mr. Somerset. She was no trouble at all . . . Yes, I'll tell her, sir."

He hung up and slipped the phone into his jacket pocket.

"Tell her what?" asked Magdalena.

The security guard pointed toward the black Range Rover speeding across the tarmac. "Mr. Somerset would like a word with you in private before we leave."

————

He braked to a halt a few yards from the Sikorsky's tail and popped the Range Rover's rear door. Magdalena took inventory of the cargo before climbing into the passenger seat. Phillip stared straight ahead, hands gripping the wheel. An unlocked cell phone lay on the center console. It was not his usual device.

At last he turned and looked at her. "What happened to your face?"

"Apparently, I said something that offended the sensibilities of your friend." Magdalena paused. "We were never properly introduced."

"Silk," said Phillip. "Leonard Silk."

"Where did you find him?"

"Smith and Wollensky."

"Chance encounter?"

"There's no such thing where Leonard is concerned."

"What was the occasion?"

"Hamilton Fairchild."

"Buyer?"

Phillip nodded.

"Which painting?"

"*Saint Jerome.*"

"Follower of Caravaggio?"

"Circle of Parmigianino. I dumped it on Hamilton in a private treaty sale arranged by Bonhams."

"I was always fond of that picture," said Magdalena.

"So was Hamilton until he showed it to an art dealer named Patrick Matthiesen. Matthiesen told Hamilton that, in his learned opinion, the painting was the work of, how shall we say, a later imitator."

"I assume Hamilton wanted his money back."

"Naturally."

"And you refused?"

"Of course."

"How did the situation resolve itself?"

"Regrettably, Hamilton and his wife died in a single-engine plane crash off the coast of Maine."

"How many others were there?"

"Fewer than you might imagine. Leonard handled most of them with an envelope filled with naughty photographs or incriminating financial information. And not just buyers. Investors, too. Why do you think Max van Egan still has a quarter-billion in the fund?" Phillip took up the phone and refreshed the web browser. "How long before the story appears?"

"I'm surprised it hasn't already. When it does, Masterpiece will go up in flames."

"You're as guilty as I am, you know."

"Somehow I don't think your lenders and investors are going to see it that way."

Phillip tossed aside the phone in anger. "Why did you do it?" he asked.

"I was arrested an hour after I purchased the Gentileschi. It was an elaborate sting operation by Gabriel Allon and the Italians. They gave me a choice. I could spend the next several years in an Italian prison, or I could give them your head on a platter."

"You should have asked for a lawyer and kept your mouth shut."

"You wired ten million euros into a Carabinieri-controlled bank account. They would have eventually traced the money back to you, with or without my help."

"I suppose the redemptions were Allon's doing, too. He baited me into committing an act of bank fraud over a compromised phone."

"I told you to put the painting on ice," said Magdalena. "But you wouldn't listen."

"You put a rope around my neck and walked me to the gallows."

"I had no other choice."

"You were a drug dealer when I found you. And this is how you repay me?"

"But they were real drugs, weren't they, Phillip?" Magdalena took a long look over her shoulder. "I don't suppose Lindsay is in one of those suitcases."

"It's just the two of us."

"How romantic. Where are we off to?"

Phillip looked down at the phone; Magdalena, at her Cartier wristwatch.

It was half past nine.

70

Downtown

On the twenty-fifth floor of One World Trade Center, in a conference room overlooking New York Harbor, war had been declared. The combatants were five in number and were broken into three opposing camps. Two were senior editors, two were lawyers, and the last was a reporter with an impeccable track record for accuracy and click-generating copy. The piece under deliberation contained allegations of financial impropriety by a prominent figure in the New York art world. Complicating matters was the fact that the prominent figure's hired henchmen had deleted the only existing draft of the story. Furthermore, it appeared that the prominent figure was at that very moment attempting to flee the country.

Nevertheless, insisted the lawyers, certain legal and editorial standards had to be met. Otherwise, the prominent art world figure, whose name was Phillip Somerset, would have grounds to file a lawsuit, as would his investors.

"Not to mention his lenders at JPMorgan Chase and Bank of America. In short, it has all the makings of a legal clusterfuck for the ages."

"My source is a freelance employee of Masterpiece Art Ventures."

"With a rather dubious personal history."

"I have recordings."

"Provided to you by a former Israeli intelligence officer who was using a highly controversial cell phone hacking malware."

"New York is a one-party consent state. She knew she was being recorded when she met with Phillip."

"But neither Phillip nor Ellis Gray of JPMorgan Chase consented to being recorded. Therefore, their conversation regarding the art-backed loan is inadmissible, as it were."

"What about the paintings in the warehouse?"

"Don't even think about it."

With that, a temporary truce was declared, and work commenced. The reporter wrote, the editors edited, the lawyers lawyered—one paragraph at a time, at a pace more akin to an old-fashioned wire service than a storied cultural-and-current affairs monthly. But such were the exigencies of magazine publishing in the digital age. Even the staid *New Yorker* had been compelled to offer its subscribers daily content. The world had changed, and not necessarily for the better. Phillip Somerset was proof of that.

At half past nine they had a draft in hand. It was limited in scope but devasting in impact. The story appeared on *Vanity Fair*'s website at 9:32 p.m., and within minutes it was trending on social media. In the aftermath, much would be made of its final line. Phillip Somerset, it read, could not be reached for comment.

––––––––

When the first text messages detonated on Lindsay's phone, she assumed they were from Phillip and ignored them. There was a brief pause, followed by a second barrage. Then all hell broke loose.

Reluctantly Lindsay reached for the device and saw a stream of venom and threats, all sent by some of her closest friends. Attached to each of the texts was the same article from *Vanity Fair*. The headline read THE FAKE: INSIDE PHILLIP SOMERSET'S MASTERPIECE OF A PONZI SCHEME. Lindsay clicked on the link. Three paragraphs was all she could take.

She opened her RECENTS, found the number for Phillip's burner, and dialed. The background whir of the Sikorsky's turboshaft engines told her that he had not yet departed East Hampton Airport.

"Have you read the article?" she asked.

"I'm reading it now."

"I can't face this alone."

"What are you saying?"

"Don't leave without me," said Lindsay, and snatched her car keys from the kitchen counter.

The chartered Bell 407 was over the waters of Long Island Sound when Evelyn Buchanan's article popped onto Gabriel's phone. He skimmed it quickly and was relieved to find that neither his name nor Sarah's appeared in the text. Neither, for that matter, did Magdalena's. Her allegations were attributed to an unnamed freelance employee of Masterpiece Art Ventures. There was no mention of her gender or nationality. For the moment, at least, she was in the clear. Phillip Somerset, however, was finished.

Voice calls were prohibited onboard the helicopter, so Gabriel shot a text message to Yuval Gershon and requested an update on Phillip's position. Yuval's reply appeared a minute later. Phillip was still on the tarmac at East Hampton Airport.

"Why hasn't he left yet?" asked Sarah over the drone of the Bell's engines.

"It seems Lindsay has had a change of heart. She called him two minutes ago and told him not to leave until she arrived."

"Perhaps it's time you had that chat with the FBI."

"I'm afraid there's a complicating factor."

"Only one?"

"Magdalena is there, too."

The helicopter remained over Long Island Sound until they reached the old Horton Point Light, where a turn to starboard carried them over the town of Southold and the waters of Peconic Bay. A ferry was crossing the narrow channel separating Shelter Island and North Haven. On the eastern shore of the peninsula, Phillip's now-abandoned estate was ablaze with light.

"It looks as though Lindsay left in a hurry," said Sarah.

They passed over Sag Harbor and commenced their descent toward East Hampton Airport. Directly beneath them, a white Range Rover was headed toward the airfield along Daniels Hole Road. It was Lindsay Somerset, thought Gabriel. And she was definitely in a hurry.

———

She made the final turn into the airport with deliberate care. Hand-over-hand on the steering wheel, a gentle acceleration mid-arc. Just the way her father had taught her when she was a girl of fourteen. The gate at the edge of the tarmac was open. The guard waved her through. Magdalena stood next to the Sikorsky; Phillip, at the open rear door of his Range Rover. He hoisted an arm in greeting, as though waving from the deck of his sailboat. Lindsay switched off the headlights, put her foot to the floor, and closed her eyes.

PART FOUR

Unveiling

71

East Hampton

The call came through on the emergency line of the East Hampton Town Police Department at 9:55 p.m. Sergeant Bruce Logan, a twenty-year veteran of the department and lifelong resident of the East End, braced himself for the worst. It was Mike Knox calling from the airport.

"Helicopter or plane?" asked Logan.

"Actually, it was two Range Rovers."

"Fender bender in the parking lot?"

"Fatality on the tarmac."

"You're shitting me, Mike."

"I wish."

The department's headquarters were located on the southern edge of the airfield, on Wainscott Road, and the first officers arrived at the scene just three minutes after the initial call. They found the victim, a white male in his mid-fifties, lying on the tarmac in a bay of his own blood, his legs nearly severed, surrounded by several hundred carefully packaged five-hundred-gram gold ingots. The driver of the vehicle that had struck the man was an attractive, fit-looking woman in her thirties. She wore leggings, a Lululemon hoodie, and neon-green

Nikes. She had no wallet and seemed unable to recall her name. Mike Knox supplied it for her. The woman was Lindsay Somerset. The dead guy with the nearly severed legs was her husband, a rich investor of some sort who owned a weekend palace in North Haven.

Death was formally declared, an arrest was made, a statement was issued. The news broke at midnight on WINS radio, and by nine the following morning it was all anyone was talking about. The real estate mogul Sterling Dunbar was in the shower when he learned that Lindsay Somerset had run down her scoundrel of a husband; the retailer Simon Levinson, still in his bed. Ellis Gray of JPMorgan Chase, having endured a sleepless night after reading the *Vanity Fair* story, was in his office overlooking Park Avenue. Two hours later he informed senior management that the firm was now on the hook for $436 million in loans issued to Masterpiece Art Ventures—loans that, in all likelihood, had been collateralized with forged paintings. Senior management accepted Gray's resignation, effective immediately.

By midday the FBI had assumed control of the investigation. Agents searched Phillip's homes, sealed his warehouse, and raided his offices on East Fifty-Third Street. The firm's three female art experts were taken to Federal Plaza and questioned at length. All denied any knowledge of financial or art-related impropriety. Kenny Vaughan, Phillip's wingman from his days at Lehman Brothers, was nowhere to be found. Agents seized his computers and printed files and issued a warrant for his arrest.

Phillip's crimes were global in scope, and so was the fallout. Two prominent European dealers—Gilles Raymond of Brussels and Konrad Hassler of Berlin—were arrested and their inventories seized. Dealers in Hong Kong, Tokyo, and Dubai were likewise taken into custody. Under questioning, all admitted that they were part of a far-flung distribution network that had been flooding the art market with high-quality forgeries for years. The French Ministry of Culture grudgingly acknowledged that four of those forgeries had found their way into the permanent collection of the Louvre. The museum's president abruptly resigned, as did the director of the esteemed National Center for Research and Restoration, which had declared all four works to be authentic.

But who was this master forger who had managed to deceive the world's most sophisticated art laboratory? And how many examples of his handiwork were now circulating through the bloodstream of the art world? Evelyn Buchanan, in a follow-up to her original exposé, reported that Phillip's warehouse likely contained more than two hundred forged paintings. Hundreds more, she wrote, had already been foisted upon unsuspecting buyers. When a partial list of those works appeared anonymously on a much-read industry message board, panic swept the art world. Collectors, dealers, curators, and auctioneers—having relied for generations on the pronouncements of connoisseurs—turned to the scientists to help them sort through the wreckage. Aiden Gallagher of Equus Analytics was so inundated with requests for evaluations that he stopped answering his phone and responding to emails. "Mr. Gallagher," wrote an art reporter from the *New York Times*, "is the scandal's only winner."

The losers, of course, were Phillip's well-heeled investors, the ones who had seen hundreds of millions of dollars in paper wealth wiped away in a matter of hours. Their lawsuits, countersuits, and public lamentations earned them little sympathy, especially from art world purists who found the very concept of a fund like Phillip's abhorrent. Great paintings, they declared, were not securities or derivatives to be traded among the superrich. They were objects of beauty and cultural significance that belonged in museums. Not surprisingly, those who made their living buying and selling paintings found such sentiments laughable. Without the rich, they pointed out, there would be no art. And no museums, either.

A federal judge appointed a trustee to sift through Phillip's assets and dole out the proceeds to those he had defrauded. Three hundred and forty-seven investors sought restitution. The largest claim was $254 million by the industrialist Max van Egan. The smallest was $4.8 million by Sarah Bancroft, a former curator from the Museum of Modern Art who now managed an Old Master gallery in London.

One of Phillip's investors, however, filed no claim at all: Magdalena Navarro, thirty-nine years old, a citizen of Spain who resided in the upscale Salamanca district of Madrid. According to documents seized from the offices of Masterpiece Art Ventures—and to sworn statements given to the FBI by the three cooperating employees of the firm—Navarro was a European-based freelance runner who purchased and sold paintings on Phillip Somerset's behalf. Her last recorded account balance was $56.2 million, a great deal of money to leave lying on the table.

As it turned out, the FBI knew more about Magdalena Navarro than it had revealed in public, which was nothing at all. It knew, for example, that the European art dealers Gilles Raymond and Konrad Hassler had identified her as the link between their galleries and Masterpiece Art Ventures. The Bureau also knew that Navarro had been in New York at the time of the hedge fund's spectacular collapse, having arrived on a Delta Air Lines flight from Rome and departed—less than twelve hours after Phillip Somerset's death—on a flight to London. Interestingly enough, she had been seated next to Gabriel Allon, the legendary former director-general of the Israeli secret intelligence service, on both legs of her journey. The art dealer Sarah Bancroft, who also happened to be a former clandestine CIA officer, had accompanied Allon and Navarro on the flight to Heathrow.

Investigators also established that all three had stayed in separate rooms on the twentieth floor of the Pierre Hotel during their brief visit to New York. And that Magdalena Navarro was likely the source of the exposé in *Vanity Fair*. And that Navarro departed the Pierre Hotel shortly before the article's publication—without luggage or a handbag—and traveled to East Hampton Airport aboard Phillip Somerset's Sikorsky helicopter. And that she subsequently left East Hampton Airport, in the chaotic minutes following Somerset's grisly death, aboard a Bell 407 chartered by Allon and Bancroft. The pilot delivered them to JFK, where they spent the night in the airport Hilton. And by eight the following morning, they were gone.

All of which suggested to the FBI that a friendly chat with Allon was in order. Finding him proved less difficult than they imagined. The FBI's legal attaché in Rome simply rang the offices of the Tiepolo Restoration Company in Venice, and Allon's wife arranged a meeting. It took place in Harry's Bar—which was where, unbeknownst to the legal attaché, Allon's involvement in the affair began. While sipping a Bellini, he told the FBI officer about a private inquiry he had undertaken at the behest of an old friend whom he refused to identify. This private inquiry, he said in conclusion, led him to Magdalena Navarro and, ultimately, Phillip Somerset's $1.2 billion forgery-based Ponzi scheme.

"Where is she now?" asked the FBI man, whose name was Josh Campbell.

"Somewhere in the Pyrenees. Even I don't know where."

"Doing what?"

"Painting, I assume."

"Is she any good?"

"If Phillip hadn't got his hooks into her, she would have been a major artist."

"We'd like to question her."

"I'm sure you would. But as a personal favor to me, I'd like you to let her get on with her life."

"The Bureau isn't in the business of granting personal favors, Allon."

"In that case, you leave me no choice but to call the president directly."

"You wouldn't dare."

"Watch me."

And so Special Agent Josh Campbell returned to Rome empty-handed, but with a fascinating tale to tell. He wrote it up in a lengthy memorandum and fired it simultaneously to Washington and New York. Those who knew of Allon's past exploits were dubious as to the document's accuracy—and justifiably so. The report made no mention, for example, of a forged portrait by Anthony van Dyck. Or a recently deceased Frenchwoman named Valerie Bérrangar. Or a Parisian antiques dealer and art thief named Maurice Durand. Or the Swiss violinist Anna Rolfe. Or the notorious Corsican crime figure Don Anton Orsati. Or the lecherous but lovable London art dealer Oliver Dimbleby, whose fictitious rediscovery and record-setting sales of three Venetian School masterworks had recently set the art world ablaze.

By the end of July, all three canvases were hanging in the apartment of the forger who had created them, along with two versions of Modigliani's *Reclining Nude*, a Cézanne, a Monet, and a stunning version of Van Gogh's *Self-Portrait with Bandaged Ear*. On the easel in his studio was a painting with an L-shaped tear, 15 by 23 centimeters, in the lower left corner. After repairing the damage and retouching the losses, the forger shipped the work to a small gallery near the Plaza Virgen de los Reyes in Seville. Then, early the next morning, he disappeared.

72

Adriatico

For the first five days of the trip, the *maestral* prevailed. It was not the cold and blustery aggressor that had laid siege to the island of Corsica the previous spring, but a temperate and dependable companion that propelled the Bavaria C42 effortlessly down the length of the Adriatic. With the seas calm and the wind blowing across the stern of his spacious vessel, Gabriel was able to provide Irene and Raphael with a smooth and pleasant introduction to maritime life. No one was more relieved than Chiara, who had prepared herself for six sun-drenched weeks of moaning, groaning, and seasickness.

Their days lacked shape, which was their intention. Most mornings Gabriel awakened early and got under way while Chiara and the children slept in the cabins beneath him. Sometime around noon he would drop his sails and lower the swim platform, and they would enjoy a long lunch at the cockpit table. In the evening they dined in portside restaurants—Italy one night, Croatia or Montenegro the next. Gabriel carried his Beretta whenever they went ashore. Chiara never addressed him by his given name.

When they reached the southern Adriatic port of Bari, they spent the night in a comfortable boutique hotel near the marina, did a large load of laundry, and restocked their stores with food and plenty of local white wine. Late the following morning, when they rounded the heel of Italy, a warm and sultry *jugo* was blowing from the southeast. Gabriel rode it westward across the Ionian and arrived at the Sicilian port of Messina a day earlier than he had anticipated. The Museo Regionale was a short walk along the waterfront from the marina. In Room 10 were two monumental canvases executed by Caravaggio during his nine-month stay in Sicily.

"Is it true he used an actual corpse?" asked Chiara as she pondered *The Raising of Lazarus*.

"Unlikely," answered Gabriel. "But certainly not beyond the realm of possibility."

"It's not one of his better efforts, is it?"

"Much of what you see was painted by studio assistants. The last restoration was about ten years ago. As you can no doubt tell from the quality of the work, I wasn't available at the time."

Chiara gave him a look of reproach. "I think I liked you better before you became a forger."

"Consider yourself lucky that I didn't attempt to forge a Caravaggio. You would have thrown me into the street."

"I have to say, I rather enjoyed my afternoons with Orazio Gentileschi."

"Not as much as he enjoyed his time with Danaë."

"She would love to have lunch alone with you before this trip is over."

"Our cabin is too close to the children's."

"In that case, how about a midnight snack instead?" Smiling, Chiara directed her gaze toward the Caravaggio. "Do you think you could paint one?"

"I'll pretend I didn't hear that."

"And what about your rival? Is he capable of forging a Caravaggio?"

"He produced undetectable Old Master paintings from every school and period. A Caravaggio would be rather easy for him."

"Who do you suppose he is?"

"The last person in the world anyone would ever suspect."

Their midnight snack turned out to be a sumptuous feast several hours in length, and it was nearly ten in the morning by the time they set out for Limpari. Their next stop was a little cove along the Calabrian coast. Then, after an overnight sail that included a snack on the Bavaria's foredeck, they arrived at the Amalfi Coast. From there, they island-hopped their way across the Gulf of Naples—first Capri, then Ischia—before venturing across the Tyrrhenian Sea to Sardinia.

To the north lay Corsica. Gabriel charted a course up the island's western side, into the teeth of a freshening *maestral*. And two days later, on a cool and cloudless Wednesday evening, he guided the Bavaria into Porto's tiny marina. Waiting on the quay, their arms raised in greeting, were Sarah Bancroft and Christopher Keller.

———

The sun had set by the time they reached the well-guarded home of Don Anton Orsati. Clad in the simple clothing of a Corsican *paesanu*, he greeted Irene and Raphael as though they were blood relatives. Gabriel explained to his children that the large, expansive figure with the dark eyes of a canine was a producer of the island's finest olive oil. Irene, with her peculiar powers of second sight, was clearly dubious.

The don's walled garden was strung with decorative lights and filled with members of his extended clan, including several who worked in the clandestine side of his business. It seemed the arrival of the Allon family after a long and perilous sea voyage was cause for celebration, as was the first visit to the island by Christopher's American wife. Many Corsican proverbs were recited, and a great deal of pale Corsican rosé was drunk. Sarah stared unabashedly at Raphael throughout dinner, entranced by the child's uncanny resemblance to his father. Gabriel, for his part, stared at his wife. She had never looked happier—or more beautiful, he thought.

At the conclusion of the meal, the don invited Gabriel and Christopher upstairs to his office. Lying on the desk was the photograph of the man who had tried to kill Gabriel and Sarah at Galerie Georges Fleury in Paris.

"His name was Rémy Dubois. And you were right," said Orsati. "He had a military background. He spent a couple of years fighting the crazies in Afghanistan, where he became quite familiar with improvised explosives. When he came home, he had trouble getting his life together." The don glanced at Christopher. "Sound familiar?"

"Perhaps you should tell him about Rémy Dubois and leave me out of it."

"The organization for which Dubois worked is known only as the Groupe. The other employees of this organization are all former soldiers and intelligence operatives. Most of their clients are wealthy businessmen. They're very good at what they do. And quite expensive. We found Rémy in Antibes. A nice place near the Plage de Juan les Pins."

"Do I have to ask where he is now?"

"You probably passed over him as you approached Porto."

"How much were you able to get out of him?"

"Chapter and verse. Apparently, the attempt on your life was a rush job."

"Did he happen to mention when he got the order?"

"It was the Sunday before the bombing."

"Sunday evening?"

"Morning, actually. He had to assemble the bomb so quickly that he didn't have time to buy a burner phone to use as the detonator trigger. He used a phone he picked up on another job instead."

"It belonged to a woman named Valerie Bérrangar. Dubois and his associates ran her car off the road south of Bordeaux."

"So he said. He was also involved in the murder of Lucien Marchand." Orsati inclined his head toward an unfinished Cézanne-inspired landscape leaning against the wall. "We found that in his apartment in Antibes."

"Who paid for the bullet?" asked Gabriel.

"An American. Evidently, he was a former CIA officer. Dubois didn't know his name."

"It's Leonard Silk. He lives on Sutton Place in Manhattan." Gabriel paused, then added, "Number fourteen."

"We have friends in New York." Orsati fed the photograph into his shredder. "Good friends, in fact."

"How much?"

"You insult me."

"Money doesn't come from singing," said Gabriel, repeating one of the don's favorite proverbs.

"And dew won't fill the tank," he replied. "But save your money for your children."

"Little children, little worries. Big children, big worries."

"But not tonight, my friend. Tonight we have no worries at all."

Gabriel looked at Christopher and smiled. "We'll see about that."

———

Downstairs, Gabriel found Raphael and Irene propped against Chiara, their eyes glassy and unfocused. Don Orsati begged them to stay a little longer, but after a final exchange of Corsican proverbs he reluctantly acquiesced to their departure. He could not hide his disappointment, though, over Gabriel's travel plans. The Allon family intended to spend a single night at Christopher's villa, then set out for Venice first thing in the morning.

"Surely you can stay for a week or two."

"The children begin school in mid-September. We'll barely make it home in time as it is."

"To where will you sail next year?" inquired the don.

"The Galápagos, I think."

With that, they said their goodbyes and squeezed into Christopher's battered old Renault hatchback for the drive to the next valley. Gabriel and Chiara sat in back with the children wedged between them. Sarah sat in the passenger seat next to her husband. Despite the gaiety of the evening, her mood was suddenly tense.

"Have you heard from Magdalena?" she asked in the overbright voice of one who feared imminent disaster.

"Magdalena who?" replied Gabriel as the headlamps illuminated the enormous horned goat standing in the center of the track near the three ancient olive trees owned by Don Casabianca.

Christopher applied the brakes, and the car slowed gently to a stop.

"Would you mind awfully if I had a cigarette?" asked Sarah. "I feel one coming on."

"That makes two of us," murmured Gabriel.

Irene and Raphael, somnambulant a moment earlier, were suddenly alert and excited about the prospect of yet another adventure. Christopher sat with his hands upon the wheel, his powerful shoulders slumped, a picture of misery.

His eyes met Gabriel's in the rearview mirror. "I would prefer if your children didn't watch."

"Don't be ridiculous. Why do you think I sailed all the way to Corsica?"

"We've had a rough couple of weeks," explained Sarah. "Last night . . ."

"Last night *what*?" probed Irene.

"I'd rather not say."

Christopher said it for her. "He got a clean shot at me. It was like being hit with a pile driver."

"You must have provoked the poor thing," said Chiara.

"As far as that creature is concerned, my very existence is a provocation."

Christopher tapped the horn and with a cordial movement of his hand invited the goat to step aside. Receiving no response, he lifted his foot from the brake and inched the car forward. The goat lowered his head and drove it into the grille.

"I told you," said Sarah. "He's incorrigible."

"That's no way to talk about Christopher," interjected Gabriel.

"What does incorrigible mean?" asked Raphael.

"Incapable of being corrected. Depraved and inveterate. A hopeless reprobate."

"Reprobate," repeated Irene, and giggled.

Christopher opened his door, igniting the interior dome light. Sarah appeared stricken. "Perhaps we should all check into a hotel. Or better yet, let's spend the night on that beautiful boat of yours."

"Yes, let's," agreed Chiara as the car shuddered with the impact of another blow. Then she looked at Gabriel and said quietly, "Do something, darling."

"My hand is killing me."

"Let me," said Irene.

"Not a chance."

"Don't listen to your father," said Chiara. "Go right ahead, sweetheart."

Gabriel opened his door and looked at his beautiful wife. "If anything happens to her, let it be on your head."

Irene clambered across Gabriel's lap and leapt out of the car. Fearlessly she approached the goat and, stroking his red beard, explained that she and her family were sailing back to Venice tomorrow morning and needed a good night's sleep. The goat clearly found the story implausible. Nevertheless, he withdrew from the track without further contest, and the situation was resolved peaceably.

Irene squeezed into the backseat and rested her head against her father's shoulder as they resumed their progress toward Christopher's villa.

"Reprobate," whispered the child, and laughed hysterically.

73

Bar Dogale

Against all better judgment, Gabriel agreed to remain in Corsica through the weekend. He insisted, however, on spending Sunday night aboard the Bavaria, and by the time Chiara and the children awakened on Monday morning, he had put Ajaccio behind them. With the *maestral* at his back and his spinnaker flying, he reached the southern tip of Sardinia at sunset on Tuesday, and by late Thursday afternoon they were back in Messina.

That evening, while dining at I Ruggeri, one of the city's finer restaurants, Gabriel read with relief that prosecutors in New York's Suffolk County had dropped all charges against Lindsay Somerset in the death of her husband. Locked out of her homes, her bank accounts seized or frozen, she faced an uncertain future. There was speculation in a Long Island weekly that she intended to open a fitness studio in Montauk and settle permanently in the East End. The largely favorable local reaction suggested that Lindsay, with her act of madness at the airport, had emerged from the scandal untarnished by Phillip's fraud.

Three nights later, in Bari, Gabriel read that Kenny Vaughan, Phillip's fugitive chief investment officer, had been found dead of an apparent drug overdose in a New Orleans hotel room. Still unaccounted for was the money that Phillip had drained from the firm's cash reserves during the final hours of his life. According to the *New York Times*, any attempt to sell off the hedge fund's inventory of paintings would likely prove disappointing, as collectors and museums were skittish about acquiring anything Phillip had touched. A team of experts from the Metropolitan Museum of Art had conducted a survey of the warehouse on East Ninety-First Street in an attempt to definitively determine which of the 789 paintings were forgeries and which were authentic. Consensus had proven impossible.

Accompanying the article was a photograph of the last painting Phillip acquired before his death: *Danaë and the Shower of Gold*, purportedly by Orazio Gentileschi. The FBI had determined that it was shipped to New York from the Tuscan city of Florence, doubtless in violation of Italy's strict cultural patrimony laws. Whether it was a forgery or a genuine lost masterpiece the connoisseurs could not say—not without rigorous scientific testing of the sort conducted by Aiden Gallagher of Equus Analytics. Nevertheless, US authorities had acceded to an Italian demand that the painting be returned immediately.

Fittingly enough, it arrived in Italy the same morning that Gabriel, after a moonlit final run up the northern Adriatic, eased the Bavaria into its slip at the Venezia Certosa Marina. Four days later, after watching Chiara board a Number 2 at the San Tomà vaporetto stop, he escorted Irene and Raphael to the Bernardo Canal *scuola elementare* for the start of the fall term. Alone for the first time in many weeks—and having nothing else on his schedule other than a visit to the Rialto Market—he made his way through empty streets to Bar Dogale. Which was where, at a chrome table covered in blue, he found General Cesare Ferrari.

The waiter delivered two *cappuccini* and a basket of sugar-dusted, cream-filled *cornetti*. Gabriel drank the coffee but ignored the pastry. "I've been eating nonstop for a month and a half."

"And yet you look as though you haven't gained a kilo."

"I hide it well."

"Like most things." The general was attired in his blue-and-gold Carabinieri finery. Standing upright next to his chair was a shallow portfolio case typically used by art professionals to transport drawings or small paintings. "Somehow you even managed to conceal your involvement in the Somerset affair."

"Not exactly. That FBI agent gave me an earful."

"It is my understanding that the interview was conducted over Bellinis in Harry's Bar."

"You were watching?"

"You don't think we let FBI agents wander around without an escort?"

"I certainly hope not."

"Special Agent Campbell gave me a good going-over as well," said Ferrari. "He was convinced the Art Squad was somehow involved in your shenanigans. I assured him that we were not."

"The swift return of *Danaë and the Shower of Gold* suggests he believed you."

The general sipped his cappuccino. "A rather remarkable development, even by your standards."

"Where is it now?"

"Still at the palazzo," said Ferrari, referring to the Art Squad's Roman headquarters. "But later today it will be taken to the Galleria Borghese for analysis."

"Oh, dear."

"How long will it take them to conclude it's a forgery?"

"According to the *Times*, it passed muster in New York."

"With all due respect, we know a bit more about Gentileschi's work than do the Americans."

"The brushwork and palette are his," said Gabriel. "But the minute they subject the canvas to examination by X-radiography and infrared reflectography, I'm cooked."

"As well you should be. That painting needs to be exposed as a forgery and destroyed." The general exhaled heavily. "You realize, I hope, that your fictitious sales through Dimbleby Fine Arts of London have added new works to the oeuvres of three of the greatest painters in history."

"As of yet, none of the pictures that Oliver purportedly sold have found their way into the artists' catalogues raisonnés."

"And if they do?"

"I will immediately step forward. Until then, I intend to remain out of the public eye."

"Doing what?"

"I'm going to spend the next month cleaning crumbs and other assorted debris from my boat."

"And then?"

"My wife is considering allowing me to restore a painting."

"For the Tiepolo Restoration Company?"

"Given the perilous state of my bank account, I'm inclined to accept a lucrative private commission first."

The general frowned. "Perhaps you should just forge something instead."

"My brief career as an art forger is now officially over."

"And to think that it was all for naught."

"I brought down the largest forgery network in the history of the art world."

"Without finding the forger himself," the general pointed out.

"I would have if Lindsay Somerset hadn't ruined a perfectly good Range Rover killing her husband."

"Be that as it may, it's a rather unsatisfying conclusion to the story. Wouldn't you agree?"

"The guilty were punished," said Gabriel.

"But the forger remains free."

"Surely the FBI must have some idea who he is by now."

"Young Campbell says not. Clearly, your forger covered his tracks well." General Ferrari reached for the portfolio case and handed it to Gabriel. "But perhaps this might help solve the mystery."

"What is it?"

"A gift from your friend Jacques Ménard in Paris."

Gabriel balanced the case on his knees and popped the latches. Inside was *A River Scene with Distant Windmills*, oil on canvas, 36 by 58 centimeters, purportedly by the Dutch Golden Age painter Aelbert Cuyp. There was also a copy of a report prepared by the Louvre's National Center for Research and Restoration. It stated that the center, after weeks of painstaking scientific analysis, had been unable to render a definitive judgment as to the work's authenticity. On one point, however, it was certain in its findings.

A River Scene with Distant Windmills contained not a single fiber of navy-blue polar fleece fabric.

Gabriel returned the report to the portfolio case and closed the lid.

"Bon voyage," said General Ferrari with a smile.

74

Salamanca

Contrary to the statement that Gabriel made to Special Agent Josh Campbell of the FBI, Magdalena Navarro was not in hiding in a remote village in the Pyrenees. She was holed up in her apartment on the Calle de Castelló in the elegant Salamanca district of Madrid. At half past twelve the following afternoon, Gabriel thumbed the appropriate call button on the building's intercom panel, then turned his back to the camera. Receiving no answer, he pressed the button a second time. At length the speaker crackled into life.

"If you do that again," said a sleep-heavy female voice, "I'm going to come down there and kill you."

"Please don't, Magdalena." Gabriel turned to face the camera. "It's only me."

"My God!" she said, and unlocked the door.

Inside, Gabriel climbed the stairs to her apartment. She was waiting in the open doorway, wearing a gauzy cotton pullover and little else. Her raven hair was a tangled mess. Her hands were stained with paint.

"I hope I'm not intruding on something," said Gabriel.

"Only on my sleep. You should have warned me that you were coming."

"I was afraid you might try to flee the country." He looked down at the two matching Vuitton suitcases standing on the tiled floor of the entrance hall. "Which one has the cash?"

She indicated the bag nearest the door. "It's all the money I have left."

"What happened to the four or five million you had hidden in bank accounts around Europe?"

"I gave it away."

"To whom?"

"The poor and the immigrants, mainly. I also made a rather large donation to my favorite environmental group and another to my old art school in Barcelona. Anonymously, of course."

"Perhaps there's hope for you yet." Gabriel eyed her attire disapprovingly. "But not dressed like that."

Smiling, she padded barefoot down a corridor and reappeared a moment later in stretch jeans and a Real Madrid jersey. In the kitchen she prepared *café con leche*. They drank it at a table overlooking the narrow street. It was lined with luxury apartment buildings, designer clothing boutiques, and trendy bars and restaurants. Magdalena certainly belonged in a place like this, thought Gabriel. It was a pity she hadn't come by it honestly.

"Your skin is the color of Spanish saddle leather," she informed him. "Where have you been?"

"Circumnavigating the globe on my sailboat with my wife and children."

"Did you make any new discoveries?"

"Only the identity of the forger." He looked down at her paint-smudged hands. "I see you're working again."

She nodded. "Late night."

"Anything good?"

"A soon-to-be rediscovered Madonna and child attributed to the circle of Raphael. You?"

"I've turned over a new leaf."

"Not even tempted?"

"To what?"

"Forge a painting or two," said Magdalena. "I would be honored to serve as your front woman. But only if you agree to a fifty-fifty split of the profits."

"Perhaps I was mistaken," said Gabriel. "Perhaps you're a hopeless case, after all."

She smiled and drank her coffee. "I'm not a perfect person, Mr. Allon. But I've turned over a new leaf as well. And in case you're still wondering, I'm not the forger."

"If I thought you were, I would have arrived here with a contingent of Guardia Civil to take you into custody."

"I've been expecting them." She took up her phone and opened the web browser. "Have you read the news from Germany lately? Herr Hassler is now cooperating with federal prosecutors. It's only a matter of time before they request my extradition."

"I prevented a major terrorist attack on the Cologne Cathedral not long ago. If it becomes necessary, I can call in the chit."

"What about the Belgians?"

"Brussels and Antwerp are the organized crime capitals of Europe. I doubt the Belgian police will seek your extradition over a few fake paintings."

"Surely the FBI knows about me."

"And me as well," replied Gabriel. "For the moment, at least, they're inclined to keep our names out of it." He looked up at the unframed painting leaning against the wall. "Yours?"

Magdalena nodded. "It's the one I painted after Phillip and Leonard Silk tried to kill you in Paris. Self-portrait of a front woman."

"It's not half bad."

"My new canvases are much better. I'd love to show them to you, but I'm afraid my studio is filled with half-finished forgeries at the moment."

There were no forgeries, of course—only wildly original works executed by an artist of immense talent and technical skill. Gabriel drifted from canvas to canvas, spellbound.

"What do you think?" asked Magdalena.

"I think Phillip Somerset's greatest crime was depriving the world of your work." Gabriel placed a hand thoughtfully to his chin. "The question is, what should we do with them?"

"We?"

"I would be honored to serve as your front man. I insist, however, on receiving no share of the profits."

"You drive a hard bargain, Mr. Allon. But how do you intend to bring the works to market?"

"With a show at a premier gallery, in a major art world hub. The kind of show that will turn you into a billion-dollar global brand. Anyone who's anyone will be there. And by the end of the night, everyone will know your name."

"For all the right reasons, I hope," said Magdalena. "But where will this show take place?"

"Galerie Olivia Watson in London."

Her face brightened. "Would you really do that for me?"

"On one condition."

"The forger's name?"

He nodded.

"It was me, Mr. Allon. I executed all those undetectable Old Master paintings between shifts at El Pote Español and Katz's Delicatessen." She threw her arms around his neck. "How can I possibly repay you?"

"By allowing me to buy one of your paintings."

"Only if you promise never to sell it for a profit."

"Deal," said Gabriel.

75

Equus

Exactly forty-eight hours later—after yet another transatlantic flight to JFK and a brief stay at a Courtyard Marriott in downtown Stamford, Connecticut—Gabriel slid behind the wheel of a rented American-made sedan and drove into a blinding sunrise to Westport. It was a few minutes after seven when he arrived at Equus Analytics. Aiden Gallagher's flashy BMW 7 Series was nowhere in sight.

Gabriel lowered the portfolio case to the asphalt, drew his Solaris mobile phone, and dialed. Yuval Gershon of Unit 8200 answered instantly. "Ready?" he asked.

"Why else would I be calling?"

Yuval remotely unlocked the door. "Enjoy."

Gabriel slipped the phone into his pocket, picked up the portfolio case, and headed inside.

———

The laboratory was in darkness, the shades tightly drawn. Gabriel switched on his phone's flashlight and directed the beam toward the painting mounted on the Bruker M6 Jetstream spatial imaging device. A portrait of a woman, late twenties or early thirties, wearing a gown of gold silk trimmed in white lace. Any fool could see that the dimensions of the canvas were 115 by 92 centimeters. Gabriel snapped a photograph of the woman's pale cheek. The appearance of the craquelure gave him a funny feeling at the back of his neck.

He placed the portfolio case on an examination table and climbed the stairs to the second floor. There was a single room, identical in size to the lab below. At the end overlooking Riverside Avenue were some twenty wooden shipping crates, each containing a painting awaiting examination by the esteemed Aiden Gallagher. Only one of the crates had been opened, the one that had been used to ship the painting now secured to the Bruker. It had been sent to Equus Analytics by the Old Masters department of Sotheby's in New York.

At the opposite end of the room was an easel, a trolley, and a portable fume extractor. The drawers of the trolley were empty and spotlessly clean. The easel was empty, as well. Gabriel played the beam of the flashlight over the utility tray. Lead white. Charcoal black. Madder lake. Vermilion. Indigo. Green earth. Lapis lazuli. Red and yellow ocher.

Downstairs, he removed the riverscape from the portfolio case and laid it on the examination table. Next to it he placed two reports. One was from France's National Center for Research and Restoration; the other, Equus Analytics. Then he switched off the flashlight and waited. Two hours and twelve minutes later, a car drew up in the parking lot. They would settle the matter quietly, thought Gabriel, and never speak of it again.

———

The museum-grade alarm system emitted eight sharp chirps, and a moment later Aiden Gallagher strode through the door. He wore khaki trousers and a V-neck pullover. He stretched a hand toward the light switch, then hesitated, as though aware of a presence in the laboratory.

Finally the overhead fluorescent panels flickered into life. Aiden Gallagher drew a sharp breath of astonishment and backpedaled. "How did you get in here, Allon?"

"You left the door open. Fortunately, I happened to be in the neighborhood."

Gallagher started to dial a number on his mobile phone.

"I wouldn't, Aiden. You'll only make things worse for yourself."

Gallagher lowered the phone. "Why are you here?"

"You owe my friend Sarah Bancroft seventy-five thousand dollars."

"For what?"

Gabriel lowered his gaze toward *A River Scene with Distant Wind-mills*. "You assured us that there were polar fleece fibers embedded in the surface paint, ironclad proof that it was a forgery. But a second analysis of the painting has determined that you were incorrect."

"Who conducted this review?"

"The National Center for Research and Restoration."

Gallagher offered Gabriel a half-smile. "Isn't that the same labora-tory that mistakenly authenticated those four forgeries that ended up hanging in the Louvre?"

"Theirs was an honest mistake. Yours wasn't. And by the way," added Gabriel, "I knew that Cranach was a forgery the instant I laid eyes on it." He pointed toward the painting attached to the Bruker. "And I certainly don't need a spatial imaging device to tell me that Van Dyck is a forgery as well."

"Based on what I've seen thus far, I'm inclined to accept it as authentic."

"I'm sure you would. But that would be a miscalculation on your part."

"How so?"

"The smarter play is to take all of your forgeries out of circulation, one by one. You'll be the hero of the art world. And you'll get even richer in the process. By my calculation, the paintings upstairs alone will add a million and a half dollars to Equus's bottom line."

"Thanks to the Somerset scandal, my fee is now one hundred thousand for rush jobs. Therefore, those paintings represent two million in new business."

"I didn't hear a denial, Aiden."

"That I'm the forger? I didn't think one was necessary. Your theory is ludicrous."

"You're a trained painter and restorer, and a specialist in provenance research and authentication. Which means you know how to select works that will be accepted by the art world and, more important, how to construct and execute them. But the best part of your scheme is that you were in a unique position to authenticate your own forgeries." Gabriel looked down at *A River Scene with Distant Windmills*. "If only you had authenticated that one, you and Phillip might still be in business." He paused. "And I wouldn't be here now."

"I didn't authenticate that painting, Allon, because it's an obvious forgery."

"Obvious to me, certainly. But not to most connoisseurs. That's why you and Phillip decided that I had to die. You told us that you had found fleece fibers in the painting because it's the most common mistake made by inexperienced forgers. It's also something that could be discovered during, say, a hurried preliminary examination conducted over a weekend. When we collected the painting on Monday afternoon, you asked when we were planning to confront Georges Fleury. And Sarah foolishly answered truthfully."

"Do you realize how insane you sound?"

"I haven't arrived at the good part yet." Gabriel took a step closer to Gallagher. "You are a member of a very small club, Aiden. Its membership is limited to those lucky souls who have tried to kill me or one of my friends and are still walking the face of the earth.

So if I were you, I'd stop smiling. Otherwise, I'm liable to lose my temper."

Gallagher regarded Gabriel without expression. "I'm not the man you think I am, Allon."

"I *know* you are."

"Prove it."

"I can't. You and Phillip were too careful. And the condition of your atelier upstairs suggests that you have gone to extraordinary lengths to conceal the evidence of your crimes."

Gallagher indicated the French report. "May I?"

"By all means."

He picked up the document and began to read. After a moment he said, "They weren't able to reach an opinion as to the authenticity." There was a trace of pride in his voice, faint but unmistakable. "Even their foremost expert on Golden Age Dutch painters couldn't rule out the possibility that it's real."

"But you and I both know it isn't. Which is why I'd like to borrow a laboratory knife, please."

Gallagher hesitated. Then he opened a drawer and laid an Olfa AK-1 on the tabletop.

"Perhaps you should do it," suggested Gabriel.

"Be my guest."

Gabriel grasped the high-quality knife by its yellow handle and cleaved two irreparable horizontal gashes through the painting. He was about to inflict a third when Gallagher seized his wrist. The Dubliner's hand was trembling.

"That's quite enough." He relaxed his grip. "There's no need to mutilate the bloody thing."

Gabriel sliced the painting a third time before ripping the swaths of canvas from the stretcher. Then, knife in hand, he approached *Portrait of an Unknown Woman*.

"Don't touch it," said Gallagher evenly.

"Why not?"

"Because that painting is a genuine Van Dyck."

"That painting," said Gabriel, "is one of your forgeries."

"Are you prepared to wager fifteen million dollars?"

"Is that how much Phillip got for it?"

Receiving no answer, Gabriel removed the painting from the Bruker and cut it to ribbons. Looking up, he saw Aiden Gallagher gazing at the ruined painting, his face bloodless with rage.

"Why did you do that?"

"The better question is, why did you paint it? Was it only for the money? Or did you enjoy making fools of people like Julian Isherwood and Sarah Bancroft?" Gabriel laid the laboratory knife on the examination table. "You owe them seventy-five thousand dollars."

"The contract specifically said that the money is nonrefundable."

"In that case, perhaps we can reach a compromise."

"How much did you have in mind?"

Gabriel smiled.

————

It did not take long to arrive at a figure—hardly surprising, for there was no negotiation involved. Gabriel simply named his price, and Aiden Gallagher, after a moment or two of sputtering remonstration, wrote out the check. The Irishman then requested reimbursement for the Van Dyck. Gabriel laid a five-euro banknote on the examination table and, check in hand, went into the sunlit Connecticut morning.

He took his time driving back to JFK but still managed to arrive four hours before his flight was scheduled to depart. He dined poorly in the food hall, purchased gifts for Chiara and the children in the duty-free shops, and then wandered over to his assigned gate. There he removed the check from the breast pocket of his handmade Italian sport coat—a check for the sum of $10 million, payable to Isherwood Fine Arts.

Included in the final settlement was $75,000 for the fraudulent report from Equus Analytics, $3.4 million for the forged Van Dyck, $1.1 million for the forged Albert Cuyp, $100,000 for the Old Master canvases that Gabriel used for his own forgeries, and $525,000 in assorted expenses such as first-class air travel, five-star hotel rooms, and three-olive Belvedere martinis. And then, of course, there was the $4.8 million that Sarah Bancroft had lost in the collapse of Masterpiece Art Ventures.

All in all, thought Gabriel, it was a rather satisfying end to the story.

He rang Chiara in Venice and gave her the good news.

"Reprobate," she said, and laughed hysterically.

Author's Note

Portrait of an Unknown Woman is a work of entertainment and should be read as nothing more. The names, characters, places, and incidents portrayed in the story are the product of the author's imagination or have been used fictitiously. Any resemblance to actual persons, living or dead, businesses, companies, events, or locales is entirely coincidental.

Visitors to the *sestiere* of San Polo will search in vain for the converted palazzo overlooking the Grand Canal where Gabriel Allon, after a long and tumultuous career with Israeli intelligence, has taken up residence with his wife and two young children. The business office of the Tiepolo Restoration Company is likewise impossible to find, for no such enterprise exists. The Andrea Bocelli song playing in the Allon family's kitchen in chapter 6 is "Chiara," from the 2001 album *Cieli di Toscana*. I listened to the CD frequently while writing the first draft of *The Confessor* in 2002 and gave the name to the beautiful daughter of the chief rabbi of Venice, Jacob Zolli. Irene Allon is named for her grandmother, who was one of the early State of Israel's most important artists. Her twin brother is named for the Italian High Renaissance painter Raffaello Sanzio da Urbino, better known as Raphael.

The fictitious Umbrian estate known as Villa dei Fiori appeared for the first time in *Moscow Rules*, a novel I conceived during an extended stay on a similar property. The staff took wonderful care of my family and me, and I repaid their kindness by turning them into minor but important characters in the story. Regrettably, several shopkeepers in the town of Amelia suffered the same fate in the novel's sequel, *The Defector*.

There is indeed a suite named for the conductor Leonard Bernstein at the Hôtel de Crillon in Paris, and Chez Janou is without question one of the city's better bistros. Nevertheless, the Swiss violinist Anna Rolfe could not have sent a low murmur through its brightly lit dining room, because Anna is the product of my imagination. So, too, are Maurice Durand and Georges Fleury, the owners of a disreputable art gallery in the Eighth Arrondissement. The art squad of the Police Nationale is in fact known as the Central Office for the Fight against Cultural Goods Trafficking—it definitely sounds better in French—but its personnel do not work in the historic building located at 36 Quai des Orfèvres.

Thankfully, there is no art-based hedge fund known as Masterpiece Art Ventures, and the crimes of my fictitious Phillip Somerset are entirely my creation. I included the names of real auction houses because, like the names of great painters, they are part of the art world's lexicon. It was not my intention to suggest in any way that companies such as Christie's or Sotheby's knowingly trade in forged paintings. Nor did I wish to leave the impression that the art-based lending units of JPMorgan Chase and Bank of America would accept forged paintings as collateral. Deepest apologies to the head of security at the Pierre for Gabriel's unconscionable behavior during his brief stay. The historic hotel on East Sixty-First Street is one of New York's finest and would never employ the likes of my fictitious Ray Bennett.

The madcap menagerie of London art dealers, museum curators, auctioneers, and journalists who grace the pages of *Portrait of an Unknown Woman* are invented from whole cloth, as are their sometimes questionable personal and professional antics. There is indeed an enchanting art gallery on the northeast corner of Mason's Yard, but it is owned by Patrick Matthiesen, one of the world's most successful and respected Old Master art dealers. A brilliant art historian blessed with an infallible eye, Patrick never would have fallen for a forged Van Dyck, even one as skillfully executed as the painting depicted in the story.

The same cannot be said, however, for many of Patrick's colleagues and competitors. Indeed, in the past quarter century, the multibillion-dollar global business known as the art world has been shaken by a series of high-profile forgery scandals that have raised unsettling questions about the oftentimes subjective process used to determine the origin and authenticity of a painting. Each of the forgery rings utilized some version of the same hackneyed provenance trap—newly rediscovered paintings emerging from a previously unknown collection—and yet each managed to deceive the experts and connoisseurs of the commercial art world with remarkable ease.

John Myatt, a songwriter and part-time art teacher with a knack for mimicking the great painters, was raising two small children alone in a run-down farmhouse in Staffordshire when he made the acquaintance of a clever trickster named John Drewe. Together the two men perpetrated what Scotland Yard described as "the biggest art fraud of the twentieth century." With Myatt supplying the canvases and Drewe the counterfeit provenances, the pair foisted more than 250 forgeries on the art market—for which Drewe pocketed more than £25 million. Many of the forgeries were sold through venerable London auction houses, including several works, purportedly by the French painter Jean Dubuffet, that went under the gavel during a glamorous evening sale at Christie's in King Street. In the audience that night, feeling slightly underdressed, was the forger who had created them. The Dubuffet Foundation, caretaker of the artist's oeuvre, had declared the works to be authentic.

On the other side of the English Channel, two other forgers were simultaneously wreaking havoc on the art world—and making millions in the process. One was Guy Ribes, a gifted painter who could produce a convincing "Chagall" or "Picasso" in a matter of minutes. According to French police and prosecutors, Ribes and a network of crooked dealers likely introduced more than a thousand forged paintings into the art market, most of which remain in circulation. Ribes's German counterpart, Wolfgang Beltracchi, was similarly prolific, sometimes producing as many as ten canvases a month. It was Beltracchi's wife, Helene—not my fictitious Françoise Vionnet—who effortlessly sold a forged "Georges Valmier" to a prominent European auction house after only a brief examination.

Within a few short years, the Beltracchis were selling forgeries through all the major auction houses, all purportedly from the same hitherto unknown collection. In the process, they became fabulously rich. They traveled the world aboard an eighty-foot sailboat, cared for by a crew of five. Their real estate portfolio included a $7 million villa in the German city of Freiburg and a sprawling estate, Domaine des Rivettes, in the French wine country of Languedoc. Among their many victims was the actor and art collector Steve Martin, who purchased a fake Heinrich Campendonk for $860,000 through Galerie Cazeau-Béraudière of Paris in 2004.

One might have assumed that Knoedler & Company, the oldest commercial art gallery in New York, would have been resistant to the virus spreading through the European markets. But in 1995, when an unknown art dealer named Glafira Rosales appeared at the gallery with a "Rothko" wrapped in cardboard, Knoedler president Ann Freedman apparently saw no reason to be suspicious. In the decade that followed, Rosales sold or consigned nearly forty Abstract Expressionist works to Knoedler & Company, including canvases said to have been painted by Jackson Pollock, Lee Krasner, Franz Kline, Robert Motherwell, and Willem de Kooning.

As it turned out, Glafira Rosales was the front woman for an international forgery network that included her Spanish boyfriend,

José Carlos Bergantiños Diáz, and his brother. The forger was a Chinese immigrant named Pei-Shen Qian, who worked out of his garage in Queens. According to prosecutors, Bergantiños Diáz discovered Qian selling copies on a street in Lower Manhattan, and recruited him. Qian was paid about $9,000 for each forgery, a tiny fraction of what they fetched at Knoedler. Besieged by lawsuits, the storied gallery closed its doors in November 2011.

With all due respect to the Abstract Expressionists, whom I revere, it is one thing to forge a Motherwell or a Rothko, quite another to execute a convincing Lucas Cranach the Elder. For that reason alone, a French judge sent shockwaves through the art world in March 2016, when she ordered the seizure of *Venus with a Veil*, the star attraction of a successful exhibition at the Caumont Centre d'Art in the southern French city of Aix-en-Provence. An exhaustive 213-page scientific analysis of the painting—the crown jewel of the enormous collection controlled by the prince of Liechtenstein—would later conclude that it could not have come from Cranach's workshop. Among the many red flags cited in the report was the appearance of the craquelure, which was said to be "inconsistent with normal aging." Representatives of His Serene Highness took issue with the findings and demanded the painting's immediate return. At the time of this writing, *Venus* was listed on the official website for the Princely Collections and on display in the Garden Palace in Vienna.

But it was the identity of the painting's previous owner—the French collector-turned-dealer Giuliano Ruffini—that so unnerved the wider art world. Several previously unknown works had recently emerged from Ruffini's inventory, including *Portrait of a Man*, purportedly by the Dutch Golden Age painter Frans Hals. Experts at the Louvre examined the painting in 2008 and declared it *un trésor national* that should never be allowed to leave French soil. Their counterparts at the Mauritshuis in The Hague were similarly rapturous, with one senior curator calling the painting "a very important addition to Hals's oeuvre." No one seemed overly concerned by the thinness of the provenance. The canvas, said the experts, spoke for itself.

For reasons never made clear, the Louvre chose not to acquire the painting, and in 2010 it was purchased by a London art dealer and an art investor for a reported $3 million. Just one year later, the pair sold the portrait to a prominent American collector for more than three times what they had paid for it. The prominent collector, after learning that *Venus* had been seized by the French, wisely subjected his $10 million "Frans Hals" to scientific testing and was told, in no uncertain terms, that it was a fake. Sotheby's quickly agreed to return the prominent American collector's money and sought restitution from the London dealer and the art investor. At which point the lawsuits began to fly.

As many as twenty-five suspect Old Master canvases, with an estimated market value of some $255 million, have emerged from the same collection—including *David with the Head of Goliath*, purportedly by Orazio Gentileschi, which was displayed at the National Gallery in London. It was not the first time the esteemed museum had exhibited a misattributed or fraudulent work. In 2010, the gallery aired its curatorial dirty laundry in a six-room exhibition called "Fakes, Mistakes, and Discoveries." Room 5 featured *An Allegory*. Acquired by the museum in 1874, it was thought to be the work of the Early Renaissance Florentine painter Sandro Botticelli. In truth, it was a pastiche executed by a later follower. More recently, a Swiss art research company utilizing a pioneering form of artificial intelligence determined that *Samson and Delilah*, one of the National Gallery's most prized paintings, was almost certainly *not* the work of Sir Peter Paul Rubens.

The National Gallery purchased the painting in 1980—at Christie's auction house in London—for $5.4 million. At the time, it was the third-highest price ever paid for a work of art. In today's market a sale of that size would hardly be newsworthy, as soaring prices have turned paintings into yet another asset class for the superrich—or, in the words of the late Manhattan art dealer Eugene Thaw, "a commodity like pork bellies or wheat." A. Alfred Taubman, the shopping mall developer and fast-food investor who purchased Sotheby's in 1983, cynically observed that "a precious painting by Degas and a frosted mug of root beer" had much in common, at least when it came to the potential for profit. In April 2002, Taubman was sentenced to a year in prison for his role in the price-fixing scheme with rival Christie's that swindled customers out of more than $100 million.

Increasingly, much of the world's most valuable art resides not in museums or private homes but in darkened, climate-controlled vaults. More than a million paintings are reportedly hidden away in the Geneva Free Port, including at least a thousand works by Pablo Picasso. Many collectors and curators are troubled by the degree to which paintings have become just another investment vehicle. But those who are in the business of buying and selling art for profit are just as likely to disagree. "Paintings," the New York gallery owner David Nash told the *New York Times* in 2016, "are not a public good."

Most change hands under conditions of absolute secrecy, at ever-increasing prices, with little or no oversight. It is little wonder, then, that the art world has been beset by a succession of multimillion-dollar forgery scandals. The problem is doubtless made worse by the apathy of the courts and police. Remarkably, none of the forgers and their accomplices mentioned above received more than a slap on the wrist for their crimes. Front woman Glafira Rosales was sentenced to time served for her role in the Knoedler scandal. John Myatt and Wolfgang Beltracchi, after serving brief prison terms, now make their livings selling "genuine fakes" and other original works online. Beltracchi, during an interview with the CBS News program *60 Minutes*, expressed only one regret—that he had used the inaccurately labeled tube of titanium white paint that had led to his exposure.

The French forger Guy Ribes was likewise able to put his talent to legitimate use. It is Ribes, not actor Michel Bouquet, who mimics the brushstrokes of Auguste-Pierre Renoir in a 2012 film about the final years of the painter's life. Ribes also executed the "Renoirs" used in the film's production—with the assistance of the Musée d'Orsay, which granted him a private viewing of the Renoirs in its possession, including several not on public display. James Ivory lamented the fact that the notorious French art forger had not been available to work on the 1996 motion picture *Surviving Picasso*. Said the legendary director: "It would have been, visually, a different film."

Acknowledgments

I am grateful to my wife, Jamie Gangel, who listened patiently while I worked out the intricate plot and twists of *Portrait of an Unknown Woman* and then skillfully edited the first draft of my typescript. My debt to her is immeasurable, as is my love.

Anthony Scaramucci, founder of the investment firm Skybridge Capital, took time out of his busy schedule to help me create a fraudulent art-based hedge fund propped up by the sale and collateralization of forged paintings. London art dealer Patrick Matthiesen patiently answered each of my questions, as did Maxwell L. Anderson, who has five times served as the director of a North American art museum, including the Whitney Museum of American Art in New York. Not to be outdone, renowned art conservator David Bull—for better or worse, he is known in certain circles as "the real Gabriel Allon"—read my nearly 600-page typescript in its entirety, all while rushing to complete the restoration of a canvas by the Italian Renaissance artist Jacopo Bassano.

Legendary *Vanity Fair* writer-at-large Marie Brenner gave me invaluable insight into her work and the New York art world; and David Friend, the magazine's editor of creative development, shared harrowing stories of past investigations into the affairs of powerful men. I can say with certainty that there is a conference room in *Vanity Fair*'s newsroom on the twenty-fifth floor of One World Trade

Center—and that it overlooks New York Harbor. Otherwise, the chaotic sequence of events depicted in the climax of *Portrait of an Unknown Woman* bears little resemblance to the way *Vanity Fair* reports, edits, and publishes consequential pieces of investigative journalism.

My Los Angeles super-lawyer Michael Gendler was, needless to say, a source of wise counsel. Louis Toscano, my dear friend and long-time editor, made countless improvements to the novel, as did Kathy Crosby, my eagle-eyed personal copy editor. Any typographical errors that slipped through their formidable gauntlet are my responsibility, not theirs.

I consulted more than a hundred newspaper and magazine articles while writing *Portrait of an Unknown Woman*, far too many to cite here. I owe a special debt to the reporters of *Artnet*, *ARTnews*, the *Art Newspaper*, the *Guardian*, and the *New York Times* for their coverage of the most recent Old Master forgery scandal. Five books were especially helpful: Anthony M. Amore, *The Art of the Con: The Most Notorious Fakes, Frauds, and Forgeries in the Art World*; Laney Salisbury and Aly Sujo, *Provenance: How a Con Man and a Forger Rewrote the History of Modern Art*; Noah Charney, *The Art of Forgery: The Minds, Motives and Methods of Master Forgers*; Thomas Hoving, *False Impressions: The Hunt for Big-Time Art Fakes*; and Michael Shnayerson, *Boom: Mad Money, Mega Dealers, and the Rise of Contemporary Art*.

We are blessed with family and friends who fill our lives with love and laughter at critical times during the writing year, especially Jeff Zucker, Phil Griffin, Andrew Lack, Noah Oppenheim, Esther Fein and David Remnick, Elsa Walsh and Bob Woodward, Susan St. James and Dick Ebersol, Jane and Burt Bacharach, Stacey and Henry Winkler, Pete Williams and David Gardner, Virginia Moseley and Tom Nides, Cindi and Mitchell Berger, Donna and Michael Bass, Nancy Dubuc and Michael Kizilbash, Susanna Aaron and Gary Ginsburg, Elena Nachmanoff, Ron Meyer, Andy Lassner, and Peggy Noonan.

Also, a heartfelt thanks to the team at HarperCollins, especially Brian Murray, Jonathan Burnham, Doug Jones, Leah Wasielewski, Sarah Ried, Mark Ferguson, Leslie Cohen, Josh Marwell, Robin Bilardello, Milan Bozic, David Koral, Leah Carlson-Stanisic, Carolyn Robson, Chantal Restivo-Alessi, Frank Albanese, Josh Marwell, and Amy Baker.

Finally, my children, Lily and Nicholas, were a constant source of inspiration and support. Nicholas, now a graduate student at the Security Studies Program at Georgetown University's School of Foreign Service, was once again forced to reside under the same roof as his father as I struggled to complete this, the twenty-fifth novel of my career. And one wonders why neither he nor his twin sister, a successful business consultant, has chosen to pursue a career as a writer.

About the Author

Daniel Silva is the award-winning, #1 *New York Times* bestselling author of *The Unlikely Spy, The Mark of the Assassin, The Marching Season, The Kill Artist, The English Assassin, The Confessor, A Death in Vienna, Prince of Fire, The Messenger, The Secret Servant, Moscow Rules, The Defector, The Rembrandt Affair, Portrait of a Spy, The Fallen Angel, The English Girl, The Heist, The English Spy, The Black Widow, House of Spies, The Other Woman, The New Girl, The Order,* and *The Cellist.* He is best known for his long-running thriller series starring spy and art restorer Gabriel Allon. Silva's books are critically acclaimed bestsellers around the world and have been translated into more than thirty languages. He resides in Florida with his wife, television journalist Jamie Gangel, and their twins, Lily and Nicholas. For more information, visit www.danielsilvabooks.com.